LOVE NOTES & LIFELINES

SINGLE DAD HOTLINE
BOOK 1

AVERY MAXWELL

That's What She Said Publishing, Inc.

ISBN: 979-8-88643-941-0 (ebook)

ISBN: 979-8-88643-942-7 (paperback)

032224

This book is for anyone still searching for where they belong.

And for Dang-it Daisie, my one-year-old Bernadoodle. One day you will stop trying to walk on top of my feet.

AUTHOR NOTE

Dear Reader,

There's always a villain, and in Stella's world, that's her ex, Silas—a narcissistic bully.

And like so many bullies, when his words don't cut as deep as he'd like, he finds other ways to tear her down.

The thing I love so much about Stella is that even though she found herself in a terrible situation, she still sees love and kindness in those around her—even her irritatingly handsome boss, Becker Hayes—and the mother she's losing one memory at a time.

Beck is dealing with his own childhood trauma that makes him choose isolation over trust, but when he suddenly becomes guardian to his estranged sister's two children, he quickly learns that trust is an inevitable part of being a family.

When he realizes his young niece has witnessed the cruelty her mother endured, he does everything in his power to make sure that nothing will ever hurt her again.

This is a story of four lost souls finding a place to belong in the hearts of each other.

If you or someone you know are struggling, please know you're not alone, and someone cares—I care.
If you need help taking the first step, please reach out:
https://www.alz.org
https://www.thehotline.org
https://www.samhsa.gov/mental-health
And if you need a friend, please join us in my reader group:
https://geni.us/AverysLUVclub

CHAPTER ONE

STELLA

Kissing the boss is never a good idea.

It didn't matter that I'd clocked out for the last time, my contract as a temporary employee was over, and he wasn't my boss any longer.

Because it wasn't *just* a kiss. He consumed me, owned me, and for two whole hours with him in that bar, I felt free from the confines of responsibility.

It was completely out of character for me, but that night, I'd just wanted to be the girl without a noose around her neck. I was fully prepared to go right back to my life full of landmines.

Fast forward a year. Now my rule is *never kiss a man in a stupidly expensive suit.*

Because now that man is my boss. Again.

Months after the best night of my life—and *that* mind-altering kiss—I unexpectedly received an offer for a full-time position as an administrative assistant to the general counsel at Crystal Waters' corporate headquarters.

It had been half a year since that one night with Becker Hayes, the company's CEO. When I had temped in that office, he'd been traveling or working at other locations. The offer came when I desperately needed consistent income and benefits to support my mother, so I said yes faster than I could blink and assumed I could easily avoid a CEO who was never in the office anyway.

Rule number two is *don't make assumptions without having all the facts.* All the travel Mr. Hayes was doing during my time as a temp wasn't his normal schedule.

I've learned that six months completely away from him *and* six months ignoring the awkwardness of seeing him nearly every day, especially since my desk in the executive suite's reception area is mere feet from his office, has done nothing to help me get over him.

Get over that kiss.

The possibility of running into him keeps me on high alert as I exit the elevator on the top floor of the Hayes building. Constantly scanning my surroundings has become part of my rather strict morning routine. This job is the only thing keeping my mother in her assisted living facility. I can't lose it because my libido has a thing for my boss.

"Oh, thank God you're here," Kara from marketing says the second I step off the elevator.

I'm a mess. But I'm a mess with a job, so I focus on the obstacle in front of me.

Kara's a nice girl with dirty blond hair and blue eyes. She'd make a perfect Barbie for Halloween, and she's as smart as she is beautiful. I hear she's somewhat of a marketing prodigy, which makes me want to be her own personal cheerleader, but unfortunately her marketing skills don't transfer to her knowledge of office equipment.

So far this week I've fixed her phone, un-jammed the copier, and helped her remove her blouse from the laminating machine.

"Hi, Kara. I love your dress. What's up?"

She glances down at the light pink silk garment and shakes her head. I'm sure she thinks I'm absurd, but I'd kill for an hour in her closet.

"It's the 3-D printer. It went a little...haywire," she says, ignoring my obvious dress envy.

"Stella, could you help me with the fast copier?" Teddy from in-house counsel asks as Maria catches sight of me from the opposite direction.

"Stella. I don't know what I did, but the coffee machine is making mud pies in all the mugs," Maria says in a rush.

This has also become my morning routine—fixer of office equipment.

"Right," I say, juggling the bags in one arm and the scrapbooks I'm bringing to my mother later in the other.

I hurry to my desk and take one second for myself to ensure everything is in its correct spot. If anything on my desk is out of place, I get sweaty.

"Kara, go unplug the 3-D printer," I call while fitting the scrapbooks into the bottom drawer of my filing cabinet and wishing it had a lock. "I'll be right there. Teddy, don't touch anything, I'll go there next, and Maria, I'll make a fresh pot on my way to help Kara."

My lunch goes on the shelf behind me and my purse tucks into the only lockable cabinet I have access to, then I check it. Twice.

"Thank you," Maria says. She's a lovely woman in her sixties and the new, very impressive, and unnecessarily expensive coffee machine makes her twitchy. "What ever happened to plain old drip coffee?" she mutters, turning on her heel.

Kara and Teddy head in opposite directions, and I inhale deeply as they go. The moment to breathe should be relaxing, but I sense my coworker Elijah laughing at me.

I hold up my palm in his direction without looking. "Elijah, don't say it. Everyone needs a little hel—" The words get caught in my lip gloss when I finally lift my head to find Elijah behind his desk—he and I share this entry area of the executive suite—and Mr. Hayes leaning against the doorframe of his office with one ankle draped casually over the other. But then he crosses his arms over his chest. It's an oddly sexual pose and heat creeps across my cheeks.

I know what his lips feel like on mine, and that is not what I should be thinking about first thing in the morning at work.

He's smirking at me. I really wish he wouldn't even look at me, let alone smirk. Smirking should be off-limits when you've had your body pressed up against someone. I thought we were in a very necessary standoff, where he takes the long way around to enter his office through another department and I pretend that I don't know how his dick pulses when he's aroused.

Ah, dang it. Is brain bleach a thing? I hope so, because I need something to erase his rock-hard body from my memory banks. Today his sleeves are rolled up, and since he has shockingly little arm hair, the tendons in his forearms stand out like a naked cowboy in Central Park.

"I didn't say anything," Elijah says. He thinks he's hiding his laughter, but it bounces along with every word. As Mr. Hayes's long-time executive admin, he's much more comfortable in this space than I am.

Oh crap. I suck in my lips and bite them. Hard. I've been staring at the CEO for how long now? Flustered, I turn forty-five degrees to my right so I can only see Elijah, but that doesn't stop the heat of Beck's gaze from setting fire to every inappropriate thought rushing through my mind.

No, no, no. Not *Beck* with his silky brown hair and eyes that sparkle like emeralds. Mr. Freaking Hayes.

These are the days I wish I'd had another option—but I was at rock bottom when Elijah showed up at my apartment with a job offer. Thank God I took my original contract position here seriously because Elijah's full-time offer came just in time.

And luckily, shockingly, Mr. Hayes and I have a silent agreement to keep our distance, which means I rarely speak directly to him—it's better that way.

I haven't been this close to him since our initial meeting after I was hired. The one where I told him I would keep things professional—pretend our kiss never happened— and he agreed. Even the meetings that have followed have allowed for more space than this.

Most days I can almost convince myself that he's not real because I see him so infrequently. But now he's standing there sizing me up and making me sweat in very unladylike places, so I glare at Elijah.

"I didn't say anything," Elijah repeats with a grin.

"But you were going to," I scold just above a whisper. I don't even know why. Mr. Hayes is six feet away and can hear everything I say. Instead of bickering with my new best friend, I turn on my heel and go save the day for people who actually need me.

THE DOOR TO THE UTILITY CLOSET SWINGS OPEN AND I NEARLY choke on my pickle-and-pimento-loaf sandwich.

"What are you doing in here?" Elijah asks. His sigh of

disappointment is overly dramatic, even for him, but I know he's worried when he runs his thumbs along the underside of his green suspenders.

When my heart starts beating again, I wave him in while furtively peering behind him. "I'm eating my lunch where Caleb won't find me. If he sees me in the break room, he'll consider this a working lunch, and I really, really need to find another part-time job." I knew when I accepted the job that Caleb Fairfax, Crystal Waters' general counsel, was cool and direct, but I'd had no idea how strict, harsh even, he would be as a manager. Though it's not as if I would have refused the job offer, even if I'd been assigned to Lucifer himself.

"Stella," Elijah says gently, then turns a bucket upside down and takes a seat next to me.

I hold up a hand to stop him. "No, thank you. You have no idea how much I appreciate you allowing me to use your car to make extra cash driving all over Raleigh for Up-Lift, but I need something more stable."

"I know." Something about the way he says those two words makes my last bite of questionable meat stick in my throat. "I have something for you." Elijah pushes his suspenders aside, reaches into his shirt pocket, and pulls out a black card.

He must own a thousand sets of suspenders because they always match his socks.

He waves the card in front of my face, but I raise both hands, even the one holding a half-eaten sandwich, in the air. "What is that?" And why does it look like a freaking credit card?

"This is an opportunity for you, take it. And put your hands down. I'm not holding you at gunpoint."

Slowly, I lower my arms to my lap. When I don't reach

for the card, he slips it into the collar of my blouse, and I raise one brow.

"Do I need to tell Samira you're getting frisky?" I grin. His wife would tease him about it for a decade, and we both know it.

"Don't you dare," he hisses but flashes a debonaire smile. He and Samira have one of the strongest—healthiest—relationships I've ever witnessed.

I plop the last bite of sandwich into my mouth and wince. I really wish this stuff would grow on me. Brushing off my fingers on my pant leg, I retrieve the card.

"Why are you eating that shit again?" he asks. Elijah is not a man who has ever had to shop sales.

My nose scrunches up before I can answer. "It was buy one, get two free."

He shakes his head, pinching the bridge of his nose. "For crying out loud, Stella."

I hear his voice but not his words as I try to make sense of the metal business card he's handed me.

It's heavy and black with baby-pink text: *The Single Dad Hotline*.

"What is this?" Turning it over in my palm does little to ease my apprehension. The back is blank.

He lets out a long, scoff-like exhale. "I told Lottie she needed more information on those cards. It's nothing pervy. It's a hotline for new single dads who have no clue what they're doing but are suddenly responsible for a child or children. It's nationwide now, and soon she'll expand to offer nanny services, but for now, it's just hotline helpers."

"What? Who's Lottie?" Pain pulses between my eyes. Whoever said stress headaches could be cured with deep breathing exercises has obviously never met me.

"Focus, Stella. I've known Lottie for years, and she'll take good care of you, I promise. She runs a hotline for single dads who have no idea what they're doing. Email her. Tell her I sent you, and she'll set you up. You'll get a monthly salary based on how many clients you match with, but remember, you're at their mercy twenty-four seven, so don't be an asshole and think you can handle twelve at a time. Just start with one or two clients, okay? It's not ideal, but at least with this position you can do it from home, and I don't have to worry about you taking the bus all over North Carolina."

He shakes his head, then tugs on the back of his neck. "Listen, you're running yourself into the ground to care for your mother. You're strong, Stella, but you need a hand. That card is a step in the right direction to getting you back on your feet."

"Will she have mannies too? What about single moms?"

Elijah tugs so hard on his suspenders they might snap. I lean out of the way just in case. This is a sure sign that he's getting frustrated.

"Okay, Miss Skeptic, yes, Lottie will have mannies, though I don't think she calls them that. Lottie will kill me for making her business personal," he mutters. "And she does have a five-year plan for single moms, but she built her business from the clientele she had access to through her father—rich, single men." He frowns. "I think she started it because her own father was a single parent, and he was a nightmare who never asked for help. She hopes that through her company she can help other children in similar situations."

I'm rubbing my temples, attempting to process all this information, when the door is wrenched open again. I hold my breath while Elijah steps in front of me. I love this man. I know he's trying to shield me in case it's Caleb, but he's not much bigger than I am.

"Elijah?"

My insides coil into a tight knot. They do it every time I hear that man's voice.

"Stella? What are you two doing in here?" Mr. Hayes stares at me sitting on an overturned bucket with a fabric lunch box at my feet. "Are you eating lunch in here? Why are you two eating lunch in a utility closet?"

"Better question is, why are *you* in a utility closet?" Elijah counters.

But we all know the answer to that question. This is where he hides his chocolates—the man has an incurable sweet tooth. I normally refill his drawer for him, but he's been in his office at odd hours this week and I didn't want to risk being caught.

He proves me right when his gaze darts to the basket above my head, and my lips twitch. Elijah thinks he keeps them in here because he has no self-control, but I'm not so sure. I think Mr. Hayes is in control of every situation he encounters, and I hate that I find it so frustratingly sexy.

"I...spilled my coffee," he says reaching for the mop to my left.

I grab it just as he does. Our fingers twist around each other's, and our eyes meet, but I can't hold his gaze when his nostrils flare. He's the pot of gold under a rainbow. No matter how close you get, he's always out of reach.

His fingers press into my knuckles, and my body zings to life. His energy zips through my veins like a drone that only he controls.

"I'll get them—it, I mean. Elijah said you have a meeting at one. I'll take care of it."

My voice is as shaky as I feel. It makes me sound weak,

and it's irritating. I wasn't always this way around men of authority. I used to have a spine—I probably even knew who the hell I was at one point.

He lets go of the mop and my hand as though it bit him. His glare is hot and steely when he addresses me. "You understand that your job is to assist Caleb, correct?"

My head snaps up at his tone. He sounds almost...angry. What the hell? Over the last few weeks, he's become increasingly irritated around me, and I don't know why, but it makes my stomach hollow out. *I need this job.*

Instead of answering him, I nod. He's so close that if I moved my knee an inch we'd touch, but I know we'd set fire to this place if I did. It's all too much.

And why does he have to smell so good? Who would have guessed that at twenty-nine years old I'd salivate for fresh-cut grass and the ocean? But seriously, he has a high-pressure job with hundreds of people depending on him—maybe thousands of people. He should stink like stress sweat, but it's quite the opposite. The more balls he has in the air, the better he smells.

Well, that's what the girls say in the break room anyway.

He crouches down in front of me so we're eye to eye. If I remembered how to breathe, we'd be sharing air.

"You're not obligated to clean up messes or fix printers or make other peoples' days easier." His breath blows my hair away from my face. Why is *he* breathing so hard? Did he run laps before coming in here to yell at me?

I press my lips into a thin line—he's been watching me, too.

"Don't be a dick just because you're having a bad day, Becker." Elijah and Mr. Hayes have been friends for years. I can't imagine using that tone with a boss, but Elijah knows what he can get away with.

He slips between us, forcing his friend to stand, and I can finally inhale again. With only inches separating us, I was having a hard time finding my words.

Elijah presses his hand to Beck's chest only to have it flicked away. "Go to your office, and I'll get you a cup of coffee."

"I get my own coffee, Elijah, and you know it," Beck grumbles.

"Then do it," Elijah says with his hands on his hips. Shockingly, Beck turns on his heel and leaves.

"Aren't you afraid he'll fire you one of these days?" I mutter, staying seated because I'm pretty sure my knees would give out if I stood.

Elijah's laugh is light and carefree. "He won't ever fire me, Stella belle." He holds out a hand and helps me stand. "Remember when I told you we all have issues?"

Images of my mother in a rage on the street make my eyes well. That was the day Elijah offered me the job here. The day he learned most of my secrets.

Too afraid of the messy emotions sitting in my throat to speak, I nod.

"Well, he has trust issues. Big, fat, ugly, painful trust issues. His childhood wasn't as idyllic as most people assume. His family was pretty messed up when he was a kid. He needs me, and that's why I'm here."

"You're a good friend." I fiddle with the mop in the bucket.

"I didn't say that was the only reason I'm here. It helps that it pisses off my father. No son of his should be a secretary." He makes air quotes on the last word.

I only know a little about his family, but he's made it clear that his father would have disowned him if he weren't the only male heir.

Heir. The word is so…old. Who worries about heirs anymore?

"But you are a good friend," I say.

"Yes. I am. I'd better go make sure he isn't abusing any other employees with his glowers." He leans in for a hug. "You unsettle him, Stella. He's different around you—that's a good thing. Are you okay?"

I sink into his touch. You forget how much you crave affection when it's used as a weapon against you for so long.

"Yeah. I'm fine."

He stares into my eyes, and for the briefest moment I wish I understood what he sees when he looks at me, but it's impossible. I'm not even sure who I am anymore. He kisses my cheek and exits the closet.

I slowly lower myself onto the bucket and pull out my phone. Opening my email app, my hands shake as I type in Lottie's email address.

To: Lottie
From: Stella
Subject: Elijah

Dear Lottie,

Elijah Sinclair gave me your contact information and he said I would be a good fit for your hotline. I would love to discuss it with you at your earliest convenience.

Stella Anderson

There, done. I'm still not sure how I feel about this opportunity, but I trust Elijah, so I jump in headfirst. Lottie's response comes through before I even close out of my email.

To: Stella
From: Lottie
Subject: RE: Elijah

Dear Stella,

Thank you for your interest. Elijah is...helpful, isn't he? Please take your time filling out this questionnaire. It is intensive and thorough, so I encourage you to be thoughtful in your answers. Once it's complete, I'll be in touch to let you know if you're a good fit for the SDH.

Sincerely,
Lottie

The attachment she included is seventy-two pages of questions. I gulp. Well, it's not like I had anything else to do tonight.

For now, I push everything to the back of my mind—it's something I've become a pro at, especially when it comes to Mr. Sexybeck—and hurry to fill his chocolate drawer before he returns with his coffee and an attitude the size of Texas.

CHAPTER TWO

BECK

"ALL I'M SAYING IS I HATE PEOPLE DOING THINGS FOR ME. I'M perfectly capable and—"

"She's a helper, Beck. It's her love language. Get over yourself. What you witnessed last week—her helping all those people in *your company*—that's who Stella is."

Horror must show on my face because Elijah picks up a notepad and hits me in the chest with it.

"Love language, you asshole, not that she's in love. It's how she measures her value. Being needed by people gives her purpose."

"Right." I scoff. He's been listening to self-help books again. Feeling my body tense, I cross my arms over my chest, hoping it hides the way my hands shake. "And I suppose you'll tell me everyone has a love language?"

He nods with a smug expression that tilts his nose to the sky and makes me want to throw a pie in his face. "We do."

Taking two steps, I prop one hip against Stella's desk and stare at him, but I'm distracted by the sweetness of her scent again—apples. One goddamn kiss a year ago and she's imprinted herself on my mind. It's fucking stupid. Can I ban apples from the office? HR banned peanut butter when someone from the third floor had an allergy. Are apple allergies a thing?

I peek under my arm at her desk and then behind me, but I can't find the source of the scent. "What's mine then?" I ask, surreptitiously scanning her space. Everything is so… tidy.

He reclines in his chair with his hands clasped behind his head. A vision of him falling over makes me ridiculously happy.

"You don't know your own love language because you don't allow anyone close enough to show you what you need or allow yourself to learn how other people's love languages affect their daily lives."

He leans forward and clasps his hands on his desk. "Hell, I love you like a brother, and have for over twenty years, but you hide that part of yourself away, even from me. If I had to guess, and based on your pre-Sailport Bay exile, I'd say you have two love languages—touch, which is a fairly common one, and acts of service."

"You're out of your mind."

"Am I?"

"Yes. I don't go around touching people to see if my love button is broken."

He shakes his head. "Last week when we went to lunch and our server was berated for nearly ten minutes, what did you do?"

How am I supposed to remember some random server?

When I don't answer, he does it for me. "You stood between her and the jackass, then took the coffee from her hand and held her arm until she stopped shaking."

"For fuck's sake, Elijah. Are you telling me I'm in love with a server from a restaurant I can't even remember?"

"No, I'm saying you show your love and compassion with touch and protection. That's your love language because you do it without realizing it, just like Stella making herself invaluable to everyone around her is an unconscious act."

The phone rings just as Caleb's door opens and Stella exits his office. Elijah answers the phone and Stella does an incredible job ignoring me as I openly stare at her. There's something about this woman that makes me want to know her—really know her—and I'm struggling to even process that.

Elijah's face contorts, and he holds the phone out to me. "It's about Cally."

I stand, with my hands in the air, and walk toward my office.

"I don't care how many times she calls, Elijah. She pulled her money out of this company without so much as a phone call and nearly bankrupted me, then she chose enemy sides. As far as I'm concerned, I no longer have a family."

A soft gasp has me clenching my jaw before I turn away from Elijah's desk. Directly across from my assistant stands the woman I've actively avoided, only to have her commandeer my mind every goddamn night.

This has been going on for months! And my balls are blue to prove it.

I don't even know why I go to such lengths to avoid her other than she makes me feel things. Damn it. She's weaseled her way into the fringe of trust simply by doing... things.

Things like refilling my chocolates, my coffee, stapling my end-of-day reports vertically instead of at an angle. I've never even once told anyone that was my preference. When does she even have time to do this shit? It's not her job, but if I can't catch her being *helpful*, how can I tell her to stop it?

Elijah snorts behind me, but I can't drag my scowl away from the woman with wide eyes and mouth agape.

A mouth I never got to sink my cock into.

Jesus, Beck. Get your head out of the gutter.

But I understand Stella's reaction. Hearing that someone has disowned their family is probably shocking, but she doesn't know my history, so she doesn't need to be so dramatic about it. The sad expression on her face holds my attention though.

Her fingers twitch against her thighs, and butterflies flutter in my chest. Why do her actions still cause such a clusterfuck of reactions within me? What it is about this woman? I'm drawn to her even more now, almost a year after our shared kiss at my company party Elijah made me host, and the unrelenting attraction is exactly why I rarely make eye contact. I also actively avoid conversing with her because when I do, I morph into a leering pervert who stares at her lips. But I watch, and I learn.

Okay, fine. And sometimes I stand behind my door when I hear her laughing with my assistant. Fucking Elijah. He gets to stare at her all day long.

Shaking my head, I turn back to the man who is now wearing an annoying smirk. He thinks he knows what's going on in my head, but he has no idea the mess swirling around up here.

When I turn my glower his way, he has the grace to check himself. "It's not your sister this time, Beck. It's her attorney."

What the hell? I haven't spoken to my sister in seven years—not since my mother's funeral. What could she possibly be suing me for? I bet it's not even her—it's probably her jackalope husband, Davis.

"What does he want?"

"He said he needs to see you immediately. And if you're not in his downtown branch within an hour, he'll have the police escort you there."

"Caleb," I shout.

Stella drops the stapler with a clatter. Why is she so jumpy around me? Obviously, if I haven't fired her yet, I'm not going to. She gets along so well with Elijah, but with me, she's a hot mess of accidents waiting to happen.

So what if she very obviously prefers my married assistant over me? Why do I even care? I don't need her attention. In fact, that's the very last thing I *need*.

Elijah winks, and I can't control the rumble in my chest.

Fine, yes, I'm a jealous asshole. But he doesn't know how her nipples pebble when she's turned on—I do.

Caleb slinks out of his office like a black cat. He's dressed head to toe in the color—he always is. He says it's the New Yorker in him, but all it conjures for me are funerals and black-tie events, and I actively avoid both of those things.

"You bellowed." He curls his lips into a sneer, and his tone is condescending as hell, but he's head counsel for a reason. He cuts Stella down with a glacial glare that has my fists curling and my left brow twitching. It isn't Stella's fault that I'm on a razor's edge.

The pulse in my throat throbs.

Poor Stella. What drives her to put up with Caleb's shit? Whatever it is must be important because she's lasted longer than Caleb's last four assistants combined. She has grit, I'll give her that.

Even my thoughts carry a thread of fondness for this woman. It's fucking insanity.

Caleb clears his throat and I finally tear my gaze away from Stella. I might need to switch offices if I don't figure out how to get her out of my head.

"My sister's attorney is demanding a visit to his office. Now," I explain, "or he'll arrange a police escort for me."

Caleb's eyes glow like a wolf. When he goes into attack mode, they're downright terrifying. "If he believes that's a viable threat, it's something more than a missed signature. Give me a minute. I'll grab my jacket and tablet. If you have any idea what this is in reference to, now would be the time to tell me."

I've been wracking my brain for the last three minutes, but I truly don't. I gave anything and everything left to us by our father to my sister before I left Sailport Bay seven years ago. The way everyone in my life there betrayed me was branded in my mind. The last thing I wanted—or needed—was a physical reminder of that.

I scrape a hand over my face. "I have no idea."

"I don't appreciate going into things blind," he snaps. Forget personal and professional boundaries, it might be time for HR to step in and see if he needs the stick up his ass surgically removed.

"Do you think I do?" My teeth make a crunching noise and I'm sure the vein in my neck is bulging with irritation. Whatever my sister's playing at is testing the limits of what little patience I have left.

Caleb is in his mid-forties. He lost his wife a few years ago but never even mentioned to anyone that she was sick until he had to take time off for her funeral. He has no other family or friends that I'm aware of, and he's also started forgetting who owns this company too often.

I've cut him a lot of slack because of what he's gone

through, but Elijah has mentioned multiple times that he has concerns, so maybe it's time to rein him in.

"Beck." Elijah's tone is cautious. I won't like what he's about to say—that's the cadence he uses to drop bombs I haven't thought of yet. Now I'm thankful the foyer between mine and Caleb's offices is semi-private—though I don't particularly relish the idea of airing my dirty laundry in front of Stella or Caleb either.

But Elijah is a completely different story. He knows everything about me, right down to why I left home and never returned.

"Just spit it out, Elijah." My patience is a tightrope about to snap.

Stella reaches a hand toward me and almost immediately snatches it back. Was she going to touch me? For what? Comfort? My skin sizzles under her scrutiny. Her first reaction to my upset was to comfort me. Why would she do that?

I swallow hard and find it difficult to blink because once I do, I'll have to turn my back on her. Instead, we stand in this weird limbo—studying each other.

"Cally has attempted to reach you over thirty times in the last month," Elijah says gently. I drop my chin and stare at the floor. "And each time she sounded, I don't know, more distressed? Weaker, maybe. Perhaps she's sick and wants to talk to you."

A sucker punch of emotion I'm not prepared for steals the air from my lungs, and I stagger back a step. Stella's entire body leans toward me, then I lose focus and blink feverishly.

It's not the first time Elijah has mentioned something similar, but it's the first time he's said it when she wasn't on hold. Something about that makes this hit harder. Growing up, my older sister was my best friend. I don't think we even kept secrets from each other, which was why her choosing the Delacroix family absolutely gutted me. Marrying Davis I could have dealt with, but taking over Delacroix Holdings, my biggest competitor, the family that took everything from us, was a betrayal I'll never be able to see past.

"Delacroix Holdings is the future, Beck. I know you want to believe you're the best at everything, but not this time. You can't compete with an established company like this. You're just not cut out for it. The business of luxury is cutthroat, and you don't have what it takes."

That was the last time I spoke to my sister. I swallow hard, trying to clear my throat and mind. Calista is only forty-three, but Davis is six years younger than her and a lifetime less mature. She probably has a cold, and Davis is off on another death-defying stunt.

It's nothing serious.

Swallowing, the tension gets lodged in my throat. What if she is sick? Does that negate their betrayal?

Out of the corner of my eye, I observe Stella standing quietly—her face is full of sympathy. It's embarrassing that my attention locks onto her when my foundation is unteth-ered—I don't *need* anyone. I don't rely on anyone. And yet, here I am, wishing I knew what she's thinking and pissed off that I don't.

Elijah crosses the room to stand in front of me, but my attention is drawn to the emotions I find in Stella's gaze.

Abruptly, she turns to her right, breaking our connec-tion, then floats around the space like a ghost only I can see. Stella hands Elijah a folder while he checks something on his phone, fills Caleb's to-go mug with coffee and hands it to him, then returns to sit at her desk.

How are they not paying attention to her? Or at the very least saying fucking thank you.

Dog whines until Stella pushes her chair back enough for the mutt to jump into her lap. She pats Dog's ears, even though the Bernadoodle dwarfs her in the chair, then Dog nuzzles into Stella's warmth as though she's done it a million times. Even my dog takes comfort from this woman.

I hadn't meant to keep the beast. Some asshole dropped her off in my parking garage and all the no-kill shelters were full. One week turned into another and she just became mine. Elijah is pissed I named her Dog, but I won't change it.

"Stella?" Caleb's gruff voice drags my attention off the bewildering assistant. "When you're done with that pile, there's another on my desk." He nods toward a stack of folders that must be close to two feet high. "And it's *one hour* for lunch. Not an hour and ten minutes."

"Caleb." I'm surprised by how calm my words are because my stomach is a volcano ready to erupt. "I don't run an army barracks, for Christ's sake. Ten minutes will not collapse us."

His expression is colder than a witch's tit in a brass bra. Stella, surprisingly, holds her head high, exposing the delicate column of her neck. She's nervous around Caleb, but she's not afraid of him. It's interesting, and probably fucking stupid.

"Let's go," Caleb orders, and I follow more obediently than Dog because there's a foreboding sensation hanging over me, something telling me my world is about to crumble —again.

"What do you mean?" I ask for the third time. My gaze is glued to Harold Sterling as he bounces a baby on his aging knee. I've known this man since I was the little girl's age. He's been my family's attorney for even longer, but I don't ever remember him using the Raleigh office—my dad always saw him in Sailport Bay.

"I'm sorry, Becker. Calista communicated that she attempted contact multiple times before she passed. She left this letter for you, and she named you guardian of Emmy and Ruby."

My heart is beating so fast I'm lightheaded. I've never had a panic attack before but I'm pretty sure I'm about to pass out. "How?" My throat is scratchy, and my voice is a detached version of my own.

"She had glioblastoma, son, brain cancer. She fought a valiant battle, but—"

"Why isn't Davis taking care of his girls?" My jaw aches. It turned to stone the second I saw the girls. The oldest is the spitting image of my sister.

The old man's features morph into a sadness I can't begin to fathom. The little girl in the corner of the room lays on her belly with markers in both hands as she colors in a book on the floor. Her feet are pointed to the ceiling and she swings them side to side. Cally used to do her homework that way—hell, she talked on the phone that way too.

"You truly haven't kept in touch with anyone in Sailport Bay?"

"You understand why I haven't," I say through clenched teeth. Something cracks. It could have been my neck or a molar, I have no idea. My entire body is threatening to crumble as if I'm an old building and a wrecking ball just crashed through my center.

He nods, only once, and the disappointment in his features causes my knuckles to clench. Caleb has stayed shockingly silent since we walked in and were ambushed by crying children. I swear his left eye twitches in time with the little one's drooling.

"Davis was killed in an accident before Ruby was born."

My fist lands on my heart and pounds against my chest as though I'm trying to jumpstart it myself.

"Cally said you're the only one she trusts with her babies. She's relying on you to give them the life she no longer can."

An image of a teenage Cally ushering me away from our house with angry, shouted words trailing us strikes my conscience like an aggravated snake.

Where the hell did that come from? Was it real? I don't have many memories from my childhood. My therapist said I blocked them out, but why would I do that? I just assumed it was normal. Who remembers stuff from thirty years ago?

"What if he refuses them?" Caleb speaks, drawing my attention, but his face is an icy mask of indifference. Even the seemingly happy baby curls in on herself.

I may behave like an asshole most of the time, but even I know there's a heart buried under all this denial. There's no way I could turn away innocent children—my nieces.

My fucking nieces.

"The next living family member is Danica Delacroix," Harold informs me with raised brows—silently communicating that he's aware of how vile that woman is. "And she wants the girls."

Fuck. Who would she turn them into?

Cally made her choices. She told me our father was right to disown me, that I'd only bring the company down. She said she was choosing the Delacroix family over me, and she always would, but she wasn't a bad person—not really —not the Cally I grew up with. This is too much. It's all too much. I can't process anything around me.

"Perfect. There's your out, Beck. Let's get the paperwork started and leave Mr. Sterling here with these—these—things."

"Mr. Fairfax, I implore you to take a moment with your clie—"

"They can't go to that woman." My voice is monotone but clear as a lightning strike.

"I was hoping you'd say that." Harold visibly relaxes. "Danica is..."

"A piece of shit," I supply.

His face turns crimson.

"Are you still the Delacroix's attorney as well?"

"I can't speak about other clients, Becker, you know that."

"It's Beck," I snap. "My father called me Becker. He's dead and so is that name."

Elijah uses it now to rile me up, but this—this is something different.

The little girl in his lap watches me with wide eyes and a trembling lower lip. Damn it. I didn't mean to scare her.

"I don't know the first thing about children." My voice wavers with insecurity.

"Exactly why allowing someone else to care for them is best," Caleb says.

Harold is quick to cut in. "I've gathered all the information you'll need, as well as what we could grab from their home, given the circumstances. Cally made sure the girls were well taken care of with your cousin until it was time for me to bring them to you."

What was she thinking?

"Beck, you have three new properties opening this year. This is not the time to—"

"The time to what?" I hiss, finally releasing the vitriol

swirling in my chest on someone. Caleb may be the best damn attorney I've ever had, but I can only handle so much shit from him today.

"The time to lose my sister?" I seethe, leaning in closer as the rage takes root. "The time for these little girls to become orphans? Exactly what kind of time are you talking about, Caleb?" I feel borderline maniacal, but I press on. "Where's your moral compass?" I'm on a roll, anger spiking every word. "Does loyalty mean nothing anymore?"

I study every flinch, every twitch of his eye, and the intensity of my tone hits exactly as I intended it to. Feigning indifference, he brushes lint off his pant leg, but his clenched fists let me know I've made my point.

"Mark my words, Beck. You're giving your competitors exactly what they want. With you distracted, they'll move in on every project you don't have your finger on. We're talking millions of dollars."

There's a small tug on my suit jacket, and I turn from Caleb to find a spitting image of my sister. My rage dissipates like rain hitting hot pavement. This little girl is my niece, and I don't even know her name. I've gone from jerk to next-level asshole in the span of one meeting.

"Mommy told me 'bout you."

Salty tears sting the back of my throat.

"She did?" I croak.

The little girl nods. I look to Harold for help.

"This is Emmy, Beck. She's four and little Ruby here just turned one."

Emmy—our grandmother's name. My stomach hollows out, and my heartbeat thrashes in my chest.

Ruby shakes some kind of bottle, or maybe it's a cup, I have no idea, but little droplets of milk fly everywhere.

"Mommy said you'll be a good daddy if you twust

yoself," she says with a head nod that accentuates each word, then hands me a piece of paper. Moisture pricks at the corners of my eyes, blurring the colors, but I get the gist. Emmy drew me a picture. On the grass stands a stick man with two little girls, and two people—her parents—sit in the clouds.

Caleb huffs next to me. "This is a family matter now, Beck. You don't require my assistance for this."

I barely hear him as I stare into eyes so similar to the ones that once protected all my childhood dreams.

Another flash of Cally climbing into bed with me and covering my ears picks at my heart like a scab that won't heal. Why are these memories assaulting me now?

Emmy smiles up at me, and my heart cracks a little more.

"You look just like your mommy," I choke out, and her entire face lights up.

She nods aggressively with happiness, showing off her bright white teeth. She's missing one in the front. "Before mommy turned gway, she said we was twinsies."

"Gray," Harold informs me, understanding I might not speak kid. But the knowledge that Cally was gray at all blasts my chest wide open.

She died alone. She tried to reach out to me, and I ignored her out of spite. Now I'll never have the chance to make amends.

What kind of monster does that make me?

My insides shake as though someone has grabbed ahold of each lung and is swinging me around the room by them. I rub my tingling palms roughly on my thighs, but it doesn't ease the sensations eating me alive.

Harold goes through a pile of toys and contraptions, explaining what everything is. Then he orders me a car and has security help me to the sidewalk with all their stuff.

"If there's anything else you need, you'll find it at the house in Sailport Bay. This is just enough to get you started. The house..."

Harold keeps talking about Cally and the house, but the rising tide of my panic drowns him out. Is he just dropping me at the pavement with a farewell and good luck? Is this really happening?

When the car pulls up, he hands me a crying little girl and places Emmy's hand in mine while security loads the trunk.

Where do I even go from here?

CHAPTER THREE

STELLA

MY PHONE DINGS WITH AN INCOMING UP-LIFT RIDE AND I accept it immediately, then pull out onto Hillsborough Street. They're close enough that I can squeeze in one more customer before I return to work, and bonus points because we're headed to the same block.

I'm still not sure why Elijah allows me to use his car like this, or why he won't even accept gas money from me. I also didn't expect that at almost thirty, I'd be a rideshare driver in my spare time, but every penny counts these days, and I can't afford to question generosity—even if it's a hit to my pride every single time.

I keep a mental tally of everything I take, and I've vowed to pay him back. Somehow.

After a two-day onboarding session with Lottie—thankfully over the weekend since I'm sure Caleb wouldn't have approved the days off without advance notice—I had my first call a couple nights ago with a sweet dad named Marcus. I wasn't expecting to get a call so soon after I was accepted into SDH. He was already pretty hands-on and only wanted to know how high a fever should be before contacting the doctor. He hasn't called back since.

GPS says my customer is straight ahead, so I pull up next to the sidewalk and a moment later, the back door opens.

I work quickly, adjusting the GPS to take us to our destination, and shimmy in my seat a little because it's finally my lucky day—this guy is heading to the Hayes building. Take that and stuff it, Caleb. Not even Mr. Freeze can complain about my lunch hour now.

The door slams shut, and whimpers fill my ears next. Did this jerk bring a dog into Elijah's car? He'll kill me.

"Harold?" I ask lifting my gaze to the rearview mirror, then spin around in horror.

"No, sorry," Beck says, shifting a little girl in his lap and searching for a seat belt. "That's my attorney, he ordered the ride for me." He finally lifts his head, and we both freeze, staring at each other with our mouths hanging open.

"Stella?" He looks around as if he's being pranked. No such luck, big guy. This is really happening. "Why are you driving strangers around?" He glances at the interior of the vehicle and zeroes in on the monogrammed floor mats. "Is this Elijah's car?"

My face heats, but I will myself to sit tall. "It is. I don't have a car, so he lets me borrow it to make some extra cash." I sold mine two months ago to pay for my mother's health-care facility.

Times are more than desperate.

Beck's face shows every ounce of confusion that must be running through his mind right now.

"Don't we pay well?" he asks while the baby in his arms attempts to stick her fingers up his nose. Seeing him dodge her assault is quite funny, but I bite my lip to keep from laughing at him.

Then his question registers and I exhale an uncomfortable giggle-snort. That's what he's worried about right now?

I stare pointedly at the little girls who have wide, terrified eyes, and I give them what I hope is a reassuring smile. "Hi there, my name's Stella. What's yours?"

The oldest searches Beck's face, and her shoulders sag when he doesn't say anything. "I'm Emmy," she says sadly. "She's Wuby. She cwies. Uncle Beck is our new daddy."

Beck splutters unintelligible words, and I'm pretty sure all the color just drained from my face, but I try to pull it together for a number of reasons, none of which are the fact that my boss's boss, who destroyed me with a kiss, is now staring at me like I have three heads.

"Well, it's very nice to meet you girls. I'm sure—ah—Uncle Beck—er—Daddy will make a great—daddy."

These must be his sister's daughters. The one who kept trying to reach him? The reality of what that must mean for him hits me in the heart with a painful thunk.

Beck makes a choked sound in the back of his throat, and I quickly face forward. "Do you have car seats for them?"

"What?"

"They need car seats. Maybe it's different with taxis or rideshares, but they'll need car seats if you want to take them anywhere."

"Add it to the list," he says dryly.

Shaking my head, I check the locks on the car doors, turn on my blinker, and pull out onto the street.

"Are you Uncle Beck Daddy's fwiend?" Emmy asks, her voice filling with a little more confidence.

I chance a peek at her in the mirror, but my gaze snags on Beck's. I'm guessing his blank stare has more to do with his sudden parentage than me being the one to pick him up on a street corner.

"Sort of," I say sweetly. "I work for his company."

"Mommy says Uncle Beck Daddy is vewy smawt."

My lips curl up at her pronunciations. She's a cutie.

"Um, how about just Uncle Beck. Or Beck," he says absently, and my shoulders roll in while my face scrunches up on his behalf. "What? What did I say?" he whispers.

My gaze flicks back and forth from the road to his in the rearview mirror. I shrug, but his eyes plead with me for answers and my mouth opens without my permission.

"I don't know exactly what's happening here, but I'm guessing there's a lot of f-e-a-r," I spell out. "And a-n-x-i-e-t-y too. Too much change all at once probably isn't good for them."

Damn it, Stella. Why the heck do you have to help everyone?

"You know a lot about kids?"

I shrug but catch sight of the littlest one in the rearview mirror. She has her fist in her mouth and drool covering every inch of her.

"In college I nannied for a family with five kids, and in another life I was a kindergarten teacher," I say. Insecurity and embarrassment over my past crash into me.

"What happened?" He sounds genuinely interested, but it's probably because he could use any distraction he can find right now. Emmy sits with her attention on me in the mirror, but the baby is all up in his face and he's struggling to hold her still. She's a wild one.

I shrug. "It wasn't enough money." The lie almost rolls off my tongue now.

His brows furrow, and it takes a second longer for the scent of feces to hit the front seat, but when it does, I shudder. He's probably wearing her leaky diaper. Beck gags and claws at the window button.

"What the hell is that?" he chokes out.

"Wuby pooped," Emmy explains. She's remarkably calm as I pull up to his building.

"That's my name," Emmy says excitedly, pointing at the sidewalk where giant mirrored letters stand tall. "H-a-y-e-s," she spells.

His head whips in her direction. "It is?"

The little girl nods. "Just like Mommy."

Beck remains silent.

"Very good, sweetheart," I say to break the tension. "Um, why don't I pull into Elijah's parking space, and then I'll help you get the girls upstairs?"

"Yes," he blurts before I've even finished speaking.

Sweat beads at his hairline and a taut muscle in his neck twitches. Has he ever been around children? From the panic taking over his features, I'm guessing no. The SDH card crosses my mind, but I shut it down immediately. It's against the rules to talk about my third job with anyone, and I desperately need that money. He'll figure it out, or Elijah will tell him. I'm sure of it—mostly.

By the time I pull into the parking space, Ruby's very unhappy, and she lets everyone know it. Beck leaps from the car, holding her in front of him with straight arms, and the sounds of Ruby's cries echo uncomfortably against the concrete walls of the parking garage.

"What's wrong with her? Is she hurt? Did I hurt her already?" Each word rises an octave higher than the last.

The fear in his tone pinches at my heart. I stare at him for a beat too long. He truly has no idea what to do. I make a mental note to create a list of emergency phone numbers for him, just in case.

"No, Be—ah, Mr. Hayes. She's poopy. No one wants to sit in their own filth."

"I don't have a fucking clue what I'm doing here. Why would she do this to me?" He's spinning in circles and talking to the ceiling, so I assume he isn't expecting an answer from me.

Emmy sits perched on the edge of the back seat with her feet dangling out the car door. I take Ruby from Beck. At least the diaper didn't leak. Then I lean down to talk to Emmy.

"Hey, sweetie. Have you seen the diaper bag?"

"Diaper bag?" Beck repeats in a near squeal. Perhaps this is all sinking in for him right now.

I throw him an expression I hope reads, *calm the heck down*, but end up rolling my eyes. He's gripping his hair with both hands. Dramatic much? This man is rich enough to hire nannies around the clock. It's not as though he'll be the one personally taking care of them.

I return my attention to Emmy. She's scrambled across the seat and is hefting a large bag with pink flowers all over it.

"Thanks, Ems. You're a great little helper. Now, can you scoot back so I can lie Ruby down to change her diaper?"

She nods and scoots back, then lowers her face to her baby sister's and starts humming a tune I recognize, "Never Grow Up" by Taylor Swift.

"Does your mommy sing that to you?" I ask, and her little face floods with sadness, a tear slipping free.

"It's a very special song," I say, pulling out a few wipes and undoing Ruby's diaper.

Heat at my back makes my spine tingle. Beck leans over me to see what I'm doing and gags again, so I elbow him to back up.

What a baby.

"Do you have a copy of that song with you?"

More tears fill Emmy's eyes. "It's at home."

Beck is behind me again. "All your stuff is at home? Where? In Sailport Bay? We'll just buy new stuff." Then his body heat is replaced with cool air.

"I don't think that's the point, Mr. Hayes," I say through clenched teeth. If I roll my eyes any harder, I'll be glaring at him from the back of my head. Geez. All these girls need is a little compassion and love right now, can't he see that?

I fasten a new diaper onto Ruby, pull up her cute little leggings covered in daisies, and tug her into my arms. My nose immediately goes to her hair. Baby smells are the best.

She also has the chubbiest cheeks. The kind that are meant for kisses, so I kiss them, and she giggles in return. Beck stands far off to the side with eyes so wide I'm sure they'll fall out like a Saturday morning cartoon soon.

The fear, the sadness, the need for love shows in Emmy's haunted expression. She needs affection too, so I offer it, feeling a connection with her that makes my throat itchy.

"Hey, Emmy, have you had a hug today?"

Taking charge is not my smartest option. I've spent months hiding behind people and odd jobs so no one would question me, but their needs trump my own.

"Mr. Sterling gave me a hug when I cwied."

I drop to my knees in the dirty parking garage and open my left arm. She crashes into me as though she hasn't been safe her entire life and my heart finds a little crevice just for her.

Beck stands ten feet away, his face going twelve shades of gray. I stay crouched down until Emmy pulls away.

"You give really good hugs," I tell her. "I might need a lot of those. Would that be okay?"

She flings herself back into my arms and we stay huddled together until my legs cramp and I have to stand or lose the ability altogether.

Emmy instantly grabs my left hand. With Ruby tucked on my hip, I stare at Beck. This man puts all my teenage crushes to shame, yet he stands gawking at us. "Ah, if you can grab the bags, I'll bring the girls up to your office."

His swallow is visible from here, but he agrees and moves toward the car, giving us a wide berth.

"They don't bite," I say. "Well, Ruby might, but she'll grow out of it."

He blanches, then runs his tongue along his front teeth. Is he gauging how much damage human teeth can do? I almost feel bad for laughing, but not so much that I don't do it. I can't help it. This gazillionaire is scared of two sweet little girls.

"Come on, ladies. I'll show you where Uncle Beck Daddy's office is."

His groan causes a tingling heat to spread through me as a memory attempts to surface. I give in to the awkward shiver overtaking my body, ridding myself of those pesky images, and guide Emmy to the elevator, holding it open for Beck.

He approaches us warily, and when he steps inside holding at least eight different duffel bags, the heaviness of what he's dealing with falls over us.

I'm a jerk for laughing at him. I don't have to know the details of what made him an Uncle Daddy to understand that whatever's happened is devastating for all three of them. But I hope he has a good support system in place—at least one better than he has at work.

He doesn't rely on anyone in the office, except maybe Elijah. We're very similar that way.

Will he even remember anything I tell him? His glassy eyes and dazed expression point to no. He must be in shock.

Maybe I'll write down notes for him in addition to the emergency numbers.

I lift my head to find him staring at me in the mirrored walls, and my entire body flares with heat.

"Thank you," he mouths. The sincerity in his expression hits me like a kiss in a rainstorm.

I simply nod. Whatever the heck is going on with him will take a whole lot of help and patience.

Two things I haven't seen Beck excel at since I've worked here—but my body knows he's capable of.

Ruby snuggles into my side at the same time that Emmy tightens her grip around my leg, and we make the rest of the ride to the top floor in silence.

CHAPTER FOUR

BECK

I'M THE LAST TO STEP OFF THE ELEVATOR AND I DO IT WITH A heavy heart. My sister died. Alone. And she expects me to raise her girls? Does she even know me?

She doesn't know you because you locked the door on your relationship and threw away the key, my conscience spits.

Guilt gnaws at my lungs, making it difficult to breathe.

"Ah, what's this?" Elijah asks, moving around his desk to take some bags from me. Thank God it's only Caleb and me at this end of the building. The next few weeks are going to turn my life upside down and inside out.

Caleb sticks his head out of his door. "There you are," he grumbles to Stella, but stops short when he finds her carrying both girls. "What's going on here?"

Stella stands still and hitches Ruby up higher with an impressive little hop that lifts her blouse to show the tiniest sliver of bare skin.

Dog prances around them and the girls squeal in delight. One point for Dog.

"Beck?" Caleb asks.

"Stella's helping me out," I say, then hold my breath as

the woman in question lowers herself to one knee in front of Dog. Emmy rests against her knee while she holds Ruby at her side. She's like a fucking octopus.

"Whatever you have scheduled for her, cancel it or do it yourself." I ignore Caleb's huff. "I need her help with the girls right now." My tone is unforgiving, but I don't regret it. The more I listen, the more I really hear how he speaks to his assistant, and it irritates me more now than ever. I'm fully aware that nothing concerning Stella should matter to me, but I'm at the very limit of giving a fuck today and, whether I want to admit it or not, Stella matters. Whatever magic she wields has lodged itself like an ice chip you didn't mean to swallow.

"Shit," I curse. If I don't ask for Stella's help, then I'm no better than Caleb. At least I remembered my damn manners before it was too late. "Ah, is that okay, Stella?"

The beautiful woman who prefers to navigate life in the shadows narrows her eyes and glances at the girls. "Unless you want little girls who get kicked out of preschool for having potty mouths, you need to watch yours."

Caleb, Elijah, and I all stand up a little straighter. Her tone was hushed, but I'm surprised by the steel in her delivery. Good for you, Stella!

Caleb scoffs indignantly—presumably at Stella's tone—and takes a step forward. He's a dark cloud amidst a sea of rainbows. Ruby throws a plastic toy at him, and he retreats as though his ass is on fire. The great Caleb Fairfax is afraid of children, and it almost makes me smile.

When Caleb opens his mouth, I hold up a hand before this can get out of control, but I can't contain my smirk. "She's right. Miss Anderson, would you mind, *please*, helping me with the girls while I sort out this...stuff?"

Her lips move but no words come. Eventually, she

releases a long sigh and angles her head toward the ceiling. "Sure," she says. "But I can't stay later than five. I have other obligations and I can't be late."

Tilting my head, I study her, allowing my face to relax when she stares back. "More rides to give?"

My words conjure a vision of her riding my dick, and Elijah elbows me in the side. What? I was talking about her rideshare job. Could they hear my thoughts too?

"Something like that," she says, then turns away from me and ushers Emmy to the far corner where an armchair and ottoman sit.

"Caleb, you're dismissed. Elijah, my office. Now." My attention is drawn to Stella in the corner with both girls in her lap and Dog splayed across her feet. Something about that scene pulls a "please" from my lips which causes Elijah to outright laugh.

I shove him through the door. This is what I get for allowing him to believe we're friends. I should have fired him a long time ago.

He doesn't say anything, but keeps his grin plastered to his face and settles into the wingback chair across from my desk, then waits for me to sink into the plush leather of mine.

I drop a few bags beside his chair, grab a folder the attorney had given me out of one of them, then set it down on my desk. The second my ass hits the chair, I go into a catatonic state. I don't even blink until Elijah waves a hand in front of my face.

"What's going on out there, Beck?"

For a moment, I'm too overwhelmed to speak, so I shake my head. Take a breath. Then manage, "They're my—my sister's girls. She's dead." The weight of those words hangs resonant in the air.

His face falls and contorts as he processes my words. "I'm so sorry," he says, as stunned as I am.

"Cancer." I hear my voice, but it's stilted and strange. "It happened a few days ago. She asked for her cremation to take place before they contacted me. She didn't want a service. I—I guess the girls were with my cousin until now."

Elijah rises from his chair and walks purposefully toward the bar in the corner of my office. He fills a glass with ice cubes and two fingers of bourbon before returning to me. I've never enjoyed straight bourbon, but today I'll make an exception.

A squeal of pure joy comes from one of the girls and the level of responsibility I'm tasked with punches me in the throat. I can't drink right now. Not when I have to figure out their shit. My gaze lingers on the door separating us until Elijah breaks my concentration.

"They're in good hands. Stella can handle this."

Stella. "That's it," I say, standing so quickly my chair rolls into the wall of windows behind me.

"Ah, what's it?"

"Stella. She can be their nanny until I figure this out."

Elijah's face contorts, and it creates a heavy, uncomfortable pang in my chest. I'm aware of how close they've become, but what is he privy to in her life that I'm not? Never in my life have I wanted to belong to a clique as much as I do now.

Want, not need. It's an important distinction.

"There are other options, Beck. Ones that will probably work better for the both of you," he says, focusing on his suspenders. "She has a lot on her plate. A lot of responsibilities that mean she keeps a tight schedule, and your schedule is anything but stable."

"Is that why she's playing taxi in your car?"

"Yes," he states curtly with no further explanation.

I stare at him until he shrugs. "It's not my story to tell. She deserves privacy too, but know this. Every day is a struggle for her, and she never asks for anything from anyone. Do not make things more difficult for her with Caleb."

I sigh and drag the chair back to my desk, then sit. "My sister died, and I wasn't there." I drop my head to my desk. "And she died alone because fucking Davis went rappelling two years ago. They called it a freak accident. Found his mangled body at the bottom of a ravine. She had to handle that grief on her own too—while raising a toddler and being pregnant."

Why didn't I pick up the phone? Just once—that's all it would have taken.

He sits quietly and allows me to grieve out loud. He has always believed I was wrong for ignoring Cally's phone calls, and now I'm drowning in guilt because he was right. I should have picked up the phone.

"So," he says after a long silence. "You have two options." I sit upright and pinch the bridge of my nose when tears obstruct my view.

"What's that?" I ask, leaning so my forearms rest on the cool surface of my desk. I'm too antsy to sit still and too angry to move. Instead, I open the folder that contains everything left in those little girls' lives.

Passports that have never been used.

Birth certificates. Emmy and I share a birthday—March 25th. My chest constricts.

Note after note from my sister, listing all their likes, dislikes, and everything in between. She planned for her death.

"You allow the guilt to consume you, or you become the

man your sister expected you to be." He holds a small black card in the air.

"What is that?"

Elijah slides it across my desk. In swirling baby-pink script, it says *The Single Dad Hotline*.

"What the hell is that? I'm not a dad. Is this a sex line?" Holy shit. When you become a parent do you automatically lose your sex life too? Can I do that?

Who am I kidding? I haven't had a sex life in—well, since the night I explored every inch of Stella's mouth. Not because of her, but because...of work. I don't do relationships, and one-night stands are trickier in the age of social media.

The lies we tell ourselves. Get a grip, Beck—you're spiraling.

"Would I give you a sex line number?" he asks. I raise a brow. "Fine, I probably would, but that's not what this is. It's a hotline for single dads and new dads of a certain wealth. You reach out, explain your situation, and you're assigned a helper that will be available to you twenty-four hours a day. If someone falls and you don't know what to do, you call. If someone gets sick at two in the morning, you call. If you need to hire a nanny and don't know what questions to ask, they'll help you. They'll guide you through all the hiccups of first-time parenting."

I turn it over in my fingertips, but everything is a blur. My mind is too crowded with memories vying for my attention. Memories of Cally and me. Images of these two mini-humans I'm expected to care for.

I cough to clear the emotion clogging my throat and use the girls' medical records as a distraction. Why would they have two pediatricians? The one in Sailport Bay I recognize, but the one here in Raleigh—she must have done that for my benefit.

Flipping to the final page, I pause at the sealed letter from my sister. Her penmanship is shaky, but I'd recognize the way she writes the B in my name anywhere.

"You'll do great things one day, Bear, so your name should start with a flourish." If I concentrate really hard, I can almost hear her voice. A barricade breaks and tears flood my cheeks. I hated her for choosing the family that destroyed our own, but I loved her too. Growing up, she was the most important person in my life. I love her and hate her and I—I loved her.

How could I let her die this way? I should have saved her.

Time passes slowly as I read the instructions from Cally, then hand them to Elijah so he can take notes of his own, which seem to consist of making lists full of baby supplies.

I can't bring myself to open her letter because I'm a coward.

Whatever's in there will break me.

"I let her down," I say quietly.

"You were hurting."

"It's been seven years since my mom died, Elijah. Seven years since I found out she planned to marry Davis and pulled the rug out from under me and my company. And now it's too late—they're both gone."

Ruby cries on the other side of the door, and I stand on instinct. No idea how to help her, but the sound tugs on something inside me, urging me forward.

"So what are you going to do?" Elijah asks.

Freezing in the middle of the room, I look down at the metal business card still clutched in my fist. "I'm going to take a crash course in parenting and hope I don't sink them or my company in the process."

Maybe focusing on the girls' needs will make it easier to ignore the guilt trying to suffocate me.

"The Single Dad Hotline," Elijah says with a wink. "It's been growing in popularity in our circles for about a year. It'll cost you a pretty penny, but it'll be worth it if the baby starts teething and you have no idea how to calm her down."

I flinch at his words. "I've never been around kids. What was she thinking leaving them to me?"

He shrugs, but sympathy shines in his eyes. "What was her alternative?"

A disgusted growl vibrates in my chest. "Danica Delacroix. For some reason, my cousin, Tabby, isn't an option."

"Oh, Beck. She really didn't have a choice, did she?"

No, she didn't. It was me or a woman who puts the devil to shame.

"No," I say, then exhale a long breath. "I have to do this, right?"

It's an idiotic question. Of course I do. There's no telling what kind of life the girls would have with Danica, but I do know it wouldn't be healthy or happy. And somewhere, buried deep, lives a need to do this for my sister.

Reaching for the door, I turn back to him. "Wait. How do you know about the Single Dad Hotline?"

"From a friend of mine," he says elusively.

"Care to expand on that? Did it work? Is it worth it?"

"Yeah, Beck. It's worth it. Have you ever even held a baby before?"

Fuck. Not until the car ride back with Stella.

Returning to my desk, I place the card face up and pull out my cell phone. "There's only an email address. What the hell kind of business is this?"

"I think it's one that will save your ass. And I know you, Becker Hayes. Your mind is running in hyperdrive because you'll try to do this all by yourself, but newsflash, that's not how families work. Families are plural for a reason—it takes a village, so lean on yours. You're not alone in this."

He lifts his iPad in the air. "I'll start by having this stuff shipped to your penthouse. After you contact the Single Dad Hotline, research babyproofing. In your house, that's a priority."

Babyproofing? What the hell is babyproofing? I'm typing *babyproof* into my phone when he reaches the door and Dog barks.

I groan while Emmy scolds her. "No, Daisie Dukes. Inside voices."

Did she just rename Dog? Two kids and a dog. Who the fuck am I?

"Elijah?"

He pauses in the doorway and raises a brow in my direction. "Can you help with Dog tonight? I—I don't think I can handle all three of them."

"You know I will. I've got your back, Beck." He shuts my office door with a near-silent click.

In the privacy of my office, I drop my head into my hands. "I'm so sorry, Cally." Her name sits rusty on my tongue. But I mean every word. "Why me? I'm not cut out to be a father. Aren't you afraid I'll mess them up?"

Dog whines and scratches at my door. I picture Emmy with her little finger pointing at Dog, and I smile.

The envelope addressed to me mocks me from my desk, but I'm still not ready to open it. Instead, I slide it into the inside pocket of my suit jacket and wake up my computer to compose a new email.

To: Lottie
From: Beck Hayes
Subject:

What the hell do I say?

Subject: ~~*Two Girls, a Dog, and me*~~
Subject: ~~*Someone made a mistake*~~
Subject: ~~*I'm fucked*~~

Grow some balls, dude. It's just an email, but I'm not an idiot. Once I send this email, everything changes.

Dog whines, and I become a father with a few strokes of my keyboard.

Subject: Help

Dear Ms. Lottie,

My name is Beck Hayes. I've recently been awarded guardianship of my two nieces. I've never been around children and to say I'm ill-prepared is an understatement. My friend, Elijah Sinclair, said you may be able to help.

I await your response,

Beck Hayes

CHAPTER FIVE

STELLA

Come on, come on! Seriously, get out of the way.

I don't say it out loud as my rideshare driver friend weaves through traffic, trying to get me to Mindful Moments, but I shout it in my head like a demented people-eater.

I have a love-hate relationship with five o'clock now, but if I have any chance of my mom remembering me, it'll happen around that time.

Each visit becomes harder. I hate this disease that's slowly eating away at her mind until she's nothing but a shell of who she once was. And sometimes it turns her into a person she's never been—angry, violent, and sad.

Even though I rationally understand it all stems from fear, it doesn't help when it's happening in the moment.

Finally, Eddie pulls up in front of Mindful Moments. He has an uncle here, so I stop in to visit Uncle Joe in exchange for the ride. So far, the deal has worked out for us both. Eddie visits once a week, and I check in on him the other days. It's hard to experience the slow deterioration of someone you love, so I never hold his choices against him, and he allows me to cry silently in the back seat without trying to comfort me.

There is no comfort for this disease.

"Thanks, Eddie."

"Thank you, kid. You sure you don't want me to come back for you?"

I glance up at the sky, happy it's clear after so much rain. "Nah, thanks. I'll take the bus and walk the rest of the way. It gives me time to process."

He simply nods because he gets it. I wait until the car pulls away, suck in a deep breath, and send up a little prayer that today will be a good day.

But I still drag my feet to the front entrance as though my legs are trudging through three feet of mud. My mother's my best friend, but some days, the ones where I'm a stranger, drain all hope from my heart. I'm losing her, and I have a front-row seat to see it happen in slow motion.

Lucía rounds the corner when I pick up the tablet to sign in. "Oh, Stella, hon. I'm glad I caught you. I'm sorry, sweetie. We had to sedate her about an hour ago."

Tears sting my eyes. "What happened?"

"She was hitting other patients, and she clawed at one of the guards. She still believes Mrs. Jones stole her blouse. We tried to calm her for close to thirty minutes before making the call."

I shake away her pity and take away her guilt. "It's okay. Can I still sit with her for a few minutes?"

These are the times I can cry for a loss that's already happened without confusing my mother more.

"Of course, hon. Take your time."

I've memorized the sterile halls that lead to my mother's room over the last few months. As I follow the yellow walls on each visit, I silently pray I'll be able to earn enough money to keep her here when the bribe I accepted runs out.

Laura Anderson was once the life of the party. The hostess with the mostest even though we had little to our name for as long as I can remember, but she'd give you the shirt off her back even if it were her last. We're so different, but I've never loved anyone more than I love her.

Would she find me a disappointment if she knew how I hid at parties or that I was rarely invited in the first place? Did she ever find it odd that I preferred time with her to birthday parties with other kids? Did she know I made those decisions so she didn't have to pick up an extra shift to put cake into the mouths of girls who made fun of me behind my back?

When my mother passes, I'll be an orphan, just like Beck's nieces. That thought causes a flood of emotion that nearly knocks me off my feet. Even at twenty-nine, I feel the weight of being completely alone in life.

God, those poor little girls. I don't pray often, but tonight, as I lower my face to my mother's bed and purge myself of sadness, I beg for them to be spared any more pain.

<hr>

IT'S DARK WHEN SOMEONE NUDGES MY SHOULDER. LIFTING MY head from my mother's bed, I find her beautiful face smiling down at me. "Go to bed, dear," she says with a shaky voice. She's far too young to be taken by this horrible disease. "You're going to do great things in college, Stella. And I'll only be a phone call away."

Her eyes drift closed as I stand. It's the same memory

she replays often. The night before I left for college. I was terrified, but she held me close.

The lump in my throat cements itself in place, so I lean over and tuck her in, then carefully kiss her cheek.

"I love you, Mom." It's a whisper that's met with silence like so many times before.

What I wouldn't give for her to tell me she loves me just one more time.

I hadn't meant to fall asleep, so by the time I check in on Uncle Joe, he's been out for hours. I tiptoe out of the facility that's bleeding me dry but keeping my mom comfortable. I don't care if I have to sell a kidney to keep her here. I'll do whatever it takes—I have done whatever it takes—regardless of who that makes me. She gave me life, so the least I can do is make sure her time left is comfortable.

The cool air of an early spring evening slaps me in the face when I step outside. I've never thought about the scents of seasons, but spring does carry something like hope on its cool breezes.

It's after ten, and all my fears kick in to overdrive as I walk into the darkness. It's too late to call Eddie and I just missed this hour's bus, so I duck my head, lengthen my stride, and count my steps while I wish I had ears like Dog's that could listen in every direction for an unknown threat. Finally, thirty minutes later, I step onto the walkway leading me home.

I'm just turning the fourth lock on my door when my phone rings. SDH pops up on the caller ID and nervous energy makes my palms sweat. I've only had a handful of calls so far, and they're all routed through the Single Dad Hotline—Lottie said it was to maintain our privacy.

I run to the sofa and answer in the way I was mentored. "Single Dad Hotline, I'm your helper. How can I help you?"

Heavy breathing then a song I heard earlier is muffled through a crackling connection. No. No. No. This can't be happening. Hitting the speaker button, I scroll through my emails.

There's no way Lottie would approve him this fast, would she?

"Hello?" he asks, and a cold sweat covers my exposed skin.

"Y—Yes, how can I help you?" Can Beck hear the panic in my voice? Crap, does he recognize my voice? I hold out my phone, put it on speaker, then determinedly roughen my tone.

"I, ah, I'm new. To all of this, I mean." His chuckle is humorless, and I can envision his hands mussing up his hair. "I was given two girls today, and this is ridiculous, but I don't know how to get them to bed. Emmy, she's the oldest, says there's a routine, but I don't know what it is. I left their instructions in my office because they were starving, and hungry kids cry—a lot—and loudly. It's my first night, and I don't want to call my assistant to get it. I have to be able to handle this shit."

I find the offending email from Lottie just as he stops talking.

From: Lottie
To: Stella
Subject: New Client!!!!

"Okay, take a deep breath," I say, hoping I sound calm and in control and nothing like myself. "How long have you been attempting bedtime?"

He curses under his breath. "Since seven."

"Wow. Okay. It's been a rough night. You said Emmy?" I

ask, playing dumb. It's a stupid idea, but until I can get him transferred to someone else, I need to help the guy without completely embarrassing him or breaking my four-hundred-page contract.

"Yeah. Ah, she said I need to brush their teeth, and I tried, I really did, but the little one bites on the bristles and won't let go. She's worse than Dog."

"Daisie," a little voice corrects, and I cover my mouth with both hands. Emmy has a delightful stubborn streak a mile long.

"Ah, anyway, then I read them stories. So many stories. But what do I do now? There's some song, a woman who works for me was kind enough to put it on my phone, but there are a million songs on my phone, and I can't find it," he grumbles.

I try to shrug off the icky feeling I have for deceiving him in this way.

"Okay, no worries." I hope the gravelly nature of my fake voice is enough to keep him from recognizing me. With the exception of one night I'm sure he hasn't thought of since, and the chaos of today, we've barely spoken. There's no way he could pull my name from this conversation now—still, I find myself crossing my fingers and toes. "What did you say your name was?"

"Beck Ha—" He stops short of his last name. Is he remembering Lottie's rules about oversharing?

"Well, hello, Beck. It's nice to meet you."

"And you are?" he asks over the sound of Ruby's cries. "You sound—"

"Ah, Jane. I'm Jane," I answer with my middle name like a squeaky robot. This is wrong—so wrong. What am I doing?

He chuckles. "It's not your real name, is it?"

"No, but rules are rules. Now, am I on speaker? Can I talk to Emmy?" Sniffling fills the silence. "Emmy? You there, sweetheart?"

"Y—Yes." I can picture the tremble of her lip and I pout in sympathy. These girls must be terrified. "Can you sing the song for me? Maybe I'll know it."

She hums the chorus, and after a few beats, I jump in. "Today is your lucky day, sweetie. That song happens to be one of my favorites. If, ah, if Beck plays it for you, do you think you'll be able to go to sleep?"

"Yes, Stella," she whispers, and I hold my breath.

The silence nearly suffocates me. How the heck did she recognize my voice?

"Uncle Beck Daddy is back. Can you tell him?"

"Sure. And Emmy?"

She doesn't answer, but I hear her sniffles.

"You're going to be just fine, okay? I know you will. Your Uncle Beck Daddy will keep you safe. Try to get some sleep, okay?"

"Mm-hmm."

It's quiet. Ruby's no longer crying.

"Beck?" I murmur when the silence of dead air takes up my entire living room.

"Yeah?" he whispers back.

"The song is by Taylor Swift. It's called 'Never Grow Up.' Did the baby fall asleep?"

"Finally," he sighs. "This is hard, Jane."

"You've got this. Where did you put the baby?" Visions of her rolling off a bed have my heart racing.

"In some foldable crib thing that took four YouTube videos to set up."

I laugh softly. "That's great. You're doing a good job. Once you get through the adjustment period, it'll be smooth sailing. How about you put that song on for Emmy, and I'll hang on the line until she's asleep in case you have any other questions."

Careful, Stella. Geez. I don't offer this to other dads. And this is why I could never be a double agent—I get too invested and I have a big mouth.

"I'd appreciate that. Thank you." Exhaustion bleeds from his tone, and it makes me a little weepy.

There's a rustling sound, and someone yawns.

"Oh, Beck?" I whisper.

"Huh?" Poor guy. I think I startled him.

"Are you putting Emmy to bed in the same room as her sister?"

"Night-night," she says, but it's garbled. Hopefully that means she's drifting off.

"No, I have plenty of guest rooms," he says.

"That's not my point." We're both whispering like a nun at church is about to catch us. "They'll probably sleep better if they're together. There's been so much upheaval, I mean, I'm guessing, since you said you were new to this. They need all the comfort they can get."

"Hmm. Do you want to sleep in Ruby's room, lovebug?"

His endearment is surprisingly sweet and totally unexpected.

"Mm-hmm," Emmy says followed by a yawn that probably swallows her entire face.

"Good night, lovebug," he whispers. A few seconds pass and then Emmy's song plays in the background.

"Crap," I whisper-yell. "Did you put a nightlight in that room?"

"I did," he says, and I can almost picture the pride beaming from his face.

"Good. That's good. What are you doing now?" Did that

sound dirty? Oh, God. I hope it wasn't dirty. All this time drooling over my boss and now we're speaking intimately late at night. It's a terrible, terrible idea and I'm going straight to hell for it.

"Honestly?" I make a sound for him to continue while chewing my lip raw. "I'm sitting outside their door wondering what the fuck I'm doing."

"You'll get the hang of it." I'm not whispering, but my voice is low, cozy, comfortable. "My first suggestion is to make an appointment with their doctor if they have one. If not, find one near you. They'll be able to give you a crash course in child safety. In the meantime, pick up a baby book or two. They're very helpful."

"Thank you, Jane." He sighs and I wish he knew it was me. "Do you ever feel like you've let down the only person who ever truly loved you and now there's nothing you can do about it?"

My heart beats against my chest so hard I can't catch my breath—this isn't part of the program. This isn't the Becker Hayes I know. He doesn't share, he doesn't open up, he doesn't do this.

"Every single day." He has no idea the power those words hold over me. "You can't change the past, but you can do everything in your power to do better."

"I guess."

"You should get some sleep. Littles are known to be early risers. Is there anything else I can help you with tonight, Beck?" I need to stop saying his name. It's too intimate, too reckless. His name conjures his taste, his scent, his whole being in my mind when I say it, and it's an addicting memory to cling to.

"Um, what the hell do I feed them for breakfast?"

It's so unexpected I laugh. "Sorry, that was rude of me."

"No, I'd probably laugh at myself too. I look like a giant asshole over here. Ruby puked all down the front of me. There are smashed peas in my hair, they smell like vomit, by the way, and I'm still wearing my suit pants."

I can envision it so clearly—his crooked smile that doesn't show often, but warms the entire building when it does, and his green, green eyes that sparkle even when he's angry.

"You're not an asshole," I say softly forgetting to mask my voice.

"I only knew what to get them for dinner because it's what my sister used to make me. She left very explicit instructions for my first night with them, and I couldn't even remember to bring them home. What if I forget one of the girls one day? I couldn't even get them to bed. How will I get them to college?"

"Whoa, slow your roll, big guy. College is a lifetime away. For now, focus on one moment at a time. Baby steps are still steps in the right direction."

"My sister knew I'd fuck this all up."

"You think so?" I lie back on my sofa and stare at the ceiling. "Raising two girls is a pretty big ask for someone she thought would mess it all up."

He's silent for a long moment, so I answer his original question. "Scrambled eggs are a safe bet as long as they don't have any allergies."

"That she wrote down twenty-seven times—no food allergies."

"Good. Then scrambled eggs it is. You can do this. They need you, so be patient with yourself, okay? It sounds like this is a huge shock for you all, so it will take some time for all of you to fall into a routine. Give yourself grace."

"I'll try. Thank you, Jane. Will I get you the next time I call, or will it be another Jane Doe?"

It can't be me.

"I'm not sure. I'm kind of new here too. But whoever answers will be able to help you."

"Good night," he whispers on a yawn.

"Good night, Beck."

I disconnect before I say something stupid, then reopen my email and send Lottie a response.

To: Lottie
From: Stella
Subject: RE: New client!!!!

Lottie! Beck Hayes needs to be assigned to someone else. I know him. Like in real life. I can't be his helper.

Stella

Her response is immediate. Does she ever sleep?

To: Stella
From: Lottie
Subject: RE: RE: New Client!!!!

Stella,

I understand your hesitancy, and in any other circumstance, I would agree. However, you're a perfect match, and I don't have anyone else who even comes close at this time. Beck is yours.

Lottie

Freaking Lottie and her seventy-page personality assessment—does it really matter how well we align? According to her, yes.

Is it weird that I've never spoken to this woman in any way other than email? Yes. Is it weirder that I know nothing about her? Also yes. But when Elijah handed me her card, I jumped at the chance. She pays well, and she pays on time, and that's really all I care about.

Well, that and how the heck I'm going to see Beck at the office and talk him down at night. *Why did I give him a fake name?* But I know the answer. In Lottie's onboarding session, she said the number one rule was to keep a professional distance from our clients so they don't become too attached, and I panicked when I heard his voice. Beck will see this as a betrayal—I know he will. So he can never, ever find out.

This has disaster written all over it—*The Parent Trap* had nothing on this.

CHAPTER SIX

BECK

THE GIRLS HAVE BEEN IN MY HOME FOR THREE DAYS NOW. That's three days of them in my office, playing with Stella, which means three days of Caleb up my ass about her workload piling up.

But it also means three days in which Emmy has retreated from the world, and three days of no sleep for me. I exhale sharply and allow my head to hit the door behind me.

I own the most exclusive spas and luxury brand in the world, and I'm sitting on my ass in a hallway, in front of the girls' room while they sleep. I have every type of baby monitor known to man, but I'm terrified of what will happen if I don't hear them when they need me.

I scroll through my phone and respond to the emails I can, but Caleb's right. Work is piling up, and I'm breaking down. How did Cally raise these girls herself?

It's so damn hard.

Daisie Dog flops her big body over the top of my legs. At least I have her when all hell breaks loose. She's turned out to be better than a magic trick when the girls spiral, which isn't often, at least not Emmy. Ruby is on another planet, and I mean that in the best, most loving uncle-ish way possible. But they love Dog—well, Daisie Dog. Emmy doesn't speak up often, but she will not call her Dog.

Daisie Dog paws at my leg relentlessly. Squinting one eye, I reach down with one hand and scratch her ears. "What am I going to do, girl?"

She makes a doggy noise I interpret as, "We've got this," as I reopen my email app with my free hand.

Twenty-two emails from Caleb. Each one more important than the next, and all I can do is stare at them—even understanding their importance, I simply have nothing left to give tonight. I've spent the last twelve years of my life building a company I could be proud of, one that would restore the Hayes name and eclipse the crumbling Delacroix Holdings brand that was once Hayes and Delacroix.

And I've done it. They're so far down the list they're not even on the same page as me. How could Cally have seen something so different in them?

What did she see that I cannot?

A sound I don't recognize has me jumping to my feet and tiptoeing into the girls' room. Ocean sounds play while fish and waves dance and glow on the ceiling as they move around the room from a projector on the dresser. That was the best fifty dollars I've ever spent.

Both girls appear to be sleeping, so I check the corners and the closets while Daisie Dog sniffs behind me. I'm not sure what I'm searching for, but this is what Cally used to do for me, and she's the only point of reference I have for this shit.

"Uncle Beck Daddy?"

That ridiculous name makes my chest burn every time,

but I cross the room in two long strides. "What's wrong, Emmy?"

Her giant green eyes brim with tears. "I miss my mommy," she sobs. I can tell she's trying to hold it in, so she doesn't wake Ruby, and it slices me wide open.

I lift her from the bed and hug her tightly as I carry her to the family room. I hug her like I'll never let her go. I hug her like she's mine.

Like she's mine. That log in my throat rolls over and jams itself into my esophagus.

"I'm so sorry, lovebug. I know you miss her." Sadness pinches my words—real, extensively brutal sadness. "I miss her too."

"I wanna go home." Her broken little voice is the last straw. New tears stain my cheeks because I don't know what to do. I don't know what to say. I can't fix this, and I can't make it better.

So I hug her.

Daisie Dog jumps onto the sofa, earning a scowl. She's not allowed on the furniture, but when Emmy flops a little arm around her neck, I allow it—for tonight.

"I'm trying, Emmy. I don't have all the answers, but I'm trying." My body sways in time with hers the same way Cally used to do for me when I scraped my knees or was frightened by a storm. These memories have made themselves known in recent days—Cally took care of me more than my parents did. I'm thankful the rocking motion soothes us both, and before long, her breathing evens out and she turns to dead weight in my arms.

I can't imagine what's going on in her head. We're going to visit the pediatrician first thing in the morning. Maybe they'll need therapy. They probably need therapy, at least Emmy—and maybe me too.

I hold her tiny hand in mine, thankful for the connection. Her wrist has little dimples in the skin where it meets her hand, and it's softer than anything I've ever touched. I rub gentle circles on it for a long time. I need the comfort of the moment almost as much as she does, but eventually, I stand and carry her back to bed, then take up guard outside their doorway with Daisie Dog.

Just in case they need me.

Then I call Jane. My world is crumbling around me, and she's one of two people who I think understands that. The other I can't call in the middle of the night without having to report to HR.

"Single Dad Hotline, I'm your helper. How can I help you?" Her voice is drowsy with sleep, but she still remembers to answer the damn phone like a professional. Her words wash over me, soothing my jagged edges. I don't understand the connection I have with her, but she puts me at ease. She feels...familiar.

"Jane?" I always ask, afraid one day it'll be a different Jane.

"Yes."

"Is it really necessary to answer like that?"

"I need this job, so I follow the rules." Her voice sounds farther away now, and I strain to hear every syllable. "What's the matter?"

The old grandfather clock in my entryway chimes three times. Three in the morning. What the hell am I doing waking her up?

"Uh, nothing really. I'm sitting outside the girls' room in case they need me."

There's a long pause before I hear her voice again, and when I do, it's muffled as though she's placed her hand over the receiver. "You don't have a baby monitor?"

"I do," I admit. "But every little noise has me jumping out of bed. And there's a lot of static that comes through those things. I'm probably getting more sleep sitting out here."

"You have to sleep, Beck. You can't take care of them if you're not taking care of yourself."

"Why do you need this job so badly?"

She sucks in a breath, reminding me that I'm crossing lines not meant for me.

"It pays well, and I have someone who depends on me."

My stomach swirls with that admission. Who is she taking care of? A husband? A sick child? Why the fuck is it any of my business?

"I don't know what I'm doing, Jane."

"You're sitting outside your little girls' room in case they wake up and are afraid. You're doing what every first-time parent does. The anxiety will ease with time, I promise."

"How are you so sure of yourself?"

"Oh." She laughs, and that niggle of familiarity hits me in the chest again. "Trust me, I'm not. My life is a hot mess and it's one bill after the next."

"Tell me?" I murmur.

"About my life?"

"Something. Anything that isn't focused on my new parenting role that has my body in a life-or-death fight every waking second. Tell me why you're so good at helping single dads."

"Well." She pauses and there's a scratching sound on the speaker. "I was raised by a single mom. It's basically the same thing except I had someone who knew how to do my hair. But." At her silence, I lean forward, hoping I can pull her truth through the phone. "I've always wondered if I could *be* a good mom." It's a whispered confession that throat-punches me with its sadness. So she's not caring for a sick child. "Anyway, I'd always planned to work with children, they make me happy, but life had other plans for me, so this job keeps me connected to them."

Three long breaths pass before she continues. "Try viewing the world through their untarnished eyes and tell me it doesn't change...everything. There's magic in their innocence that gets lost with age. Hopefully, by doing this, I can be the one to help them hang onto it for a little longer."

I envision Stella shrugging and shake my head. I'm so fucking tired my wires are getting crossed.

"What else?" I ask, then lie down until I'm flat on my back with my feet crossed at the ankles and one hand behind my head. With her in my ear, I can almost forget that I'm on a hardwood floor.

"Well, at one of my jobs, I work for this guy I can't figure out. The files he gives me never match the ones in his office, but don't ask me how I know that. There's this other guy who works down the hall. He's very young, but he would give me a funny look anytime I gave him something directly because my boss prefers to be the go-between. Anyway, it took a while, but now we're on the same page, we just can't pinpoint what's wrong. It's all very cloak-and-dagger stuff and we're probably wrong anyway."

"You should tell someone," I say.

"Hmm. We will when we're sure it isn't an error on our part. Like I said, he's very new, and it's not really my field of expertise."

"Good." Words are getting harder to say. I close my eyes.

"It's late, Beck, and you need to sleep."

"Why do you have two jobs?"

"I've got to pay the bills."

"Do you have anyone to lean on?"

She doesn't answer and I'm suddenly as alert as if I'd heard a fire alarm.

"Jane?"

"Yeah, sorry. I'm here."

"Do you have someone you can lean on?"

Her sigh races through the line as if her lips are pressed to my cheek and not the phone. "Not anymore. Life's hard. You're experiencing that firsthand right now. But I do believe you're exactly who those girls need. It'll be rocky at times, but lead them with love, and the rest will fall into place."

"I'm going to take them to the doctor tomorrow. Emmy was sad tonight and tried to hide her grief."

"I'm sorry to hear that. You're doing the right thing, though," she says quietly. She's always quiet, and so damn gentle.

"Jane?"

"Yes."

"I think I let a fifteen-year-old grudge take my sister from me."

She makes a choking sound, and her sadness carries through the phone. "You can go down every what-if road, but it won't change the past. Learn to forgive yourself for whatever's causing you pain, then move forward. If you don't move forward, neither will the girls."

"Have you heard of Delacroix Farms?" Shit. Here goes another line of personal information I promised not to cross.

"I have," she says cautiously.

I ignore the questions rattling around in my mind. The ones asking why it's easy to tell this virtual stranger things I don't tell anyone else.

"Well, it used to be Hayes and Delacroix. My dad was in

a car accident when I was almost twenty, but he had already planned to leave the company to Vincent Delacroix in a trust that was doled out to us at Delacroix's discretion. He gave us just enough to survive, then when my mom passed away a few years later, he took the entire damn company. My sister fell in love with his son—and then they took over the company."

Her silence squeezes my heart in a way I can't explain. It's as if somehow, she's sharing my burden. I have no idea why I'm telling her this. I don't know her. Maybe it's because she's signed the same rock-solid NDA that I have, or maybe it's because needing someone isn't a choice I can ignore anymore, and needing a stranger feels a hell of a lot safer.

"I'm sorry. I shouldn't be burdening you with all of this."

"Sometimes it's easier to tell a faceless stranger you'll never meet. It's healthy to get things off your chest. It sounds as though you've been holding onto that anger and hurt for a long time."

I nod, even though she can't see me.

"The girls are very lucky to have you. Remember that."

"Thank you." I laugh and clamp a hand over my mouth. That sounded slightly hysterical. "I might owe you extra for a therapy session."

"No need. This is what I'm here for. It's hard being a single parent. It's even harder when you're thrust into it with no warning. The hotline is here for the dads as much as the kids."

Right, because she's there for multiple dads. I'm seriously sleep-deprived if I'm jealous of a faceless woman I'll never meet having a connection with other men.

"Thank you, Jane."

"You're welcome, Beck."

"Tell me your real name?" The words are a desperate

plea for something I don't even understand, but she doesn't laugh in my face.

"I can't do that. It's against the rules."

"And you need this job," I repeat.

"See, you're a fast learner. You'll have this parenting thing down in no time and then you'll have no use for me."

"Don't sell yourself short. I think you're seriously overestimating how much I can handle. I have a business to run that's sinking quickly in my absence, and two little girls who don't know if I'm their uncle or their daddy."

"Talk to the pediatrician, and you can always call the hotline if you get stuck. Is there anything else I can help you with tonight?"

Is there? I've accumulated a million questions to ask her in the past couple of days, but I can't recall a single one at the moment.

"No, I think that's it."

"Good night, Beck."

"Good night, not-so-Jane."

Her laughter rings in my ears, stirring up a familiarity I can't place. The line goes silent when she hangs up, but her words buzz through my veins. I just can't tell if it's a warning, or a promise—or what either option would mean.

CHAPTER SEVEN

STELLA

"So," Elijah drawls. "I hear Beck has a hotline hottie helping him at night."

"Shh," I hiss, sprinting to his desk before his smirk has fully formed. "He doesn't know it's me, does he? How did you know it was me? Oh, God. I'm going to lose both jobs, and Mom has another payment due in two weeks."

"Stella, take a breath or twelve. He doesn't know. He just said that this mystery woman felt familiar, and she's saved his ass more than once. I connected the dots, and you just confirmed my suspicion."

I drop my head into my hands. "What am I doing, Elijah? This is wrong on so many levels. He's confiding in me because he thinks he'll never meet me. What if he finds out? It's an invasion of privacy. It's a betrayal, but every time I email Lottie, she says she doesn't have anyone else for him."

"That's Lottie. She hand-selects every helper with every dad based on the questionnaire you both filled out."

The muscles in my face pinch together. "Elijah," I say through clenched teeth. "Why do you know more about

Lottie than I do? I thought you weren't connected to the hotline. You said you were just helping out a friend."

He waves me off, but it's too late.

"You've been manipulating this entire thing. Is this some kind of game to you?" Is he just like my ex, Silas? Hurt burrows into the deepest recesses of my soul. I've been emotionally alone for so many years now, but Elijah was quickly becoming someone I counted on.

"No, it's not like that, I promise. Lottie needs sources all over the world to run her business. I'm simply a middleman."

"Are you the reason I got Beck—er—Mr. Hayes. Geez, Elijah! Who am I right now?"

"Seriously, lady, calm down. It's not some big conspiracy theory."

"Easy for you to say." I pout. "You're not the one being deceived, or the one deceiving. Holy crap, Elijah. I'm both of those."

"Lottie created that personality assessment specifically to find matches that work in a family environment. She painstakingly tweaked and tested it until she got it right. Part of the reason she's so successful is because she only takes clients if she has the right match. I didn't betray you— I would never do that to you."

I hear the truth in his words and heat erupts over my skin in an overwhelming flush. Too hot. Too over-whelmed. I fan my face with both hands, and he tosses me his keys. "Go. Get a couple of rides in. Clear your head. I'll make up an excuse for the Ice King if he ever shows his face today."

Grabbing my purse, I scurry out of that office faster than the gingerbread man. I don't have to be told twice.

Twenty minutes later I'm cruising to North Hills for a

rideshare when my phone rings. I glance at the screen and cringe. This had better be freaking Lottie.

Pressing the green *accept* button, I drop the phone into the cup holder. "Single Dad Hotline, I'm your helper. How can I help you?"

"For fuck's sake, I'm really starting to hate that greeting. Just say hello, Jane."

"What's wrong?" I immediately pull into the closest strip mall.

"Everything. Everything's wrong. I missed three meetings this morning interviewing nannies. I think the first one asked if we'd be sleeping in the same room. The second one had a rule about not changing shitty diapers, and the third one? The third one showed up to my house in a dress cut to her navel refusing to contain her boobs."

Eesh. Is he advertising on Penthouse Daddy?

"Hold on. What nanny agencies are you using and what are you telling them? That's too awful to be bad luck."

"I don't know. TakeCareOfBaby dot com or something like that. I simply said who I was, how old I was, what I do for work, what I'm looking for in a nanny, how old the girls are, that I have thoughts on rewards and punishments I'd like to discuss, the hours I need childcare but also that they should be available at my discretion, and that I'm suddenly raising my nieces alone—or something like that."

I can't help it. It's not professional, and it's not kind, but a burst of laughter rolls out of me. This man—this man who single-handedly changed the landscape of luxury, doesn't understand that he's essentially created a hire-me-daddy campaign.

"What? Why are you laughing?"

"Beck." I wheeze. "Did you submit a photo too?"

"It was required," he mutters.

"And you don't see anything wrong with some of that information?"

"No," he barks. "I don't. Why do you sound so far away?"

"I'm in the car."

"Pull over," he demands.

"Geez, Dad! I am pulled over. Calm your hissy fit."

He doesn't say anything, and I hold my breath.

"Calm my hissy fit?" he eventually says. "Calm my hissy fit."

"Yes," I say in return. "Beck, that doesn't sound like a reputable nanny agency. You need to start over with a vetted, reliable one, preferably one that comes from a personal recommendation. That was—well, I don't know what that was but I'm guessing it's some kind of kink site."

"What? Are you shitting me? No, I would have... fuck me."

Biting the inside of my cheek so I don't laugh in his face again, I ask, "Where are the girls?"

"They're in my car watching some weird talking puppy cartoon, but don't worry, I'm staring at them through the window. I can't get them into the doctor until next month because they're technically new patients. Next month! Isn't this an emergency? What if Emmy's sad? And I mean really sad. These doctors are supposed to be helpful and they're not. I need to ask Elijah, that's my assistant, to find me a goddamn concierge doctor for them. They have those, right?"

"I'm sure they do, but you still need to calm yourself. You're spiraling, and that won't help the girls. They're probably freaking out that you're not in the car with them, too. They just lost their mom. They need to know that you're there for them in new situations."

A door slams a second later. "I'm in the car." His voice is pitched low and happy music plays in the background.

"Good. Take a deep breath." I listen while he does. "Do you feel better?"

"No. This *feels* like an emergency."

"Are they bleeding?"

"What?"

"Are they bleeding?"

Ruby happily babbles in the background.

"No, of course they're not bleeding. Why would they be bleeding? Do they just bleed randomly? Holy Christ. When do they get periods? Is that what you mean? I can't change a diaper and talk about periods too."

"Beck, are you listening to yourself?" Of course not. He's a smart man who's drowning in fear right now.

"What?" he asks again.

"You just asked me if the girls were getting their periods. I'm sure you took health class in high school. When do girls get their periods, Beck?"

"Shit. When they're teenagers. Then why would they be bleeding?"

"I was trying to make a point and didn't realize you'd already jumped off the deep end. They aren't bleeding. They're breathing, eating, and sleeping as well as any other time you've seen them, correct?"

"Yes." That one word heaves with grumpiness.

"Then this is not an emergency. They need love, Beck. And they need stability in an unstable time. Give that to them."

"I'm trying," he says more calmly than I've heard him today.

"I know you are."

"Why does your voice soothe me?" he asks, and the fear locks my muscles again.

"I just have one of those tones. Are you okay now? I have some other appointments I need to get to."

"Yeah, I'm okay."

"Good. Take a nap with them today. It'll do you some good."

"Fine. Okay. We're heading into the office this afternoon, so maybe I'll grab one while my attorney's assistant watches them. She's the only one I'm comfortable leaving the girls with and she keeps turning the nanny position down."

Crap. It's true, but I need the benefits this corporate job at Crystal Waters offers—and as far as I can tell, nannies don't get that. Working as a nanny was the first thing I thought of when I lost my teaching job, but I axed the idea when I found out I'd need to have a very flexible schedule, not to mention health insurance, which costs a fortune.

"I'm sure she has her reasons," I say. "Everyone has a story, and not all of them are easy to share. Deep breaths— you've got this."

I hang up before he can say anything else and immediately call Elijah.

"Hello, sweetheart. How are the passengers today?"

"I want to go see my mom. Can you cover for me if Caleb has a meltdown?"

"I've got you, babe! Do what you've gotta do. But heads up, Beck's coming in with the girls at two."

I glance at the clock. That means I'll have thirty minutes with Mom. "I know. He just told *Jane*. I'll be back before he is." I say it like a curse and am so tempted to hang up, but because I'm in his car I hold my tongue. "Thank you, Elijah."

"Anytime, Stella."

I drop the phone to my lap, then make my way to Mindful Moments, silently praying that today will be the day she remembers me because I need my mom more than ever, and the sad reality is, I may never have her again.

"How is she today, Lucía?" I ask as I approach the front desk.

"She's been in and out, but mostly happy. I hope you get a few moments with her."

Part of me wishes Lucía wouldn't share her optimism, because it only hurts more when it doesn't happen.

"That's great. I'm happy to hear it."

I sign in, then walk down the halls that smell of death. Morbid but true.

It's quiet when I enter my mom's room. Eighties hits are playing in the background and when I find her, her foot is tapping to the rhythm her mind might not remember, but her body will never forget.

"Laura? Are you awake?"

Her lashes flutter open, and she smiles. "Now why are you calling me Laura? Are you too cool to call me Mom?"

My entire body shakes with emotions I've learned to keep sheltered because I never know if she'll be able to handle them.

"Oh, baby. I'm sorry. Are you okay?"

I run to her and drop my face into her chest where she clings to me.

"Mom. I—I've missed you."

"Now college can't be that bad." And just like that, my heart breaks into a million tiny pieces. It's becoming harder to recover from these heartaches, but this time, my heart has broken for the last time. There's no putting me back together again.

"It's not, Mom. It's great, actually. I'm very happy. I met a guy."

Her eyes light up at this news. I never shared it with her when I was in college. She'd want to meet him, and it would have been a whole thing, and now I'm sad I'll never get that experience with her.

"Is that right? Tell me about him."

So I tell her about Beck, minus his nieces and his own drama. I tell her the fantasy she always wanted. The one where the girl got the guy and happily ever after was forever.

CHAPTER EIGHT

"Stella?" I yell like a bad rendition of an old action movie. Daisie Dog darts past me, knocking over Emmy and almost taking out my legs. "Dang it, Daisie. Calm the fuck down." The damn dog runs straight for Stella's desk.

I'm holding the elevator open with my foot while I wait for Emmy to shuffle out in front of me. Tuesdays and Thursdays are her favorite days right now because she gets to see the one person who has been able to pull a smile from her —Stella.

And speaking of the devil, Stella's beautiful face pokes around the corner as though she's playing peek-a-boo, Daisie Dog sitting like a lady at her side. Traitor.

I shake my head when Ruby squeals and reaches for Stella who is, in fact, playing peek-a-boo.

Has she always had a slight hint of red in her light brown hair? She stares at me with those amber orbs that tell a million stories and make you believe in the happy ending. I stand immobile and mute.

Ruby punches me in the face with the toy phone she has

in her hand, and I almost drop her but recover quickly—thank God. At least she broke my trance and not my nose.

One would think that after two weeks with little to no sleep, I'd be somewhat adapted to life with kids. But I'm not. Not by a long shot.

Emmy sprints into Stella's waiting arms and Ruby wiggles so much I finally give up on the cringe factor of her crawling on this floor.

Note to self—ask the cleaning crew to bleach the floors every day.

"Thank you for doing this," I say. Her reaction is guarded as she nods but keeps a soft smile on her face for the girls. "Has the temp I hired been able to take over most of your responsibilities when they're here?"

She looks at me briefly and nods again. Has she always been this shy? Not at the party where we shared a kiss, but in the office? I vaguely remember how odd I found it that she was babbling the day I became an uncle-daddy, but I can't recall a single word from that day, or even what her voice sounds like at a normal volume.

Pulling out my phone, I leave myself a note. *Ask about sounds. Does lack of sleep make you forget random shit?*

Because it's only the random shit I'm forgetting. Not the sound of Stella moaning into my mouth, no, that sound is so engrained in my memory not even pure bleach could wash it away. And yeah, I'm even more fucked up now because, in my head, she sounds like Jane and Jane looks like Stella.

Before the girls, I simply stormed by her desk every day without a hello. Now, I'm surrounded by her, and it consumes pieces of my brain I don't have to spare. My body refuses to forget how she pressed against me, even if my mind tells me it has to.

"Are you girls ready to play today?" she says into the

crook of Ruby's chubby little neck right where I found a random Cheerio earlier. If I were ten feet away, I wouldn't hear her.

But I remember how she sounds when she melted into me, and it's fucking glorious.

Jesus, Becker. Grow up. That's not helping anything.

Then her gaze is on me again and my body heats as though I'm being roasted over an open flame.

"Caleb said he can't deal with the temp today and insists I stay at my desk." Is she trying not to roll her eyes?

My lips twitch and I do it for her. "Did he give a specific reason why?"

Stella shakes her head.

"Well, I'll let you in on a little secret then. Caleb prefers control, and when he doesn't have it, he gets pissy." I take a few steps closer, and angle my head, silently inviting her in to hear my secrets. Her scent invades my senses—fresh and sweet. Apples.

I stand upright and clear my throat. Lack of sleep, that's what's making me think with my dick. It has to be because never once, in all of my life, has one make-out session, in a bar full of people, taken control of my entire life as Stella has.

"The best part about being the boss," I say, pretending I didn't just inhale her, "is that I can shuffle employees anywhere I like." Involuntarily, I take one tiny step closer and bask in this heady sensation when her pupils dilate. "Do you mind watching the girls for a few hours today, Stella?"

God. Damn. Even her name tastes sweet on my tongue.

"No," she whispers with a shaky exhale. "I don't mind."

With that, she turns, takes Emmy by the hand, and leads her into the large room separating my office from Caleb's.

She doesn't get two steps before Caleb's voice cuts through the air with the precision of a whip. "Not again. I needed you at your desk today. Having too many people mess with my filing system disrupts everything." He doesn't quite hiss, but my body responds like it's a personal affront anyway.

Daisie Dog jumps between them and snarls at Caleb. It actually causes me to back up a step. She's made unhappy sounds before, but this is a warning—a warning to stay away from Stella and the girls.

Maybe the damn dog isn't so bad after all.

"Daisie," Emmy scolds with that little finger outstretched. The dog backs into Emmy but keeps her teeth bared in Caleb's direction. "Good, Daisie." The little girl embraces Dog's neck and whispers something with a small smile.

"This isn't a farm," Caleb huffs.

I pointedly ignore the farm comment by crouching down beside Emmy and placing a hand on the mutt's head. "Is there a specific reason you can't make do with the temp, Caleb? I know you're very particular about how you do things, but surely, it's not so difficult that someone else can't do it."

His face blanches for a millisecond at my cold tone before his mask falls into place. "But Ms. Anderson wasn't hired to be a nanny," he grumbles.

"Well, that's only because she keeps turning me down." I'm taunting him now, but it's also the truth. I'd give my left nut to have Stella in my home playing house with the girls.

Fuck me.

The muscles around Caleb's mouth pull tight, and I can tell it's an effort to keep his mouth closed.

"So as I was explaining to Miss Anderson," I continue, "if

she has no objections, she will be in charge of the girls while we bust out *my* three meetings."

The new girl Elijah trained yesterday is sitting at Stella's desk, and I nod, but she's no Stella.

"I'm sure her assistant can handle everything for a few hours, and if she has a question, Miss Anderson is right here." I point to the corner of the room that now has a basket of toys, an art easel, a dog bed, and a dollhouse.

I glance at Elijah, and he winks.

"My assistant has an assistant now? What is this madness?" Caleb's tone is even, but I can tell it's taking him great effort not to lash out. He truly hasn't been the same since his wife died, but his reactions to Stella are out of character, even for him.

I advance on him slowly to shield the girls from some harsh truths. "It's called having your sister die and then getting thrown into the sea of fatherhood without a life vest. If Stella agrees to be that lifeline a few times a week? Then. So. Be. It. Understood?"

Caleb's ears turn redder than a sunburn, but he nods and walks stoically into my office.

Turning to Stella, I give an apologetic shrug. "I think I packed everything on your list, but..." I fade off because I honestly have no idea what happens in the mornings. My house currently has dishes and diapers and so much pink everywhere that I could have packed the TV remote for all I know.

"I've got it," she says, and there's that tingle of awareness again. Am I making this all up in my head because I remember how she tastes? I've never had to follow up this personally before with a...with a what? We made out—kissed and danced all night. I didn't even sleep with her so I can't call her a one-night stand.

Shaking my head, I walk into my office and promise myself I'll get a full night's sleep tonight. I have to, otherwise I'll end up drooling all over Stella. Or worse, embarrassing the fuck out of myself around her. And she's one person I can't afford to lose.

"THIS IS AN EMBARRASSMENT, CALEB. DELACROIX FARMS? You know why I won't work with them. Did you think I wouldn't realize that Legacy Inc. was owned by them?" My hands shake as I hold his proposal in my hands. "Why now? Why is that waste of sperm contacting me now?" I demand, fearing I already know the answer—the girls.

He doesn't even pretend not to understand who I'm talking about. "Danica's proposing a very good deal that will make you both a lot of money. It's good business. Just look at the reports I put together. The numbers make financial sense."

He's pushing this too hard. Is this more than a crisis in his private life or does he have one foot out the door and I've been too distracted to notice?

Or you didn't want to admit that you've been stupid enough to trust the wrong person—again.

Peals of laughter outside my door have my body relaxing. Maybe if I offer Stella more money she'll consider nannying.

"Beck," he snaps. "Are you even listening to me or are you off fantasizing about my assistant again?"

This has me sitting up taller. "Consider your place, Caleb," I say through clenched teeth. He may have more leeway than most because he and Elijah stuck with me in the beginning, even when I couldn't pay them much, but he's dangerously close to crossing a line now, and he knows it.

He backs away from my desk with his palms out. "Fine, I apologize. That was out of line. But I do firmly believe you need to get your shit together before we start losing important deals."

What is it with people in my life giving me spidey tingles lately? It's not the same as it is with Stella. No, Caleb is making the hair on my neck stand on end like animals who sense they're being hunted too late.

Never going to happen. I created this company with my blood, sweat, and tears, and I'll keep it at the top of its game, even with lovebug and Ruby-rolls in tow.

Ruby-rolls. Huh. I've been feeling guilty about giving Emmy a nickname and not the round little terror that's Ruby. She certainly has the market on squishy baby limbs. Ruby-rolls fits, but it's definitely not PC. Rubella? Wait, is that a disease? The little girl in question laughs and it hits me—Ruby-roo. She's got the energy of that tiger in *Winnie the Pooh* too—always on the go. It's not perfect, but it fits, and it's one less guilt weighing on my conscience.

Caleb stands with his hands on his hips, shaking his head. Shit. I zoned out worrying about a freaking nickname for a baby.

He's wasted enough of my time today though.

With a heavy sigh, I stretch my neck from side to side, pleased with each crackle that releases. "It's not happening, Caleb. There will never be a day when I work with Danica Delacroix. Not one. In fact, I'm going to bury her and everything marked by the Delacroix name. Is this all you had for me today?"

Anger fills every word that leaves my mouth. My gut riots as each possibility comes to light, and intuition has never steered me wrong before. Something big is coming, and it's happening right under my nose—I feel it. Maybe Elijah was right to be wary of him, and I was too stupid to open my eyes.

The problem is, I have no idea where Caleb's head is at. He could be preparing to quit or...

No. Caleb's a lot of things, but he's not as diabolical as the Delacroix family. Regardless of what happens next, Caleb's a professional, of that, I'm sure.

I'll have Elijah put his sleuthing skills to work and find out why he's in cahoots with Danica on these deals, but if he's betrayed me?

"It's not a deal to dismiss so easily, Beck." Controlled anger underlines his words.

"I said no. Did you have anything actually worth my time, or is this it?" So much for hiding my suspicions. There's no masking my pissed-off tone.

Caleb gathers the papers strewn all over my desk. "That's it," he bites out. "Perhaps my assistant, or her assistant, can find a better deal for you."

"Are you—Are you jealous that I *need* Stella right now? Is that what this is?"

Caleb is the kind of man who has to feel like your right hand, your number one, and if he doesn't, all hell breaks loose. We found that out after the first six months of working together, but over the years he's come to terms with the fact that Elijah will always be my right-hand man. Is he feeling displaced—by Stella? Everything about him right now, from his barbed tongue and shitty attitude to his ill-disguised dislike of Stella, says jealousy is his motivation.

His laughter is cold and detached. "Not even a little. However, it's interesting that she's Stella now. It takes most people years to be on a first-name basis with you. Be careful there, *Daddy*. What would your colleagues say?"

Standing, I press my white knuckles to the flat of my desk and lean forward. "I'm not sure what's gotten into you today, but I seriously encourage you to take a long look at whatever's ruling your actions. We've had a wonderful working relationship for years. Don't ruin it now."

"Oh, our working relationship is just as it's always been. You're the boss. I haven't forgotten."

"Caleb," I say in warning.

He seems to come to his senses and waves me away. "I'm sorry," he says too contritely. "Things have been—hard. And you know I don't do well with change and this..." He points to my door. "Is a lot of fucking change."

"It is, and I'm sorry about that. I'm doing the best I can, and I will find a permanent solution soon, but until then, you will respect my decisions."

Caleb mutters under his breath but exits my office as Elijah walks in.

"What was that about?" he asks.

"Another deal with Delacroix."

Elijah sighs and runs his thumbs on the undersides of his suspenders. "What are your thoughts on Caleb now?"

My shoulders tense. "I'm not sure." Lowering my voice, I scan my office as though I'll find prying ears. "I don't under-stand what's going on with him. He's excellent at his job, he always has been, but something has shifted with him. He doesn't talk about his personal life, ever, so perhaps he and the woman he was seeing broke up. I'm the last person to give anyone the benefit of the doubt, but he's been with me for ten years, Elijah. He helped me build this company from the ground up, same as you, and he's probably still grieving. His loyalty over ten years has to account for something."

"But do you think he's still loyal?"

I rub the heels of my hands into the side of my head. "I don't know. But I don't have proof either, so where does that leave me?"

He shakes his head as if I'm an idiot, but he and Caleb haven't gotten along since the early days when the hours we worked didn't add up to the paycheck I could afford. I've always been the mediator, so his skepticism is nothing new. But this is the first time I've been disappointed in Caleb's work performance. Bringing me Delacroix-adjacent deals is beneath him, and we all know it.

"I'm not sure, but you can't let his attitude continue to carry on that way. It's not fair to the rest of your employees, and it's not a great look for you."

Pinching the bridge of my nose, I lean back into my chair. "I know. I just haven't decided what to do yet," I admit. "He's known for ten years that Delacroix is off limits. So what's changed?"

My door opens with a crash, and a smile tugs at my mouth at the sight of Emmy's little face.

"What's up, lovebug?" I ask.

Daisie Dog barrels in after her, licking at her sticky fingers, and Emmy trips over her feet to stay upright. The damn dog is a menace.

"Can I haves this?" She almost, almost smiles as she holds up a giant lollipop.

"It looks as though you already are. I'm guessing Stella meant for you to ask permission before it went in your mouth?"

Stella appears a moment later. "Sorry," she mutters, and I lean forward to catch every syllable. "I was changing Ruby behind my desk and had to hold her down with both legs to do it—you really need to install changing stations in the restrooms, by the way." She shakes her head with wide eyes and her cheeks heat pink. "Sorry," she says again. "Emmy was excited."

An invisible weight lifts from my shoulders. "No problem. We were done anyway. I may need you to show me the diaper-changing leg maneuver though. It's like wrestling a pissed-off donkey getting a new diaper on that kid."

She smiles, and I swear I forget to breathe. The sun filtering in from my floor-to-ceiling windows showcases the smattering of freckles that cover her cheeks, nose, and forehead. It's actually painful to drag my gaze away from her face.

"Give me ten minutes and I'll be ready to take the girls home. I just have to grab a few things to work on after they're in bed."

Emmy's shoulders droop with my words, but Stella takes her hand and leads her out of the room with Elijah trailing behind.

Daisie Dog sits glaring at me with disapproval in her upturned nose. "What?" I ask.

She pants. I cross the room to push her out, but she jumps through my legs and I crash into the bookcase. "Dang it, Daisie. Seriously, what's gotten into you?"

She licks my leg, then exits with exaggerated swagger no dog should have.

I need to find a damn nanny. And maybe a dog sitter.

I called a new nanny agency and they told me this was the busy season for them so it would take a bit longer than normal, but something's gotta give. None of us can keep this up forever. The one thing all the baby books agree on is that kids need routine—and that's the one thing I haven't been able to give them.

CHAPTER NINE

STELLA

"HAVE YOU FINISHED TRANSCRIBING ANY OF THESE FILES?" Caleb's loud voice startles me, and I jump. For as big as he is, he's scarily stealthy.

"Yes, of course. Here you go." I hand him a stack of folders and he retreats to his cave, only to return a moment later to drop an even bigger stack in its place.

"Your *assistant* did these incorrectly, and since they should have been done yesterday, you'll need to stay until you're caught up."

Panic makes my lungs deflate. It's okay. It's only one night. Mom will be okay.

"Sure." I give him a plastic smile.

He turns to enter his office and kicks his door shut on the way by.

"He's worse than that Chucky doll from the eighties," Elijah whisper-yells on his way to my desk. "Here, give me half of them."

I place my hand over the pile. "It's okay, I've got it. I don't want you to get behind too." He flicks me in the forehead.

"What the heck, Elijah? You can't do that." I rub the sting out of my skin.

He comes at me with his thumb and middle finger ready, and I release the stack of folders.

"I've got this. With Beck 'working'"—he uses air quotes and shrugs—"from home, my to-do list is cut in half. We'll bust this out so you can still see your mama today."

I swallow the emotion sitting in my throat. Or try to, anyway. Even though Elijah found out about my mom by accident, I can't deny that having someone on my side is a comfort I didn't think I'd ever have again.

The day he showed up outside my apartment as I was trying to get her into the car was one of the worst days of my life. It was probably all kinds of illegal for him to pull my information from HR, but I've never been more grateful for anyone's snooping abilities, and he's been a shoulder to lean on ever since.

I only have two more months until I get full benefits for me and my mom. That's when I go from a contracted worker to a full-time employee, but it's always felt like probation, especially when Elijah said my hiring process was unusual. But I guess that's what happens when you're hired by the most precision-driven man in North Carolina.

No one can ever say that Beck isn't generous with his benefits. Insurance for me is one thing, but insurance for my mom? It's more than I could have asked for.

Elijah takes half of my stack back to his desk, and moisture pools at the corners of my eyes before I can stop it. At what point in my life did accepting help from a friend become a foreign concept?

We work in silence—the only sounds in the room coming from our fingers clicking away on keyboards. It's strangely calming, but it's broken when Caleb exits his office talking noisily on his phone.

I don't bother shifting my gaze away from my work. He's using that tone that means his lunch hour will be extended and it's anyone's guess when he'll return.

As soon as we hear the elevator ding, Elijah leans forward on his desk, and so do I. I love this man. The only person who might be able to beat him out for top spot is his partner, Samira.

"Something's seriously wrong with that man," he says with a sly grin.

"Really wrong," I agree. "Why does he get away with such bad behavior?"

He shrugs. "Beck is as loyal as they come. Caleb has been here since the beginning, so Beck feels like he owes him something."

I wrinkle up my nose but keep my comments to myself.

Elijah is the closest thing I've had to a best friend since I was sixteen years old and it's in these quiet moments when it hits me just how lonely I am.

My phone vibrates on my desk, and I glance down. "Oh, crap. Oh no."

"What is it?" Elijah asks. "Is it Laura?"

I shake my head and turn my phone to face him.

"It's SDH. That means it's probably Beck."

"Oh, let me get the popcorn! I've known that guy since I was ten years old, and I've never seen him lose his composure like he does with you, so let's see if Jane gets the same reaction. I cannot wait for this show."

I roll my eyes but answer the call, internally cringing because Elijah is about to hear my horribly fake impression of myself. "Single Dad Hotline, I'm your helper. How can I help you?"

Elijah covers his mouth, and I glare at him, but his shaking shoulders convey his laughter, so I drop my chin to my chest and stare at the floor.

"I don't know what to do with her. She's a pooping little terror."

"Beck?"

Elijah laughs out loud this time, and I shoot him a death glare while holding up one finger to my lips.

"Oh, shit. Not again," Beck whines.

"What's going on? Is everyone okay?"

"It's Ruby." He's panting like he's working out, though I'm sure he's not. "She hates me. She must. Why else would she continue to strip naked and take a dump on the floor? Is she part dog? Is this a thing that people don't talk about? Help me, Jane. Please. I cannot clean up one more pile of human shit full of corn. And don't get me started on Daisie Dog. She keeps sniffing around it as though she's considering eating it and then I will vomit. I will. I swear it."

It's hard to keep my laughter in when I can so clearly envision him in full-on distress. His dark brown hair is for sure standing on end and his green eyes are panicked but determined.

"Deep breath, Beck. Remember, you've got this."

"You keep saying that, and every time you do, one of them takes it to the next level just to fuck with me."

"First, does Ruby have a new diaper on?"

He snorts. "Hell yes, she does. I duct taped that thing on her good."

"Oh no. It's not too tight, is it?"

"No, she's rolling around in applesauce on the floor while I gag over the giant turd she left in front of the door." He's so loud I pull the phone away from my ear and his voice still fills the room.

Elijah has fallen out of his chair and is rolling in laughter. Probably not too different than Ruby.

"Where's Emmy?"

"She standing here, holding the bag open for me."

Beck wretches, and I hear Emmy giggle.

"What a good helper, Emmy."

She doesn't get a chance to respond because Beck is back and nearing hysterics.

"What am I doing wrong? This can't be right, right? People wouldn't do this over and over again if this was normal. I think she's trying to break me. I see it in her little eyes, and I hear it when she laughs after I step in her shit. She thinks this is all funny. But news flash, it's not. Not even a little. Please tell me what to do. Help me before I step in any more corny shit."

Elijah can't control himself and runs from the room. I hear his howl of laughter a few seconds later.

"This is a phase she's going through. Not all kids do this exactly, but it won't last forever. She might be ready to start potty training. Some kids basically do it themselves pretty early, but I admit, this is probably a little too early."

"Oh no."

I hear a loud thud and my heart rate accelerates. "What was that? Did someone fall?"

"Only my pride, my dignity, and my head hitting the floor. I'm barely keeping them alive, Jane. I'm not ready for potty training."

"You can work up to it. In the meantime, check to see if she has any one-piece pajamas with a zipper."

"She does," he groans. "All her laundry is on the floor in the hallway."

"It's what?"

"I had it in a basket and was moving her room to room

while I put it away. But then I had to help Emmy with her hair, that was a nightmare by the way, and when I turned around, Ruby had dragged all her clothes into the hallway, probably with her teeth because they all had round wet marks the size of her mouth. I'm too damn tired to do anything about it, so they'll stay there until the cleaning service comes."

As that mental image sinks in, I don't fight the smile that accompanies it. "I know it's hard right now, but it will get easier."

"It would be easier if you or Stella would just agree to be my nanny."

Guilt closes my throat, and thankfully, he speaks so I don't have to.

"I have them, now what do I do?"

Rolling my shoulders, I begin to pace. "Do they have feet attached?"

"Feet?" he asks. His voice is unnaturally high, and I envision him as a preteen.

"Do they have material that would cover Ruby's feet, I mean."

"Yes. They have feet."

"Okay. That's okay. What you need to do is get some scissors and cut the feet of the pajamas off. Then take them with Ruby to the bathroom and clean her up. After that, put her diaper on as normal, no duct tape, and then put these pj's on her backwards so the zipper is in the back. She won't be able to reach it that way, so her clothes will stay on."

"Seriously?"

"Seriously. It's that easy."

"You always have the answer." There's a hint of awe in his tone that warms my body.

Elijah reenters the room, having composed himself, but I turn my back on him.

"I don't always, but I try."

There's a beat of silence, then two.

"Thank you for talking me down and for helping me not step in poop again."

"On the bright side, you must have gotten her to eat corn."

His laughter finds its way through the phone and weaves around my heart like a tourniquet.

"That is a bright side for sure. Do you always find those too?"

My heart races uncomfortably and my armpits could use more deodorant. "That's harder for me to do, unfortunately, but I wish I could."

"Jane?"

"Yes, Beck?"

"Thank you." It's the most sincere thing anyone has said to me in a very long time and it cocoons me in an embrace I desperately need.

"You're welcome. You know where to find me if you need me."

"I do—No Ruby-roo, no! Get your hands out of your diaper."

Ruby's baby giggles are the last thing I hear.

I count to ten before I turn around because the weight of Elijah's stare bores into my back.

"He likes you," he finally says. "He doesn't like many people, and he likes both of you."

Sadness rips away Beck's virtual hug. "He wouldn't if he knew I've been lying to him. Don't you feel guilty?"

"Honestly? No. I've known Beck for twenty-five years, and in all that time, I've never seen him this way. You're making him human again, Stella, and for that, this will all be worth it. I respect your decision to pass on a nanny gig that would pay more than working for Caleb but take a moment to consider if it's worth it. Sometimes the hardest decisions are the right decisions."

What he's saying would make sense for most people, but I need the flexibility to see my mom at a moment's notice—I can't be tied down with two little girls if she needs me, and I need the insurance I get working for a corporation this large. I can't give up the last few months of my mother's life —even if she never remembers me again.

CHAPTER TEN

BECK

"Okay, girls. That was a—well, it was something, wasn't it?"

I can't see Ruby's face because apparently, her car seat is supposed to face backward. YouTube is my best friend right now, but Emmy stares at me with wide eyes. In the daylight, I can see the shadows in them as she holds on to her sister's hand for dear life.

Rubbing my temples does nothing to ease the headache brought on by stress and lack of sleep. I've spent the past two nights watching how-to-parent videos, and I missed two meetings today.

Daisie Dog nudges my hand from the passenger seat, and I begrudgingly pet her ears.

I hate that Caleb may have been right about my company, but I didn't have a choice—these girls need me. All the people I've interviewed for a nanny position over the last month are seriously lacking—Cally's girls deserve nothing but the best I can give them. I owe it to them and to my sister.

You haven't liked the nannies because they're not Stella. My inner voice is a prick, but it's not wrong. For weeks, Stella's pulled double duty helping me out on the days I go into the office.

Shit. I should call HR and have them give her a bonus—what would they label it as? A bonus because the owner of the company can't stop thinking about you? Or a bonus because the owner of the company is seriously abusing his power and remembering what you felt like in his arms?

Jesus.

She's so good with the girls, but she's turned down both of my offers, and it's probably because she can sense me perving out over her every time I see her. But even freaking Jane turned me down. If the situation weren't so dire, it might be a hit to my ego.

The final straw was at the pediatrician's office today. One whole month after taking custody, I find out the girls are in a state of shock and need stability. Stability, possibly in the form of the home they lived in with my sister. My childhood home in Sailport Bay.

That won't be happening.

I understand what Dr. Bomburg was saying, but she's also a little hippie-dippie, so I'm not sure how much I should be listening to her advice. I can't believe my sister would have even chosen her.

Turning in my seat, I stare at Emmy's sad face. "Ready to go home, lovebug?"

Cally used to call me lovebug when I was a kid, and the nickname suits Emmy, too, even though she's the spitting image of my sister. Her eyes are bright and hopeful even when they're sad. I don't understand it, but it doesn't make it untrue. "To my house," I clarify. "With the fancy elevator?" All the light leaves her face, and she rests her head on her sister's car seat.

"I'm trying my best here, Emmy." She doesn't respond because she's four and doesn't understand the complexities surrounding our situation. So I drive us to my penthouse in silence for another dinner of mac and cheese because it's the only thing I can get them both to eat.

What were you thinking, Cally? What made you think I could do this?

<hr />

THE COMPANY I HIRED TO BABYPROOF AND FURNISH MY HOME with anything and everything kid-related we might need finally finished up today. My apartment now resembles a child's play area with foam rolls covering every corner and sharp edge.

It's only by the grace of God that I figured out the baby carrier, and that has been a lifsaver. Strapping Ruby into the kangaroo pouch took a lot of trial and error, but Emmy was happy to let me borrow her stuffed bunny.

"Emmy, why don't you bring your backpack to your room? I have to piss, ah—pee, then we'll figure out dinner, okay?"

She nods but stays put with her little hands outstretched wide as though she's waiting for me to drop Ruby. Wrestling the little girl into the carrier on my chest is not an easy feat, and I'm covered in sweat by the time her legs are through the holes.

But Jesus Christ. Does Emmy have that little faith in me?

"I won't drop her, Emmy. I promise." Her gaze drifts from my hand holding Ruby still, to Ruby's wildly waving limbs, and she doesn't lower her arms. "I promise. I've got this," I repeat, securing the last clasp of the contraption.

Emmy frowns, looks from one buckle to the next, then

picks up her backpack and walks to her room, thank fuck. I've had to piss since we arrived at the doctor's office, but I couldn't figure out where the hell I was supposed to set Ruby down. Now I understand what Stella was talking about, and changing stations will be installed at Crystal Waters as soon as fucking possible.

When Emmy turns into her room, I dart across the hall to the guest bathroom and freeze.

What the hell is on my toilet?

I bend at the knees, careful to hold Ruby's legs out of the way, something I learned the hard way last night when she kicked over the box of pasta, but the lid won't open. A white plastic arm-like thing holds the seat in place. It shoots out from the toilet's cistern and stops in the center of the lid with a wide circle keeping the lid shut.

Seriously, *what the fuck* doesn't cover it. I have to piss so badly sweat is beading down my back. Spinning in a circle, I look for something, anything that will help me understand the complete and utter chaos that is my house right now.

I find nothing.

Dancing around on my tiptoes like a toddler, I aggressively try not to cup myself, but I'm in danger of peeing my pants for the first time in over thirty years.

Groaning, I pull back the shower curtain.

Last night I had to take a hammer to the child lock on the pantry before I figured out there was a magnetic key. Is there one in here too?

Ruby laughs, and I swear it's at my expense—she's a little devil, this one.

I shake the lid harder. I don't care if it breaks, it has to open. I slide two fingers under the lid and lift like a body-builder. The first crack sounds like relief. The second crack happens just before the plastic lock dislodges and the lid opens with a deafening snap.

Thank God.

Now I'm faced with a mirror that runs from the vanity across the wall to where I'm standing, and Ruby sees everything through her drool and squeals of delight. She would think this is funny.

"You can't watch me piss, Ruby. How the hell do people do this shit?" I'm starting to miss those first few weeks of ignorant bliss—the ones before I knew you couldn't leave a one-year-old in the care of a four-year-old for thirty seconds while you pissed for the first time in twelve hours.

Now I know better, which means I wear Ruby whenever possible.

She doesn't reply, but my bladder is in an all-out war and I'm out of options.

"Okay, kiddo. Desperate times and all that." I place a hand over her eyes with my left hand, unzip myself with my right, and I'm pissing before I've even grabbed ahold of myself.

Please let me hit the bowl...please let me hit the bowl.

I glance down, but all I see is Ruby. I can't even see my feet. Is this what it's like to be pregnant?

"If I have to clean up my own piss, I'm pretty sure it'll push me over the edge. A man can only handle so much shit, Ruby."

The little girl beats her tiny fists against the fabric of the baby carrier while I relieve myself.

Today I've hit an all-time low.

I close the lid without looking. If there's a mess, I'll deal with it later. I wash my hands, then exit the bathroom without looking back.

Please don't let all the toilets be locked down.

"Emmy, are you ready for dinner?" I call down the hall. She exits her room a second later with Daisie Dog beside her, and we walk to the kitchen without speaking. Emmy closes the gate behind us. It's quickly becoming a habit because if we don't, Ruby will find a way to escape.

At least I can walk over the baby gates. The cabinets, drawers, and now toilet seats are a different story.

Who the hell comes up with this stuff? Emmy sits on the floor with her head resting on Daisie Dog while I reheat last night's pasta.

"Okay, girls. Let's get you into your seats," I say, placing bowls with suction cups on the bottom of them on the table. These I approve of. Especially after I learned Ruby's penchant for tossing bowls overboard.

I lift Emmy first, and she slides into her booster without a fuss—she hasn't been talking much the last few days. It's been weighing heavily on me, and the hippie-dippie doctor's advice was less than helpful.

"Taking them home will give them a sense of security they're lacking right now."

Is it possible Quackburg's right?

Ruby's next, and getting her out of the carrier is worse than wrestling a pig in mud. She wiggles and bites and then laughs about it all. By the time I buckle her in, I'm breathing heavily.

"Will she grow out of biting soon?" I ask Emmy, who shrugs and focuses on her bowl of pasta. Her downturned lips and empty gaze are so sad it kills me.

Would she have been better off with Danica?

No. I cut that train of thought off before it can fully form. But I do have a cousin, Tabby. Why didn't Cally consider her?

Daisie Dog paces behind the girls, ratcheting my frustration higher. What would Stella do?

She'd hug them. And Elijah says *my* love language is touch. He doesn't know what the hell he's talking about.

"Emmy?" I ask, and she lifts her head from her bowl. "Do you need a hug?"

Tears spill from her green pools that are replicas of my own, and I'm hugging her tightly a second later. We cry together while Ruby flings orange pasta everywhere. I need to hug this kid more. Will that be enough though? I'll add it to my list for Jane.

Jane or Stella. They're equally important to the girls' happiness right now, but only one of them feels like a betrayal of the other.

"We'll figure this out, okay, lovebug? We will. I promise." By the time she pulls away from my embrace, I'm horrified to see what Ruby's done. Pasta is smashed into her hair, which is already filthy because I've been too scared to give her a real bath, so she's been getting a mix of showers with me in a swimsuit, and baby wipes, but even I think we've gone past what's sanitary and it's time to soak her. Pasta's everywhere. On the walls, the floor, even the ceiling.

This is what I get for having a neutral-colored apartment.

"Do you think she got any of it in her mouth?"

The faintest hint of a smile turns Emmy's lips up when she shrugs.

"Probably not, huh?"

She shakes her head and puts a spoonful of pasta in her own mouth while I grab more for Ruby. This time, I feed her, and it goes about as well as it did when she fed herself.

When dinner's over four million years later, I'm ready to admit defeat.

Emmy tugs on my pants. "Uncle Beck Daddy?"

I glance down and wish I knew what to do to take that sadness away from her beautiful little face. She's too young to carry all this heartache. "Yeah, Emmy?" I ask while wiping Ruby's hands and face before hefting her into my arms. I carry her to the family room and place her down on a mat that plays music when she moves.

"Wuby needs a tub."

A tub. A bath.

With a heavy sigh, I nod and fake a smile. "Let's call Jane and see if she has some pointers."

Emmy's eyes light up as she runs to her sister. "Yes," she whispers. "Stella. Stella."

"Stella? No, Emmy. We'll call Jane." She carries on as though she didn't hear me, so I make the call...as visions of Stella fill my mind.

"Single Dad Hotline, I'm your helper. How can I help you?"

Her voice gives me pause. It's the cadence—there's something so familiar about it that a chill works down my spine.

I'm losing my damn mind, because now I'm hearing Stella in Jane's voice.

Shaking my head, I focus my attention on the phone in my hand. "Don't you know it's me by now? I've only called you four hundred times. You don't have to do the whole spiel every single time."

"Oh, but I do. All I see on caller ID is SDH, so it could be you, or it could be another dad in the middle of an emergency. I have no way of knowing."

"You have other clients now?" An unfounded and completely idiotic stab of jealousy sits in my gut.

"Not right now," she admits. "But I don't think it's unheard of for us to have multiple at a time."

"Huh."

My hand is on my hip as I stare at the girls. Emmy sits crisscross next to Ruby, smiling up at me with so much sunshine she nearly blinds me.

"Did you need help with something tonight, Beck?"

At my name, I stand to attention because this time I'm not imagining it. She does sound like Stella.

"I think I'm losing my mind. Emmy asked for an assistant who works in my office tonight, and when you said my name it sounded—never mind." It's lack of sleep that's making me batshit crazy. "Um, so I need to give the girls a bath, and I've never bathed anyone except myself."

"They haven't had a bath at all?" The horror in her tone tells me I've screwed up.

"Well, I took them into the shower. I wore a bathing suit every time," I point out. "And I let the water spray over them. But it's nearly impossible to hold a kid that's all soaped up, so no. They haven't had a real bath. But I'm keeping them clean. Cleanish. Mostly."

"Okay. No problem," she says, but her tone tells me this is a major problem, and I'm smart enough to know better. "This is an easy one. The only thing you need to remember is to never, and I mean never *ever* leave them alone in the bathtub. You must be within arm's reach at all times. Kids can drown in only a couple inches of water."

"Jesus, I wasn't aware this was a life-or-death situation. It's a fucking bath."

"Language, Beck."

My spine prickles, and I immediately drop my gaze to Emmy, who's smiling up at the phone.

"Are you...do you...never mind. Hit me with the bath instructions."

Forty-five minutes later, I have Ruby sitting in some kind of plastic seat that's supposed to keep her contained, while Emmy fills cup after cup of water. I'm sweating and could use a shower myself. I had no idea kid stuff was so, just so...much.

"Did Baby Corp. bring you shampoo and all that stuff?" Jane asks. She has the patience of a saint, but it doesn't escape my attention that she now sounds a million miles away.

"Yes." I grab a bottle of Aveeno baby wash that smells of flowers and oatmeal. I'll have to evaluate why I'm hearing Stella everywhere another time.

"Good, so wash them like you'd wash yourself. With Ruby, you may have to spread her rolls a little to make sure she's really clean because she's still in diapers. You don't want any poop or anything settling there."

I sit back on my heels and shake my head.

"Are you fuc—messing with me? That will get me arrested." Wait. How does she know Ruby has rolls? Did I call her Ruby-rolls on one of our phone calls?

She laughs and it's a beautiful melody I already know. I'm so fucking confused. Do I have the hots for Jane or for Stella? Or am I so tired that I'm making everything up in my head?

Stella versus Jane. Then there's Stella as Jane. And in my dreams, it's an inappropriate version of them both.

When Leah in accounting was pregnant, HR told me that pregnancy brain was a real thing and we needed to make accommodations for her. Maybe that's what's happening here, too.

"You won't get arrested." Jane's voice is filled with mirth.

"You're their guardian. It's your job to make sure they're clean."

"No way. I'm not doing it."

"You're cleaning her everywhere when you change her diaper, right?"

"I clean what I see as quickly as possible without looking."

"Beck. This is serious. If you don't make sure there's no poop remnants, she'll get an infection."

"What if I turn on the jets and just swish her back and forth a bit?"

There's that laugh again. The one that makes my cock jolt and the hairs at the base of my neck stand on end.

"You can do this. Make sure you wash their hair and behind their ears. They're just mini people."

"I'm going to hell for this."

I drop a cloth into the tub and start with Ruby's feet. She laughs and kicks, splashing us all with water.

"You could have mentioned that bath time is for everyone. I'm getting a shower over here," I grumble.

"Didn't I mention that? It's nearly impossible to come away dry."

Jane talks to Emmy while I tackle the little linebacker. Every muscle in my body aches by the time Ruby's clean.

"Okay, your turn, lovebug."

"Wub you, Stella," Emmy says with the cheerfulness you'd expect from a four-year-old, but this time my ears are awake. She called her Stella, and now Jane is talking a mile a minute.

"So Emmy should be a lot easier. But you'll need to teach her how to clean herself properly—"

"Jane?" I interrupt.

"The same with brushing her teeth. She should make the first attempt and then you brush them after her."

"Jane," I say more firmly.

"You'll also want to make sure you put extra ointment on Ruby's little bum if she still has that rash. I think that's it for now. You've got this, Beck."

I'm about to open my mouth when Ruby tips over the tub seat and I drop the phone to fish her out.

Bath time's over. I've got some shit to figure out. First and foremost, why an executive assistant I know is very well-compensated has so many damn jobs. Because one thing is for sure, Jane is my Stella—I hope.

I pause with Ruby held out at arm's length. She gives me a funny smile, and just as I'm bringing her close to drape a towel around her, the kid pisses all over me.

CHAPTER ELEVEN

STELLA

"Laura, it's okay. Take a deep breath."

Today is the worst day I've had with my mom yet, and it's only seven in the morning.

"Who are you?" she screams. "Are you the little slut who stole Charlie from me?"

Charlie. My dad.

I clench my teeth to keep the tears from falling. It's true, what Anna Kapern said in PE when I was thirteen years old —he didn't love me enough to stay. I'd told my mom, and she had said it was ridiculous mean girl nonsense, but we never stayed in one place long enough for me to make any kind of connection with anyone else after that either. Chasing fun was our motto and when life wasn't fun anymore, we moved on.

"Remember, Stella, just because she says it doesn't mean it's real," Lucía whispers as she readies my mother's medication.

It shouldn't be this way. She shouldn't be here, requiring another sedative to calm her down. It's so freaking unfair.

I can't look away from the syringe Lucía is preparing.

Mom's palm hits my cheek hard enough to snap my head back like a rag doll. "That's what homewreckers get," she wails right before Lucía injects her with medicine to calm her down.

The results are not instantaneous, so it takes some cajoling to usher her into the bed, but by the time she's leaning back, and we raise the guardrails, her stare is vacant. I don't know what's worse—the rage that filled her moments ago or this.

At least we didn't have to call security.

"Are you okay?" Lucía asks, pinching my chin and inspecting my cheek like a loving grandmother. "Let's get you an ice pack."

"No." I choke back a sob. "It's—It's okay. I have work. I'll be late if I don't leave."

"Stella, at least take one for the road." The compassion in her voice breaks down one of my remaining walls. I can barely hold it together as it is. It would be easier if she just ignored me.

"Honestly, I don't even feel it." My voice pitches higher with each word because I do feel it. I feel it right down to every nook and cranny of my heart. I'm being erased from my mother's mind, and it rips me in two. My entire existence fades with each of her memories.

Lucía reaches for me, but I back away, wishing I could sprint from my life and wake up in an alternate universe where my mother was still my mother, and I didn't have to hide in my own life.

I hold myself together until I get to the street, then run in the direction of my office. It'll take close to an hour to walk, but I need the exercise right now. I need the fresh air. I need to feel like I'm not suffocating in loneliness and sadness and grief that hasn't even hit me yet.

My legs burn with the effort. I'm not a runner, but right now the physical pain is welcomed, so I focus on that because the emotional pain is more than I can take.

I'm out of breath after ten minutes. I slow my jog to walking at a clipped pace and use the remaining time to focus on my breathing. To focus on the good memories and refuse to allow these few bad ones to be what I remember about my mother.

My phone vibrates in my purse, and I pull it out. It's a text message from SDH.

SDH: Jane? I need you to call me as soon as possible.

Beck leaves his phone number in the next message.

But I don't call him back. It's against the rules, and if nothing else, I am still a rule follower. I can't afford to lose any of my jobs, not when I'm barely scraping by as it is.

I clutch my phone to my chest, loving that someone in this world needs me, but vowing not to answer it—I can't—not yet.

My heart thrashes wildly in my chest.

It's not her fault.

It's not her fault.

I repeat it a hundred times, and then say it again when I arrive at the office. I'm sweaty and blotchy, but I'm here. I'm doing it. One step in front of the other. I will make it through to the other side of this.

Pep talk complete, I drop my phone on my desk, place my purse in the cabinet drawer, double-check the lock, then walk into the ladies' room with my head down. The reflection I find in the mirror isn't me. This girl is sad and close to breaking. This girl has never felt more alone in all her life.

My makeup is smeared from wind and tears, so I take a

few minutes to scrub my face clean. My hair clings to my neck and face as though I ran a marathon, but there's nothing I can do about that now. The elastic I usually wear around my wrist snapped when my mother first attacked me.

It's not her fault. She isn't in there anymore.

By the time I've emerged from the restroom, the sounds of baby babble fill the air. But when I round the corner to where my desk faces Elijah's, I find Beck holding two phones, and everyone turns their attention to me in slow motion.

One of the phones in Beck's hands is mine—and it's ringing.

No, no, no! There go two of my three jobs. What the hell am I going to do now? My mind spirals with potential backup plans and worst-case scenarios, but honestly, this is rock bottom—there's nowhere else to fall. I swallow the first of many sobs that will inevitably attempt to break free.

I am stronger than my circumstances. I am stronger than my circumstances.

Beck is wearing Ruby in a BabyBjörn, and I'm momentarily struck with pride that he figured that one out on his own again. But then he's standing before me, tilting my chin to face him, and everything about his demeanor changes in an instant. His eyes are dark and angry. His jaw ticks like he's trying to control himself.

"Who touched you?" His hand on my face softens as he runs a fingertip over the side of my face, but it scorches my skin, swirling and sparking through my entire body.

The handprint. On my cheek. I knew it was there, but I didn't expect to be called out this way. I jerk my chin free and flash him a warning I hope isn't hidden by tears. He's being inappropriate—it doesn't matter that I love it.

"Who. Did. That?" Each carefully articulated word sucks the air from the room. This version of Beck is different—protective, dangerous even. This is the man who engulfed me on the dance floor then encouraged me to let down my walls for a few short hours, and it causes a shiver to work through my body.

But I also steel my spine because I'm out of options. I can't lose this job, so I power through with false bravado.

"It was a misunderstanding. I have makeup in my bag. I'll cover it with powder, and it'll be gone by lunchtime. I'm perfectly capable of doing my job."

"And which job is that, *Jane*?" His voice is silvery and lethal. It carries a command in a tone I've never heard, but he doesn't move away, doesn't give me space.

He sucks in a breath, but we're too close—the mint of his toothpaste tingles my nose when he exhales. Then he bends his knees, and it brings us to within inches of each other. Ruby's feet kick against my chest as he stares in one eye, then the other. Whoever he's searching for is gone. I'm not the girl I was last spring. I never will be again.

The silence is so thick I can't breathe.

"My office. Now," Beck growls. Daisie Dog growls. Ruby roars. Elijah hisses in Beck's direction. Emmy tries to blend into the wallpaper. And Caleb smirks, then follows Beck to his office while I watch the pieces of my life slowly drift into a fire.

"Where are you going?" Beck asks when he turns at his doorway. He doesn't quite snarl, but it wipes that smug expression from Caleb's face. In fact, he's turning an impressive shade of red I've never seen on anyone else.

"Based on your attitude, you'll need your attorney present for whatever Miss Anderson has done now."

Now? Like I've done something before?

Beck's gaze flicks back and forth from me to Caleb, and my external cringe has nothing on the internal one happening at the same time. He's remembering what I stupidly told him in one moment of weakness where I foolishly allowed myself to believe I was part of a team again.

"Who is the junior associate, Stella?" Beck snarls.

I bite my lip and shake my head. But he snaps the same question again. "Who is the junior associate, Stella?"

Ruby cries, Emmy whimpers, and I crack.

"Teddy Park," I say. Both Beck and Caleb's eyes flash murderously.

"Elijah, make sure that from now on, Teddy Park shadows Caleb—on everything." I don't lift my gaze from the floor, but the air shifts and I'd bet he's facing him fully now. "We're all about teaching the next generation around here. Isn't that right, Caleb?" His name slithers from Beck's tongue and I expect a sharp retort.

"Beck, don't be ridiculous," he says, but his tone carries a sense of unease, and we all hear it. "I've been with you since the beginning."

"Then you won't mind mentoring our most promising associate." Beck's body vibrates with rage.

"Be—um, Mr. Hayes." *Shut up, Stella, shut up.* "The girls feed off your energy. They feel whatever you're feeling."

"Mr. Hayes?" he snarls. "We're past that now, *Jane*, don't you think? My office. Now."

I nod and hurry across the room. Elijah squeezes my upper arm on the way by. "It'll be okay. I'll talk to him when he's calmed down."

"You knew?" The vein in Beck's neck pulses with each word. "Of course you knew. I should have known better."

Elijah, who is much smaller than Beck, goes toe-to-toe with him. He's close enough that Ruby reaches for his suspenders and gives them a snap, which makes him yelp and her laugh, but it doesn't deter him.

"Think before you speak, Beck. There may be lines drawn in the sand, but I have never once held that stick, and I'm not doing it now."

"Elijah, it's okay. It's my fault." I shake my head and enter Beck's office. I made my bed and now it's time to lie in it.

Hope—it really is a fickle thing.

<hr>

WE'VE BEEN IN BECK'S OFFICE FOR ALMOST FIFTEEN MINUTES, and he hasn't said a word. He's pacing behind his desk and patting Ruby's belly mindlessly, which she seems to enjoy. She's already let out three impressive burps, and she's well past the stage of assisted burping but she thinks it's funny.

She's a great distraction because the need to fill the silence is overwhelming, but I have no idea where to begin. Everything has gotten really complicated, really fast.

"Who hit you," he says after an eternity.

My mouth tastes like cotton balls, and I swallow twice before speaking. "Respectfully, sir, that's none of your business." I try to shift in my chair, but Daisie Dog is sitting on my feet.

His posture stiffens and so do the lines around his eyes, but he rounds his desk with measured strides until he's standing, looming over me.

"Sir?" he asks.

"Don't be a jerk. I don't know what to call you. I was just as confused as you are now. I wasn't expecting my boss's boss to call the hotline. What are the freaking odds of that, anyway? Though, after talking to stinking Elijah, I have a feeling the odds were pretty high."

He leans over and places his hands on the armrests of my chair, caging me in, throwing gasoline on my fears.

And my desire.

I drop my gaze to my lap before he sees the unrequited lust lurking behind my quickly crumbling walls.

"I. Don't. Work. With. Liars. Stella. So tell me one thing…"

I gulp, and the sound makes Ruby laugh. Since she's inches from my face in this position, I reach out and squish her perfectly chubby thighs.

Beck pulls back so she's out of reach, and it hurts more than it should, but Emmy catches my attention. She's crouched down in the corner, clutching a little blue book to her chest.

Daisie Dog stands and trots to Emmy's side—at least they have each other.

"It's okay, sweetheart. Sometimes big people have big voices." I smile and wait for her to respond.

"It's scawy," she whispers. Beck's head whips in her direction before he deflates like a sad balloon.

"I'm sorry I scared you, lovebug. I didn't mean to. Stella's right. My voice just got too big for a moment. I'll do better next time."

She nods and takes a seat on the floor, but I see how small she tries to make herself. She's a lot like me.

"What, Beck?" I tear my gaze away from the little girl in the pretty blue dress. "What do you want me to tell you?"

He takes a step back and rests his hip against his desk, but he wears an unreadable mask. "Are you playing me?"

It's so absurd, I laugh. "Playing you how, Beck? I'm working twenty-four hours a day. Name one single thing I've gotten from you that would benefit me in any way that I haven't earned."

He narrows his eyes. "Why are you working so many hours?"

Damn it. Why did I open my mouth with this guy? The one time I break the rules, and this is where it lands me.

I shake my head when my words won't come. I was here —I saw how poorly he reacted to the news of his sister even calling. His own sister. Every time she called, he got angry. He never lashed out, but it was there in his body language. Hopefully the girls will soften him, because if you'd asked me a month ago, I would have said Beck Hayes is adamantly against family and the emotional baggage that always follows. If his reaction to my mother is a quarter of that, I won't have a job anymore.

"Was it Caleb you were speaking about? One of your jobs with the sketchy boss?"

I'm quick to nod and even quicker to respond, "But I don't have proof of anything. Neither does Teddy—yet."

"But you were certain enough to risk speaking to a junior associate about it?"

I nod.

"Why didn't you tell Elijah?" His face remains impassive, but his voice hitches on his friend's name.

How the heck do I tell him this? My chest aches—all those broken pieces of my heart slice against its walls.

"I needed to be sure first. Elijah's the only friend I have, and I..." I hate that my voice cracks. I should be stronger than this. "He's all I have. I couldn't risk losing him and I couldn't guarantee that he'd believe me."

His Adam's apple bobs violently as he studies me. "Why do you work three jobs? I pay you very well."

"It's none of your business." There's steel in my tone that's been missing for a very long time. "I work because I have to, just like anyone else. I have bills to pay and things to do and people who depend on me, just like you."

"The difference, Stella, is that I'm not working around the clock." His voice is aggressive, but his posture is guarded. This man confounds me.

My shoulders fall forward in defeat. "What do you want from me? My resignation? Do you want me to call Lottie and tell her I broke her rules? Well, that one I can't do because I've never actually spoken to her. She's connected through connections and there's no direct access to her except for email."

Emmy pops her head up from behind Beck's desk and we both do a double take. She walks quietly to my chair then climbs into my lap and kisses my cheek.

"I lub you, Stella."

Her words suck all the air from the room.

Beck hefts himself up so he's sitting fully on his desk. His stare is akin to a hawk's—he doesn't miss a thing.

"I don't work with liars, Stella."

I bite my tongue to keep from crying, but my words quiver with my chin. "I'm sorry that's what you think of me. If there was any other choice—"

"I have to take them home." His shoulders droop and his voice is quiet, introspective. He speaks as though he's unsure, and it's a tone I've never heard from him before. I've only known this man to be confident in everything he does. "To Sailport Bay," he adds quietly.

That stings more than it should—I'm truly losing everyone this week.

"But my business won't run itself, and from the looks of things, there's some shady shit happening I wasn't aware of."

The taste of copper fills my mouth when I bite down harder because I don't know what to say to that.

He observes me for so long that my skin itches. His eyes crinkle at the corners and his upper lip twitches. Does he do that on purpose? Is he aware of how he affects me?

"What will it take for you to come with us?" he drawls. A southern accent he works hard to suppress seeps out thicker than I've ever heard it.

"Excuse me?" I ask, choking on the excessive amount of saliva in my mouth.

"Name your price. Help me help these girls so I can save my company from what I fear is going on behind my back. Name your price."

"You don't work with liars."

He raises a brow. "Are you a liar, Stella?"

"Not intentionally. Not when I have a choice. I—"

"That's what I thought."

"W—Why me?"

He stares again in that way that makes me think he's seeing to the very heart of me and isn't afraid of what he finds.

"Because you're you, Stella. You're the only person all three of us are comfortable around, and that's not something that comes to me easily. I spent hours last night wondering if I was losing my mind. When I was mostly certain you were Jane, I spent the rest of the night trying to figure out your angle here, and unless you're the best goddamn con artist in the world, I can't find a single thing that would harm me, the girls, or my company. You helped me because you needed a job, and you're damn good with kids. You're playing taxi driver because you obviously need money, but I see no signs of drug use or unsavory debts."

I scoff indignantly. "I'm not a petty thief or a con artist. I'm not a bad person and I've never once touched drugs of any kind. I hardly even drink." I straighten and tilt my chin up. I may be a lot of things, but I'm done allowing other people to paint my story for me—not anymore.

A slow smile creeps over his face. That crooked one that makes me want to throw caution to the wind, but it's his dimples that wreck me. There's one on each side, and it makes him seem so much younger when they're on display.

"That's the same conclusion I came to, Stella Jane. So I'm assuming it all boils down to money. How much do you need to live comfortably without forty-five different jobs?"

My chest beats and rattles like a snare drum. *How much do I need?* The idea has never been plausible before. What the heck do I ask for? Emmy snuggles in closer and it's hard to breathe.

"It's not just money, though." I need time to consider this. "I have obligations here that I can't miss."

"Name your terms." He's so cool and confident and I'm unraveling faster than my ex's lies.

I stand with Emmy on my hip and practically run to the opposite wall, hoping the distance will kick my brain into gear. What do I need? *Think, Stella, think.*

All the while his gaze sets my body ablaze as he studies me with Emmy.

"I need Saturdays off and a way to get back to Raleigh for the entire day."

His brows furrow, but he nods. "Done."

What?

"And I need to come back one night a week. Same deal. I need reliable transportation back and forth. I don't even know where Sailport is."

"Sailport Bay," he says. "It's in the Outer Banks."

That makes me pause. "Like the TV show?"

This stinking man rolls his eyes. "Yes, like the TV show without all the drama. What else?"

"Um." I bite my lip so hard I almost break the skin. "Ah, well. There's always the chance I'll have to rush home. If there's an emergency, I mean."

"Obviously. Are you expecting many of those?"

I shrug. "That's the thing, there's no way to know."

He nods slowly but studies me so intently that I swear I can feel his gaze ghosting over my body. "We'll make a contingency plan for *emergencies*."

Crap. Oh, crap. He's really serious about this. Guilt claws at my chest. I won't be able to see Mom every day. On the other hand, if he pays what I need, I won't have to kill myself trying to afford her care.

"How much do you need, Stella?"

I quickly tally my mother's care, her meds, my rundown apartment, and all my miscellaneous bills, then blurt out a number I have no right speaking. "Twelve thousand a month."

His lips twitch again. Don't look, Stella. Don't look. He's a human solar eclipse—if you're not careful, you'll go blind.

"That's one-hundred and forty-four thousand a year," he says. Is he laughing at me?

Oh, crap. Twelve times twelve is…freaking math. I only make four thousand a month as Caleb's assistant. And I'm close to making the same with SDH. That's eight thousand a month, maybe I should have matched that. But I can't. Not with the schedule of a nanny and being so far from home.

"Done," he says, shocking me so much I lean against the wall for support.

He stalks closer with gleaming eyes, and I shift Emmy to the opposite hip.

"But—but," I stutter and take a step to the left, tripping over the dog.

"Dang it, Daisie." He grabs my bicep before I land flat on my face.

"My insurance. My benefits…"

"You'll remain an employee. I'll take care of that." His gaze bores into me. We're standing so close our thighs touch, and my heart rate skyrockets.

Trying to catch my breath, I inhale deeply and am hit with a hint of spice that triggers memories that are definitely not safe for work.

"Do you know why my mother named us what she did?" he asks silkily, then brushes a piece of Emmy's hair behind her ear.

Becker and Calista? I have no freaking idea. What does that have to do with anything?

"My mother had a funny sense of humor. Our nicknames, Beck and Cally."

It takes a moment for it to register, but when it does it comes out on a whisper. "Beck and Call."

"Yeah." He runs one long finger over the imprint of my mother's hand, causing a Pavlovian response—my body will never forget his touch, but I still have no idea what the hell he's talking about. "You'll have your time for whatever secrets you're keeping, but for twelve grand a month, I need you all in with the girls. I have a feeling there's a war brewing, and I haven't been invited to the battle."

"What? What do you mean? With Caleb?"

"What was it you said to me? None of my business? Use that phrase here. Just promise me you'll be available to the girls at a moment's notice any time except your previously stated days off."

"Beck and call," I say mindlessly. "You want me to be at your beck and call?"

A groan escapes and he pinches the bridge of his nose. "Not mine—the girls'."

My gaze drifts lower and is that—is he? Is he having the same reaction to me?

"I don't know how this works with the hotline," I say dumbly. I keep my lashes lowered—anything to not make eye contact with him again. "There's probably a hefty fee for canceling our contracts, and she doesn't have a nanny service yet." Am I really trying to talk him out of this?

"Let me worry about that. Trust me, if she'd had a nanny package, it would have saved us a lot of trouble. But then again, I wouldn't have gotten you."

Holy hotness. Holy, holy, swoon. He's so close, my body breaks out in a hot flush, so I speak just to keep my mind occupied.

"The nanny option is coming next year, but it wouldn't have mattered for you because she doesn't have anyone else right now that matches with you."

His lips curve into a cocky grin. "You tried to get rid of me?"

"I—I didn't want to lie. I..."

"And that is why you're still here when I don't work with liars, Stella." My name rolls from his mouth like a lover's caress.

"But..."

Why am I even arguing? It's not like I have any other options. But am I really going to live with this man? Holy crap. I'm going to live with this man. In the same house. And he's groped me, intimately. Geez, I really wasn't myself that night.

"Okay," I agree quickly. Yup, I guess I am. I can't even believe this is happening right now.

"Done. I'll have a contract drawn up by morning." He

takes a step back, and the cold air that washes in leaves me weak in the knees. He turns at his desk. "By someone not named Caleb." He winks, and my jaw nearly unhinges.

"You're not the only one with secrets, sweetheart."

Sweetheart.

Sweetheart.

Stupidly, that becomes my new mantra as I make the long walk home.

CHAPTER TWELVE

BECK

"SHOW ME," I SAY REMOVING MY SUIT COAT AND DROPPING IT over the back of my chair. We're in the conference room with the blinds closed and have taken advantage of every available surface while Elijah babysits Caleb.

Teddy, who doesn't look a day over twenty, nods like his head's on a spring and he can't stop the movement.

"Teddy, are you nervous?"

He lets out a breath that shifts papers across the table, and a chuckle bubbles up in my chest.

"Okay. There's no need to be nervous," I say, attempting to keep my tone light. "Stella told me the gist of her hunch, now I need you to show me what you've found."

For the next two hours, this kid walks me through the files and numbers that don't match up.

What the hell is Caleb up to? He's shifting money and deals around, but it's not missing from anywhere, and the deals that do go through have all been approved by me.

"Sir?" Teddy speaks up with a crackle in his voice. How long have I been sitting here staring at this one file?

"I'm sorry. Go ahead." A new headache builds, pressure forming at my temples.

"Well, I don't know for sure, but my guess is that he's shifting money to set you up for something big, and not necessarily good." That was my thought too. "My father is a cynical man, and he would say there's a deal coming that will blow up in your face, and when it does, they'll leave a trail leading straight to you. I think he's angling to prove that you've been embezzling from your own company."

He places three more files on my desk, and it paints a pretty clear picture, but it doesn't tell me what deal or when. It's a never-ending circle of messes. The one thing it does give me is ammunition to cut Caleb loose.

It will be messy, but it'll be fast.

"Your father sounds like a very smart man," I say. "You must be aware that I recently became a father—or father figure—to my nieces."

"Yes, sir. My dad was a single parent. I can appreciate how much work it is." He has more optimism than Daisie Dog when she sits beneath Ruby's highchair.

I really like this kid.

"I appreciate you, Teddy. And I'll be honest with you. The girls aren't doing well in my penthouse, so I'll be bringing them home to the Outer Banks for a while. This office will remain open with Elijah in charge, and I'll be in one day a week until we find a more permanent solution."

He nods, and he might be holding his breath, so I push on quickly.

"But Caleb will be leaving us shortly, and I'd appreciate it if you'd take over his office." He pales, and I chuckle. "Not his job, not yet anyway, but after this, I can assure you that you'll be fast-tracked here. For now, I want you in that office, following every single thing amiss in these folders. You only report to me or Elijah. Is that clear?"

"Yes, sir." The smile on this kid is blinding.

"Okay. I'll have Elijah make sure your office is ready for you tomorrow."

"T—Tomorrow?"

"I may be distracted by family obligations, but I didn't get to where I am by dodging the tough stuff. So unless you want to be witness to the bloodbath that will be getting Caleb out of the building, I suggest you take the rest of the day off and come back tomorrow ready to help dig us out of this mess."

"Yes, sir." He almost salutes me before hurrying to pack up his files with a red face. Now I understand why Stella likes him so much—he's got a good head on his shoulders and a heart that's in the right place.

I'm rooting for him—and that's something new for me too. The Stella effect is real.

"Oh," I say when he's almost to my door. "Cut out the *sir* shit. I'm only thirty-five. My name is Beck."

His eyeballs might pop right out of his skull, but I've made the right decision. Don't ask me why I'm putting all my faith in a girl who lied about her identity for six weeks when I've spent my entire adult life avoiding trust and complications, but I am. I follow my gut with business, and following that same logic, for whatever reason, Stella Anderson is the easiest decision I've ever made.

I ENTER THE PENTHOUSE AT QUARTER PAST TEN EVERY KIND OF exhausted there is, but it's replaced with worry when faced with the family room. I spin in a circle, searching for a point of reference.

Is this my apartment?

Stella's been here since seven this morning, but this is not how I left the place, and she's been busy today. She sent updates in picture form throughout the day of the girls at the park, reading books, and even making freaking dinner. It softened the thorns that have been in my chest since I took custody of the girls.

But that's not what has me backtracking to make sure I entered the right apartment. The place is spotless, and the cleaners don't come until Friday.

I move through the quiet space to the kitchen, and that's where I find Stella, standing on a kitchen stool, scraping macaroni off my ceiling.

"Elijah's all I have." Her admission locked around my heart, and I can't find the key.

"What are you doing?"

She gasps, spins, and every cliched romantic comedy my big sister ever made me watch comes to life when she falls. I run to catch her, but Daisie Dog chooses that moment to run circles around my leg, tripping me up, so by the time I make it to Stella, we're both tumbling to the floor.

It's nothing like the movies.

At least I cushioned her fall, but she knocked the wind out of me, and I'm wheezing while she scrambles to untangle herself from my arms and legs.

"Dang it, Daisie," I groan.

"Oh my God. I'm so sorry. You scared the crap out of me. You said eleven. I had forty-five more minutes. Geez. Warn a girl, Beck." She scolds me as if I'm a toddler and I feel my cock thickening beneath her weight.

Horribly inappropriate and dizzyingly fantastic in the same breath.

She stands quickly and I'm thankful for it—mostly. Our situation is already complicated enough.

"Beck," she snaps, while I lie there smiling like a buffoon with Daisie Dog preening behind her.

There's something about hearing her full, beautiful voice that softens more of those thorns around my heart. It's not the muted version, the one I got through a speaker phone, bad connection, baby babble, anger, or a whisper. It's a reminder that she sheltered herself away from me, either to deceive me or protect herself—probably both.

And apparently, I don't care about her motives.

I don't immediately move from my sprawled-out position, but my smile widens. In the movie, I'd be the lovesick fool fawning over a girl way out of my league.

My life is getting messier than Ruby in a mud puddle.

"Your deception should piss me off," I say, using a jovial tone that feels foreign on my lips as I sit up. "But hearing your voice makes me happy."

She shakes her head and offers me a hand. There's no way her tiny frame could possibly lift me from the floor, but I take it to feel her skin against mine, then rise to my feet while currents of electricity pass through our joined fingers.

She's so damn soft, and her small hand is delicate in mine, but there's a strength to her that's sexy as hell. It's difficult to let go of her, but I do before it becomes uncomfortable.

I crave being this close to her—close enough to count her freckles—close enough to be inappropriate. I should have taken into account what having her in my space would do to me. Or maybe I did and allowed lust to fog my decision-making abilities.

Dads, even uncle-daddies, do not fall for the nanny. *Say it again louder for those of us in denial back here.* There's a power dynamic at play—a thousand and one ways this is all wrong, and not a single part of me cares.

Fuck.

"We've been over that," she huffs, stepping around me. Damn this version of her. The real her—Stella and Jane combined to make one perfectly imperfect soul. "I didn't set out to deceive you, so either you let it go and move on or you find another nanny."

"Oh, no you don't. You signed a contract," I grin. "One that pays you handsomely. I'm not losing you now." My voice is too deep, too sultry, so I take a step back and loosen the tie around my neck.

Elijah's teasing voice sings in my head. *"You didn't think about your attraction when you strong-armed her into living with you."*

But how could I? Everything we've done has been at warp speed. Our one night that was cut short after she received a phone call and ran off. Elijah hiring her. My uncle-daddy status. It's all unbelievable, really.

"How did it go with Caleb?" She worries her lip, then steps back onto the stool as though she's going to try again.

I reach her before she stands upright, wrap my arms around her thighs, and lower her to the ground. It's a slow decline down my body that pumps blood everywhere but my brain. "Don't do that again." My voice needs a memo of its own—don't use that husky tone when her body is pressed against yours. "You can't wrestle Ruby with a broken arm, and I don't want shit all over the furniture."

I take the spatula she was scraping with and the towel she's using to catch pasta pieces then step onto the stool myself, realizing too late that my Oxfords don't have great traction.

"It went about as well as you're imagining," I say over my shoulder, struck by how domestic this is. "He's been with me a long time, but I wasn't expecting the amount of animosity he was hiding behind." My sigh is heavy with loss—I relied on Caleb. "I don't know what his motivation was. We've always worked well together, but this company was always my baby. I've paid him fairly, generously even, but apparently that wasn't enough for him."

"Did Teddy help?" There's a fondness in her tone that has me glancing down. A giant boulder rolls around my gut and is gaining speed.

"You care about him." The words come out hoarse and painful.

She nods. "I do. If I had a younger brother, I think he'd be just like Teddy—shy but sweet and a hard worker. We stumbled onto the files at about the same time, but he's the one who put it together while I scouted for inconsistencies. So...was he helpful?"

I frown as I scrape at the ceiling. "Let's just say he looks very good in Caleb's office."

"What?" Stella screeches then covers her mouth and runs to the baby monitor set up on the counter. A low chuckle vibrates in my chest. When she's sure she didn't wake the girls, she turns to me. "For real?"

"Yes, Stella. For real." Her smile is a hit to the nuts. I fucking love making her face shine. "He'll work in Caleb's office so he has access to every file he can get his hands on. Caleb was escorted out empty-handed today, so hopefully Teddy will find something."

I pause with my arm outstretched to the ceiling. There's no denying Caleb was misappropriating funds, but it's so unlike the man I know. Sure, he's a hard-ass, but he's always been an ethical hard-ass. It's why I hired him in the first place.

"Beck?"

Stella's voice jolts me into motion, and I clear my throat. "Elijah's packing up his personal belongings and will leave them at the front desk, but I doubt he'll come for them. His fate is in the hands of the legal system now—if we're right, he'll never practice law again."

"That's good, right?" she mutters while chewing on her bottom lip, stealing my attention from the job I'm doing on the ceiling. It's impossible to be in her vicinity and not be drawn to her—not when she's so close. Her amber eyes shine with unshed tears, and they're pointed right at me.

My reaction to her tears is so visceral they could knock me on my ass again.

"What's wrong, Stella?"

Daisie Dog whimpers at her feet, and I step down from the stool.

"Huh? Oh, nothing. It makes me happy when good things happen to good people. That's not usually the case, and Teddy is good people. I'm sad for Caleb and whatever caused him to inflict pain on someone else, but I'm not sorry to see him go, so that probably makes me the complete opposite of a good person."

Elijah's words about love languages and protective tendencies flash through my mind, but I ignore them when she shrugs, then moves to the sink to load the dishwasher.

How could she possibly believe she isn't a good person? It makes me want to shake some sense into her. She should see herself as I see her. Personified hope.

She doesn't hear me approach, but when I touch her shoulder, she jolts, then melts into my hand. It makes me crave more of her, and I know instantly that I need to lay some ground rules for myself around her. Immediately.

"Why were you following those files?" I ask, cataloging her reactions and committing them to memory. "Were you expecting a raise? A promotion? What did you hope to gain from it?"

She spins on me in a fiery ball of anger. Exactly what I was hoping for. Her nostrils flare and her chest heaves, bringing us closer on each violent inhale. "Nothing, Beck." She spits my name and the muscle in my cheek twitches. "I wasn't hoping to get anything out of it. I didn't even know if I was right, but it was the right thing to do."

"Let me make sure I understand." Even though my tone is gentle, it's now apparent how close we're standing, so I reluctantly step back. It's no small feat either because my entire body is charged when she's near. "You put yourself out there to stick your nose into something that could have gotten you in trouble because 'it was the right thing to do'?"

"Yes." Her nose scrunches up the second the word leaves her lips. "It's not the same."

"It's exactly the same. You did it because you're a good person. Just like Teddy. Just like Elijah, the double-crossing asshat."

She winces. "He wasn't expecting this to happen either. He was honestly trying to help me and...he—"

"Elijah knows your secrets." Though my tone is light, my stomach clenches as if it's trying to heave.

"It's different."

"How?"

"He and Samira happened to show up at my apartment one day when I needed help."

Now my entire body tenses. "Are you in danger?"

What does that mean for the girls? For me? For her?

Her hair swishes side to side when she shakes her head adamantly. "No, I wouldn't be here with the girls if I were."

I don't quite believe her. She may not be in physical danger, but there's something—something she refuses to tell me that has fear rolling through my airway. There's no doubt she'd protect the girls, but would she protect herself?

"Then tell me who hit you."

She bites her lip when her chin trembles. "If I tell you, you have to promise to drop it after."

"Fine." We both hear the lie. There's not a chance in hell I'll allow her to be in danger.

She fidgets with her wrist and her shoulders curl in. "Do you promise?"

I lift my brows but don't utter a word.

"It was my mom, but it's not her fault. It was a misunderstanding." The words spill out in a rush and her hands ball into fists. I take an involuntary step forward. Comforting her is engrained deep, but I stop myself from reaching for her. This goddamn relationship is messy as hell.

You don't do relationships. Yeah, I'm pretty sure that ship has sailed.

"So the house is clean," she continues quickly. "The girls are packed, and I'll be back in the morning at eight." Then she spins to face the dishes again and says over her shoulder, "I've never been to the Outer Banks, so I'll bring a few things and switch them out when I return on Saturday if I need to."

"Sailport Bay is very laid back and beachy. You and the girls will love it," I say, attempting to drown out the wild thoughts in my head—the ones screaming about relationships and relations and nannies and parenthood.

My life is a fucking Judd Apatow film.

Stella pauses her attack on the dishwasher and places a

hand on her hip. She's the flame and I'm the moth, drawn to her in unimaginable ways. I lean against the counter, facing her, but even leaving the open dishwasher between us, there's a gravitational pull to be in her orbit.

"Then why don't you like Sailport Bay? Elijah told me you haven't been home in years."

"Elijah has a big mouth."

She waits expectantly, and I give a halfhearted shrug. Stella Jane is a sorcerer pulling truths from me before I'm ready.

"I haven't been back to Sailport Bay because I have a feeling the memories that haunt that house are not good ones. After my relationship with Cally crumbled, there was nothing left there for me."

Her lashes flutter wildly, and her eyes showcase her sadness—but it's not just hers. She carries sadness on my behalf, and I don't know what to make of that. No one but Elijah has done anything on my behalf since my mother died.

"Um, I'm sorry to hear that." She takes a step forward, then pauses as though she wants to say more, but shakes her head. "That's really terrible, and I'm so sorry you had to go through that." When I don't respond, she offers an awkward wave. "Um, I'll see you in the morning then."

She slips along the counter and away from me, but I jingle a set of keys.

"What's that?"

"The keys to the SUV you'll drive in Sailport Bay. I don't want you walking home this late, and it'll be easier if you pack your stuff at your place."

She crosses her arms and juts out her hip. It's a little sassy, but the way she bites her bottom lip betrays her nerves. "What if I can't drive an SUV?"

I relish the fire that comes from her when I least expect it.

"I have a feeling you can do anything you set your mind to, so I'm not worried about it," I say, playing along because I love this banter.

"Yes, I can drive an SUV," she says with a whimsical laugh. "If you ever need a ride, I'm only a phone call away."

"I'll keep that in mind," I say dryly. "But I'm hoping for what I'm paying you there will be no more rideshares in your future. And I know we haven't worked out the logistics of you coming back to Raleigh on your days, but we will. It's a three-hour drive, and I'll adjust my schedule so you have a fair amount of time here for...whatever it is you're doing." Even my words pout, but when her eyes crinkle at the corners, my heart expands three sizes.

"I know you will, Beck."

My brows wing up into my hairline. "You do? How?"

One slim shoulder lifts with a sexy shrug. "I guess I just trust you."

I stand frozen as she turns to leave. I don't move until I hear the front door close, then hear her using the key I gave her. She wiggles the handle three times before silence descends.

"I'm glad you trust me, Stella. I just don't know if I can trust myself."

CHAPTER THIRTEEN

STELLA

"We might have to rent a van," Beck says. "Freaking Daisie will take up an entire row, and there's so much... everything. I should have had the second SUV delivered here and not in Sailport Bay." He lifts a plastic teething ring with one finger as if it repulses him.

He's dressed more casually than I've ever seen him and it's messing with my ability to concentrate. His navy-blue shorts and polo shirt with a pink whale on it are so far removed from his suits and ties that I'm finding it difficult to reconcile both sides of him. He looks...normal. And sexy. Super sexy, but I'll never, ever say that out loud.

"What do you think?" He turns suddenly, placing a hand on my forearm, and heat creeps up my neck to settle in my cheeks.

I can't remember what the heck he said, so I peer around him at the pile of stuff he has in his family room. It's everything the company he hired to babyproof brought over and then some.

"So this house we're going to, in Sailport is—"

"Sailport Bay," he interrupts. "It's a big thing there. Sailport is another town in South Carolina and neither likes to be mistaken for the other—it's a big rivalry."

I lift my brows, waiting for an explanation, but he's back to crossing his arms and drumming his pointer and middle fingers on his opposite bicep. I've seen him do this in the office a few times, but it's so much different when I can see his forearms.

No wonder the guy lifted me so easily last night. When the heck does he have time to work out?

Behind him, Ruby is in a bouncy seat, trying to launch herself into outer space. That kid has a lot of energy. Emmy sits beside her sister on the floor with a book she keeps close by but has never let me read—It probably holds a special memory of her mom.

Emmy tucks her knees into her chest, making herself even smaller.

Someday soon we need to teach Emmy that it's okay to live loudly and to take up space.

"Wow," I finally say. "That's a lot of stuff."

Beck spins on me with a scowl. "You're supposed to be the expert here. Are you telling me I didn't need to buy all this shit?"

I haven't rolled my eyes this much since I was in middle school. "No, Mr. Grumptitude. You do need it here. But do you need it in Sailport?"

"Sailport Bay, Stella. Sailport Bay," he cries in exasperation. "I'm telling you, there's no faster way to get the townsfolk to turn on you than mess up the town name. It's worse than cursing in church." There's that Southern drawl again.

"Townsfolk?" I can't quite keep the humor from lacing my words.

He closes his eyes and his nostrils flare. His behavior is

out of character, even with all the upheaval in his life right now.

"Are you nervous to go home?"

He finally opens one eye and glares. "I'm not afraid of anything."

"Okay, hotshot. Well, I did some research on Sailport *Bay*. It's not what I was expecting. What do people do there in the winter?"

This question has him showcasing his crooked and highly addictive smile. "The townsfolk," he teases, leaning over to pull a piece of teething biscuit off my sleeve, "get all up in your business. All day. Every day."

His little touches are as maddening as they are comforting, and it takes me a moment to register what he's saying. Thank God he avoided me in the office for so long. I would have had to pack extra panties every day.

Wait. What did he say?

They'll get in my business? No, no. I like privacy. I've spent the last year trying to hide in plain sight. I don't know if I can handle a small-town circus right now. I lift my gaze to his, and whatever my face is doing right now has his interest, because his eyes turn molten as he studies me.

"Does that scare you?" he asks.

I gulp. "I just...I have a lot happening in my life right now, too. There's a reason I don't have many friends. There's a reason I work so much. My life does not belong to me."

His thick brows pinch together as he scrutinizes me with such determination that I'm sure he can read every note of my heart. "Someone stole your trust," he says quietly.

His hands twitch at his sides, and he lifts them as though he's reaching for me before dropping them to his sides again.

Touch me, I want to scream. Instead, I straighten my

spine, prepared to defend myself, but his expression turns contemplative. Why do we keep standing so close?

"Well, Stella Jane," he murmurs, leaning into my personal space, "that makes two of us—but you're a step ahead because I don't trust anyone."

"That's not true," I say and lift Ruby from the bouncer seat to put some space between us. She shares her happiness with a loud babble that demands attention. I tickle her belly and fit my nose into the crook of her neck, inhaling deeply before turning back to her uncle.

There's just something so soothing about the scent of a baby.

Embarrassment washes over me when I realize he caught me sniffing the little girl—again.

"There's something about the way she smells, huh? I thought it was just me being weird."

I don't quite laugh, but it's there, bubbling in my chest. I move to sort through the ridiculous amount of stuff he piled here while Ruby attempts to rip everything out of my free hand.

"Why do you think I trust people?" he asks.

I stand up straight with a bath visor that's supposed to keep soap out of their eyes. "Look at Elijah—even Caleb. And just yesterday what you did with Teddy. You placed so much trust in that kid, based on what? What some random nanny you barely know told you? Maybe you're too trusting."

"Are we keeping this?" He removes the visor from my hand. I nod and wade through more stuff.

"That's not trust, Stella. That's business. You cannot run a business as large as mine without placing some responsibility on other people. Responsibility does not equal trust."

"Elijah is your friend though. You trust him."

He shrugs. "I've known him since I was ten years old."

"And you trust him," I say with an epic eye roll.

"Fine," he sighs. "Yes, I trust him."

"And for some reason you trust me."

He doesn't reply, and when I face him, his expression is haunted.

"At least on some level, you must trust me, right? With your nieces?"

Beck frowns and his Adam's apple bobs unnaturally.

"I outsource," he finally says. "It isn't the same thing as trust."

My stomach drops as though I've been kicked, and I don't know how to respond to that or why it stings like a personal insult, but it does.

"It's not just you," he clarifies. His hand lands heavily on my shoulder. It takes every ounce of willpower not to shrug him off. "I outsource what I can't do so trust on a personal level is unnecessary—my life is Crystal Waters."

I nod and can't quite make my lips sit normally. They're pressed together so tightly that I'm probably frowning in that exaggerated way that clowns have. "You can call it whatever you want, but at its foundation, the definition is the same." Turning to Emmy, I lean down to dislodge his hand from my body. "Emmy? What do you want to take with you, sweetie?"

She holds up her book in one hand and places her other around Daisie's neck.

"Anything else?"

Emmy steps forward and reaches for her sister.

"You just want the book, Ruby, and Daisie? What about any of these toys?"

She shakes her head. "Wuby and you."

Well, if that doesn't stab my eyeballs with emotion.

"*She* trusts you," Beck says. "That's what matters."

I stand and hold Emmy's hand. "If you say so, Beck. But having a live-in nanny isn't the same as hiring an attorney who has their own office. It's personal. That means you have some level of trust in me too or this will never work."

Beck shutters his eyes behind an emotionless mask, and I take a step back.

Am I doing the right thing? Moving in with a complete stranger?

SDH did a background check on him, sure. But how thorough are they?

"I don't do *personal* anymore, Stella. Even when I want to."

He walks out of the room and takes his lie with him.

CHAPTER FOURTEEN

BECK

A PACIFIER HITS THE WINDSHIELD AND I DUCK EVEN though it's already on the dashboard. "How the hell can she throw it backward like that?" I ask over Ruby's cries.

"Maybe you should pull over and I'll sit between the girls back there. Ruby can't see anything sitting backward, and she obviously isn't happy about it."

I groan at the same time my stomach rumbles. Why the hell is there so much traffic? It's not even summer yet. "We've already stopped six times in two hours."

Stella reaches into the diaper bag at her feet and hands me a granola bar. "Welcome to parenthood, Beck. Pull over. What the heck did Daisie eat anyway? She's as much to blame as Ruby."

"Who the hell knows. She's become a savage at dinner time. And why is she just Daisie now? Don't I get to name my own damn dog?" That was whiny. I need to grow the fuck up.

"There's a rest area up ahead. Go there." She points through the windshield. "You named her Dog, Beck. *Dog.*"

"I didn't mean to keep her," I mutter, and the dang dog huffs as though I insulted her.

"But you did, and you'll have to take up her name with Emmy." She smirks and slips out of the car as soon as I park.

I stare at Emmy in the rearview mirror. She sticks up her chin in challenge. For crying out loud. I can't win against a four-year-old and Stella knows it.

My fists are clenched on the steering wheel as I try not to stare at Stella while she climbs over Emmy's car seat, but my fucking eyeballs have a mind of their own.

A flash of skin at her waist. The denim clinging to her ass. My mind is telling me not to be an asshole, because I literally just told her that I don't do personal, but every other organ and muscle in my body believes otherwise.

"All set," she says, lifting a brow.

Shit. She caught me staring. Again.

There's not even a reason to look in the rearview mirror because the back is filled to the roof, but my gaze drifts to her as though she already has me on a leash.

"Are you sure we don't need that other stuff?" I ask, pulling back onto the road. Focus on the girls, Beck. Not on how unfairly hot the nanny is or how sweetly she would come for you.

Damn it.

Emmy's belly laugh draws my attention back to the mirror. Stella makes a funny face and both girls giggle.

The car vibrates violently—a safety measure that alerts me when someone in front of me is slowing down.

Jesus, Beck. Eyes on the road.

"I'm sure," she finally says. "The girls have always lived in this Sailport *Bay* house, right?"

"Ah." Regret coils in my chest as potent as acid reflux. "I'm not sure."

I sense her watching me. It's a goddamn magic ability I didn't ask for, but I focus my attention on the road.

"Let's assume they have," she says. "That means all their stuff, all the things that feel like home will be there too. Unless...who owns the house? Has anyone cleared it out?"

"It's always been in the family." I think, unless my father willed that away to Delacroix too. "I called my cousin, Tabby, last night. She's making sure it's ready for us."

"Good! Then I'm sure we'll be fine, and I can get anything we're missing when I go home on Saturday."

My nose wrinkles on the word home. Where do I consider home? The penthouse has always been just that, the penthouse. Home hasn't been part of my vernacular in years.

I nod but allow my mind to wander as we drive for another hour in silence. Well, not silence—Stella keeps the girls entertained singing inane songs about monkeys and being happy.

And they laugh. They laugh more in this hour than they have with me the entire time I've had them.

See, Stella! I don't do personal. Not with you, and not with them—they only laugh like that for you.

My sister's face flashes before my eyes. But it's a distorted version of her and it's gone just as fast.

Fine. Lying to myself has never been this habitual before. So yes, I'll do whatever I can to give these girls a happy childhood—even if that includes allowing a modicum of trust—for them. I can do that. I had a happy childhood...didn't I?

Perhaps I shouldn't have given up on therapy so soon.

But how do you give something that you no longer understand? Adulthood stole my young innocence the day I walked away from Sailport Bay—the day I walked away from everything that made me who I am.

Stella's hand lands on my shoulder and I almost swerve into the breakdown lane. She actively avoids contact with me most of the time, and it's for the best.

Does she remember how explosive we were? Is that why?

"Are you okay? Do you need me to drive for a bit?"

I shake my head, running a hand through my hair. "I'm good. Sorry, I was thinking. We'll be there soon."

When I sneak a peek in the mirror, she's already watching me, but I can't hold her gaze. Something is happening to me that I can't get a handle on, and I need to be at the top of my game. For the girls, for my company, and for myself.

"Okay," she says softly, but her tone tells me she doesn't believe me.

You don't know me, Stella Jane. Not at all.

A SIREN TO OUR RIGHT WAILS WHILE CONFETTI SHOOTS OVER our car. Daisie stretches over the middle seat to hang her dopey head out of Emmy's open window.

"What is this?" Stella asks with wide eyes while I drive at a snail's pace because the entire town of Sailport Bay flanks my car.

Stella and Ruby are as loud as I've ever heard them. It figures they'd love the chaos. Cally always did too.

A pit lodges itself in my throat. This is why I haven't come back here. Being in the one place where my family and I were a team—until we weren't—makes it hard to remember why I walked away.

"Tabby," I say through clenched teeth.

Stella's hand lands on my shoulder again, and this time she squeezes, then uses the delicate finger of her free hand to point straight ahead. The warmth of her touch has me relaxing my jaw while I finally take a full, unrestricted breath.

She can't be the one who chases away my demons.

The car rolls to a stop and I squeeze my eyes shut tight for a full twenty seconds before creeping forward again inch by inch.

We're rolling down Main Street in our very own fucking parade. On every business and every flagpole are posters, signs, and banners welcoming us home.

Us specifically. Our names are plastered everywhere, even Stella's.

"So much for making a quiet entrance," I grumble.

The crowd files into the street ahead, blocking the road, so I roll to a stop in the middle of it, right in front of Coastal Comfort, the town's general store. God forbid an ambulance needs to get through.

"Are we supposed to get out?" Stella's voice trembles, and I immediately turn in my seat.

My cheeks puff out like a blowfish as I release a breath. "You don't have to be afraid of these people. They're nosy fuckers, but they care. When the summer rush dies down there's not much here but the community they've built."

A shiver works through me, and I fight hard not to let the weakness show. There was a time when I was proud to help build this community.

"That sounds...nice," she says, but her gaze still darts from one person to the next until a knock on my window has us all jumping. Her hand on my shoulder squeezes one more time, and when she removes it, I try not to acknowledge how bereft I feel.

I drop my chin to my chest and count to ten while Tabby stands outside my window, spinning her hand like she wants me to roll down my window. I freaking told her I wanted to come back quietly. That's why I don't trust anyone in my family, not even my quirky cousin, Tabby.

"I should have known," I say, then lower the window enough to hear what she has to say for herself.

Tabby is the spitting image of my aunt Imogen, right down to her jet-black hair, patchwork dress, and mismatched flip-flops. The apron tied to her today says *Bake the world a better place*, and it matches the lopsided grin we both inherited from that side of the family.

It's nearly impossible to look at Tabby's happy persona and not smile. She opens her mouth but is cut off by a voice I've known since I was a child. Oliver Shines announces our arrival over a loudspeaker in his silky radio announcer voice as if he's introducing his next segment.

"Small-town magic," he says in that buttery tone that hasn't changed with age. "Through tragedy we find hope. Welcome home Becker, Emmy, and Ruby. And a very special Sailport Bay welcome to our newest resident sweetheart, Stella Anderson." He drags out her name gameshow-style.

My gaze lands on Stella in the mirror and my heart twists when I take in her pale complexion. "Tabs, what did you tell everyone?"

I pop the car in park, and it's all the invitation she needs to open my door and throw herself at me for a hug. She's a whirlwind of activity that somehow manages to unbuckle me and drag me from the car at the same time. When my feet hit the pavement, she hugs me even tighter.

I'm not sure if she ever grew to five feet, but her personality makes her feel giant. Even if I tower over her in height, she'll always beat me in enthusiasm.

My muscles relax when she grins up at me, and my lips almost tilt up to match her expression.

"I told them what you told me," she says, then releases me and opens the back door. Emmy breaks into a sob while reaching for my cousin with both hands.

"Hi. I'm Tabby," she says, reaching over Emmy and offering a shell-shocked Stella her hand. "I'm Becky Bear's cousin."

California can hear my groan.

"Come on out. Everyone wants to meet you."

Stella's eyes are not capable of opening any wider, but when Tabby removes Emmy from her booster seat, Stella scrambles into action removing Ruby, crawling out, and holding her close.

"What exactly did you tell them?" I ask again.

"That you were coming home with the girls, and you were bringing a girl with you." Tabby attaches herself to Stella. "I'm so glad you're here. We're going to be the best of friends."

Stella's entire body is a tightrope, but she nods and searches my face, the street, even the dog, silently begging for an escape. What does she expect me to do? She looks near panic, so I tug her away from my cousin and into my side.

The entire town erupts into applause—or that's how it sounds anyway, and now it's my turn to search for an exit.

"Are they filming a Heartmark movie?" Stella whispers into the side of my chest, and my body vibrates with something foreign, yet familiar, but definitely not nostalgic.

Oliver's voice cuts through the noise. "Cherish these moments, kids. Sometimes the simplest connection will lead to extraordinary happiness." His voice is replaced with quiet background music.

Across the street are hot dog vendors and cotton candy. In front of us is a giant bouncy house and merry-go-round.

In less than twenty-four hours, they've created a goddamn festival for a homecoming that's not permanent.

I lean in to whisper in her ear. "I'm not sure Heartmark could handle Sailport Bay. The people of Sailport Bay swear too much for that wholesome happy horseshit."

She chokes on a laugh and buries her face further. It's... nice. Daisie barks but thankfully is semi-contained in the SUV.

"There he is," a familiar voice says to my left—Wanda Williams. A smile crawls onto my face when I turn in slow motion with my arm still holding Stella tightly. We called Wanda the Weather Witch when I was a kid because of her uncanny ability to predict storms. And not only of the rain and wind variety.

"Mrs. Williams," I say as a million memories hit me all at once. The candy she'd slip me when she thought no one was around. The advice she'd give that I'd never take and always, always end up wishing I had.

This is insanely overwhelming.

"It's too much, I know," she says, then reaches up and pats my cheek. Her skin sizzles against mine and her eyes dance with mischief. "You're home."

She removes her hand and inches closer to the girls. Emmy clings to Tabby, while Ruby climbs Stella like a tree.

"Yup," she says. "Welcome home, girls."

Then she turns, gives me a loud-smacking high five, and marches back into her store with her pointy little elbows swishing with each step. Coastal Comfort hasn't changed since I was five.

"Tabby," I say when my wherewithal returns. "What's going on here?"

"It's not every day the golden boy returns home with a gorgeous partner and his nieces. We wanted to commemorate the occasion, and you can't take that away from us. We missed you, Bear."

"I'm not the golden boy, and I'm not home—not permanently." I ignore the gorgeous partner bit.

My cousin makes a show of staring at my arm tucked protectively around Stella and she quirks a brow. "Whatever you say, Bear."

"Stop calling me Bear." My words come on a terribly concealed growl and she smirks, hands Emmy to me, then stands with her hands on both hips. "Did you read the letter?"

The noise of the festival fades, and her words swish in my ears.

"I didn't think so. Then trust me, you'll want this," she says, pointing between me and Stella, "to be your truth soon enough."

My arm snaps back from Stella's shoulder so quickly my watch gets caught in her hair and she yelps. Shit. "Sorry," I mutter while Tabby tries to untangle us. "What do you mean, Tabs? What are you talking about?" I ask, trying not to notice how Stella rubs at her scalp.

Emmy's grip on my shoulder tightens at the same time her little feet dig into my side.

"Em—"

Daisie Dog growls and barks from the open window of my car. It's so aggressive it cuts through the noise of the parade.

"So it's true." The words slither from Danica Delacroix's lips like the snake she is. Daisie goes nuts, but Leo, my childhood friend, raises his hand in greeting from across the street, and I know he's got Daisie. If I'm going to let Tabby back into my life, I have to let Leo in too.

This town is so fucking messy.

Danica comes to a stop on the sidewalk a few feet away from us. Her face curls into a cruel expression as she sizes up Stella, then each girl in turn. Emmy whimpers and hides her face in the crook of my neck. The need to protect sizzles in my veins with Hulk-like energy.

Emmy's little body trembles. Why the fuck is this little girl so terrified of her own aunt?

CHAPTER FIFTEEN

STELLA

THE WOMAN CURRENTLY GLARING AT ME AND THE GIRLS MAKES me want to hug everyone in my vicinity. And it's not only because Emmy's attempting to climb inside of Beck's chest. It's because this woman stands like a bully about to throw the first punch—and I'm done with bullies taking advantage of innocent people.

I have personal experience with bullies of all ages, and I'm still trying to recover from them.

"Hey, Emmy," I murmur. The little girl lifts her damp eyes from Beck's shoulder and practically launches herself at me.

Beck steadies her on my hip because I'm still holding Ruby on my other side. The angry blond woman scoffs but doesn't move closer. A million questions pass between Beck and me that neither of us has the time to answer. But there's a shift in our relationship in the span of a breath. A connection is reinforced as we stand united against this clear threat.

"I'm going in there," I say, nodding to where Mrs.

Williams just entered. The building in question has brightly decorated windows displaying everything from candy to fishing bait, so I'm assuming it'll have something to distract the girls. "It looks like there's some...something in there...for them. Maybe."

He nods, but we both turn our heads when Daisie barks again. A man in his mid-thirties gets into Beck's car and pulls it to the side of the road.

I open my mouth, but Beck waves me off. "It's fine. That's Leo."

My brows must reach my hairline.

"Welcome to Sailport Bay, sweetheart."

"Sweetheart," the horrible woman hisses. "That's convenient."

I ignore her, and if Beck's not worried that a man just drove off in his car, I won't be either. The woman in front of me opens her mouth, but I cut her off by walking through the center of our strange little circle, heading for the store.

"Go with her please?" Beck asks, and before I know who he's talking to, his cousin Tabby cuts in front of me and opens the door.

Thank God. The girls are little, but I'm seriously out of shape. Carrying them both makes my muscles shake.

Entering the store is like being transported back in time. Penny candy lines one wall. Though it no longer costs a penny, it's still cheap enough that even I can afford it.

All the outside chatter fades to white noise when the door swings shut. I release a long breath, then step to the side and kneel while keeping my arms around the girls.

Tabby flops down in front of us with her legs criss-crossed and a smile that would tell anyone she's related to Beck.

Mrs. Williams walks toward us wearing a *Sailport Bay is for Lovers, Sailport is for Losers* T-shirt. She's carrying chocolate lollipops, which makes me relax in relief. She hands them to me, then slowly lowers herself to the floor too.

My mouth might be gaping because this is the oddest welcome I've ever experienced. "Thank you," I say.

"That was Danica the devil eater." Tabby throws her thumb over her shoulder.

I nod politely but focus on unwrapping the lollipops, which takes more effort than it should because grabby-hands Ruby is climbing my arms to get to it.

After handing Ruby the first lollipop and silently praying it doesn't end up in my hair, I offer the second to Emmy. Lowering myself to a sitting position, I spread my legs and both girls crawl between them.

By the time we're all settled, both women are staring at me with obvious interest.

"I told ya, Tabs," the older woman says with a weathered smile.

"You did. I wouldn't believe it if I didn't see it with my own eyes, though."

It's obvious they're talking about me, but it's best if they keep their theories to themselves.

"Who was that woman, and why are they"—I indicate the girls with my chin—"scared of her?" Asking questions is easier than deciphering their riddles.

Their shoulders tense in unison and my skin prickles with awareness. Tabby shakes her head while plucking her bottom lip, and the older woman nods thoughtfully. Then they both turn to me, but they're interrupted by Emmy.

"Auntie Dani doesn't like me."

Auntie?

I look at Tabby. Does Beck have another sister?

"Danica isn't n-i-c-e," she spells, and I'm grateful Emmy isn't old enough to read yet. "But she is their aunt on their father's side. It's...complicated," she continues. "She's never had anyone's best interests in mind except her own—and that's especially true for the girls. She made her brother do a DNA test on them, for crying out loud."

The door flies open, and Beck calls out over our heads because he's scanning every nook and cranny, but not looking down. "Stella? Stell—"

"Down here, Bear."

He rolls his eyes, but his frown clears the second his gaze lands on me and the girls. Beck nods once, then shifts his focus to the other two women.

"What did she do?" he demands. If he's talking about the lollipop all over Ruby's face and hands, he can suck it. I gave the girls candy, big whoop. His expression darkens like a storm cloud rolling in at a frantic pace, not caring what it destroys in its path. Crap. He isn't talking about me—he's talking about the woman outside.

Beck is in protector mode and he's willing to tear down the world to make sure he succeeds.

Daisie lurches forward and her leash slips from his hands. He scrambles after her, but Daisie skirts our circle and sits behind me.

"Cally did what she had to do, Beck. You'll see. She said everything she did was to protect the girls." Tabby lifts her sad gaze to his. "And to protect you. But that's all I know. She was very confused at the end."

"Bullshit," he seethes. "She sided with the fucking enemy. Again." His gaze shifts around the room as though he's searching for an outlet for his rage, and it makes me want to hide. "Stella!" I flinch at his tone, and both girls immediately cling closer to my legs.

He sees it too and scrubs a hand over his face. His nails leave marks down his cheek like he's trying to claw away layers of skin. "Sorry. As much fun as the welcome home party has been, we should get the girls to their house."

If it's odd to anyone else that he doesn't call it home, they don't say anything. I'm too shocked to form any opinions, so I stand with an apologetic shrug. Both girls' alarmed faces turn to me, and my stomach hollows out a little.

"It's okay, girls. We're okay. You're coming with us."

Beck reaches down for Daisie's leash, and Emmy rushes to grab my leg, while Ruby sits unusually still until I pick her up. "Thank you for the candy," I say. "How much do I owe you?"

The older woman's eyes crinkle at the corner. "Just a promise to keep lovin' on those babies. It's nice to meet you, Stella. I hope you find your place here."

She's so sincere, and Tabby nods in agreement at her side. There's a lifetime of history in this town—history I have no part in, but for the first time in a long time, I wish my future would outshine my past. Maybe one day, I'll find happiness in a small town like this—one where neighbors truly care about each other. But for now, when my life is all about managing chaos and heartache, I'm not sure there's a fairy tale for me.

And then I see the war raging inside Beck too. How fragile is this foundation he's building? And where will I land when it all comes crumbling down?

"THIS? THIS IS YOUR CHILDHOOD HOME?" I KNEW BECK WAS wealthy, but this is an actual oceanfront estate.

"It's a house, Stella. It hasn't been a home in a long time, and it will probably never be a home again. At least not for them." His gaze stays on Emmy. She's on my back clinging to my neck as though she's about to fall—like I'd ever let that happen.

She doesn't trust it yet, but I'll always catch her.

"That's—"

"It is what it is." Beck has never truly been cold with me. Not even the day he demanded I follow him into his office. But he's cold and detached now. It's unnerving, and I'm not the only one who senses it.

The girls cling to me like the last remnants of a baby blanket that's well past its prime, and Daisie trots next to us.

He sticks a key into the lock and the enormous front door swings open. Beck stares at something above my head but holds his hand out, gesturing for me to enter with the girls.

When I step inside my fears evaporate as calming comfort envelops me. Everywhere I turn the soft ocean theme beckons me forward. The teals and grays with hints of navy throughout make me want to sink into the oversized sofa with a book and never move.

Emmy slides down my back, then tugs on my hand, and I follow her farther into the house. In the corner is a doll-house bigger than she is, and when she flips a switch on the side of it, tiny lights glow in every room. Her shining eyes find mine and I smile. She falls to her knees and sets up a tiny table in the tiny kitchen with a chandelier hanging above it that shoots rainbows across her face.

Ruby kicks and tries to roll in my arms until I find what she's reaching for. Hanging in the doorway is a jumper swing. I carefully check that it's attached properly then buckle her in.

The second I step back she runs her little legs to push herself back as far as she can go then she lifts them and swings through the extra-wide doorway. Daisie lays on the floor in between them with her paws crossed, watching them both.

This is home to them. It's home to Beck too, but he's still standing in the doorway. One foot on the porch and one on the threshold. He's frozen, but his gaze darts from the ceiling to the walls, landing on nothing. I can't decide if he's trying to categorize it all or forget it ever existed.

"Beck?" I ask hesitantly.

He blinks feverishly before focusing on me in the center of the room.

"I've—I mean. I don't know where their rooms are. Or where anything is. Can you get them settled? Do...whatever they need. Okay? That's what you're here for. Can you do that?"

His words push me back a few steps, but I nod so he can't tell how he's affected me.

"Good." He steps into the house, closes the door, then stalks down the hall away from me—from us. He takes a sharp turn into a room and slams that door closed, but it bursts open a second later. He reappears, his expression wild as he spins in place.

His chest heaves for oxygen, but when he catches me staring, he points, obviously ready to yell, then turns and storms off. A second later, a third door slams, and because we're surrounded by windows, I catch him stomping toward the beach.

Curiosity gets the better of me. I take a quick peek at the

girls to ensure they'll be safe for thirty seconds, then quickly slide down the hall to the door that spooked Beck.

The second I open it, my heart trips over itself in my chest. It's a study, or an office, perhaps it even served as a library, but it's most recently been used as a makeshift hospital room. An IV bag still hangs in the corner from a metal rack, and a freshly made hospital bed sits waiting for its next patient.

The room is cloaked in death. The scent of it permeates the walls and weighs heavily over me.

"That's Mommy's room," Emmy says quietly. "The water." She points to the wall of windows that overlook the ocean.

"Your mommy liked the ocean?"

She nods, heartbreak covering every inch of her expression. "When she could see it."

Her little hand slips into mine and she leads me back to the family room where Ruby's still running and swinging.

That's where their mom died, and Beck knew it the same way I did—you never forget the scent of death.

I glance toward the open ocean, unable to fathom the depth of his emotions. I can't console him, but I can be there for these girls, so I surround them with love while they give me a tour of the house.

In Emmy's room, there's a note on hot pink paper taped to her nightstand.

Remember, Emmy. Even when you're sad, Mommy loves you always.

Without turning my head, I find six more love notes scattered throughout the room.

Cally filled this house with love so her girls would feel it even after she was gone.

She didn't want them to forget her, and after witnessing

my mom slowly lose her memories of me, I understand why. It's the most painful thing to be wiped from someone's life as though you never existed.

I vow then to make sure these girls will always remember their mom. For as long as I'm around, Cally's memory will be kept alive.

Hopefully it doesn't break Beck in the process.

CHAPTER SIXTEEN

BECK

THE HOUSE IS DARK BY THE TIME I LIFT MYSELF FROM THE damp sand. Night fell when I wasn't paying attention.

Standing at the threshold of that house wasn't what I was expecting. Though if I'm honest, I really hadn't given it much thought. So when my mind flashed with a story—one that may be a memory—I froze.

"Get him out of here. Your mother is such a fucking mess. Get him out of here, and call an ambulance." For the first time in years, I remembered my father's harsh tone and harsher words. I remembered the fights and why the only memories I'd clung to were ones of Cally and me. It was all too much.

Then I went into that room—the one I spent my childhood loving, the one that stole my mother's last breath when cancer finally set her free—it spooked me after that. But seeing it that way again, for my sister, with the scent of death still clinging to every fiber of it broke me wide open.

I don't know what I expected when I went in there. That it would still be a library? It only makes sense that it's where Cally would take her final breath too.

But the bed, so similar to the one I rolled in for my

mother, siphoned the air from my lungs. Memories of crying at my mother's stiff, gray hand intermingled with images I can conjure of my sister going the same way were suffocating me.

This house—this family—is so fucked up. Is it just biology? Will I fall to the same fate? Do I not have an ounce of loyalty in me either?

Will I pass that on to those innocent girls?

I roar like a werewolf howling at the moon because I can't get Danica's words out of my head. Would my sister really do that to me? I cry out when the unfairness of it all becomes too much.

"Why the fuck did you leave everything to Danica, Cally? Why would you do that? Why would you do it to your girls?" When fresh tears fall, I swipe at them angrily. Rage, and pain, and exhaustion—they all steal pieces of me, and I have no outlet to fight back. "Why even leave them with me if you were going to give away their home, the one place that brings them comfort?"

I was in shock in Sterling's office, and apparently I tuned out a lot of details, otherwise maybe I would have been better prepared for this news. "But God, Cally, why? It doesn't make any sense." Anger rises like the tide, and I shout to the sky, "I fucking hate you. I hate you so much."

Dropping to my knees, I tunnel my fingers into the sand. A light flickers on in the kitchen, casting a long shadow over me. I don't want to look, but I'm unable not to.

Stella moves around the space with an easy grace. She's too far away for me to read her expression, but there's a sadness in the way she carries herself that beckons something dark and growing inside of me.

The lone pendant light over the island calls to the lonely —a lighthouse in the dark.

I continue to stare long after Stella's out of view.

I was an asshole, and she didn't deserve it. I have no idea what my future holds anymore, but one thing's for certain—Stella is as essential to our survival as air, and it scares the hell out of me.

Needing people leads to betrayal every single time.

And she has a secret she won't share with you. "Yeah," I say to the wind. "But I wouldn't share secrets with me either."

An hour later, I walk on dead legs back to the house.

Tiptoeing up the deck stairs, I leave my sandy shoes on the porch as quietly as possible. The glass door slides open with a low scratching sound that will only get worse if opened any wider. Or at least, it did when I lived here, so I turn sideways to slip inside.

The kitchen is the same as it's always been. The only upgrades are the appliances. Nostalgia and grief swell at the same time, but I shake them away and wash the sand from my hands in the sink.

Stella must have made dinner. Of course she made dinner. I told her to take care of everything, didn't I?

Leaning against the sink, I dry my hands with a towel and take in the room that once felt like home. Almost nothing has changed, and it makes me irrationally angry. Life moved on. It should have moved on without me. I moved on without it—without them.

But the only thing out of place is the silver tray covered by a dome lid. It sits in the center of the island, highlighted by the single light source. This is what Stella was doing in here? Leaving me dinner?

Lifting the cover, I find a giant piece of lasagna, garlic bread, and a salad.

My mouth waters and guilt sucks the liquid down greedily with a painful swallow.

Why would she go to that trouble after I told her to do her job like a servant?

Heating it up will only waste time. Suddenly I'm too ravenous to wait, so I carry the entire tray toward the sofa. It hasn't changed either. It's big enough for a football team and has cushions you can get lost in—my mother searched for one big enough for this room for two years. She was manic in her search too. It's strange that I remember that, but not a single family moment that didn't instill unease. This is where Cally checked in with me every day after school, though, and those are the memories that have been attacking my heart since I walked through the door.

Standing frozen behind the sofa, I realize that heat from the fire warms my face. Stella started a fire too. It's still early spring, and the ocean air gives the chill more bite.

A dog snuffle catches my attention. Stella is curled up in the V at the end of the sofa with Daisie sprawled out over her feet. Stella lies on her side, hands clenched between her thighs as if she's cold. She's so small I'm not surprised I missed her. But it's the pinch of her brows that hypnotizes me. Her face contorts, then she flinches.

Immediately, I want to slay the dragons in her dreams.

Her eyelids fly open, and we're caught in this weird trance. She's sucking in deep, labored breaths, but mine are too shallow. Daisie climbs up to place her head on Stella's hip. As her eyes focus on me, our breathing evens out, but still, we stare.

Sella sits up and adjusts her shirt.

"Are you okay?" she asks. Her voice is a soft melody that flitters across my skin.

"You made a fire." I've lost the ability to carry a conversation.

"Yeah. I hope that's okay." Stella tucks her feet in close

and rests her chin on her knees. Daisie grunts and flops off the sofa, heading toward the stairs.

"And you opened the flue."

Her face scrunches up. "I grew up in upstate New York with frigid winters. I know how to start a fire." I lean forward, starving for any bit of her I can get. "We lived in a tiny house for a while, but it was cheaper to run a small woodstove in the winter than use the oil. I'd get up in the middle of the night when I got cold and put another log on. You learn to do things pretty quickly when you have no other option."

What did it cost her to share that bit of herself with me?

"When did you move to Raleigh?" Every piece of her I get is a hit of dopamine that has my body begging for more.

Her gaze drops to her knees, and I use the distraction to sit on the other end of the massive sofa with the tray of lasagna in my lap.

"When the winters became too hard for my mom." It's a non-answer, but it tells me a little more about the mother who hits her.

"Did you make this?" I ask, lifting a forkful to my mouth. Even cold, the scent has me drooling.

She stares at my plate and then the bite on my fork. "Wait!" She reaches out with one hand, like that'll stop me.

I raise one brow in return and slide the cheesy pasta between my lips. I don't mean to groan, but Jesus, it's good.

"Did you even heat it up, or are you eating like a drunken college kid?"

Her words pull a chuckle from me even when my heart still feels so fragile.

"Drunk college kid," I reply, and take another bite.

My eyes close to savor the taste. It might be the best lasagna I've ever had.

Then my plate is snatched from my lap and she's quietly stomping to the kitchen. Is she going to toss it in the trash due to my garish manners? I scramble after her.

But nope. She wets a paper towel, lays it across my plate, then sticks it in the microwave.

"You got the girls to eat that?"

Her cheeks turn pink. "There may have been some bribery involved. But I put spinach in it, so it was worth the cookie I gave them after."

She turns and shoos me away with both hands. "Go eat your salad. I'll bring this out when it's ready."

I nod in thanks because my throat's closing on me. She's taking care of me. It's so...domesticated, and I don't completely hate it, even though I need to.

She works for you, Beck. She's not a friend. She's an employee. That's an important distinction. If she betrays you as an employee there are repercussions. If she betrays you as a friend, it would shatter what's left of you.

The voice in my head lately is nameless. It's not mine. It's not my father's. But it feels real all the same.

"Would you like a glass of wine?" I finally ask.

Her shoulders fall forward like she's relieved, and she hangs onto the edge of the island. "I'd love one, thank you. Just half a glass. I meant it when I said I don't drink often."

I grab a bottle of red from the wine cabinet beneath the island, two glasses, and an opener from the same drawer it's been in since I was twelve, then return to the safety of the sofa.

In here, we have our own corners. Opposing sides. In here, there's no temptation of more, of what-ifs. There's only my side and hers.

The air shifts, swirling around me with memories of apples. Closing my eyes, I take a moment to breathe her in before she places the tray in my lap and skips closer to the fire.

"Thank you," I mutter, then continue opening the wine while she adds another log to the blaze.

When she stands, I hand her a splash of wine and try to regulate my heart rate as she returns to her side and covers herself with a thick velvet blanket.

I eat in silence, thankful her gaze remains on the fire so I can memorize how the light dancing across her features reminds me of fireflies.

She's beautiful. She might be the most beautiful woman I've ever met. I've never wanted the complications that come with more than a one-night stand, but the strings that hang from Stella are already twining around my arms and legs.

How do I say no to the complication that is Stella Jane?

My silverware clatters when I set my plate down. "Cally and I carved our names on the underside of this table when I was six and she was thirteen or fourteen."

Then I snap my lips shut so fast I almost bite my tongue. Where the hell did that story come from? I haven't thought about that in years, yet here the memory sits, fully formed in front of my eyes.

"Did you get in trouble?" Stella asks, bringing the long-stem wineglass to her lips. When she pulls it away, they're stained a deep red. I stare at the color until she licks them, then I jerk my gaze away.

"No," I say quietly. "I don't remember getting in trouble very often." I don't remember a lot of things, but I keep that to myself.

"Do you think it's still there?" The excitement in her tone has my mood cautiously lifting.

"I'm sure it is."

Her teeth sink into her bottom lip, and I remember what

it felt like to bite that same spot. Then she jumps up, sets her glass down, and crawls onto the floor. "Let's find it."

"Stella."

"What side did you do it on?" Her energy is infectious, addicting, like winning the bid on a multimillion-dollar deal. It fills my body with adrenaline.

She scoots around on her back, trying to wedge herself between the floor and the table, and it's so absurd, I laugh.

My fingers trace the edge of the old driftwood table, and for some inexplicable reason, I sink to my knees and shimmy along the floor to the far side where the knot in the wood calls to me.

"Over there, I think," I say with a sigh.

She beats me to it, lying on her back and pushing herself beneath the table.

"Oh," she gasps.

"What? Is it—is it gone?" Is that panic in my voice? Sadness?

"No. No, it's...well, it's here."

What the hell does that mean?

Lowering myself to the floor, I slide in beside her. Stella shimmies and her side presses into mine, breathing life into me when I forget how to do it myself.

Beck + Call = Family forever is still there.

But it's what Cally wrote beneath it in black marker that clogs my lungs and burns my eyes.

Thank you, Beck. Thank you for loving the girls.

I love you always, even if it doesn't feel that way.

And my love shines forever,

Call

My skin prickles everywhere. I can't claw my way out from under the table fast enough. I can't get far enough away.

"Beck." Stella reaches out and touches my forearm, and for a brief second, the pain of betrayal doesn't sting. But then Cally's words ring in my ears, and I jerk away.

"Did you find a room? For yourself?" The words are harsher than she deserves.

"I did," she says sadly.

"Good. Good night, Stella."

I run from the room like I'm chasing my last breath. My feet fly up the stairs two at a time, then I turn down the hall and take the second set of stairs to the third floor.

I can't go to my room tonight. Is it even my room anymore? Every room in this house has memories haunting it. The only place that's safe is the bonus room up here. If memories haunt this place now, they won't be mine.

CHAPTER SEVENTEEN

STELLA

THE SPRAY OF HOT WATER SOAKS INTO MY TIRED BONES, tempting me to stay for another hour, but reluctantly, I lean forward and turn it off.

The girls will be up soon, and if last night is any indication, their uncle is in no shape to do anything with them right now.

The towel I dry myself with is freaking amazing, thick and luxurious. It's nicer than any I've ever used. Grabbing another, I bend at the waist to wrap it around my hair—

"You're awake?" a woman's voice coos through the baby monitor I have permanently affixed to my side.

Who is that? Blood whooshes in my ears as the face of the evil blond hits me like a sledgehammer, and I forget all about drying off. I secure the towel with my fist and rush out of my room, dashing down the hall to Ruby's room since her door is the one that's open.

Tabby sits on the floor in the center of the room next to Ruby, and my knees buckle with relief. Emmy sits in the center of the bed with dolls spread out around her and

Daisie across her legs. Not that I think Beck would be overly excited that his cousin's here, but the girls love this woman. That tells me to give her the benefit of the doubt.

"Tabby?" I gasp. It's embarrassing that I'm out of breath after running ten feet. "You scared the crap out of me. I wasn't expecting anyone this morning. Do you have a key?"

"Oh." She laughs. "Yeah, loads of people have keys."

"They what?"

"When *things* were happening," she says, nodding toward Ruby, "people needed access for various reasons."

"They don't require access anymore," Beck says from the doorway.

Oh, good lord. My fists clench harder around the towel as water drips down my body. The luxurious piece of cotton feels more like a dishrag against my skin now.

Biting my tongue, I lift my gaze to find Beck doing a lazy perusal up my body, and for one moment, we're frozen in each other's sphere.

"Ah, sorry. I heard—well, I thought..." The words spill from my lips in no particular order. "Sorry," I say again. "I heard Tabby through the monitor, and I thought, well—" One fist lands on my hip. "I wasn't expecting anyone, okay?"

Beck's features soften infinitesimally. "No one should have access but us," he says gently. "That goes for you too, Tabs."

"Well, technically, that's not true," she says conversationally.

A conversation passes between them, but I don't speak their language.

"What does that mean?" I ask when it becomes apparent neither of them is willing to give me information.

"Danica owns the house," Tabby blurts. "Beck still owns

the land, but it's kind of a mess, and she's a witch with a grudge so..." She shrugs and I turn back to Beck, suddenly feeling more naked than I am.

Old insecurities and new fears for the girls snake around my conscience. I never had stability as a kid. We moved from house to house and town to town while my mom chased fun and, occasionally, work.

Beck must read me easier than a large-print book because he steps forward with his arms open to embrace me but stops short of actually touching me when his gaze skates over the towel again. The vein in his throat pulses, matching the rapid beat in my ears.

We're both painfully aware that only a rectangle of cotton separates us.

"I don't know what's going on yet, but I will," he promises. The strain in his voice matches the tightly corded muscles in his forearms—they flex with each word. He's the kind of man who doesn't make empty promises.

"Cally said she explained some of this. What do you mean you don't know?" Tabby asks. Her voice is a bucket of cold water that breaks the spell we're under.

Move, Stella. Go get dressed! I don't. Instead, I stare, first at Beck, then Tabby and the girls.

"I mean I hadn't spoken to my sister since the day I left." Beck's words draw me back to him. The pull he has over me is alarming. He swallows thickly, and his entire demeanor changes. "That's what I mean. I have no fucking clue what you're going on about."

Emmy stands with a smile on her face and her hand stretched out toward Beck.

His questioning gaze asks me to translate, but all I can offer is a halfhearted shrug.

"It must be a Hayes thing," Tabby says. This woman lives in her own world and clearly has no clue about the tension floating above her head. "If you curse, you owe Emmy five bucks. Cally made the rule when I started helping out more."

"When you... Why didn't she do it before? I've said fuck about a thousand times in the past month."

Emmy steps closer with two hands out.

"Maybe she wasn't comfortable. This is home to her. You behave differently when you feel safe," I say.

He glares at me, and I clutch my towel even more tightly, but I don't back down. His expression morphs into something else—understanding, maybe? Emmy's secrets are so similar to my own, but there's no way he knows that.

The muscles in his cheek bounce when he clenches his teeth, but he reaches into his pocket and pulls out a hundred-dollar bill.

"Wait," I say. "That's crazy. She's expecting a dollar or two." Isn't she?

He shrugs as if he couldn't care less. "It's all I have."

Emmy continues to hold out her other hand, and her eyes shine as though she's captured all the stars in the sky.

"Fine," He hands her another hundred-dollar bill, and she giggles while taking it.

Smart girl.

"Dang, kid. You're going to be rich before you hit kindergarten," Tabby singsongs.

"It's too early for this sh—I need coffee," Beck mutters.

"Ah..." My head swivels from Tabby to Beck. "I need— clothes. Will one of you help the girls get dressed?"

I slip past Beck in the doorway and shiver when his forearm brushes against my bare skin on the way by.

Stupid, stupid, neglected hormones.

I'm almost to my room when Beck's voice gives me pause. "What kind of crap is she trying to pull with this house, Tabs?"

"Cally didn't tell me everything, only that anything connected to Hayes and Delacroix would stay with Delacroix. She thought it was safer that way. Everything she's done has been for one reason, Beck. She loved you enough to fight. She loved the girls enough to do whatever it took. As far as Danica? She's a pissed-off rhino because of what you've done to her company—"

"What I've done?" he roars, and the vibrations hit me in the hallway.

"And she's crazy enough to use the girls in any way she can to make you bend. Danica doesn't give a shit about any of you. She doesn't know how. Her father chose Davis over her. Davis chose Cally over her. She's never known love and kindness, so you can't expect her to have any of those qualities. Ugh," Tabby groans. "Give her another hundred, Bear. I don't have any cash."

Bear. It causes a smile to ease some of the tension pinching my face even as true fear for the girls' emotional stability weighs heavily on my shoulders.

But there's not a damn thing I can do about it standing in Beck's hallway wearing only a towel. The silence of my room allows my mind to formulate a plan of attack while I roll mindlessly through the routine of getting dressed.

How does Beck feel about teamwork?

I EXIT THE BATHROOM TO FIND EMMY SITTING IN THE MIDDLE of my bed.

"Emmy? You okay?" She lifts her head from whatever is in her lap, and the tension leaves her little body when she sees me.

She holds up a clear bag full of hair elastics and another damn pink note. It's truly the house of secrets.

"What's this?" I ask, sitting on the edge of the bed.

"Mommy's helping me." She holds the bag up to my face.

The note says, *Emmy loves French braids and pigtails.*

Huh. Maybe not all secrets are bad.

"French braids and pigtails, huh? Those are my favorite too. Do you want me to do your hair?" I ask. She nods, and sunshine beams from her face.

"Tabby pulls too hard." This drags a chuckle from me.

"Well, sweet angel, I happen to be very good at braids and pigtails. Which would you like today?"

"Bwaids."

"Braids it is. Come here." I lift her from the bed while she clutches the bag in one hand and a hairbrush in the other, then I carry her to the bathroom and set her on the counter.

Ten minutes later, she has two pretty braids going down the sides of her head.

"The braids are perfect. Are you hungry?" Her stomach chooses that moment to rumble. "Breakfast time, kiddo. You ready?"

She nods and lunges for me as if she's part spider monkey.

We're halfway down the stairs when I smell smoke and run to the kitchen. Tabby stands on the island waving at a smoke detector, and Beck's on the deck with smoke billowing from a frying pan.

"What the heck happened?" I ask, peering around Tabby

to search for Ruby. The little girl catches my eye, pauses for half a second, then makes a mad dash toward the door, laughing hysterically, but I scoop her up before she hits the open doorway.

"You're trouble, kid." She claps happily as though she understands every word.

Beck turns at my voice, and his cheeks look like they caught fire with breakfast.

"Ah, I haven't made pancakes in...ever." He tilts the pan in my direction, and the black smoke shifts in the air. The bottom of the frying pan is crusted with a thick coating of ash.

Good lord. I really am on my own here, aren't I?

Embarrassment ratchets up the heat on his cheeks, and I take pity on him. Trading Emmy and Ruby for the frying pan, I gesture toward the house while dutifully studying the scorched mess he handed me.

"Play with them for a bit. I'll fix this."

The heat of his body warms mine, and I make the mistake of lifting my gaze. Beck's attention is on Ruby, but it's his smile that imprints on my heart. Ruby has a fist in her mouth, and she's drooling more than a Saint Bernard, but he's staring at her with such undeniable love that I'm pretty sure my ovaries explode.

He angles his body to mine before I can get away. "Okay. Thank you, Stella. And I'm sorry for..."

Beck clamps his lips shut and I shrug.

"It's fine. It's cold out here though. Take them inside and give me twenty minutes."

He won't meet my gaze, but he does as I ask, and twenty minutes later, we're all sitting around the table having breakfast as a family.

Or, what I've always imagined a family to be. It's only ever been my mom and me. That knife in my gut twists another forty-five degrees.

Pretty soon it'll just be me. That thought steals my appetite, and I push my plate away from Ruby's sticky fingers and focus on getting the food in her mouth instead of on the floor.

"Isn't this...cozy." The shrill voice behind me casts an arctic chill throughout the room. Emmy drops her fork and appears to shrink in on herself, and my instincts take over.

I stand abruptly, having no idea what the hell is going on here, but this woman terrifies the girls, and I won't allow it, not if I can—not when they're finally settling into the safety of their home.

"Um, the girls and I are heading to the beach now. We're collecting stuff for an art project later."

"They cling to you like you're their mother," Danica murmurs. Her expression is hard to read. Nothing I've seen from her would indicate that she has any kind of maternal instinct, but with the way she looks at us now, a mixture of sadness and confusion, it's almost as if she's envious of the bond I have with the girls. "I hope you're not leaving on my account." Her words are clipped, but not as harsh as when I first met her.

I speak without giving her the satisfaction of eye contact. She doesn't deserve it, but I do keep my tone intentionally gentle. "My job is simply to keep the girls happy and safe— from whatever causes them harm."

Ruby rests on my hip while I hold Emmy's hand tightly, waiting for Beck to snap out of whatever shock he's in, but when our gazes align, a hint of gratitude flashes in his swirling green orbs.

That's enough for me. I shuffle Emmy up the stairs for more layers to fend off the distinct chill that covers us. But I have no idea if it's cold from the cool spring air or the secrets everyone's hiding behind.

CHAPTER EIGHTEEN

"All the food is labeled in the fridge with their names on it," Stella says for the third time.

It's seven o'clock on Saturday morning, and she's already an hour behind her schedule.

I admit, the last two days have been a complete cluster-fuck, but because she's guided us through the chaos of our lives, I attempt to be respectful that there's something about Saturdays that are important to her, so I'll make it through the day. Granted, I should have paid more attention to how she ran things yesterday, but I was too busy avoiding this house, this town, and her.

I also haven't slept much since we arrived. It's this damn house and all the memories that jump out of every crevice. Haunted houses have nothing on my childhood home.

Stella spins in place before dumping another pile of diapers on the changing table I carried into the family room late last night. I wouldn't have bothered, but when I caught her in the act, halfway to the stairs with a piece of furniture bigger than she is, my heart jackhammered in my chest.

She thought it would be easier if I kept everyone in one

location, but she could have asked for fucking help. She's lucky she didn't break her neck trying to maneuver that thing to the stairs.

She's also probably right, but I'd prefer she not think of me as an invalid.

"I took care of them on my own at the penthouse," I remind her, then internally cringe at my sulky tone.

Stella's lifting a packet of baby wipes, and her hand freezes in the air. "Um, yes, you did." She sets the wipes down next to the diapers. "But you're, I don't know, different here. No one has really settled into a routine. I'm sorry I'm leaving. But I need—"

"This was a condition of your employment, Stella. I understand what that means. You can go now," I say curtly because I can't keep the bite out of my tone. She makes me lose control, and it simply can't continue.

But when hurt flashes across her face I want to kick my own ass. Why do I insist on pushing her away when the only thing she's guilty of is caring, maybe even too much, for my nieces?

"Uncle Beck Daddy?"

My entire body seizes. We can't keep using that name.

Stella's small, warm hand lands on my arm.

Love language. Maybe Stella has two of them.

"Emmy, honey. Come on down." To me, Stella says, "We'll address your name when I get back. There's a lot of things we need to talk about. They need a united front. Even though I'm *just* the nanny, they need to feel as though we're a team in everything that concerns them."

Emmy runs across the room with Daisie trailing behind and flings herself at Stella. "Don't go. Don't go," she cries.

Boulders clog my throat and sit heavy in my gut simultaneously. My thoughts skip back to what Stella said. She'll never be *just* the nanny.

Daisie glances between me and the girls, then lies down at their feet. I can't even be all that mad about her choosing sides anymore.

Even Stella is startled by the fragile emotion spewing from the little girl. Is this what she means by teamwork? I'm not someone who shares feelings or brainstorms solutions. If I don't understand something, I learn—on my own—or outsource.

"Shh," Stella coos, gently running a hand over Emmy's hair.

I drop onto the sofa and observe as Stella cradles my niece in her arms.

Teamwork requires partners, equals. The way Stella soothes Emmy now isn't something I'll learn in a book or a TikTok video. This is feelings and emotions. It's human connection. It's what I've actively blocked from my life.

"I'll only be gone a short time. I'll be home before you wake up in the morning. I promise," Stella whispers. Her face is calm and soothing, but her hands shake as she lightly smooths Emmy's hair over her shoulder. The dichotomy of the two actions untethers me. Every vibration of her delicate fingers transfers energy through the air and straight to my heart.

She more than cares for these little girls—she loves them.

Emmy clings tighter to Stella, and my lungs burn with the need for more oxygen—but every breath hinges on the woman before me.

"Listen, sweet pea. Uncle Beck has my phone number. If you need me for anything, you tell him and he'll call me, okay?"

"Don't go." Emmy's broken words slice me open.

"Emmy, lovebug. I'll be here all day, okay?" Even though I'm trying, putting everything I have out there, I'm not as comforting as Stella.

Right on cue, Ruby starts babbling. The sound crackles in the baby monitor on the side table.

Stella kisses the side of Emmy's head, then walks her to me.

"Listen, Em." Something's changed in her tone as she speaks now. Her eyes twinkle and the expression they share shouts, *can you keep a secret*? "Uncle Beck will need a lot of help today."

"Hey," I bark, but she rolls her eyes. How fucking rude. It doesn't matter that she's right, she didn't need to announce it to the one person I'm supposed to make feel safe.

"But I told him…" Stella glares at me, and I scowl right back while my mind shouts *traitor, traitor, pillow fort raider*. A flashback of Cally and me as vivid as the scene before me blurs the lines of past and present.

Cally standing outside my pillow fort while I taunted her. *Traitor, traitor, pillow fort raider. Traitors can't come in.* My fist lands on my chest. Cally was heading to college, and I was so scared—she was leaving me for long stretches of the day for the first time in my life.

I was ten, but I'd never felt so unsafe. Home was just a house without her to protect me, and that was with her coming home every night. Why the fuck did I think I'd be unsafe?

Emotions burn hot in my eyes, but Emmy's soft giggle drags me to the present.

"I told him what a good helper you are," Stella tells her little coconspirator, and it's hard not to be sucked into her story. "Ruby's too little, but I told him you were a big girl, and you knew where everything was, and that you would be an excellent helper. Am I right?"

This magical nanny fairy does what I'm not capable of—she makes Emmy believe she's safe in her home and with me. Emmy's entire demeanor changes as she casts a shy, mischievous smile in my direction.

Emmy assesses me as if she's now the teacher and I'm her troublesome pupil. "He needs our help."

My jaw hits the floor.

"You'll keep him in line, right, Emmy?" Stella winks at the little girl, and my heart reaches for her. Thump. Thump. Thump.

Emmy's little fists land on her hips, and I narrow my eyes even as my lips twist with the beginnings of a smile. Her stance mimics Stella's as they scrutinize me.

"Yup." She hugs Stella tightly one more time. "Come home."

Stella's hand pauses its soothing gesture, but the muscles around her eyes twitch. "I will, Ems. Before you even wake up. Be good for Uncle Beck, okay?"

Emmy nods, pulls away from Stella, then walks to me with slumped shoulders and tight fists.

Stella gets sunshine and rainbows, and I get a cumulonimbus cloud. The competitor in me stirs to life. I don't want her to be sad skies and dark clouds around me. I want her to be sunshine, and I'll find a way to be the fucking rainbow too.

We stand together and watch Stella leave the house. Emmy's body is wound more tightly than any four-year-old should experience. I don't need Stella to tell me that. Then Ruby cries, and we make our way up the stairs to get the little maniac.

I immediately regret sending Stella on her way the second we enter Ruby's room.

"No, Ruby," I cry. "What the hell are you doing?"

"I gots this, Uncle Daddy, and I don't need monies today." My eyes are bugging out of my head as Emmy pushes up the sleeves of her jammies and crosses the room wearing a stern expression that makes the craziness break free from my chest. I laugh—hard.

But come on, a stern-looking four-year-old is funny.

"Wuby. Poop is nots paint." Emmy wags her finger at her little sister who sits in a pile of shit, laughing her head off.

"Maybe there's something wrong with her. No kid should play in shit as much as she does."

"Bad word." Emmy waves the same disapproving finger at me.

Attempting to wrestle my amusement into a somber expression, I manage a chagrined, "It was. I'm sorry."

"Okay," she says, with her schoolteacher persona in full swing. She crosses her arms, and her mannerisms are so similar to Stella's that I misstep.

"Come on, kid, can you help me give her a bath?"

Emmy wrinkles her nose, but then she sets her jaw and her mother's determination flares to life in her eyes—she's a true chameleon.

Oh, Cally. I hate you and love you and miss you all at the same time.

"What's our plan?" I ask Emmy after strapping Ruby into her rocket launcher.

I swear this swing is hazardous, but Stella promises it's safe.

The second her squishy little feet hit the floor, peals of laughter echo in the room as she winds up and swings through the doorway—she has no fear.

Just like me. Or younger me anyway.

"Do you wanna play with me?" Emmy asks hesitantly. The insecurity in her voice claws at my conscience. If I'd been part of her life while Cally was alive, she'd already believe she could trust me.

But she doesn't. Our relationship is still new, and while I hope she trusts me to protect her, I don't think she's figured out where I fit into her life.

"Sure do, lovebug. What are we playing?" I spin in place, searching for a board game or building blocks in the sea of pink that follows us everywhere. "What's your favorite color, Emmy?"

"Pink," she says without hesitation. "But Wuby likes puw-ple."

"Huh. Okay, lay it on me. What are we playing?"

She holds up two naked dolls, and I shake my head. "Your mom used to let me play with my army men in here." I swallow hard. "This was her dollhouse when she was little."

"I knows it," Emmy says with her head down. She's forcing a doll arm into a hot-pink dress but hasn't figured out that the fingers are stuck.

I sit beside her and stare at the tiny working chandelier that matches the one in our foyer. My mom had this made for Cally—the light fixture was her favorite thing about this house.

A memory tries to take root. Again. There's something that I'm missing, or something that I've forgotten, but it's gone before I can grab it.

Everything about this house is familiar, but my memories here are fragmented. Bits and pieces of my childhood are clear as day, but they're just that—bits and pieces. I can't recall fully formed memories until my late teens, and surely that's not normal, but I haven't given it much thought— until now.

Daisie joins us on the floor with an old slipper in her mouth. Emmy and I chased her for nearly thirty minutes, but she wouldn't release it, so we gave up and decided this one time she could use it as a chew toy.

Emmy releases a frustrated sigh and shakes the doll a little.

"Want help?" I ask.

She nods in earnest. "Yes please." Emmy hands me the doll and the dress, and that's pretty much how the next hour goes. Her handing me dolls to stuff into inappropriate outfits and shoes while Ruby swings and spins and drools.

Note to self, Google why she drools so much.

Just when my ass is beginning to go numb, Emmy places her head in my lap, and I rest my hand on her hair. I pat her head awkwardly, like she's a new dog and I'm attempting to gain her trust, but it feels right.

Cally would definitely not appreciate me comparing her daughter to a dog, and a small smile tilts the corner of my lips.

"Everything okay, lovebug?"

Her body deflates in my lap. "I miss Stella."

Ruby squeals beside us, obviously voicing her opinion too. Even Daisie lifts her head from the slipper and whines.

"She's pretty great, isn't she?"

Emmy crawls into my lap and rests her ear against my chest. She's so small, so delicate, yet so very brave. "I lub her."

A porcupine climbs into my throat, poking and stabbing me with emotional quills, so I remain silent.

Emmy loves Stella. Want and need pick up their pitchforks in my mind. I don't *need* anyone. And I haven't wanted anyone either, but there's something about Stella that's unknotting years' worth of baggage, and I'm afraid of what she might find when she releases the final string.

"Pwetty nails?" Emmy asks, holding up my hand. My answering scowl has her standing and kissing my cheek. "Let's make you pwetty."

"Ah, what does that mean, exactly?"

Emmy runs from the room and returns a second later. She kisses Ruby's nose on her way by, and it unlocks something hot in my chest. But when she holds up a bottle of bubblegum-pink nail polish, reality slams into me with the strength of a heavy-weight fighter—my life has truly, and forever, changed.

It's ten thirty before both girls fall asleep. I still haven't figured out how Stella manages to get them both down at the same time, but this is a win for me, and it's only because I allowed Daisie to curl up on Emmy's bed—just this once.

My fingernails sparkle. So do my fingers, and places on my knee where Emmy missed my nails completely. For some reason, I thought she'd have better control, so this mess is on me.

But *I* was *fun*.

From playdough that Ruby ate, to painting fingernails, wearing makeup, and sand pies at the beach that we pretended to eat, we had fun.

And it was so flipping exhausting that I won't be moving from the sofa any time soon.

But maybe exhaustion is simply the excuse I'm using to not open the letter from Cally that's been burning a hole in my pocket for weeks.

A dirty martini sits on the coffee table in a puddle of condensation, untouched. Perhaps I was hoping Stella would come home and interrupt me.

When Stella comes home? Jesus, what a mess.

After tugging on the ends of my hair, I down the martini in one gulp and instantly wish there were another nearby. Instead, with shaky hands, I open her letter.

Dear Beck,

Of all the things I wish I'd done differently in my life, you are at the top of my list. I wish I'd found a way to tell you every-thing before it was too late, but we never had all the evidence, so it was a risk I couldn't take. Now, unfortunately, I'll never get it for you.

What is she talking about? Evidence of what? My lungs burn inside my chest, but I can't seem to fill them.

After Mom died, I went through the library searching for answers I didn't fully understand the questions to—our lives have never been what they should have been. Not when Dad died. Not with Delacroix, and not for you.

I know you believe Davis and I betrayed you. You think Dad betrayed you. But that's not how it was, Beck. We all loved you. We were all protecting you. I wish I could have found the proof sooner. And I'll never forgive myself for pushing you away the way I did, but I didn't have any other options. Please know I never meant a word of what I said to you that day. You are amazing, and strong, and meant for great things in this world.

And the one thing I know as truth is that Dad handed over Hayes and Delacroix to Vincent, not because he didn't trust you, but because he knew if you took it over, they would sink you too. And we all knew that if you'd known the truth, you would have fought to keep it—to make it right—because that's what you do.

Even at twenty, you were a better man than Vincent Delacroix. I wish I could have told you this in person. I wish I'd found a way to protect you in a way that didn't rip you from my life, but please understand that everything I did was because I loved you as though you were my own. I raised you when Mom's depression refused to let go of her, and it was one of the greatest pleasures of my life.

Images burn my retinas. Ones of Cally bringing food into my parents' bedroom, of my dad begging my mom to shower, of Cally ushering me away from it all. They tear open a wound I hadn't remembered existed.

With great effort, and angry swipes at my eyes, I return to my sister's letter.

Dad knew what a great man you were and would be. He didn't want to hold you back. And he didn't want you to get caught up in lies and deceit the way he had. Vincent was laundering money for years, and Dad believed it better for you to hate him than to get caught up in a fight that wasn't yours.

Vincent took on shady deals that Dad spent years shielding the company from, but when that car came out of nowhere, he couldn't do it anymore. He made plans, almost as if he knew his death was imminent, so he made sure we were only paid employees. If anything happened, and Vincent Delacroix was the sole owner, he would take the fall.

Sickness stabs at my gut. This can't be true. It can't. That would mean I lost everything and everyone I loved because they didn't trust me enough to tell me the truth. They...loved me enough to protect me while paying the highest price of all—our relationship—and they never gave me a choice.

*Please, Beck. If you believe anything, believe that I loved you and I'm begging you to keep Danica away from my girls. She's worse than her father. Assume everything she says is a lie or is for her benefit. She has **eyes** everywhere.*

*Davis gave me proof that my hunch was correct. We were trying to make things right by taking over Delacroix Holdings. We just ran out of time. Forgive my riddles and clues, but for your sake, and the sake of my girls, I can't take any chances. You'll find what you need **where the stars shine bright.***

I love you, little brother. I always have, and I always will.

Cally

What are you talking about, Cally? I turn the page over, hoping for a sign, a clue, something to tell me what she's talking about.

Her penmanship is shaky. Is it possible she wasn't thinking clearly when she wrote this? The date on the envelope tells me she wrote it two months before she passed. But I have no idea what to do with any of the information.

Where the stars shine bright?

I open my palm and the letter floats to the table, then I drop my head into my hands.

Cally couldn't possibly believe I'd be afraid of Danica, would she? Haven't I proved that over the years? What I've done to their company so far is only the beginning. But if what my sister is saying is true? What I've done will be a grain of sand at the beach compared to what I will do.

Emmy's bottle of nail polish sits on the other end of the table. Cally died fearing for everyone she loved. I can't do anything about what I didn't know, but I can do something for these innocent little girls.

This house and all its secrets are trying to crush me, and I'm finding it difficult to sit still. But if I missed out on my sister's short life because the Delacroix family was trying to hurt us, I'll burn their world to the ground and stomp on the ashes.

Rage is a powerful motivator, but so is fear, and maybe even love. It hits me how powerful it can all be when the front door opens and Stella walks into the darkened room.

CHAPTER NINETEEN

STELLA

THE BANDAGE ON MY FOREHEAD PULLS AT MY SKIN, AND I scratch lightly around the adhesive. They keep my mother's nails short now, but today they weren't short enough.

"Every time I visit, she becomes more violent. Is it me? Is it my fault?"

Lucía, my mother's favorite nurse, sits down beside me. "You know it's not. Your mother has always loved you, but she lashes out now because she's scared. Nothing's familiar, so everything's terrifying. It's a cruel way to die. God gives you this amazing life, then takes everything from you one memory at a time."

"Sometimes I don't even know if I should keep coming." Something inside me dies with that admission.

"She still has some good moments, but they're few and far between." She slips me a folder I've dreaded since we got here.

Hospice.

It never occurred to me that I'd lose my mother before I hit thirty. She was older than I am now when she had me, but she's never once felt old. She was vibrant and full of life.

She found the fun in everything we did, even if sometimes the fun overrode a bill or two.

New tears burn tracks down my face.

"I know it's hard, honey."

"H—How long do I have?" I ask through thick blobs of emotion clinging to my mouth.

"I'm not sure. You'd have to ask the doctor," Lucía hedges.

"I'm asking you," I plead. "What's your guess?"

She sighs beside me, takes my hand in hers and gives it a gentle squeeze. "A few months. Six, maybe."

Even knowing it was coming doesn't make it hurt any less.

"I should be here," I cry. Lucía knows why I'm not, and she even encouraged me to take the job with Beck, but I still worry my mother will feel abandoned on the off chance she remembers me and I'm not here.

"Stella," she says gently. "No one questions how much you want to be here, and you shouldn't either. I encourage you to come as often as you can, but the reality is, you're young, and you have to do what will be best for your future. If that's taking this new job that makes it harder to be here daily, but gives you some stability, then that's what you do. Don't carry guilt for doing what's in your best interest. What would your mom say?"

Lucía was around for enough good times with my mom to know exactly what she'd say.

"She'd ask me if my boss was hot and single, and if I said yes, she'd kick me out the door and tell me to bring back some grandbabies."

Lucía laughs, and it breaks a sad chuckle free from me too.

"I can hear her saying that. You're the only one who can

make this call. It's hard, and it's not fair, so no one will judge you no matter what you decide, but if this new job makes anything in your life easier, then I think you should hold on to it. Life doesn't always have to hurt."

"My mother never liked Silas," I admit. "She wanted grandbabies, but she never mentioned them with Silas."

The ring I grabbed from my apartment earlier—the last remaining tie to Silas—sits like a beating heart in my pocket. I'd only picked it up to try and sell it, but now I wish Silas had demanded it back. I don't want it anywhere near me.

"Mothers usually know the truth, Stella. We spend years learning our children so we'll know how to help them when they need us." She kisses the side of my head and leaves me alone with my mom.

"This isn't fair, Mom," I sob as soon as Lucía closes the door. "You're supposed to be here for me. You're supposed to help me pick wedding dresses and baby strollers. You're not supposed to leave me all alone."

Two more hours pass before I can pull myself from her bedside.

It's not her anymore. She's not in there. She doesn't mean it.

But that mantra is hard to believe when she still looks like the mom I've always run to.

I leave Mindful Moments full of hate and anger and sadness. Hate for the world that is so cruel. Anger at the doctors for not being able to save her. And sadness for what my life will be when she's no longer my responsibility.

THE HOUSE IS COMPLETELY DARK AS GPS GUIDES ME UP THE last of the long and winding driveway. Thank God.

I'm not ready for an inquisition, and I'm not strong enough to store my feelings in an airtight vacuum yet.

Every time I think I've built back an ounce of strength, I'm reminded of how fragile I am—of how precarious life is.

The enormous SUV crunches over gravel until it comes to a stop at the front porch. It's a beautiful home that grants me peace in its safe haven, and I'm grateful Beck had all the locks changed yesterday. The new one has a keypad with a special code for each of us. Beck said it's practical, but beneath the practicality is his need to keep the girls safe, even if he doesn't admit it.

Pressing the code he set for me, I enter the house as quietly as the chimes will allow.

Safely inside, I slide the lock closed, pausing momentarily to appreciate one lock as opposed to the four flimsy ones at my apartment, then press my back to the cool glass and suck in a breath that masks my fears.

There's a significant temperature difference between the coast and Raleigh, and now that I'm inside, I don't know if I'll ever feel warm again.

"You're home." Beck's low, throaty voice startles me. It's so dark in here I can't tell which direction it came from.

"Beck?"

A lamp flickers to life beside the sofa and I glimpse the side of his face.

"Is everything okay?" I ask, pressing myself harder into the cold glass pane of the door.

He nods while shuffling papers in front of him. I need to disappear before he looks at me too closely.

"Okay, well. It's been a long day. I'll see you in the morning," I say, then attempt to flee the scene.

I feel it the instant his gaze lands on the bandage above my left brow. The air crackles between us with an edge of danger that soothes more than it scares. It's not fair that I'm so in tune with this man, but tonight I'm a hairsbreadth away from crumbling, so I hike my large bag to my shoulder, tilt my body away from him, and break for the stairs.

He catches me before my foot hits the second step. His fingertips graze my face before catching the edge of the bandage and removing it—then everything changes.

The muscles in his forearms flex as they hold my chin hostage. His gaze darkens, and his chest expands, eating up all the space between us.

"This is the second time you've gone somewhere and come home injured." His words are stilted, and it takes a moment to realize his jaw is clenched as he speaks. There's a hint of alcohol on his breath.

"Have you been drinking?"

His eyes narrow into slits as if my question insults him. "I had one drink," he growls. "Don't deflect, Stella. What's going on?"

God, I want to tell him—tell him every sordid detail. But if I tell him about my mom, it will only lead to more questions about her facility—how I afforded the hefty deposit in the first place, or why I can no longer teach, and it all leads back to Silas. Shame makes me bite my tongue.

Beck's hands tighten around my biceps, the strength in his grip the only thing keeping me upright. His warmth seeps into my frozen bones. He's the stability I've always yearned for but never had. And maybe it's because he's strong where I'm weak, or maybe it's his haunted expression asking a million questions I don't have answers to, but whatever it is, it makes me break.

Tears flood my cheeks. My shoulders shake while my body is wracked with violent sobs.

"Jesus, Stella." His arms land at my back and under my

legs, then he carries me to the sofa while I can only cling to him. He places me on his lap, holding me while I cry, his protection silent and stoic around me. Today was exhausting, yet in the comfort of another person, I find new pains and guilts to mourn.

Eventually, I muster the courage to pull back—to tear myself away from this comfort I haven't earned—but when I do, I find my pain reflected in Beck's watery gaze.

"I'm messed up, Stella." His words ghost across my lips and nose.

"So am I."

He searches my eyes before dropping his gaze to my lips.

They go dry, and I drag my tongue along them.

Neither of us move, yet our lips touch on an inhale. We explore softly at first, testing the connection, but the second his tongue teases mine, our worlds explode, and we pour every ounce of pain we're hiding into feeling...something, anything that doesn't hurt. Something that takes the heartache away.

"Stella," he groans when I spin to straddle his legs. Somewhere in the back of my mind, someone's yelling that this is a terrible idea. Screaming that this can never be. But for the second time in my life, and in the presence of this man, I shut out all the voices that rule my actions. There's no future here, but maybe it's the danger of it all that's so thrilling.

If he fires me, I won't have to feel guilty over not visiting my mom.

If he doesn't fire me, this would be a much healthier way of coping—probably.

"I don't want to think anymore, Beck," I say as he trails kisses down the side of my neck. "I don't want to cry or make life-and-death decisions. I just want to feel this and block everything that hurts me."

"This won't solve anything, and it won't change anything either," he says against my lips even as he's lifting my shirt over my head.

"I know."

His palms land on my breasts and he squeezes them roughly before tugging down the cups of my discount store bra. I don't think he even notices the quality of the fabric because his gaze sears a hole in my skin where his thumbs run teasing circles around my pebbling nipples.

His teeth sink into the sensitive flesh at my neck before his tongue darts out to lick it better. "I'll make you feel, Stella, and you tell me no more lies. I can't handle any more lies."

He pulls back to put a few inches between our bodies and his fingers graze over my skin, leaving hot embers in their wake. But when he anchors me with his gaze, the pain he's carrying shifts to me. I feel it as clearly as if it were my own, and I'm thankful we're both trying to escape even though we know it'll come rushing back in the morning.

Beck Hayes needs to feel alive as much as I do.

"No lies," I agree, then reach forward and undo his belt. That tiny voice of reason asking me if one night is worth the risk of losing it all snaps her mouth shut and fades away.

His hands encircle my wrist, not tightly, but enough to halt my actions. "This doesn't mean I need you."

The words hit harder than my mother's hand, but I nod and lower my lashes so he doesn't witness the pain he's inflicted.

But he leans forward and lifts my chin so we're eye to eye, as if that will make his words sting any less. "It can't."

I try to jerk my head away from him, but he holds firm.

"I won't allow it."

"Jesus, Beck. I got it, okay. This doesn't mean anything to you. You don't need me even if you want me, but I want to feel something, anything to make me forget, just for a little while. I understand what this is, what it isn't, and what it can only ever be—sex, a physical release for us both. Not a relationship. I got that message loud and clear." At some point my tone turned bitter, but I don't take it back.

"No, I don't think you do," he snarls, then leans forward and pulls my earlobe into his mouth. His teeth sink into the soft skin, causing goosebumps to cover my flesh. "I can't need you." His tone is tortured, and my heart rate spikes in response. "I can't need you because everything I need in life becomes cursed. I can't do that to you. I want you as my nanny, but I can never need you as more."

He doesn't give me time to process what he's saying. Does it even make sense to him? I blink in confusion, but his lips are leaving damp kisses down my center.

My brain short-circuits when his thumbs slip beneath the waistband of my jeans, and my hips lift to him as though he picked them up himself.

His hot breath whispers across my chest, but when his teeth graze my nipple, he rips a ragged moan from my throat.

I've never felt this way with a man. He's the only one I've been able to give myself over to so completely, and none of it's real—it doesn't *mean* anything. It's *just sex.*

What will we do tomorrow?

Beck tugs on my nipple, dragging me back to the here and now. His fingers work the button, then the zipper on my pants, and my chest expands until I can't take in another breath.

I lift my hands to his shoulders, and he takes his time

scanning my entire body before he meets my gaze. The want and need I'm experiencing is reflected in his cool green irises.

"Say yes." His words hang resonant in the dead of night.

"Yes."

It's the only thing I can say—the only thing I want to say.

Whatever he's been holding back is unleashed with that one word. He strips my pants away as easily as if he sliced through them with a pair of scissors.

He shifts us, then kneels between my legs on the sofa, and stares down at my near-naked body.

"You're beautiful," he mumbles. "So damn beautiful." He says it like it makes him mad, like he wishes it weren't true, and my self-esteem takes a nosedive.

I hug my arms around myself, but I have no chance of hiding—not when he shakes his head with a determined, heavy-lidded gaze.

"No, not tonight. For one night I get all you have to offer, and then I'll spend years playing it over again in my mind."

My chest heaves. There's too much inaction. It gives me too much time to think. Too much time to question, and finally he understands. His thumbs hook into the tiny strings of my panties, and he shreds them from my body. Scraps of cheap lace slip through his fingers while his gaze eats me alive.

"Beck?" He can't just sit there staring. I'm losing my mind. I need him to move. I need...wait. If this is one night, I don't have to need anything. I can take. And trust me, I want to take.

I sit up abruptly, forcing him back on his heels as I move forward. My fingers fumble with his button and zipper, then he's lying back while I shuck his pants from his thick thighs.

Our bodies tangle and I trail kisses down his hips as I

attempt to remove his boxers. When I tug them again, revealing an inch more skin, his cock springs free and smacks me in the forehead, directly over the cut from my mother's nail.

I wince and move along quickly, but he studies me too closely. He sees everything, and before I can lower my mouth to his erection, I'm flat on my back while he kicks his legs free of his pants.

"Whatever hurts you will not be me. Not my body, or my actions, and definitely not my cock." Does he hear himself? Does he know the pain his words have already caused? Then he leans over me so his heavy erection rests against my thigh and I lose the ability to think.

My core clenches in anticipation, moisture pooling between my legs.

He's big—long and thick—and he moves his hips in a way that makes me shiver with anticipation.

His lips land softly, gently, on the cut, and he takes the opportunity to stare at it up close and personal. He drops his gaze to mine, but I'm too embarrassed to comment and stare over his shoulder instead.

"No more pain tonight, Stella Jane. One night of pleasure to remind ourselves that life doesn't have to hurt. One night."

One night. It hits like an atomic bomb, and perhaps that's what he'd intended. He's told me over and over again he doesn't need me. Perhaps it's time I started listening to truths instead of wishing on lies.

CHAPTER TWENTY

BECK

Trust doesn't come easy for either of us, and yet, we're about to do just that with our bodies.

It should register as a warning. It should trigger something in my self-control to step away and stop this, but it doesn't. It begs and teases me onward. It makes me a believer, if only for tonight.

I fucking hate that anyone or anything has marred her perfect skin and there's nothing I can do to fix it, but I can make her forget—for a little while anyway.

I kiss her forehead, the tip of her nose, the divot at the base of her neck, then I slowly, meticulously make my way down her body to her bare pussy. It beckons me forward with her scent of sex, drugging my thoughts.

My mouth waters instantly. It's a response that's out of my control because my body has been waiting for this moment for an entire year. The way she mewls and clenches her thighs claws at my self-control and it's addicting—every piece of her makes me want more.

The room is silent, save for her erratic breathing. I crave

the sound—every place I touch her causes a new beat, a new moan, a new reflex.

I stop when I reach her pubic bone and stare up her body with every dirty thought of what I could do to her racing through my mind. Her skin is so soft beneath my fingertips that I can't stop touching her—tracing small circles over her exposed body.

She lifts her head in exasperation, but when she sees my expression, her endless pools of amber fill with white-hot lust. I'm a master at hiding—at wearing an impenetrable mask—but the way she breaks through my exterior, as if she can discern all my secrets simply by being here, makes something dark and filthy beat against my chest. It's almost as though her desires and fears are inexplicably tied to mine so every push and pull we attempt lights the wick of our flame.

My body is ready to burst with desire so visceral it could have its own zip code.

"Put this under your head," I demand, tossing her a throw pillow. "Eyes on me."

She shudders, and her mewling response cascades down my body until my balls throb. That sexy mouth plays a soundtrack I want to memorize.

I learn her body by her sounds of approval as I nip, lick, and suck, but there doesn't seem to be a rule book for little Miss Stella Jane. With her, I just want it all—her sounds, her cries, her bodily reactions. I want to see how every inch of her responds to every piece of me, and I want to know how far I can take her.

"Have you ever watched a man lick you to orgasm?" My voice is husky and low, the only part of this interaction I'm in control of.

"No," she says, and it's too quiet. This is office Stella who was hiding her voice from me, and I hate it.

I glide my hands up and down her thighs. "Don't do that. I want to hear you. I want to hear and feel and experience every piece of you that's real, and nothing else."

Her eyes shine in the glow of the lone lamp behind me. Her chest expands with a deep breath, causing her tits to fall to her sides, so I reach up with both hands and press them together. Stella's hands land in my hair, her nails scratching lightly, and with each pass of her finger, a fissure of tension is set free.

"Fuck, Stella. Your hands on me—I've wanted that for so damn long."

She arches her back and presses her tits into my palms. They're the perfect size. Pressing them together leaves a gap just big enough for my cock, and the image of her licking the tip while I fuck them makes my erection bounce against her thigh.

"Beck, please." Damn. She's not begging, but she's not demanding either. She's Goldilocks—fucking perfect.

The ocean is rough tonight. It's the only sound in the house besides my heavy breathing and the aroused noises Stella releases.

"Please what? Please fuck you with my tongue? Please make you squirt and ruin the sofa? Be very specific in what you ask for, baby, because I aim to please."

"Please...with your tongue." It comes out in the rush of an orchestra hitting the crescendo and I thank my lucky fucking stars for this reprieve she's offering.

My first taste of her sends a firestorm of electric currents coursing through my veins. She tastes as sweet as she smells, like fucking apples, so I settle in with one foot on the floor and the other folded beneath me as I part her with my thumbs. I want to invade—I want to own every inch of her body.

Her hands fist in my hair, dragging me closer, and I grin against her damp flesh, then I enter her with one long finger. She's so damn tight, and wet, and so perfect my eyes roll to the back of my head when her walls pulse against the single digit.

When my cock finally enters her, it might destroy me.

She rocks her hips, using my chin and nose for friction. The wet slurping sounds of her pussy cause precum to leak from my slit—she wants this as much as I do. I stiffen my tongue and stretch it side to side until I find her protruding clit begging for attention.

Stella freezes when I clasp it between my teeth. I flick over it relentlessly with my tongue. Perspiration dots her skin, filling the room with our scent, and the animal in me roars. I want to lick every goddamn inch of her body.

"Beck. Beck. Please. I—I'm not—I can't."

But she can, her body tells me so. She twists and bucks and her thighs tremble. She's close. This is the Stella who cries out in pleasure and doesn't care who hears her. This is the Stella who unapologetically takes up space, and I treasure this side of her as much as her caring and giving nature. She's too damn perfect.

I replace my tongue with the fingers of my free hand so I can memorize her face when she comes. A beastly rumble fills my chest because I already know the motion she prefers. Her body is so easy to read if you're paying attention.

And the thing that scares me is that I am paying attention. Every fucking detail of her shines in high resolution as if the story of Stella is being broadcast in technicolor for my eyes only.

Curling my finger inside her, I make a come hither motion against her spongy walls and groan when she clenches down on me. She's already dripping, but I want more—I need more.

Her head drops to the sofa when she pulls the pillow from beneath her and covers her face with it.

Not happening, sweetheart.

I move up her body, rip the pillow away, and find her fighting to keep her startled eyes open. They flutter in time with my ministrations and my inner beast roars knowing I hold her key.

"You going to be loud, sweetheart?"

She nods while her body quivers and her hands land on my chest. Her fingertips sear my skin—a branding—as if I'll only ever belong to her. A hiss of pleasure and apprehension slips through my clenched teeth.

"It fucking pains me that I won't hear it all, but I want to hear something." Sliding my finger from her pussy, I rub her wetness over her clit while I lift my free hand to close over her mouth.

She licks my palm, then nips at the flesh, and my body flares with lust so powerful, not even a tornado could tear me away from her right now. I like it, the pleasure with a little bit of pain. And I like that she gives it to me.

Our position is awkward as hell, but I keep up the pace while covering her mouth and staring down at her, attempting not to fall off the side of the sofa. Mere inches separate us, my gaze drilling into hers until she closes her eyes, shutting me out, and rocks against my hand. She comes with the beauty of the northern lights.

I'm transfixed, bewitched, and everything in between. I can't take my eyes off her. She twists and bucks as her slick heat covers my hand. She cries out and the sound is tied directly to my aching balls. They tighten painfully with every noise she makes.

She's always beautiful, but like this, unguarded and real, she's ethereal.

Her lashes flutter with the effort of keeping them clenched tight, but tears leak from the corners. They slide down the side of her face, and I'm mesmerized by the sparkling tracks they leave—it's a beautiful memory.

Her orgasm stretches out in slow motion, but I keep my hand moving. Her musky scent is one I'll never forget. Tonight, she's mine and I want to see how far I can take her.

I need to see how far I can take her.

She gasps beneath my palm, and her eyelashes flutter but never fully open. But it's the way her body molds to mine, seeking, searching, climbing, that has my heart clenching painfully.

"One night," I groan. I can't help the pissed-off tone. I need to hear it. *She* needs to hear it.

But when her body shakes violently from her head to her toes, I say it again, this time for my benefit, because the pride that comes from making Stella mine, even for a night, makes my chest convulse. I'm the king of the motherfucking jungle—and she's my queen.

One night to want, but never to need. One night. It's a prayer, a promise, and a lie all rolled into one.

The aftershocks of her orgasm might be the most beautiful part of this encounter. The way her eyelashes flutter along her creamy cheeks. The color that rose from within to cover every inch of her skin. And the way her toes curled at the very end, tightening every muscle in her long legs? That was something to behold.

Her eyes are closed as she traces my pecs with her fingers. It's an excruciatingly delicious sensation. Each touch from her sends sparks through my body, short-circuiting my brain. There are no fears when I'm with Stella like this, and it makes me crave her hands on me everywhere.

I didn't think her skin could turn a darker shade of pink, but when she finally opens her eyes, I'm pleased to find I'm wrong. Her cheeks burn. Are they as hot as they appear?

Lowering my lips to the right side of her face, I let her heat nearly scald me, then I sigh into her.

"You're magnificent when you come, Stella Jane."

I pull back and rest on my knees. She sits up instantly but doesn't try to cover herself. There's something about sex, maybe sex with me, that causes her to shed her insecurities —the ones that make her walk with downcast eyes and slumped shoulders. The ones that have her cowering even as she bares her neck to the vultures.

It fucks with my head that I want both sides of this woman more than my next breath.

We sit there for a long moment, both naked and staring, but that insecurity slowly creeps in when I make no move to touch her again even though my cock is red, angry, and weeping for a taste of her.

"Is..." She scans the room. "Is something wrong?" Her brows form a small V between them, and my face relaxes. I'm aware of what people find when they pay attention—the crooked smile I inherited from my father. The same one that puts people at ease over a cocktail sends grown men running from the boardroom. But never have I encountered anyone who inspects me so thoroughly that I fear she catches a glimpse of the man beneath.

"Nothing's wrong. You were perfect," I say softly, perhaps even with a note of sadness.

"Were? As in it's over?" Fire—it roars to life in her eyes now.

I lift one shoulder because no, I don't want it to be over, but it has to be. "I didn't bring condoms."

She crosses her arms over her chest and pulls her knees up to her chin. I groan, and it's a pitiful sound because the way she's sitting gives me the perfect view of her pussy, swollen and ready for me.

"You're stopping because you don't have a condom." Her teeth sink down into her lower lip and my cock nods in appreciation.

"Trust me, even that almost wasn't enough to stop me," I mutter.

Her cheek twitches and there's a flash of a dimple I hadn't noticed before. She doesn't smile enough—it's a travesty. If she were mine...

"So you never planned for this to happen?"

"Of course not." Who does she think I am? More importantly, who the fuck has she been hanging around that would make her think that? "Despite the way we began, I don't—I don't expect anything from you, Stella."

She rubs her temples with a frown. When she removes her fingers, her expression is neutral once again. "And if I told you I had an IUD in place, what would you say?"

My face purses and my jaw clenches to keep every thought and word inside my head. All that does is keep me from breathing, so I choose my words very carefully.

"Then I would encourage you to be very, very intentional with your words." My jaw aches and the words sound rough as they escape through clenched teeth.

She gracefully lifts her body to her knees, tucking them beneath her now, then she lowers her arms to her sides. Her dark lashes fan out over fair skin and flutter as if she's in thought.

When she lifts her head, we're nose to nose, and she very slowly, intentionally engages my gaze as if she's waving a red flag in front of a bull.

Electricity blasts through the room, from her into me and vice versa. The air crackles around us like fireworks meeting their fuse.

She doesn't shake or waver. If anything, she lifts her chin higher, baring herself to me completely.

Her tongue dampens the corner of her lower lip before she speaks.

"I have an IUD, Beck, and no STIs. The next move is yours."

CHAPTER TWENTY-ONE

STELLA

His jaw ticks and the color in his eyes swirls like a war is brewing and he hasn't chosen a side—until he does.

Beck drops his shoulder near my ribs and before I can decipher the move, he throws me over his body in a fireman's hold. My fingers flex against his back and I press them into his flesh, hard. He groans, so I do it again.

The position pushes the air from my lungs when he reaches the stairs and a squeak of surprise wheezes out with each step he takes.

His large hand lands on my ass, not to spank but to hold me in place. But when his strong fingers knead the flesh there it draws a new moan from my lips. Up close and personal, he smells like man and sex and everything I shouldn't want.

"You can't be loud up here." He squeezes my ass harder in warning and the sensation goes straight to my clit. "The girls will wake, and then I'll have to take drastic measures."

That has me stiffening and clamping my mouth shut.

He stalks to my room, grabs the baby monitor from my

nightstand, then carries me back to the end of the hall and the stairs to the third floor.

I've searched the house, of course, to check for any potential dangers to the girls, but it's curious to me that he's taking me to the third floor instead of his bedroom or mine. I haven't even figured out what the third floor is used for, but it doesn't matter when he lays me down in the center of an overstuffed and oversized bean bag.

It's roughly the size and firmness of a queen-sized bed. Who knew they even made them this big?

He doesn't say anything while he plugs in the baby monitor on the other side of the large room and turns the volume up as loud as it will go, and the low rumble of static air fills the room.

He doesn't speak as he walks back to me with hunger radiating from his every pore, or as he lowers himself down beside me.

One night, Stella. One night. My mantras change with the wind, but this one I take as an oath.

He reaches out with a long finger to trace my collarbone and my tummy clenches. Then he goes lower between my breasts, and lower still until he presses the tip against my over-sensitized clit and I see stars.

It's embarrassing how wet I am, but he seems to like it. The groans he made as he fingered me were the catalyst for the most intense orgasm I've ever had.

My back arches into him and I cross my legs, seeking friction. When I catch him staring, he smiles because he understands all too well what he's doing to me, and if I'm honest, he already knows my body better than I do.

"Are you sure?" His voice is low and silvery, but not hurried. The man downstairs was frenzied and manic. The man before me now is in control and going at his own pace.

My body shivers in anticipation. "I am." We both seem surprised by the strength of my tone, but he slowly grins and takes me at my word. It's an ounce of trust in the sea of betrayal that surrounds his island, but it's an ounce he gives freely, and it thaws the ice that had been creeping into my soul.

"One night," he whispers so softly he probably didn't even mean to say it out loud. My heart pinches painfully.

Reaching out, I place my palm against his chest, shocked to find it beating so violently. "I get it, Beck. You don't need me, but you want me—for one night," I clarify. "I understand." My spiel would have carried more weight if my voice hadn't quivered.

His gaze scans back and forth as if he's speed-reading, but I've never seen the book, so I have no idea what he's fighting in that brilliant mind of his. I do, however, recognize the sadness lurking below the surface.

I'm about to stand and tell him it's okay, we're probably better off leaving things as they are, but the second I place my hands on the velvety material beneath me for leverage, his hands dart out to grasp my waist, and he drags me to him.

It happens in a flash. I'm sitting on his chest, facing away from him, and before me is the most rigid penis I've ever encountered. His naked skin beneath me makes my body burn hotter than ever before. He's hard to my soft, rough where I'm smooth, and I revel in the way we fit together.

His dick actually looks painful, but I lose my train of thought when he tugs me down so my back rests against his chest and his hand slides down my stomach to possessively cup my pussy.

I gasp and try to keep my eyes open. I never wanted to be

controlled again, but this—this is different—this is me willingly giving him control, and I've never been so turned on.

"You have one thing wrong with that assumption, Stella Jane. I can't need you, and I don't want to want you. It would make things easier, but that doesn't appear to be a possibility for me anymore."

I want to ask what isn't a possibility, him needing me, wanting me, not wanting to want me, but he leans forward, and it pushes me down his body until his cock bobs against my entrance and he groans into my ear. The combination of his rough sound and the hot air hitting my skin makes my desire uncontrollable.

The second his hardness touches my soft skin we emit sounds that tangle together in a carefully orchestrated symphony.

"Take it, sweetheart. Show me how much you want it."

So I do, eagerly. I roll my hips, and the tip separates my lower lips. He presses a hand to my back, urging me to rock forward, and he slides in another inch, then two.

"Show me how you move, baby girl. Show me what you need."

Placing my hands on his thighs, I shift my weight, trying to sink down to the root of him, but he's too big. I'm forced to take him in short thrusts that coat him in my arousal.

He's so damn thick.

When I'm finally fully seated, I twist my hips in a circular motion and he lurches forward, almost knocking me off him. But one of his hands holds my hips steady, while his other splays open across my collarbone, molding me to him. His warm breath tickles the back of my neck and the top of my spine.

The light flickering up from the staircase casts us in an orange glow, and I love how his tanned skin looks splayed across my fair chest. His cock pulses inside me, hitting just the right spot, and a sound I've never made before claws its way free from my throat. It's the sound of desperation—that's the only way to describe it.

The heat of his body presses into my back and he moves my hips in a sinfully delicious circular motion. First one way, then the other. It's slow, and sensual, and he reaches so far inside me I swear he's marked every organ as his own.

"Jesus, I'm in favor of what you need, baby. It's so fucking good." His voice is clear and strong. It doesn't carry the guttural sound it did downstairs, and it hits me in a way it shouldn't. It lances my heart and ties it together in a pretty bow with his name on it.

I'm screwed.

"But now," he growls, "it's my turn."

My head rests on his left shoulder, and he tilts my chin so his gaze can lock onto mine. There's something dark in his eyes that I don't understand but trust anyway. I nod against his skin and wait for his next move.

His feet hit the floor and without warning, and he thrusts his cock deep, stealing my breath and a few more pieces of my heart.

"Lift up," he says, tapping my thighs. I spread wider around him and plant my feet flat on the bed for leverage with my hands on either side of his waist, then lift myself over him while he remains lodged deep within me—part of me.

I lift and he follows. I bend and so does he. We move as one. One body. One soul. It's a connection we shouldn't have, but I'm helpless to fight it. I glance over my shoulder and his gaze bores into mine. A million truths pass in that fraction of a second before he clenches his eyes closed, shutting me out.

With the next upward thrust, he takes over. He drives into my body as though I've always been his destination. In and out over and over again. The wet sounds of sex and skin hitting skin make my nipples pebble, and he grunts each time our bodies connect.

The scent of our sex is sweet. It's something that's always felt strange or taboo to me before, but with Beck, I want to bask in it. I want to wear it like a badge so he'll always remember how good we are together.

With a brutal thrust, my gaze lowers to where we're joined. I see how his hardness parts my lips and disappears inside of me. And when he pulls out, the evidence of us has me anxious for a taste of him.

I lost my breath ten thrusts ago. I gasp and moan. Tears leak from my eyes. I've never been fucked this way. Not once in almost thirty years has anyone made me feel so much with so few words. My boobs feel heavy and full. My heart is like a runaway train. In this moment he owns me—and I allowed it—I crave it.

His heavy arm lays across my abdomen before his hand snakes down to my pussy. With two rough fingers, he slides into me, adding to the fullness of his cock already buried deep, and he takes me to the precipice of heaven while the fingers of his free hand pinch, roll, and strum against my burning clit.

I've never felt this way before. The fullness of his dick and fingers—the way he works my body like he's done it all his life—the way he groans in satisfaction when my body responds to his touch—it's all so much more than I ever knew sex could be.

He's the choreographer of my body, and only he knows my song.

An orgasm hits with no warning, and the noises coming

from my mouth don't sound human. Beck removes his fingers from my pussy but continues to slam into me while he covers my mouth.

I smell myself on his fingers. It blends with his natural scent, and a guttural sound is ripped from my throat.

"I love that you can't stay quiet, but I'm not nearly done with you and if you wake my nieces too soon, I can't be held liable for anything I do. Understand?"

I nod frantically against his palm, but he doesn't remove it. The sounds of wet, messy sex fill the room. It's us and sex and so much baggage I can't think straight.

I might lose consciousness during my next orgasm, but I come to when Beck's body shakes violently beneath me. I turn my face in time to witness his contort—his neck pulses in time with his jerky movements inside me and I clench around it. It causes my core to flutter. I feel him everywhere our bodies touch.

He's beautiful when he comes.

Hard lines and chiseled muscle, but the fear and worries that weigh him down on a daily basis are nowhere to be found.

He thrusts three more times before he lowers us both to the bean bag bed. His hand presses into my lower belly, holding me still and keeping his cock inside me.

The room falls eerily quiet. The sounds of our heavy breathing lost to the vastness of the room.

His come leaks around the sides of his penis and down my thighs. It coats us and dries to our skin, but he doesn't let go. "Do you feel that, Stella?" he murmurs into my hair. "That's us. We did that—together. This moment in time, it's ours. No one can ever take that away."

I try to move, but his free hand clamps down over the

one still holding me to him. "Don't move. Not yet. It's not over until you leave."

The sadness in his voice makes every hesitation leave my body in an audible whoosh. So I do as he asks. I lie on top of him while he holds us together.

My eyelids grow heavy, but I won't move until he does. If he isn't ready for this to end, who am I to force the issue?

The sun will rise soon enough.

Bang.

Bang.

Bang. Bang. Bang.

Daisie barks, and I jackknife awake with blurry eyes and search for the baby monitor. Where the hell?

My eyes won't focus in the early morning light even after rubbing them with the heels of my hands.

"Shit," a man groans from somewhere in the room, and the *eep* that escapes me would be comical if it hadn't come from my lips.

Reaching for my phone, I freeze. I'm naked. In bed. In a bed that's not mine.

"Oh my God." It comes out far too loud.

Where am I? I place my feet on the floor, and it all comes rushing back.

My head whirls side to side as though I've been possessed by a demon and I'm in the middle of an exorcism when Beck tugs the blanket off his face and his gaze finds mine.

"Oh, crap." I slap both hands to my lips and press tightly.

He tilts his head as he checks me out with a lazy, self-satisfied smile, and he takes his time in his perusal of my skin.

Bang. Bang.

His smile tilts into a frown and everything changes. Our bubble bursts—our desires flash naked neon signs all over the bonus room, and someone is beating on the front door with enough strength to make the wood crack. We hear the vibrations ringing through the baby monitor and down two flights of stairs.

Beck stands with the lazy self-assurance his title and position affords him, then jogs bare-ass naked down the stairs while I grab a throw blanket, tie it around my body, and follow him.

I catch him on the second-floor landing, jumping into a pair of sweatpants.

"You get the girls—I'll get the door." His jaw flexes as he focuses on the drawstring of his pants, but awkwardness is settling in around us.

I give him a thumbs up, which makes him pause and turns my face an uncomfortable shade of embarrassed.

A thumbs up, Stella? Really?

"Stella?" Emmy's sweet voice calls from her doorway, followed by unhappy babble for Ruby. I have no idea what time it is, but it's ass-crack of dawn early if they aren't awake yet.

"Hi, honey. Sorry, I was, um, getting out of the shower. Can you go chat with Ruby and I'll be in there in two minutes?"

She flashes a sleepy nod, then turns and walks next door to Ruby's room. Daisie stands in front of her, growling at the stairs. Emmy's been sleeping better with Daisie in her room, but as she walks toward Ruby's door, Daisie nudges her away from the stairs.

Crap. Way to go, Stella. The kid isn't even five years old, and you just showcased the walk of shame, complete with the scent of sex still lingering on your skin.

I dart into my room and pause when Beck answers the door with a "What do you want?"

I don't wait to see who it is. I need to get dressed and get the girls down there to distract him from whoever is currently riling him up.

Pulling on a pair of panties, a sports bra, sweatshirt, and leggings, I hurry to Ruby's room and quickly change her diaper.

I've never been so thankful for a double staircase in all my life. I can still hear Beck at the front door, so I usher Emmy down the back stairs that lead directly to the kitchen.

Daisie follows behind us, but instead of taking up residence under the girls' seats, she sits directly in the middle of the doorway. She doesn't growl, but she bares her teeth and refuses to move from her spot. What the heck is going on?

Emmy climbs into her booster with her arms raised, waiting for me to buckle her in, so I quickly set Ruby in her highchair, then secure them both.

In the cabinet I find a box of Cheerios I hope aren't stale, then drop a handful on both trays. "I'll be back in a few seconds, okay, Ems? I'm going to ask Uncle what he wants for breakfast."

"Uncle Daddy," Emmy corrects. Somewhere in the last few days, we've lost the Beck in that sentence.

"Right. Uncle Daddy."

I slip past the island and around Daisie, heading toward the front of the house when I catch sight of Beck towering over a blond woman.

And my torn panties dangling off the back of the sofa like an X-rated Christmas ornament.

Beck doesn't lift his glower from the woman, so I hurry back the way I came and tiptoe through the family room to the sofa. He sees me, I know he does, but he doesn't flinch until I lift the panties from the sofa and tuck them into the band of my leggings.

He smirks, which alerts the woman to my presence, and she turns her poison-laced glare my way.

Danica.

Thanks a lot, Beck.

CHAPTER TWENTY-TWO

BECK

"You...services are not required for this conversation," Danica spits in the most condescending tone I've ever heard.

Daisie snarls from the end of the hallway but doesn't move from her post. No one is getting between her and those girls.

Dog, you're all right.

Danica stands in designer everything but offering nothing while Stella waltzes in with discount everything and still offering all she has. Plastic women will never hold an appeal for me again—not when Stella has seeped so deeply into my soul.

Stella waits for Danica to turn to me then she frantically kicks her bra under the sofa, and my smirk widens into a grin.

What will she do with our jeans and shirts? The thought almost makes me laugh.

But it's none of Danica's fucking business, so it bothers me that Stella is running around trying to make things more comfortable for this piece of shit.

"Right," Stella says while tossing a throw pillow over her jeans, and it takes me a minute to remember what she's talking about. At least she doesn't cower at Danica's rude and wrong assessment. "The girls are ready for breakfast. Can I get you anything?"

She's asking me, but Danica answers, "Egg white omelet with seedless vegetables, no meat, and no dairy."

I have no fucking clue what seedless vegetables are, but even they piss me off.

"She's not a maid and she's not a chef, Danica," I say, wearing a scowl that grows deeper the longer she's in my presence. "You don't get to order her around."

"Touchy," she says with a fierceness that probably intimidates most.

"We have nothing to discuss, so you can show yourself out." I hold a hand out to usher Stella toward the kitchen and swing the door closed, but Danica kicks it open with a red-soled boot.

We're at the fucking beach. Who wears boots to the beach?

I stare at Stella, and telepathy might be one of her skills, because she nods, then returns to the kitchen with the girls —who may dislike this woman more than I do.

"Funny. You always were so funny." Danica's sickly sweet tone sets my teeth on edge. "The thing is, we do have things to discuss. While you got the girls, I got..." Her laugh grates. I'd rather listen to someone who's eaten nails for lunch than spend one more second with her. "Well, everything else." Her arms raise, and she spins in a circle with dramatic flair.

My teeth clench so hard my ears pop. Daisie's claws clink against the hardwood floor, but as agitated as she is, she doesn't move from her spot.

"And because I have control of those wretched little

monsters' inheritance, I thought it only fair I invest it wisely for them—it's allowed as part of the trust, you know." She turns in another slow circle. I'm staring at pure evil in flesh and blood. "Of course, the wisest investment was in Delacroix Farms—and it was a heavy investment too. Enough so that their futures will be, shall we say, dependent on the company's success."

I've never once thought about hitting a woman, but I have a sudden vision of Stella doing it for me. It's a wild, erratic, and completely out-of-control thought, and it brings me such dark pleasure my grin matches Danica's.

"You won't blackmail me into anything. So if that's why you came over here at six in the morning, you're even crazier than I thought you were. Now leave."

"I'm here because I have...business to see to in Raleigh, and you haven't heard the best part." She's full of shit—she's here to gloat. Danica has always been a little unhinged, but this is next-level. Does she realize how close I am to shutting down Delacroix Farms permanently? Is that why she was trying to make a deal with Caleb? And now this?

"Your dear, ill-minded sister trusted me. Such foolishness must run in your family. She took right after your dimwitted father." She leans in close enough to nauseate me with her perfume and lowers her voice even as it pitches higher. She's truly deranged. "She gave me everything, Becker. E-ver-y-thing. And now, when I take custody of the girls, their future will be at my whim."

"Screw you."

Emmy whimpers and for a fraction of a second, I think I see something close to sadness flicker in Danica's eyes, but she blinks, and it's gone. The pitter-patter of little feet on the back stairs releases the tension from my shoulders—the girls need to be far, far away from Danica.

"Tsk, tsk, Becker. The Hayes family has always been controlled by silly emotions." She steps further into the entryway and my fingers flex at my side. Now she's close enough to see the family room and the kitchen, so she'll see the girls if Stella tries to take them out the back door.

"Well, I do have an alternative option for you," she says casually. "Accept the deal with Delacroix Holdings, and I'll leave the house and possibly the rest of the girls' inheritance alone. It depends on how good of a boy you can be."

A sickly sensation washes over me. She'll get my girls over my dead fucking body. "They don't need that inheritance. They're not, and will never be, a Delacroix," I say menacingly. It has no effect on her level of crazy. "Even your own brother refused to give them that name. What does that say about you?"

She tuts and rolls her eyes as if I'm the inconvenience, so I change tactics and go after the one thing she'll understand—money.

"They'll get their inheritance from me, and I promise you, it'll be more money than you'll ever see in your lifetime. Because that is what you see when you look at them, correct? Dollar signs?"

Her eyes flash murderously.

"Well, newsflash, you twit, they're little girls who have their lives ahead of them, and I'm prepared to spend every cent of my fortune to ensure you never get a hand on them. Can you say the same?" Her eye twitches. "I didn't think so. So whatever scheme you're running in your chemically imbalanced brain, take it to the train station and buy a one-way ticket to anywhere but here. You're not getting them."

"Daddy Becker," she coos with a nails-on-chalkboard tone. "I never thought I'd see the day." She glances down and picks up my boxer briefs. "Playing house with the slutty nanny so soon? You're truly making the next phase of my plan so much easier. This trip is proving even more fruitful than I'd hoped. And to think, you're handing it all to me on a *silver platter*."

She tosses my underwear to the floor, and I silently curse my sister. Why did she do this?

"Enough niceties." This is her being nice? "Here are your options. Merge with Delacroix or I'll take you to court for custody of the girls and get what I need from you that way. It really is your choice."

"No court would grant you custody, you have to know that."

"No court? Maybe. But the judge? Becker, are you still so naive? I've spent a lifetime coercing people into my corner. Do you truly believe I won't have a family court judge in my pocket? When it comes right down to the loving auntie who has been part of their entire lives, the one who knows how they got every nick or scar on their fat little bodies, or the reclusive bachelor uncle who didn't even know they existed, who do you think the judge will choose?"

I feel Stella's heat at my back—she tethers me and gives me strength, but I don't want her anywhere near this woman and her baseless threats. I turn to block her from Danica's putrid face, then walk her backward until she hits the hallway. A quick glance to my right proves that Daisie's gone. I'd bet a thousand dollars she's sitting on Emmy's feet.

Stella doesn't need to be infected by Danica's vitriol, but her entire body is already shaking and the expression on her face makes me want to check every corner for ghosts.

"Marry me," I murmur under my breath. I don't even know where it came from. It's not what I meant to say, but now that I have, a plan takes root in my mind.

Her face bleeds of color and she shakes her head as if

she can't believe what I just said. "What did you say?" she whispers in alarm.

I glance over my shoulder when I hear Danica inching closer. She's a nosy pain in my ass. "Stay," I command. She opens her mouth to protest, but I return my attention to Stella.

Pressing my body into Stella's, I push until she inches along the wall, putting more space between her and Danica. It's ridiculous. This is my home, and I shouldn't have to hide to have a conversation.

"If we're engaged, I'm no longer a bachelor. Children need stability, remember?"

She shakes her head in a way that shouts, *have you lost your mind?* Then she presses a hand to my chest and steps to the side. "Sorry to interrupt," she says at full volume. "I wanted you to know that I'm taking the girls down to the beach."

If we're married, I'm no longer a bachelor. It's jumping out of a plane without a parachute, but what choice do I have? I meant what I said and will spend a fortune to protect my sister's girls—my girls—but without having all the pieces, I'm fighting an invisible battle.

What the hell was my sister talking about? *The stars shine bright.* Why the fucking riddles?

"Stella, hold on. I'll join you."

Stella stops short but keeps a pleasant smile on her face. *Marry me.* My words send a jolt of longing through me that I tamp down immediately. This is a farce. A solution to a problem, that's all.

Marry me. It's fake, but if nothing else, it's a layer of protection I don't have at the moment. Goodbye, reclusive bachelor, hello, insta-family man.

I search Stella's face, silently begging her to go along with this.

"You see, Danica," I say, but my gaze never leaves Stella's. Oh, I'm going to take great pleasure in this lie. "Your plan is faulty." My grin expands in time with Stella's eyes. She knows I'm going for it.

I raise a brow. It's her chance to jump ship, but instead, she nods. It's a barely perceptible movement, but it's a nod that I accept as a yes, and I slowly shift my attention to Danica.

"I assure you it's not." Danica's nose is in the air as if everyone and everything is below her.

"You missed the most important piece in this scenario though." My words drip with venom.

"I never miss anything." I'll give her credit, she holds her ground, but the lashes on her left eye flutter. If you weren't watching closely, you'd miss it, but it's a sign of weakness—a sign that she's not as convinced as she's pretending to be.

Her tell hasn't changed since we were kids, and my give-a-fuck-ometer is significantly depleted.

I advance on her, standing to my full height so I tower over her. "You missed Stella." Stella's name rolls off my tongue—a kiss from a lover. "Take me to court for custody, you insufferable nightmare, I dare you. Let's see who the court chooses. A single aunt who terrifies the girls just by breathing, or their uncle and his new wife who have uprooted their lives to move home because it's what was best for the children."

Her eye twitches even more noticeably and try as she might, she can't control the fluttering of that one eyelid. I bet she's regretting whatever caterpillars she has resting on her lashes now.

"You're not married." Her voice has lost some of the swagger she walked in with.

"Not yet," Stella says, holding up her ring finger. She flashes it briefly before tucking her arms behind her back, but Danica and I both saw it.

Where the hell did she find a ring—an engagement ring—and why is she wearing an engagement ring?

"They're still owners of Delacroix," Danica stutters.

"Not until they're eighteen, and if you think I won't find a way to solve that issue before their birthdays, you've underestimated the wrong man, Dani."

"That's not the only trick up my sleeve, it was simply the cleanest. But unlike your father, I don't mind getting my hands messy, so perhaps you don't know *me* very well. Did you know you have this house for five more months before I bulldoze right over it and all your sad, fucked-up memories? Davis isn't here to save you this time, and trust me, that's only the beginning of the Delacroix name tearing you limb from fucking limb. I'm so deep into this game and you haven't found the start button. So when you fall, remember this. I gave you a choice and you chose wrong."

My blood rings in my ears. I've never been this angry—rage doesn't begin to cover what I'm feeling. Then I focus on the way she said her brother's name—the hurt that surrounded it, and I hold back some of the fire coursing through my veins.

"Is this really what this is all about? Davis? You can't handle that he chose to be here, with us, rather than home with you? When we were goddamn kids?"

"He left me all alone with him," she blurts and immediately snaps her mouth shut. She blames me for taking Davis from her and leaving her alone with her father, but that's no excuse for what she's doing to my girls now, so my plan moves forward. She's had years to fix her shit and she hasn't. I won't allow her to ruin any more lives.

"I kept you afloat as a courtesy, Dani." The words rumble in my throat as I fight to keep my composure. "That courtesy has expired. Every wrong decision you've made, every bad deal, every time you thought you'd come out on top and failed, *just know* that was *me*. I've been picking your company apart since the day my father died, and this time I'll ruin you."

A little color drains from her face—she wasn't expecting that, and I'm even more grateful that Elijah suggested I hire outside counsel for those deals. They're likely the only ones Caleb didn't tell Danica about. But she knows now, and things will get messy.

"How long has Caleb been your little lap dog?"

Her sneer spreads across her face. "Your father should have taught you something about loyalty, Becker. If he had, maybe you'd still have some secrets to keep."

That's what I thought.

"You have no idea how deep my secrets go. Get out." I reach blindly for Stella and pull her into my side. "We'll see you in court."

"Only if I don't make a move first," she threatens as she walks through the front door.

I slam it behind her with enough force to shake the foundation.

Both hands fall to the wood frame and I lean forward while dragging in ragged breaths. It takes a full minute before I gather myself enough to turn around, and truthfully, I expect Stella to be gone, but she's still standing there, white as a ghost.

She shakes her head when I step toward her, then stop. We're a room apart, but it feels like miles separate us now.

"You've been tearing apart her company for revenge—to destroy her—personally."

"I had to, Stella. Her family took everything from me."

"You've been doing it for years." Her voice has an eerie quality to it I don't understand. "Even before the girls."

"I had to do it slowly, meticulously. There could be no errors."

She blinks and lowers her lashes as if she can't bear to look at me. When she finally meets my gaze, the pain in her expression guts me. "You're going to take everything from her. You'll leave her broken and alone."

It's such a strangely specific thing to say that I'm at a loss for words.

"Do you take pleasure in tearing her down?"

My jaw nearly hits the floor. "Do I take pleasure in ruining her? Yes. She's been after my family my entire life. Do I make a habit of this type of systematic takeover? No. I prefer to build things that people want—that enrich their lives. But I won't lie and say that my dedication to ruining her hasn't gone nuclear. Did you not hear what she's willing to do to the girls?"

Frustration makes my voice rise. I don't mean for it to, but I don't understand where her head has gone or how it went down this path instead of the one where I'm protecting innocent children.

"I did," she admits, then stares at her feet. Her right hand twists around her left wrist. What's going on with you, Stella? It's a long moment before she lifts her face again, and she's wearing a pain I can't begin to fathom. "How does that make you any better than her? You want me to go along with this scheme of yours, but how can I trust that you won't do the same thing to me?"

"I—"

Stella turns before I can finish my thought. "I'm getting the girls from their room and taking them for a walk. We'll be back." Her tone sets off alarm bells. Ones that tell me she's not okay, but I'm so far out of my element, I'm not even sure if we're in the same stratosphere anymore.

I don't move as she goes upstairs, or when I hear them leave through the back. I stand here contemplating how the best sex of my life turned into collusion, coercion, and the possibility of losing the little girls I'm already growing to love.

CHAPTER TWENTY-THREE

STELLA

I'm covered in a cold sweat as memories assault me from every angle even though the air still carries the chill of early spring on the coast.

At least I remembered to bundle up the girls better than I did myself, but I wasn't thinking clearly. How could I when I heard how malicious Beck was, or how easily he'll ruin her?

Will he feel any guilt at all?

Silas still doesn't. I know because he texts me out of the blue with threats from time to time. It's not enough that he ruined my teaching career. Not for him. I'm not sure anything will ever be enough.

Beck is not Silas, and Danica is not you, my consciousness reminds me. *He's doing this to protect the girls.*

Now. Now he's going after her to protect the girls, but what about before? Will destroying her career be enough? When will he stop?

"There they are," a woman exclaims. My internal battle drops its swords and I quickly place an arm around Emmy, who is positively glowing with happiness as the strangers approach.

It takes me two more seconds and blinking like a maniac to recognize Beck's cousin, Tabby. The anxiety that had crept into my shoulders relaxes, and I release Emmy.

If Tabby was so close to Cally, why wouldn't Cally have left the girls to her?

Beside her is a man I haven't met yet, but from his broad smile and open arms, I'm guessing he's part of this community too. His hair is a little too long and it blows in the breeze. He wears flowing yoga pants even though it's chilly out, and he has a distinct surfer vibe about him.

Tabby stops when she's in front of me, holding Emmy's hand, and the man reaches for Ruby in the stroller, but I'm quick to wheel her behind me.

"This is Leo," Tabby says in greeting. "He's safe, I promise. Even Beck would vouch for him."

The sweat from earlier tickles my spine in its descent south. "Ah…"

Leo holds up his hands in surrender. "I totally get it, Stella. You don't know me. These little pipsqueaks are lucky to have you."

Emmy turns to him. "'Lo," she says with a hand on her hip. "I'm four."

"Ah, gotcha," he says with a kind smile. "So that means you're too big to be a pipsqueak?"

"Mm-hmm. Right, Stella?"

My instinct is to possessively tug her back into me, but she's comfortable with them, so I try to be reasonable.

"So," Tabby says in a tone that raises the hairs on my arms.

A thicker sweater would have been a great idea. I can't

tell if I'm shivering in reaction to the situation or the weather.

I tug the collar of my sweatshirt closer, and without breaking stride, Tabby reaches into her enormous bag and pulls out a sweater, which she hands me. I stare at it, but the alternative is to return to the house, and I'm not ready for that yet.

"I hear congratulations are in order." Tabby's laughter is infectious, so carefree and happy.

I busy myself putting on her sweater so I can gather my thoughts, but it doesn't work. Confusion must show on my face when I glance up, because she's wearing the kind of smile that can make you believe there's still good in the world. When her lips curve up, her cheekbones rise and even her eyes crinkle with happiness.

Leo must sense my hesitation because he says, "We parked on the street so we could walk the beach before dropping in for a visit. We'd just gotten out of the car when Delacruel"—he winks and my defenses lower a little—"slammed on her brakes to ask if we knew."

"So we did the only reasonable thing," Tabby says, grinning ear to ear while bending down to kiss Ruby. "We lied—told her we were on our way to help you plan the wedding."

"Um, yeah. We haven't really—it sort of happened—we need to talk." It all comes out in a rush, and Tabby almost knocks me over with a hug. "What are you doing?" I wheeze. She's a heck of a lot stronger than I gave her credit for.

"You needed a hug," she says when she pulls back, but hangs onto my biceps and studies my face. Her inspection unnerves me, and her assumption has me fighting back tears because I do need a hug. I always need a hug.

She nods, then angles her head toward Leo, but never

takes her gaze off mine. "Leo, I think our girls could use a session."

Tabby pats my biceps like a mother would when the final decision has been made, and my jaw hangs open. What session? What is she talking about?

She doesn't give me a chance to ask any questions.

"Oh, good. There he is." She points to the house. I don't mean to follow her finger. I know who's up there—Mr. Grumptitude himself—but my stupid eyeballs seek him out anyway.

Beck.

He stands behind the glass doors with his hands in his pockets. I shiver because even though I can't be sure he's staring at me, my body reacts as if his hands are touching me intimately.

Daisie is standing on her hind legs with her front paws pressed to the glass beside him. Why doesn't he let her out?

Tabby grabs the stroller from my hand, but I don't release it right away. I glance back at the house. Beck has opened the glass doors and is holding Daisie on a leash. He nods, then rubs his forehead in irritation, or maybe exasperation. Is he as confused as I am about everything?

"Emmy, can you show Miss Stella your moves with Leo?"

She jumps in place and claps her little hands. Whatever they're talking about makes her happy, and it eases some of the panic that's taken up residence in my chest.

"Moves?" I finally question, but Tabby is halfway to the house.

"I'm a yoga instructor," Leo explains. "I do morning beach sessions. I moved them here when Cally—well—I moved them so she could watch, and Emmy could still participate."

"That was…that was nice of you."

His expression tells of pain and loss—he cared for Cally too.

"It's what we do around here. It doesn't take a lot to enter the mix, you just have to be a good person and the town will always rally around you through good and bad."

"And if you're not a good person?"

His face morphs into something almost playful. "Then you'll wait thirty minutes to get a menu at the diner, and you absolutely would not get a welcome home parade."

I frown. "Is that what happens to Danica?" What is wrong in my mind that I have empathy toward someone who so clearly only cares about herself?

Perhaps Silas did alter the chemistry of my brain with his gaslighting and narcissistic demands. Or this could be Stockholm syndrome, right, where I side with the wicked?

Leo waves a hand in front of my face, nods, and removes a backpack from his shoulders, pulling me from my pity party. Then he releases and unrolls two yoga mats. Who just carries around yoga mats?

"Don't go feeling sorry for Delacruel." His soft tone holds sadness but also conviction. "I promise you she wasn't born with a good bone in her body. She was trying to poison puppies when she was ten."

I gasp and shake my head. There's no way she's a cartoon villain in the flesh—her name is too coincidental for that to be true.

"I'm not lying. She had a neighbor who was a breeder and supposedly she couldn't study with all the noise, but truthfully, she did it because Cally was getting one of those puppies and she wasn't allowed to."

Thank goodness it's too cold out for bugs because the

way my jaw hangs in the sand, I would definitely be swallowing flies right now.

"Luckily the Jacobses had a security system and they caught her before she did anything, but they handed over the rat poison to the sheriff. It was the talk of the town for months. She went to private boarding school after that." He shrugs. "It's kind of hard to come back from the name Delacruel."

"She's been bullied her entire life?" My head throbs. Not everyone is deserving of empathy. I know this, but I can't seem to control it either.

"No, you're missing my point," he says. "Attempting to poison the Jacobses dogs was the least vile thing she did as a minor. Trust me when I say she would do anything to gain her father's favorable attention, and when that failed, she went in the other direction. That's when he finally started paying attention to her."

I swallow hard.

"Listen, I have sympathy for her, but she was raised the same as her brother, and he wasn't a monster. It's how she's wired. The fact that she hasn't done something heinous enough to land herself in prison yet is shocking."

"Davis was..."

"Davis grew up with Becker and me—he was two years older than us, but it never seemed to matter. It's like he took all the good genes and left Danica the evil ones. All I'm saying is, have sympathy for all she'll never have, but don't feel bad for her. Her life is her making—she's had plenty of chances to change her stripes. Come, have you practiced before?"

He waves me to the mat. Emmy is already on hers, sitting on her knees with her hands in front of her in the prayer formation.

"Do you like yoga?" I ask her when I adopt the same position.

She nods but holds a finger to her lips, and I bite my cheek to keep a serious expression that matches hers. I mime zipping my lips shut and she throws me a thumbs up.

Does who Danica is change the fact that a wealthy man is trying to ruin her?

It's not the same. It's not the same. It's not the same. This time it's Elijah's voice I hear in my head, accompanied by a wave of sadness. I miss him.

"No, Stella," Emmy says on an exhale. Her disappointment in my yoga abilities is funny.

It turns out I'm not as flexible as I thought. Emmy masters every pose, and Leo guides me through each one as though he's working with a toddler.

"May I adjust you?" he asks after I miss every verbal direction he's given me.

"Sure," I say with a shrug. Then he's behind me, spreading my arms wide and tilting my face toward the sun.

"You hold a lot of regret and loss in your heart."

My lashes hit my brows. How does he know that?

"Open your chest with a deep breath. Count to ten as you inhale, then hold it."

Adjusting my legs so I don't fall on my face, I do as he asks.

"Finding inner peace sometimes means letting go of what hurts us."

Inexplicably, my eyes sting.

"Good job, Emmy. You're doing great."

I peer over my shoulder and sure enough, Emmy's in some advanced version of the pose I'm currently failing at.

Leo walks around us—his voice is calm and as soothing as the ocean waves at night. His words hit their mark every time and somehow, he's turning yoga into an emotional release I'm not prepared for.

"Good," he praises. "Now lie on your mats, face down. Place your forehead on the backs of your hands."

Emmy does some kind of twist and suddenly she's face down.

I'm much less graceful, but when we're settled, Leo guides us through a meditation that does make my heart feel a touch less battered.

When he tells us to rise, he hands Emmy some wipes and she gets to work cleaning the mats. I stare, unsure if I should interrupt or not.

"She likes to do it," he whispers. "She used to do it with her mom."

At that, my throat closes up.

"You know, I was close with Beck growing up. We were inseparable, actually. Him, me, and Davis."

I'm not sure where he's going with this, so I remain quiet and stare at a point far across the ocean.

"He thinks he doesn't need anyone. It's how he's programmed himself in adulthood, but that's not who he is. Under all that confidence and cold exterior, he has a soft heart. He always did."

With a deep inhale that burns in my lungs, I ask, "Why are you telling me this?"

His face falls momentarily, but then he shrugs it away. "I've lost a lot of people I love." He fidgets with a hemp bracelet around his wrist. "It would be nice to have him back. It would be nice to see him happy and sharing the love that's buried under all that anger."

"But what does that have to do with me?" I ask again.

His shoulders shake with silent laughter. "Tabby said she has a *feeling*." When I arch a brow in his direction, he flashes an understanding grin because what he's saying is absurd. "But the thing is, she's rarely wrong about people and she said Beck's different with you. Different than when we were kids, and different from the indifferent façade he gives the rest of us now."

"I think she's reading too much into an interaction that lasted less than ten minutes," I say dryly.

"Maybe." He bumps my shoulder with his. "But if there's a chance that he might open up, that he'll let you in and remember that not everyone is an enemy, I'm willing to bet whatever I have to make it happen."

I don't like the sound of that. "What does that mean... exactly?"

"Wedding planning." He stares at me expectantly with rakish charm radiating from every pore. "I don't care if this is a sham. If it lets us into Beck's life, even momentarily, I'm sure as hell going to take the opportunity. Maybe a team effort will show him what he's been missing out on by living for revenge."

The word revenge makes an image of Silas flash in my mind. I blink multiple times to rid myself of it.

"You okay?" he asks as Emmy hands him a wad of wipes.

"Yeah," I say too quickly. "I got sand in my eye."

Emmy's face breaks into a bright smile and she waves with both hands toward the house. Curiosity has me glancing over my shoulder to find Beck standing as stiff as a statue and Daisie barreling toward us. If she runs into Emmy at that speed, she'll break her.

Leo and I move in unison, but I should know better. Daisie comes to a screeching halt that kicks up sand at Emmy's feet and the little girl throws both arms around her neck.

"We're on his side," Leo says quietly.

Everything in me hopes that's true—for Beck's sake.

Then he whistles loudly and rocks back on his heels. "And that's not the picture of an indifferent man. That's a man on the verge of becoming infatuated."

Beck stands with the doors to the deck wide open while he stiffly waves to Emmy. I can't make out his face, but his stance is menacing. His glare can be felt from a mile away as it sweeps over me, then Leo.

I take two quick steps to the side and Beck's shoulders visibly relax. Even I can see that from here.

Leo laughs as freely as Tabby, and I get the sense that he does it as often.

"Yeah, I have a good feeling about this," he says as he rolls up the mats. "Go ahead, I'll meet you inside."

I don't need to be told twice. Taking Emmy's hand, we walk to the man standing as our sentinel.

Too bad he's too late to protect me. I squeeze Emmy's hand and she squeezes back. It's too late for me, but there's no doubt in my mind he'll do what he says with these girls, and that outweighs my conflicted feelings about his threat toward Danica.

I have to let go of the emotions from my life that are carrying over to how I perceive Danica. We're not the same people and the situations are nowhere near the same.

It's funny how different circumstances can change a person's truth, one I've held onto with both hands—not all men leave, not all men cheat, and not all men hurt women simply because they can.

Beck is not Silas. I owe it to him, these girls, and myself to at least attempt to give him the benefit of the doubt.

He's not Silas.

Danica is not me.

Our situations are not the same—this is the truth I cling to now.

With effort, I eventually tamp down the voice asking me if the differences really matter and enter the house.

Please, Beck, don't make a liar out of me.

CHAPTER TWENTY-FOUR

BECK

MY BODY IS SO STIFF EVEN A FEATHER COULD CRACK ME IN two. Something primal, something white-hot and explosive, swirls through my body when Leo puts his hands on Stella.

Daisie whines at my side and scratches at the door.

"Relax," Tabby says behind me. She places Ruby in her jumpy contraption and begins pulling out ingredients from the pantry, saying something about cupcakes, but I can't pay attention. Not when Leo is draped around Stella's limbs like a pretzel.

My mind went completely blank when I caught sight of Stella and Leo on the beach—blinded with jealousy is probably a better description.

These feelings for Stella are dangerous. Rationally, I know this, but it doesn't negate the fact that I have them, or that Tabby sees it.

"I am relaxed," I say through clenched teeth. I drop my arms to my sides when I hear myself and shake the tension out of my hands. Even my arms ache from crossing them for so long with every muscle straining as though I'd lifted three hundred pounds.

"I see that," she says. Her laugh gives me a flashback to our youth, before everything went to hell, and it messes with my head. Allowing the good memories makes it harder to hold on to the betrayal that sent me away in the first place.

"What's he doing?" I give up pretending and allow the growl in my voice to take root.

She glances up and shrugs. "He's helping her with yoga poses."

Tabby dumps pickle juice into her bowl and I scrunch up my nose in disgust, but Daisie, the damn traitor, sidles up to Tabby, sniffing the floor for castaways.

"I thought you were making cupcakes?" I clip on Daisie's leash then open the door before she can barrel through it on her baby giraffe legs.

"I am," she says gleefully.

A smile slides from one ear to the next and another memory hits me in the chest. This one is of her, Cally, and Aunt Imogen in this very kitchen. They always allowed her to experiment, even though seventy percent of the results sent us running for the trash can.

I can't handle the messy emotions she draws from me, so I stare back out the open door with Daisie yanking and pulling on the leash. It takes me longer than it should to see that Emmy's waving. Happily, excitedly waving with her entire body.

Mine isn't nearly as energetic, but my heart kicks in my chest. The damn crazy pediatrician was right—she needed to be home. Daisie yelps, so I pull her to me and release the leash, knowing she won't venture too far from Stella and Emmy anyway.

"How did Cally choose the pediatrician in Raleigh?" The answer doesn't matter, but it's been bothering me.

Nothing about that woman would have appealed to the Cally I knew.

"Oh," Tabby singsongs as I take up residence at the kitchen island. "She didn't. I did. She was too sick to travel when she started making arrangements."

That makes a lot more sense, and it also dumps a new bucket into my well of regret. It'll be overflowing soon.

"Didn't you just love her?" Her smile reaches all the way to her eyes. Does this woman do anything that doesn't radiate fucking rainbows?

I take it back. Tabby shits, breathes, and eats those rainbows.

"She was...something," I finally tell her as Emmy barrels through the open door. The magnetic pull that is Stella Jane nearly knocks me off my feet, and only through sheer determination do I stay where I am and not at Stella's side where I want to be—or out there publicly claiming her as mine.

"Oh, good," Tabby says then bounces around the island and shoves me toward Stella. Then she's dragging my arm to drape over Stella's shoulder while Daisie stands between Stella's open legs. She's the most inconvenient dog on the planet. "Let's get a couple of candid shots for the locals."

Stella turns in my arm, straddling Daisie, and I almost laugh. An hour with Leo would confuse anyone, but add Tabby and Daisie into the mix and I feel bad about the deer-in-headlights expression she casts me now. She has no idea what's happening outside of these walls, but I do. Sailport Bay is gearing up for one of their favorite events—wedding season, and wedding season is only made better when it's one of their own taking their vows.

"I'm assuming Danica has told everyone about our engagement by now, so Tabby wants to share some photos to make it—" I almost say *make it real* but the words won't come. That's a conundrum to focus on later. I swallow and attempt a more reassuring thought. "She wants to share the photos because everyone will be excited. Weddings are a big deal around here."

She lifts her hand to brush a stray hair behind her ear, and the ring I noticed her wearing earlier flashes in the light.

I clasp her hand in mine before I make the decision to do it. My thumb rubs mindlessly over the hideous thing and when I twist it a little more, it reveals a line of green tainting her perfect skin.

"What the fuck is this?"

I'm vaguely aware that Tabby is moving around us like our own personal paparazzi, and that Leo is handing Emmy a five-dollar bill, but my focus is solely on Stella. She swallows hard, as if it pains her, and blinks feverishly to gain control of the angry emotion attempting to break free. Her cheeks are a delicious shade of pink as she glares at me and I can hear her teeth grinding, but because it's anger and not me making her flush, it threatens my ability to remain calm.

"Who gave this to you?" I ask, attempting to lighten my voice this time.

"It—it really doesn't matter," she whispers.

I was right. Some asshole gave her a cheap engagement ring. But the disaster of a ring isn't what concerns me.

"Why do you carry it around with you?" Jealousy springs to life in vibrant colors. I'm not sure what I'll do if she says she's still in love with some faceless asshole. And there is no doubt that he's an asshole.

He gave her sand when she deserves the pearl.

She shakes her head, and it takes her a minute to open her mouth. "I don't." Stella glances around the room when

Ruby's screech of delight fills the silence. Tabby and Leo must have taken the girls to the family room.

"Then why do you have it?" She scans my face, and I don't know what she finds there, but her cheeks catch fire—the light pink deepening into a crimson glow. Fuck me. That's more like it.

That shade of red is mine.

She shrugs but won't meet my gaze. "Why do you care?"

"I... It's turning your finger green," I say lamely. She narrows her eyes and places a hand on her hip. This is her fiery position—one I'm partial to, if I'm being honest.

"You're worried because it's turning my finger green. That's why you nearly broke my finger to get it off?"

"What?" I glance down. Shit. I am pinching her finger harder than necessary. I silently curse then release her hand. "I apologize."

"For what?"

Is she serious? "For—for manhandling your fake ring."

"The fake ring you're worried about because it's turning my finger green." Her ire matches my own and it's all I can do to keep my lips to myself.

"Yes. Now answer my question. Why do you have it?"

She rolls her shoulders and walks to the wall of windows. "I picked it up when I went home Saturday. I was going to sell it, but now I want to toss it into the ocean. Honestly, I was kind of hoping submerging it in the Atlantic would wash away some of the nightmares he still causes too."

My heart gallops in my chest. "Do you trust me?" I ask in disbelief. After everything, she trusts me with at least one of her secrets. Relief crashes into me like a ten-foot wave.

"I want to," she clarifies. "I wouldn't have told you that if I didn't."

She has her own war going on inside her, and like me, she doesn't let anyone in. Unlike me, I fear it's because she doesn't have anyone *to* let in.

"Elijah's all I have." Her words have haunted me, and now the truth of them steals my resolve.

Her sadness shows in her guarded posture and her expression that could break anyone's heart, but I get it now. She tries to be everything to everyone without ever letting them in—she's protecting her heart.

If they don't know her, they can't hurt her.

It's not about trust with Stella. It's about belonging in a world where good is never enough and love is tossed away like yesterday's bread.

We're a lot alike. My wounds sit fresh and deep in my soul, but now I have an uncontrollable desire to ruin whatever—whoever—hurt her so badly.

Doesn't she know she could never blend in? She's the diamond in a sea of coal.

"You're not alone anymore, Stella." Her hands tremble and the pain in her gaze is a visceral hit to my chest.

"Do you have a wedding date in mind?" Tabby yells, interrupting our moment.

Little feet slap against the hardwood floors and Emmy comes to a breathless halt in front of us. "A weddin'?"

Does she even know what a wedding is?

"Like Cindewella and her pwince?"

I guess she does.

My mouth opens and closes, but Stella drops to her knees so she's at eye level with my niece.

"Well," Stella begins, then searches my face for guidance. She's the expert here, so I shrug. "Sort of like that," she says when she turns back to Emmy, whose gaze dances with a million questions.

"Will you be my new mommy? Mommy said I'd get one and she said to be nice. But that's easy 'cause I alweady lub you."

Sweat blooms on my palms. I need to make an appointment for us all with a therapist as soon as possible. What the hell do you say to that? And what if things don't work out with Stella and me? Will that just be another loss this little girl has to suffer through?

What if things don't work out with Stella and me?

What have I done?

While I panic, Stella remains calm.

"Oh, sweetie." She pulls Emmy into a hug. "No one will ever replace your mom. She's your mom and she always will be, even from heaven. But I think it's okay to have lots of people who love you as much as your mom. How does that sound?"

Emmy's shine has dimmed a little. Does she understand how Stella just deflected that answer? Then her face lights up again. "Do I get to wear a pawty dress? A pwetty one? A pwincess one?"

This question I can field. I'll buy her a hundred dresses if she wants. I'll probably buy her anything to keep this innocent happiness on her face.

"You can wear whatever you want," I tell her, crouching down beside Stella.

There's concern in Stella's gaze when she turns to me, but it's overpowered by the happy spin Emmy does in her arms. When she leans in and kisses Stella's cheek, I fall unceremoniously onto my ass.

I've never wanted a family. Not once. I've actively avoided it by never having relationships, but I think I'd change my opinion on the matter in a heartbeat if I got to see that kind of love every day.

Emmy runs into my arms next. "I lub you too, Daddy Beck."

I'm glad I'm sitting down because if I wasn't those words would have bowled me over.

She runs back to my cousin, blissfully unaware of the bomb she just dropped.

Stella and I sit side by side in complete silence. The seconds turn into minutes before she glances in my direction.

"Are you okay?"

I shake my head. "It's too soon for her to up and call me Daddy, isn't it? I'm not prepared. I wasn't prepared. Did I even tell her I love her back?"

Stella bites her lip and I have my answer. Shit.

She shocks the hell out of me when she rests her head on my shoulder. Maybe the events of the day have drained her, too, but I'm even more surprised that I want her to stay there—I need her to stay there.

It was stupid of me to think I could have Stella and not need her as well. There's no half-assing it with this woman.

"I think she's confused," she says softly, and I place an arm around her, tugging her closer. "She's trying to make sense of her world in concrete terms she understands. Mom and Dad are safe—it's who kids want when their life doesn't make sense. That's my guess anyway."

Another memory thunders in my chest. It wasn't Mom and Dad who chased my ghosts, it was Cally.

Fuck me.

I give up and drop my chin to the top of her head. She shudders against me. She does it a lot, almost as if she's been starved for affection so it surprises her when she receives it. For someone who's very touchy-feely, she doesn't receive affection in the same easy manner in which she gives it.

There's so much I don't know about her, but my feelings for her aren't wrong—uncomfortable, yes, but not wrong. Even though it messes with every plan I've made for myself, I lean into them. Into her.

"You're a very smart woman."

"Sometimes," she says. "And sometimes I ruin everything I touch." The sadness in her voice sends me into that protector role again. It's something that's becoming normal where she's concerned.

"What do you mean?"

Her gaze is haunted when she lifts her head, and my heart crumbles when she closes herself off before my very eyes. Whatever she was about to tell me is now hidden behind a mask that I hate. I haven't given her any reasons to trust me, but I'll show her that the masks she wears aren't needed around me.

Never in a million years would I have thought I'd be singing a different tune in a matter of days, but something about this woman has me reevaluating my entire life—and I don't even hate it.

"Whoa," Tabby says, entering the room and flopping onto the floor in front of us. She always did have strange social skills. But this time, I simply shake my head because this is the Tabby I remember—no boundaries, no facades, only unconditional love. She was an innocent bystander in my self-imposed exile.

Leo enters the room with a girl on each hip.

Another casualty. But his smiling eyes say welcome home, and for the first time since I stepped foot in this place, the walls have stopped closing in on me.

"One post on Facebook and Instagram and you're a runaway train." Tabby turns the phone to us, and my throat runs dry.

The picture was taken only a few minutes ago. Tabby captured the moment I grabbed ahold of the ring on Stella's finger. Stella's staring up at me and from the angle, it truly appears that she loves me. But it's the expression on my face that has me doing a double-take.

Possessive comes to mind, but it's more than that. My face tells a truth I've been ignoring for months.

I'm falling in love with my nanny—my fake fiancé—and when I turn to Stella, the same astonishment is reflected in her gaze.

When the hell did I start falling in love with my nanny?

CHAPTER TWENTY-FIVE

STELLA

THE DAYS HAVE TURNED INTO WEEKS, AND WE'VE SETTLED into a routine. Beck has been abnormally quiet about my trips to Raleigh, especially when I didn't make it home until the wee hours of the morning on Thursday, but it was part of our deal, and he accepts that. Mostly.

I haven't told him about my mom and it's killing me. But opening up about her would lead to questions and eventually, he'd find out what I did.

The guilt is the worst late at night. If I'd known my path to Raleigh was paved in lies and gaslighting, or that it would lead to career suicide and the world being ripped out from under me, I never would have come.

The buzzer goes off on the dryer and I jump. Worrying about things I can't change is a destructive cycle I've never been able to break even after years of therapy.

My head is down as I exit the laundry room with another load, so I don't see Beck until I bounce off his solid chest.

"What are you doing?" he asks.

I peer down at the laundry in my arms, and he makes a show of checking his wrist that isn't wearing a watch.

"It's one in the morning and you have an early day tomorrow." It's not my imagination. He's annoyed by my Saturday trips home. Is it because he's in the dark, or something else?

I shrug past him. "I didn't want you to be unprepared with the girls. This is the last load."

"Why didn't you ask for help?" he demands, following so closely that his heat engulfs my back.

"Ask for help with what? Laundry? It's not really a two-person job."

"It would go a lot faster if we did it together. You should have asked. How often do you stay up doing this shit?"

We still haven't talked about what happened between us. The first couple of days were really awkward, but since the news of our fake engagement was the talk of the town, it's been easy to ignore our sexcapades. Now the more time that goes by, the more grateful I've become. I don't want to be what Silas accused me of, and I fear that the hurt Beck could cause would be more than I can handle.

To his credit, Beck has brought it up more than a few times, but we've always been interrupted, or I've turned nonurgent matters into semi-urgent ones.

Yes, okay, I'm avoiding it. But he was very clear it was one night, and I knew what I was getting. Heck, I initiated it. Just because my feelings and emotions are messy does not mean I have a right to saddle him with them.

He stands with his hands on his hips as I drop the laundry to the sofa and begin to fold. His silence tells me he's still waiting for an answer.

Shaking out Ruby's crib sheet, I tuck the corners in on themselves, and he drops to the sofa next to me.

"You do this all the time, don't you?"

It's a fight not to roll my eyes. He sounds guilty, but he has no reason to be. This is what he pays me for.

"I do it when it needs to be done," I say.

"Well, I can help. I was doing laundry myself by the time I was ten."

This surprises me. I would have guessed he grew up with household help.

He observes me closely. He always does. It's as though if he learns every line of my face, he can read every thought in my head.

"My mom would always wash my stuff with Cally's," he says. "More than once my uniforms ended up pink or blue or whatever color she'd thrown in with mine." His brow pinches but his stare is vacant, like a memory is consuming him. He shrugs and looks away when he catches me staring. "Um, my state championship was the final straw. I showed up and had no choice but to wear a tie-dyed uniform."

My eyes are wide as I suppress a laugh.

"She'd washed it with one of her latest craft projects." This time he shakes his head, but it does nothing to change the emptiness in his gaze. "She always had projects to do. But now that I think about it, I think Cally did my laundry. She...she got in trouble for ruining my mom's painted pillowcase."

"Oh no," I say.

"Yeah." He offers me a weak smile that's not enough to show even a hint of dimple. "Um, after that, I did my own. I've always been independent." He grabs a T-shirt and folds it into a perfect rectangle, but I fear the memory has made him sad.

"What sport?" I ask, changing the subject.

"Hmm?" He hums. His attention is concentrated on attempting to fold Emmy's panties.

"What sports did you play growing up?" I put him out of his misery and take the underwear from him. Emmy doesn't care if they're folded.

"Tennis, golf, and swimming. I still hold two state records from my senior year swim team." Pride beams from those crooked lips and thankfully, the sadness fades from his features.

Golf, tennis, and swimming? Has he ever utilized teamwork?

"That's—interesting."

He pauses with a T-shirt in his hand. "What's interesting?"

"Well, you chose three independent sports. You didn't have to rely on a teammate to succeed. And you're kind of the same way in your office. You do everything yourself until you can't and then you outsource it. Even then, you'd rather hire someone than ask a friend. Leo tried to help you fix the railing on the dock last week and you wouldn't let him."

"I didn't know you were analyzing my every move. And you're one to talk, by the way."

I must frown because he rolls his eyes. I snort. There's something about this man in particular rolling his eyes that makes him appear softer, more approachable.

"You are," he insists. "Case in point," he says, holding up a pair of jeans that have my bra clinging to them. I lean forward to rip it from his hands, but he pulls the clothing out of reach, removes the bra from the jeans, and holds it in his lap.

What the heck is he doing? I try to ignore the fact that he's holding my bra by folding the rest of the laundry as quickly as possible.

I attempt to stand, but he tugs on my arm, and I fall back down.

"We're very similar in a lot of ways." His voice is thoughtful.

I'm not sure I'm ready for a serious conversation with him.

"I guess," I deflect. "More different than alike though."

He shakes his head and holds up my bra. "We haven't talked about what happened upstairs."

Suddenly the temperature is about twenty degrees too hot.

"It's okay." I look at anything but him. "I'm sure you're about to say it was a mistake, and that's okay. I get it. We really don't have to talk about it."

He tugs on my ponytail until all I can see is him, and my mouth hangs open in shock. The angle exposes my neck. It draws his attention to my pulse which makes it race wildly. This close, the scent of him, fresh cut grass and spice, has my body melting into him even more.

"What are you doing?" The words are whisper-soft as I arch into him.

"Was it a mistake, though?" His gaze heats my core.

I swallow and because he's holding me to him, it makes a gulping sound.

"Wasn't it?" Every gasp of breath I take surrounds me with more *Beck*.

"It should have been," he says, lowering his day-old scruff to my cheek. He places gentle kisses along my jaw, and I exhale a shaky breath. "But I can't seem to make that connection work in my brain. Every time you've ignored this conversation for the last two weeks, I've almost lost my fucking mind, so what does that tell you?"

He runs one finger along my collarbone and pulls me

down so I'm lying on the couch, the back of my head cushioned by his legs while he carelessly tosses the folded laundry onto the coffee table, and I'm struck mute.

"There's so much about you that I don't know." He studies me as though he's memorizing every truth and lie I've ever told him.

There's so much he can't know.

"And you're right," he continues. "I've never been a team player, but something about you makes me rethink my process."

Surely he isn't suggesting...

"But there's so much you don't know about me either," he says.

"Like what?" I can't quite keep my voice steady.

"For starters, I've never been in a relationship." He's staring down at me so earnestly that he has to be telling the truth. But how? How is that possible?

I sit upright. He most definitely did not feel like a virgin when he was inside of me.

Warmth floods my cheeks, and he winks. "But how?"

"I said I didn't have relationships, but I did have relations."

"Oh." I rub at the crease between my brows. Then his meaning sinks in. "Oh," I say more loudly. "Right. Of course."

"Does that make you uncomfortable, Stella Jane?"

Why does my stomach hollow out every time he calls me that?

"No. Maybe? Is that what you want? Relations without the ship?" I'm not sure I could do that on a regular basis. I get too attached. I might already be attached.

Silas's words sliced me open. Maybe I'll never be able to

erase his voice cutting over the crowd like serrated knives intent on inflicting the most pain.

"You'll only ever be a sidepiece, Stella. Don't you see that? Mistress material but never someone you'd wife up. Am I right?" Our colleagues had all laughed uncomfortably but urged him on as though my life were an 80s frat party and bad behavior was rewarded.

"Hey, Stella. Where'd you go?"

I blink so quickly, the room becomes a blur. That's when I notice my chest heaving with sharp, erratic breaths.

Crap.

"Shh," he says, pulling me into his lap. I can't reconcile this protector side of him with the man who has *relations* without any strings.

"What is it, Stella? Tell me and I'll fix it. I will." It's there in his tone—he really would try.

"S-sorry," I stutter. "I must be tired. This is silly." I attempt to move, but he clutches me tighter, then hands me a baby towel to dry my eyes that hold moisture in the corners like I'm holding on for dear life.

"Tell me, Stella."

"It's nothing, really. It's been a lot of change, and I'm a creature of habit. Apparently I'm not sleeping as well as I thought."

"Bullshit. What about my relations sent you spiraling into a memory?"

"Nothing," I lie again, but he holds my chin hostage. It's harder to deceive him to his face.

God, am I going to do this? I've seen him determined before. If he really wants to find out, he has access to my employment history. It would take less than five minutes for him to unearth my truth.

I can't tell him about this while sitting in his lap. "It's

fine. You should probably hear it from me anyway." My voice breaks. "I really need space to tell you this."

"No. You're upset. I caused it, at least in part, so there will be no space between us."

I glower at him. *How dare he?*

"Talk, Stella. Now." His tone is exasperated, but the storm in his eyes tells a different story. Oh my God. He's angry on my behalf. He's angry because he cares—about me.

My heart hurts—it throbs and aches like nothing I've ever felt. How long has it been since someone actually cared? Elijah cares, but not like this, and it's because this is different that I talk, forcing the words I hope will be enough without giving away my entire story while I keep my gaze on a fixed point on the floor. "I'm not relationship material anyway."

His fingers press into the flesh of my hip. He's not squeezing—flexing them, maybe. Then he releases me one finger at a time.

"Who told you that?" he rumbles, and I feel it in his chest. "Who. Told. You. That?" Each word is punctuated with a pause.

I don't answer. I can't.

His hand finds my ponytail again and he tightens his grip against my scalp. I wince, not out of pain, but with desire that has no place in this situation, especially given my history, but it doesn't make what I'm feeling untrue.

God. If he were Silas, I'd be a mess, but he's not Silas. Beck is everything Silas will never be.

He leans his head closer to my face—his glare is so intense I need sunglasses.

"Beck, you're hurting me." I lie. *Will he let me go?* The rage hiding his face is gone with a blink of his eyes and he releases me immediately. I shouldn't have lied—I instantly miss his hold.

"Who told you that, Stella?" His voice shakes. Why is he so mad?

"It truly doesn't matter."

"Was it the same donkey who gave you that awful ring?"

I can't hide my flinch and he cups my face again with the tenderness of a lover.

"Give me a name."

I don't know what comes over me, but the name slips out. "Silas."

His eyes narrow and he presses his lips into a hard line. Beck's patience appears to be running thin. "Last name. What is his last name?"

This time I do pull away from his grasp and shake my head.

"Fuck. I'm fucked up, Stella, but at least I had a hand in causing it."

He thinks I'm fucked up?

"Whoever hurt you, whoever put those shadows in your eyes, is not a man. Tell me you get that."

I don't understand the anger, the emotion, the blinding fury that's swirling to life inside of him. Is it for me? Because of me? Will he tell me to leave just when I'm finally feeling as though I belong and not only because someone needs me, but because they care if I'm around?

"Beck," I say, attempting to redirect this conversation. "I'm really tired."

He leans into the sofa and studies me. "In the office, you're everyone's helper. Here, you do all the little things that make a family run, but you do it quietly, behind the scenes."

I remain silent but fear kicks up dust in my stomach.

"What did he do that makes you turn yourself inside out to be someone everyone needs but never really knows?"

He's summed up my life in one sad sentence. I leap to my feet, but he follows me.

"I'm tired." My chin trembles.

"That wasn't a dig, sweetheart. That's me fully understanding what I'm dealing with and trying to contain a rage that makes me liable to murder a man I've never met."

"I'm tired," I whisper meekly.

I swipe angrily at the emotion betraying my wants and before I remove my hand, I'm airborne and cradled against Beck's chest.

"What are you doing?"

Is that why he holds me this way? Does he think I'm so broken I need to be sheltered like a child?

"I'm taking you to bed." His voice is husky as he takes the stairs two at a time and enters my room a moment later.

He's backlit by moonlight as he lays me down, kicks off his shorts and T-shirt then slides into bed wearing only a pair of red boxer briefs.

Oh my God. Is he staying in here?

His heavy arm is a vice around my middle, and he drags me across the mattress so he can mold my body to his. I glance down and find his fist nestled between my breasts, and he uses it to keep my upper body close to his. So close that his heart beats against my shoulder blades.

We're silent for so long that I finally allow myself to relax. Only then does he whisper into my ear.

"I may not know a lot about relationships, but there are two things you need to understand. One, I'm a fast fucking learner. And two, you are relationship material, Stella Jane." His heart rate thrums faster at my back. "You might be the only kind of relationship for me. Understand?"

A response, any response, is beyond me. He rolls me to my back, cups my cheek, and scans my face. What I find in his haunted eyes should scare me—it should send me running home, but it doesn't. Instead, I curl into him even more.

Sheer determination marks every inch of his face.

"Tell me you understand."

"I understand." Though I don't believe it. He isn't supposed to get attached to me. I'm damaged, and this kind of damage would tank his reputation—and then what would happen to the girls?

You have to tell him, Stella. You have to walk away.

His eyes narrow into slits as he appraises me before lowering his lips into the most heartbreakingly gentle kiss. "You don't, but you will," he vows over my lips. Then he pulls away, rolls me back to my side, and says, "Go to sleep, Stella. You have an early morning and an even longer day."

"The laundry." Why am I putting up a fight? Survival instincts maybe?

"Leave it. You're not alone. I'm not alone. It'll be an adjustment, but we'll learn to count on one another—together, because we're in this together now, Stella. All in. Now go to sleep."

His breathing evens out, but the way he cradles me tells me he isn't asleep. I hold out as long as I can, but eventually, sleep drags me under.

CHAPTER TWENTY-SIX

BECK

THE ALARM ON STELLA'S PHONE BLARES AND SHE'S SLOW TO turn it off. I haven't slept at all because my mind wouldn't shut up. It ran through every terrible scenario my messed-up brain could muster.

Why would someone tell her she's not relationship material? Who would tell her that? An ex? The mother who hits her? My mind conjures the worst because I don't know her truth—but I know someone tried to break her. She's dealing with more than a bad breakup, and whoever did this to her still haunts her heart.

How do you know? my conscience teases. *What do you know about relationships, anyway?*

Even my thoughts are an asshole today.

Was I wrong to push her last night?

Maybe.

Probably.

But a switch flipped inside me the day I saw her doing yoga on the beach and it lit me up like a goddamn Christmas tree. And seeing her confidence fail right before my eyes last night—it broke me a little.

She's still keeping herself from me, still has walls up, and I haven't purchased a ladder yet because I'm no better. I've been trying to keep emotional distance between us. It was my idiotic way of protecting myself, and for what?

Stella finally rolls over and turns off the alarm with a groan that my cock responds to. She freezes when it reaches for her.

"Good morning," I say on a heavy exhale into the crook of her neck.

"Ah, good morning?"

Chuckling, I shake my head because something tells me waking up with Stella always makes for a good morning.

"You should get going," I tell her, but I don't miss the worry lines that appear around her eyes. "You don't want to be late, and I don't want you driving home in the middle of the night."

"Home," she mutters to herself.

But against my better judgment, this is beginning to feel like home. And I have to remember that there's still a threat against our happiness. Danica hasn't filed paperwork, as far as I understand, but she's right about getting everything except the girls. If I hadn't been so shocked by my sudden parenthood at my initial meeting with Harold Sterling, I would have known that.

I roll over her and she gasps, even though I place most of my weight on my forearms. "I'll make some coffee to take with you."

"Thank you," she says, turning her face and covering her mouth with the back of her hand. Does she think something like morning breath would keep her from me? Truthfully, if it were anyone else, it probably would, but I let her know where I stand by holding her hands in mine and kissing her, gently at first, then rougher as need consumes me.

I pull back before we get carried away though. As much as I need to have my dick inside her again, there's something about Saturdays that's sacred to her, and I won't have her miss it because of me.

A whisper of doubt settles in my heart. What is she hiding that she thinks is so terrible I won't be able to handle it? Who is hurting her and why won't she confide in me?

It's the unknown that kills me, but my gut says not to push her anymore on this for now. If I've learned anything about Stella Jane, it's that she'll never hurt me or the girls. Is that trust? I don't have a fucking clue.

"Okay," she says with a shaky exhale that makes me wish we had all day to explore one another.

Soon. We'll find that time soon.

Ruby's babble sounds through the monitor, urging me out of bed. "Get ready," I tell her. "I've got the girls and the coffee. Plus Tabby will be here this morning too." I cringe. "She's baking again."

Stella laughs, and it eases some of the anxiety swirling in my gut.

"Her pickle cupcakes were not that bad."

I stop with one leg in my pants. "You're joking," I deadpan. "Pickle cupcakes? I almost threw up in my mouth."

"Fine, they weren't great, but the lavender mousse was okay."

"Your taste buds are broken."

She climbs out of bed, patting my chest on the way by, and I finally accept how much her touch affects me. The ring of green no longer stains her finger, but I swear it's all I see on her hand, and it immediately sours my mood. What the hell would be in that ring that would cause it to stain like that?

"They weren't that bad, and I'm sure they're better than her fish-oil-infused coffee cake."

I hold up a hand. "Please stop. I have a weak stomach." But my gaze lingers on her ring finger and an idea forms in my mind—a really good fucking idea. Unfortunately, there's only one guy I trust with this and he's three hours away in Raleigh. It looks like Stella isn't the only one traveling today. "Go get ready. The girls and I have some errands to run."

"Yeah?" She hesitates. "Are you sure you're up to taking them out? Should I pack their stuff before I go?"

"Get ready, Stella. I have to learn sometime."

She's not convinced, so I finish dressing, kiss the side of her head, and exit the room. If I can't erase the stain from my mind, at least I can cover it up.

"There are jewelers closer to Sailport Bay, you know," Tabby says from the back seat where she's perched between the girls.

"Not for what I need," I say.

Leo glances at me from the passenger seat but I avoid him by glancing in the rearview mirror. Tabby has made faces, read books, sang, and played videos for the girls the entire drive.

Insecurity floods me.

"Why didn't she give them to you?"

Tabby stops mid-song and her eyes mist when they connect with mine. "Isn't that obvious?"

Turning my eyes to the road, I say, "Not to me."

"She loved you, Beck. And she trusted you more than anyone in her life, even me. I'm the backup plan, but these girls were always meant to be with you. She knew it would be hard. She knew you'd feel overwhelmed. But she also knew that no matter what, you'd always put them first."

In the mirror I see her hands holding each of the girls' little fingers. Would they be better off with her?

"And I've been going through IVF treatments," she says, surprising me. "They aren't working—they didn't work," she corrects. "It, ah, well, it hit me emotionally in ways I wasn't prepared for. I'm not in a place where I could care for them like they need and deserve."

I glance at Leo, but he keeps his head tilted toward the window.

"I'm so sorry to hear that," I say, surprised at how much I care about her pain.

"Thank you, but regardless, they're meant to be with you. I don't know all the details of what made you leave your home and everyone who loved you, but I can tell you that Cally understood, and she never held it against you. Unlike me," she teases, but I wonder if there's a grain of truth in her words when she won't meet my gaze in the mirror.

"I'm kidding, Bear," she says with an uncomfortable laugh. "But trust me, Cally never resented your choices. In fact, she was so proud of you. She loved you. If nothing else, believe that. She loved you and she trusted you with the most precious gifts in her world—her girls."

I pull into the parking lot of the jeweler with a brick of emotion lodged in my throat.

"I'm surprised you're buying a real ring for a fake engagement." Leo gives me a smirk, pulling me from my sadness. What do I say to that?

Is it fake? Yes, right? But I can't shake the fact that everything is beginning to feel so real.

"Is it fake, Beck?" Tabby leans forward and places a hand on my shoulder. "Do you want it to be fake?"

Pinching the bridge of my nose, I close my eyes. "I don't know," I admit. "We haven't known each other for very long, and she's the nanny, for Christ's sake."

"But…" Tabby encourages.

"It doesn't feel fake," I say with a sigh. "Not when we're playing house, and not when we work so well together. Not when she ignites a protectiveness I've never had before. Not when I want to crush every fucking thing that hurts her—"

"You do need to start watching your mouth," Tabby interrupts.

I'm not sure why I invited them to come with me. I never ask anyone to do anything because I prefer to be alone.

Parenting is messing with my mind. I don't believe in love, yet here I am loving two little girls and their nanny. I don't have friends, yet Tabby and Leo drone on as though we were separated at birth.

I jump out of the SUV when the walls start closing in. I should have given this one to Stella. It's too crowded.

Leo exits the car next. "Take a deep breath, Beck." I whirl on him with so much pent-up energy I might actually take a swing at him.

I'm not someone who loses control. Is this another thing parenting does? Make you fucking insane?

"Tabby will get the girls out and take them on a walk. Let's go pick out a ring for your maybe baby."

"Don't call her a maybe baby, you dick."

"What do you suggest I call her then?" he asks with a shit-eating grin on his stupidly smug face.

Mine. That's the only word I hear in my head at his question. Just call her mine.

"THAT WAS FAST," TABBY SAYS WHEN WE EXIT THE STORE. AND she's right because I knew exactly what I wanted—simple, clean, elegant, and perfect.

"Marco's the best. When I called him this morning, he already had a good idea of what I wanted for her."

Tabby smirks. She holds a sleeping Ruby to her chest on the bench while Emmy dances around us.

"I told Elijah I'd stop by the office to sign a few things while we're here, and I need to grab a few files we don't have loaded onto our server yet." Leo arches a brow. "I haven't figured out how to be in two places at once, okay?"

Leo claps me on the shoulder. "Perfect. Marco said he'd have the ring done in a few hours. Tabby and I can take the girls to the aquarium while you get your work done."

"That's..." Stella's words about trust bounce around my head. And she's right. Telling myself I don't trust people— that I don't need them—has been a deflection and a way to protect myself. But there are people in my life like Tabby and Leo who have never once done me dirty. Knowing you're wrong is a hard pill to swallow, but I choke it down.

"That's a great plan. Thank you. Let me call Elijah, then you guys can drop me off."

He nods and helps Tabby load the girls into their seats while I stand outside the car and make the call.

Elijah answers after six rings. "Hold on." His voice sends a fissure of fear along my skin. Something's wrong.

"Elijah? What's going on?"

"For fuck's sake, Beck. Hold on."

But I don't hold on. I jump into the driver's seat and am already steering us to my building when Elijah comes back on the line.

"It's Stella," he finally says, and my foot automatically slams on the brakes, causing everyone in the car to jerk forward and cars to zip by with horns blaring.

Fuck them.

"What about her? What's going on?"

"I—I don't know. I'm heading over to the facility now, but she was upset."

"What facility? Where is she?"

"Shit, Beck. Don't make me lie to you. I have to go. I'll let you know when she's all right."

"Elijah, don't you dare fucking hang up on me," I roar. Emmy whimpers and Ruby cries. "I'm already here. I'm in Raleigh. Tell me where she is, and I'll get her. I'll make sure she's all right."

Me, goddamn it. It should always be me.

"Beck, don't play with her. She's already been through so much."

His words kick me in the gut and steal my air. Stella trusts him. Stella doesn't trust me...yet. It's the *yet* that keeps me going.

"I'm not fucking playing, Elijah. I just bought a two hundred-thousand-dollar ring. Does that sound like I'm playing?"

"She might view this as a betrayal, Beck."

"Tell. Me."

"She went to visit her mom, but when she signed in, she saw that her ex was there too. Things were really bad for her with him, Beck."

"Silas," I snarl.

It takes Elijah a moment to reply. "Ah, yeah. She told you?"

"Hints. Where's her mother?"

"Mindful Moments. It's about fifteen minutes outside the city."

I hang up without a goodbye, glance at my passengers to make sure everyone is still buckled in, enter the address into GPS, and then pull a U-turn with my tires squealing.

CHAPTER TWENTY-SEVEN

STELLA

"Is he still in there?" I ask when Lucía enters the room. She's one of the most sought-after nurses, in part because she's one of the few who work in both homes and facilities, and partly because she has a little mama bear in her, and that's exactly who you want caring for your loved ones. But today she's grown to twice her size.

She's the only one besides Elijah who knows my whole sordid past, and that's only because she found me outside my mother's room the night my world collapsed, and she had to get a doctor to prescribe me a valium to calm me down.

"He is," she says with a fierceness I haven't seen from her before.

"And he didn't say what he wanted?"

She shakes her head. "Somehow he was on the visitor list, so the front desk let him through. I'm sorry. You don't have to go in there. You can wait him out in here. I'll alert the other nurses, sweetie. We've got you."

I went out to grab a bagel for lunch, and before I could sign back in, Lucía whisked me into the nurse's lounge to tell me Silas had arrived while I was out. I've been hiding out in here for close to thirty minutes.

"That's probably a good—"

"Excuse me, I'm...Stella." Silas's voice goes from sad to icy in the same sentence. He stands to his full height, which is not tall, but in doing so, his concerned mask slips from his face. "I was just in visiting Laura. How nice of you to join us." He opens the swinging door wide, obviously a silent order for me to follow.

Lucía grabs my arm, and whispers, "You don't have to go in there."

"Oh, but she does. We have unfinished business to discuss. Isn't that right, *Stella*?" My name sounds slippery and dirty coming from him.

"Stella," Lucía tries again.

"It's okay. I'll be fine." But it won't. I know it won't. Better to save her than risk exposing her to the devil.

Silas doesn't move from the doorway, so I have to turn sideways to get by. His gaze is cold and menacing—more so than I've ever seen him. The second I cross the threshold his hand grips my bicep hard. Hard enough that his fingers pinch my skin, and I can already envision the bruises that he'll leave behind.

My mother's room is only three doors down and when we reach it, he shoves me through the open door with both hands, closing it behind him.

This was a mistake. I know better than this, but when he places a chair in front of the door my body tremors and I hold my arms tightly around myself.

It's dark in here without the hallway light to guide me. Mom rests better when it's dark, but it engulfs me now. I feel like the stupid girl trapped in a horror movie. It takes all my strength to make my legs work so I can round my mother's bed, reaching out blindly for the lamp on the nightstand, and for once, I'm thankful that she's sedated.

"Are you afraid of the dark now, little homewrecker?"

His words push me over the edge of panic, but I swallow down the fear and pain he's about to cause. This man is the worst kind of narcissist, yet even knowing that, I can't shake the shame from my heart.

"You've really made a name for yourself, haven't you?" The ice in his tone eviscerates any warmth Beck has lent me. "First with me... Well, you didn't succeed in ruining me, now did you?" He laughs. My stomach rolls and I swallow bile that burns my throat. "But now? Engaged to *the* Becker Hayes? The very man you work for?" His laughter turns menacing, like the villain locked away in a mental institution. "You do have a type now, don't you, my needy little slut?"

"I'm not your anything." The words sound stronger than I feel and I mentally pat myself on the back.

He strikes like a snake. Before I can jump out of the way, he has my arm twisted painfully behind my back and he's pressing every inch of himself against me.

The bile in my throat inches higher as white-hot agony blinds me.

Lucía will get security—she will—as long as they're not on break. Please don't be on break. It's past lunchtime, right? The assisted living home is not exactly a hotbed of illegal activity. Just a few more minutes, and she'll be here.

"Why are you here?" I ask, but he twists my arm a little higher, and I cry out as the burning pain races down my shoulder and into my elbow. This is going to hurt for a while.

"You're engaged, Stella. I wanted to say congratulations. But now I wonder, does your husband-to-be know why you can no longer teach? Does he know that you ruined a family or that you ruined your reputation when I turned down your advances?" He leans in and places his face against mine. The acrid scent of his breath makes me want to vomit. "Does he know that you're a dirty little whore who will ruin his squeaky-clean image?"

"That's not true, and it's not what happened." He's not used to me talking back, and he presses on me until my face is smashed against the cement wall. His fingers grip tighter, and he uses his free hand to grab a fistful of hair. He snaps my head back like a twig and I fight to keep my tears at bay —he doesn't deserve them.

"No," he hisses into my ear. "But that's what the world believes. That's what every single person on the board believed because I am God in your world. I make the rules, you obey them, and you're a very convincing *whore*, Stella."

He tugs my arm higher, and the burning sensation erupts into a forest fire. The pain of it clouds my vision and if he weren't holding me up, I'd be a puddle on the floor. But hard as I try, a whimper he doesn't deserve still slips free. He loves it. I know he does because his gaze zeroes in on my lips and he presses his groin into my back. I'm going to be sick.

"It didn't take much convincing. You're nothing without me, you never have been. Does your new fiancé know what he has in his bed? How far you'll go to be loved. Has he experienced how desperately foolish you are?"

"You're hurting me," I say quietly. He's going to break my arm. It's stretched to the very limit of where it can go naturally—one more tug and I'll feel it snap.

"But you enjoy the pain, Stella. You positively thrive in it," he hisses. "It's why you kept coming back for more. Isn't that right?"

"No, no it's not," I cry. "I kept coming back because you lied to me over and over again."

Shut up, Stella. Shut up before he breaks you.

The old me would have stayed mute. The old me would have believed his lies, but not anymore. You can't break what's already shattered, but I can take those jagged edges of my heart and fight back. Emmy's beautiful face appears in my mind, and I draw strength for that little girl.

I suck in a sharp breath. "You twisted everything until I didn't know what the truth was anymore. You messed with my head and my heart, and you did it with the intention of breaking me, but it didn't work."

His hands squeeze harder, and the blinding pain steals the breath from my lungs. He has me where he wants me, quiet, pliable, weak, and he thinks he's won because his larger body makes mine submit, but my mind will never be his victim again.

"Get off me," I try to scream, but it's barely a whisper. He yanks, and my scalp aches. I think he may have pulled out some of my hair.

"Oh, Stella. That's not how this works. I gave you money so dear old brain-dead Mom here could live in this place. It almost cost me my family, so now that you've lured in a rich man, I want my money back, with interest."

He runs his nose up the column of my neck, but I'm stretched so painfully I can't release a gag. I had taken his money—I didn't have a choice. He made sure no school would ever hire me again. He went out of his way to burn every bridge and every prospect I had for over six months, so when he offered the six months at Mindful Moments in exchange for all the incriminating evidence of our relationship, I did it.

And shame has burned me from the inside out ever since.

"Get off…"

"They're in there," Lucía shouts.

The sound of wood splintering is followed by a voice that doesn't belong here. Not now. I close my eyes and every bone in my body turns to Jell-O.

"Get your goddamn hands off my wife," Beck roars, and my entire body convulses. What's he doing here? Oh, God. Is this another one of Silas's punishments?

Silas releases me so quickly I fall to my knees. When I can breathe, I lift my head to find that Beck has him in a choke hold, hissing something in Silas's ear while both men glare—at me. Silas's is full of rage while Beck's scans me head to toe with a different kind of rage. At me? At Silas? I can't tell.

My head droops as the pain of this day settles into my bones and makes itself known. My arm throbs where Silas's hands were. My neck aches, and the bile in my throat eats away at my mouth. Even my knees begin to ache from the momentum of my fall. But it's the emotional pain of what's to come that allows a small sob to escape.

"Beck." I raise my hand, but my words are hoarse and quiet.

"You made a mistake touching my wife, asshole."

Wife? What?

Beck very clearly has the advantage of height and weight, but Silas is too stupid to shut up. He's going to ruin my life again just to watch me fall—he gets off on it.

My eyes well as I envision the inevitable outcome.

"You should have done your research," Silas taunts. "Luckily, she's not wearing a ring. You might have time to salvage your reputation."

Beck releases him, but not before hitting him hard in the gut with his fist.

Silas stalks to the other side of the room, wheezing, and grinning like a serial killer.

"What are you doing here?" Each syllable that passes my lips scrapes against a new wound—the words are raw and rough.

Beck's entire body vibrates with tense muscles that make his dress shirt pull at the seams.

A baby cries and my body responds as if I birthed her. *Ruby*. Where are they? Who's with them?

"Tabby has them," Beck answers my unasked questions. "Lucía let us in."

"Stella, Stella, Stella," Silas tsks. "I knew your pussy was sweet, but enchanting a millionaire with it? You must have learned some tricks in my absence because you're nothing more than a two-dollar whore."

In a flash, Beck's forearm is crushing Silas's windpipe.

"You will not talk about my wife that way, and I'm a billionaire with a B, you asshole."

"Whatever. This is what she wants, what she *craves*, and it's what she deserves. Isn't that right, my little slut?"

"I'll warn you one last time. Do not speak about my wife that way."

"Your wife? Your wife?" Silas laughs, and it sounds as unhinged as Danica's. "Your wife owes me fifty thousand dollars. I paid for her mother to lose her memory in comfort. That makes me a hero, don't you think?"

Leo enters the room while nurses crowd the door. He surveys the situation, then pulls Beck off my ex before he kills him.

"You didn't," I choke out, holding onto my neck with both hands like it's leaking emotions. "You blackmailed me for information so I couldn't show the world who you really were."

Silas tsks, but otherwise ignores me. "You know," he says to Beck. "You didn't have to marry her. She's a much better mistress. It's what she's good at—too stupid to ask the right questions. Isn't that right, you dirty little—"

"Beck, no," I shout. But it's too late. He flies across the room as though wings have sprouted from his back, and he lands a punch so hard the sound of bones cracking echoes in the room.

Silas crumples to the floor with blood streaming down his face and a disturbing grin that tells me it won't end here.

My world is crashing and burning. Again. Instinct tells me to seek refuge in my mom's embrace, but when I fall beside her bed, reality sets my hope on fire as she opens her glassy eyes—I'm truly on my own.

That's when Lucía enters with two police officers. Where did she find them? Her eyes scan the room for less than a second before she points to Silas. "There he is."

"Me?" Silas chuckles. "I'm the one who was assaulted."

"Officers, my name is Becker Hayes." He aggressively tugs on the hem of his shirt and runs a hand through his messy hair. "I came to visit my fiancée and her mother, and I found him assaulting her. I'd be shocked if she didn't have bruises."

I stare up at everyone in the room in horror. How did this spiral so quickly? Lucía holds her hands out to me and she helps me rise, but I wince when pain shoots through my shoulder and elbow.

She's quick to lift the sleeve of my T-shirt where marks have already formed. "See," she says pointing to my arms.

"That's not what happened. Doesn't anyone care that I'm

bleeding?" Silas's voice doesn't sound as menacing as it did a few minutes ago.

The collective room says, "no," without ever looking his way.

Everything moves in slow motion, as though we're underwater, as the officers remove Silas and question everyone else.

I talked to them first, right after Beck insisted the doctor on-call examine me from head to toe, and now time holds no meaning as I stand here, alone, while my mother lies at my side. Her eyes are open, but the memories that make her my mom are gone today. She holds a smile on her face reserved for strangers, because today, that's who I am to her.

She's not there anymore. She loved you. This isn't her fault.

"What's wrong, dear?" The cruelty is that her voice sounds like my mom. She looks like my mom. But she's not my mom—not to her anyway.

"Stella?"

I'm wound so tightly that when I jump in my seat every muscle in my body aches.

Beck's scent envelopes me in an embrace, and then he gently places his hands on my shoulders, massaging and soothing the pain he has no part in.

"Can I sit?" he whispers.

My face is pinched when I turn my head to peer up at him. His expression is sad and full of pity.

"You're a very handsome couple," my mother says with shining eyes.

Beck nods in her direction. "Hello, Mrs. Anderson. It's so nice to meet you."

She stares at him with a plastic smile. She doesn't recognize him, but she'll pretend she does—it's how this works now.

"It's time for my walk," she says, her smile dimming as thoughts slip away from her. Then she closes her eyes. She's been doing this more and more when she can't remember words.

"Now you know my secrets." My voice sounds more like a scared little girl than my own.

"No, I don't." He takes my hand in his and runs gentle circles on my wrist with his thumb. "I know that you obviously love your mother. I know the lies and half-truths that scumbag attempted to state as facts, but I don't know anything about your secrets until I hear them from you."

"Who are you?" my mother asks.

I turn toward her so fast my head spins. But she's not asking me, she's asking Beck.

"Hello, Mrs. Anderson. My name is Becker Hayes, and I'm in love with your daughter."

She smiles, but her gaze is skittish. "My daughter," she repeats. She doesn't remember that she has one. "And who are you?"

My heart is already in ashes, and she just blew them away.

"My name is Stella. Do you need anything?" She glances around the room and the moment is gone. She stares at a TV in the corner that quietly plays her favorite music. She used to love the trivia questions that accompanied every song. Now she stares at them without seeing.

I squeeze her hand, then rise and kiss her cheek. She stares at me and for a split second I feel her—who she used to be, and then like everything good in my life, she vanishes.

"We'll let you rest," I say through a cloud of emotion.

Beck remains at my side as I exit the room. He takes my hand in his and leads me out of the building to the car I drove here.

"Where are the girls?" I scan the parking lot, searching for his other car. "What did Emmy see?"

He leans against the car and pulls me between his legs with a gentle touch. Beck's eyes are a myriad of emotions, but he doesn't speak.

It takes three tries before I make my words work, and when they do, they're choppy. "Can I at least say goodbye to them? They've already had so much loss. I don't want them thinking I've abandoned them."

He tilts his head. Is he messing with me, or does he not understand my request?

"Stella, you know what I think?"

I shake my head and clench my teeth to keep any emotions I can control in check.

"I think the girls aren't the only ones suffering great losses. I think even when you were in a relationship, you were always alone. I think life has treated you poorly, yet you give everything you have and then some."

Salty emotion gags me no matter how hard I fight it.

"I think you equate need with love, but you've taught me something about myself no one else ever could. I need you, yes, but I don't have to need you to love you. I think I love you just as you are, whether you're doing the laundry, finding a traitor in my company, or simply gracing me with a smile."

My body is telling me to back away, but the pull of his embrace is a warmth I desperately need. The urge to flee is strong, but it's not as strong as the determination I find in Beck's open expression and I sag against him.

What the hell does he mean he loves me?

"The girls are on their way home with Tabby and Leo. They'll spend the night at the house. Come with me?"

"Where?"

"Somewhere you can relax, and if you're willing, tell me what the fuck just happened in there."

I owe him that, don't I? The truth?

"I see your mind spinning, and if any part of your brain is telling you that I won't love you if I know your secrets, then you're seriously underestimating how far I'm willing to go to love you, sweetheart."

"How do you know?"

He jerks his head back. "Know what?"

"That you'll still love me after you hear what I've done? You've never been in a relationship, Beck. You've never loved anyone before. What if you're just grieving and not really feeling what you think you are?"

"So cynical," he says, walking me toward the passenger door. "In all the time you've worked for me, have you ever known me to go back on a decision once I've made it?"

No, but that's different. In business, he has stats and projections. He understands the risks before going in.

"You can't take out insurance in case we don't work out. Relationships are not as black-and-white as making a deal with a new property."

Beck's eyes crinkle at the corners, then he opens the door and gestures for me to enter. Once I'm seated, he leans on the doorframe with that crooked grin that sucks me in every time. "Then I look forward to you teaching me about all its colors. Buckle up, beautiful. It's going to be a long night."

CHAPTER TWENTY-EIGHT

BECK

WE DRIVE FOR CLOSE TO AN HOUR WITH NOTHING BUT THE radio for company. Stella is curled into the door like a wounded animal, and I'm still gripping the steering wheel with white knuckles.

Seeing that piece of shit with his hands on her broke down the last of my resistance. He hurt her. She's wearing the imprint of his hand on her wrist, and she sleeps cradling her elbow close to her belly.

Now I can't shake the image of her in pain from my mind. I thought I might be in love with her when I bought the ring, but I'd allowed my own stubbornness to cloud my truth. When I heard her whimper in pain, nothing else mattered. It was in that moment I knew I couldn't live without her, and I finally succumbed to the fact that I love my nanny. But her mom? Christ. Why didn't she tell me about her? I could have done something.

I *will* do something.

My gaze drifts back over her—she owns me now. Life has never before spiraled this quickly on me, nor have I ever been so excited to see where I'll land. But I will do anything for this woman, and for all her questions, that's how I know. I know this is right because of how she makes me experience the tiniest emotions so viscerally. It's something I've never had before. It's primal. A need that infects every inch of my body. I want to protect her from everything that hurts her. I want to erase the shadows that haunt her dreams.

But I don't just want her.

I need her, and I'm done fighting it. It should be a terrifying realization, but it's not. If anything, it's set me free.

By the time I pull into the parking lot, it's almost empty, and I'm thankful my manager here was able to quickly execute my demands. I have properties closer to the city, but this one is special. There's a reason appointments here are booked a year in advance, which, admittedly will piss off the people I canceled on and mess up the schedules of everyone who has to work late to make up for it, but I'll reward them handsomely for this.

"Stella, baby? We're here."

Her lashes flutter but don't open so I exit the car and carefully open her door. Her head was resting against the window, and it pops up when I pull it away from her.

"Hi." I keep my voice quiet. Until I know exactly what happened in her mother's room, I'll take care not to spook her. Everything from my words to my actions is gentled for her even though the rage of seeing her terrified still burns through my veins.

"Where are we?"

"Crystal Waters. My favorite property in North Carolina."

Her gaze sweeps over my shoulder, then around the parking lot. "Is it open?"

"For us, yes. Come. We have appointments."

"Why?" Her knee buckles when her feet hit the gravel,

and I bite my tongue to keep myself from lashing out in fear. Did that fucker hurt her anywhere else?

"Because that asshole had his hands on you and caused you pain. I want to erase that from your mind, so we're getting massages, ones that heal, not hurt. I called in two of my best people. I promise it'll be a massage you'll never forget."

She shrugs, but the energy has already drained from her. The spark that made her shine has dulled. "I've never had a massage, so I'm sure my first will be very memorable."

I stop short as she stares at her feet.

"You work for me."

She raises a single brow but doesn't say anything.

"One of the perks of working for me in the executive suite is the free monthly massages. That didn't stop because I coerced you into nannying instead."

"No, I've never used them."

Her words don't compute. I thought everyone took advantage of that perk. "Why not?"

"They're expensive, so the tip would be expensive."

A vision of her mother springs to mind. This is why she had so many jobs. All the pieces of her life click into place, and my gut twists and turns so painfully I nearly double over.

"Would you like to have a massage?" I ask.

She bites her lip and blinks slowly, but I give her time to collect her thoughts. "My shoulder is really sore," she finally admits. "And my wrist...and my elbow."

I've never experienced the term "seeing red" before, but I feel it in every fiber of my being today. It surrounds us like an angry aura only I can see.

"I've let them know. They're the best, Stella. They won't hurt you."

She sighs, and the weight it carries could knock over an elephant.

"Okay?" I need her to say yes. I need to make this better. For someone who has spent years not needing anything, she's the exception. I've never felt this out of control before. Another person's pain has never affected me so viscerally, and it's all because of my love for this woman.

"Okay."

We walk to the front door hand in hand, and Maria opens it as we approach. She's my top-performing spa manager, so I'm not surprised to see her here. I've never asked any of my properties for this kind of thing before.

As soon as we're in, she locks the door behind us, and Stella releases an audible sigh. Maria nods as if she understands, and Stella holds her battered arm in tighter to her side.

"Jeffry and Gretta have room twelve prepared for you," Maria says serenely.

"Thank you, Maria. This is my fiancée, Stella."

Stella isn't beside me, so I glance over my shoulder. The sheer wonder on her beautiful face is blinding.

This property is my pride and joy. It's the one that eased my fears about being successful, and it's the first to put a Delacroix Farms property out of business.

"It's pretty, isn't it?"

Pretty is an understatement, but I'm the one who gets to give her this experience, this lifestyle. That knowledge makes my heart riot in my chest. I get to give her the world.

Who the hell has she turned me into?

"Yeah, it's so pretty," she says, staring at the chandelier overhead that was hand-crafted by a master glass blower and took over one hundred hours to complete.

As I lead her through the space, her gaze jumps from

one detail to the next. The soft overhead lighting complements the cool tones that lend to the overall ocean theme beautifully. A sense of pride fills me like nothing before. I've always been proud of my accomplishments, but I've never once cared what anyone else thought.

I care what Stella thinks. I care what she feels and if she's safe. I care about her happiness more than my own, and that might be the most shocking of all.

We enter a room tinged with the soothing scent of lavender. The lights are low, and candles flicker in the dark while the sounds of the ocean are detectable if you listen closely.

Letting go of her hand, I move to the first bed and fold down the sheet. "Get undressed, then lie face down. Take your time getting comfortable. They won't enter without permission."

"Take off...everything?"

The smile I offer her is as reassuring as I can make it. "It's up to you. I'll leave mine on so I don't make my employees uncomfortable." I drop my pants and remove my shirt. "But a lot of people, especially women, leave their underwear on. Whatever you choose, you're completely safe here, you have my word. The masseuse maneuvers the sheet so you remain covered at all times."

She nods, then shucks her shirt and tosses it to the empty chair.

I can't breathe for an eternal moment.

There's a bruise on her shoulder where he gripped too hard. A matching one on each bicep. But the one on the back of her neck floods my veins with ice. She's wearing the fingerprints of a monster. To get bruises that deep, he was holding her neck hard enough to bring her to her knees.

Every ounce of willpower I have keeps my voice quiet

and steady rather than bellowing and irate when I ask, "Stella, did he do this to you when you were together?"

Visions of her bruised and battered taunt my mind like a sick house of mirrors.

"Only once." She glances away.

"Do not feel ashamed. The only one in the wrong in that situation is him." I know men like that.

Vincent Delacroix was like that—manipulative and vicious to a maddening degree.

She lowers her jeans but keeps her panties on. I almost laugh when she tucks her bra into the shirt she was wearing, but when she turns to the bed, my laughter fizzles out. It's time for healing, so I drop it—for now—while she climbs onto the bed as I instructed.

I do the same on the bed to her left. "Relax, Stella. Take deep breaths."

A knock on the door ends my pep talk as masseuses enter the room. Moving in silence, they place foam rolls under our ankles.

Stella gasps and I snap my head toward her. Gretta uses gentle sweeping motions to ease her into the touch, but I can't lower my face until her stiff muscles relax. I catch Gretta's eye when she does. She nods toward her bruises—a silent acknowledgment that she'll take good care of my girl.

We lie face down with the sounds of oil and moving hands as our soundtrack. They're still working on our bodies twenty minutes later and I'm not expecting her to speak, but I press my upper body off the table when she does.

"I didn't know he was married," she says. Her words are slightly muffled from the circular pillow she's resting her face in, and I lean toward her.

That's when I follow a single tear that joins a puddle

beneath her. I move quietly off the table, not caring that I'm being vulnerable in front of my employees. I hold my hand out to Jeffry and he fills it with oil that I rub together, then mouth, "Thank you. Go home." Holding my hands in prayer formation, I silently bow my head to them as they exit.

It all happens in less than thirty seconds, and then we're alone. I keep moving, waiting for her to continue. She's so lost in her head that I don't think she realizes they've exited the room. Or maybe she doesn't care.

"He lied to me for years. He would twist things so much I thought I needed therapy, but he twisted that too and I never went. He made me believe I was going insane. Without my knowledge or my consent, he turned me into a monster."

"Stella." Even her name is almost impossible to say. My throat is too tight, and my mind too alive with all the ways I'll ruin this bastard.

Her head snaps up and she blinks rapidly, bringing our surroundings into view.

"Shh. I sent them home. I'm here, Stella. I'm listening, and I'm not going anywhere." I hold out my oiled-up hands. "May I?"

Fresh tears pool on her lashes, but she finally nods. It takes her three deep breaths before she wipes her tears and lowers her face again.

"We worked at a private school in Raleigh. A really expensive, exclusive school. He's still the headmaster there."

I file that information away to weaponize later and slowly run my palms down her back.

"My mom had the diagnosis for a while, but that day I'd learned she'd need more care than I could offer—soon. I was upset, but he said he couldn't miss the faculty holiday party. I'd wanted to go, to get my mind off my grief, but by the time he'd left I had agreed I was being incredibly selfish, and that my time should be spent with her."

I glide my fingertips down her spine and press my thumbs into her skin on either side, then scale back up one vertebra at a time, thankful that my hands have something to do other than punch something.

"My mom still had mostly good days then. She could even care for herself with help most of the time, but it's been a rapid decline. That night she went to bed early and told me not to be silly. She wanted me to go to the party, to enjoy myself, and to spend time with Silas."

She tucks a piece of hair behind her ear, then continues. "I'd met Lucía at a support group she ran at Mindful Moments and instantly felt a connection with her, so I called her to stay with my mom and I went. I didn't even think twice about the cost, I just wanted to be someone else for a little while. I thought I was lucky because Lucía has been trained in both facilities care and as an in-home nurse. *Lucky,* can you believe that?"

She scoffs and it's a harsh, choking sound, then she's silent for a beat.

"Anyway, he wasn't expecting me, and the whispers began as soon as I entered the ballroom." She sniffles, and that one sound guts me more than I ever thought possible. "I was uncomfortable from all the attention, but I stupidly attributed it to my new dress. I felt like a princess."

Her chuckle is heartbreaking.

"He caught sight of me when I was halfway across the room, and I'll never forget how his mask slipped, or the woman who whispered in his ear. That's when he flexed his hand and I saw the ring on his finger."

Her body trembles beneath my touch as she attempts to hold in her silent sobs.

"I'm here, Stella. I don't care what lies he told. I'm here."

I don't know if it's my words or my touch that soothes the tremors, but she sucks in ragged breaths. It's probably easier for her to tell this story without eye contact. She wears her cloak of shame close, but I will make sure she discards it like the shitstain who made her this way.

"I knew something was wrong, but I couldn't make my feet move, and then everything happened so fast. All I remember is being surrounded by a group of men—coworkers I'd had coffee with—while he walked in a circle around me. Berating me. Asking if anyone needed a mistress because he had one he was throwing away. He laughed in my face when I held up the ring he'd given me."

Her tone chills and her body tenses as she gets lost in the memory. "He told me I was a stupid girl who would never be wife material. He called me names and pointed out my flaws. All the things he'd said for years to make me believe I was losing my mind. He made me appear crazy to everyone there. And not one person stood up for me, not one person cared about the pain he was causing or the embarrassment I felt at being treated like dirt."

Stella rolls over and sits up, holding the sheet to her chest. I would give anything to take away her pain. I never want to see her like this again. Her shoulders sag in defeat. Her face is devoid of the love that normally fills it. Even her voice has lost the cadence that makes her my Stella.

"He fired me and ruined my reputation by making sure every school on the East Coast knew his version of my nightmare—he called me a stalker and said I was unstable. After a few months, I was desperate. He knew I had cameras in my home because of my mom." She lifts her head but her lashes flutter against her cheekbones and her knuckles turn white around the sheet she's holding.

I reach for her, hold her face in my palms. *I'm here, Stella. I'm here.*

"It was the first thing I did after my mom's diagnosis. The cameras let me keep an eye on her for short periods of time. Then one day, he showed up and offered to pay for six months of in-patient care at Mindful Moments, but I had to hand over every piece of evidence that linked him to me."

Her lashes stick together and her chin trembles in my hands.

"I didn't have any other options. I had no job, no prospects, and Mom's condition was taking her from me too quickly. As soon as the money was transferred to my account, I gave him everything. It didn't really matter anyway. He'd already destroyed all the pieces of me that mattered."

"Not all of them, sweetheart. I promise you—he didn't take them all."

She shrugs me off, then wipes at her nose with the back of her hand.

"I kept her home as long as I could, and accepted every job I could get as a temp. That's how I met Elijah, and he was so kind, but after our, well, after our kiss..." Her lashes flutter and her cheeks pink when she glances up at me.

Oh, I remember that night well, sweetheart.

She swipes at her nose again and I scan the room for some tissues. "I didn't want to put him in a weird position after that. I never thought I'd see either of you again, and I never expected him to track me down, but when Caleb's last assistant quit, he showed up at my building. He found me trying to get Mom in the car."

"He helped you get her to the nursing home," I say, remembering his random story when he showed up late. Elijah is never late.

Her brows crease, but she nods.

"Silas's money is running out, so Elijah's helped me find other sources of revenue. He lent me his car, but only allowed me to repay him with cookies. Then he gave me an email address for Lottie. She hired me after a background check, and now, here we are."

I swing her legs over the table and step between them, then rest my forehead on hers.

"Please tell me you don't still believe his bullshit. Tell me you understand how easy you are to love. Nothing he's ever said to you is the truth. I'm willing to bet my entire fortune on that."

"But why? After all this, why? I took his money like a prostitute."

I suck in a harsh breath. He's fucked with her mind—made her see herself as someone she's not. He's left her with the impression that she's unlovable. It's hard to keep my rage at bay, but for her, I do. For her, I'd do a hell of a lot of things.

"You took the money because he owed it to you after the hell he made of your life, not because you're a prostitute, and I don't ever want to hear you call yourself that again. Not ever. You've made someone else's lies your truth, and it's time we changed that."

"He made me a mistress—a homewrecker. That's who people believe I am. What if you want the girls to go to that school someday? It's the number one rated school in the southeast."

I smile and my lips hover over hers. "No, baby. He's the homewrecker, not you. And let me worry about schools. But I'll tell you this—any place that doesn't respect you will not get a dime from me. It's funny how quickly tunes change when dollar signs are involved."

"But—"

I cut her off with a gentle kiss, then lift her off the table and place her carefully on her feet.

As much as I want to carry her everywhere, protect her from the world, something in my gut tells me she needs to be the one to take the steps forward. So I will stand beside her while she forges her path, but she'll never walk alone again.

She pauses when I tuck the sheet around her then open the door. The place is empty, so I walk with purpose, in my underwear, toward the steam room.

Once there, I place a hand to the small of her back and walk her into the room while billows of steam scented like eucalyptus engulf us.

CHAPTER TWENTY-NINE

STELLA

It takes me a few minutes to get my breathing under control. When we first entered, the scent was nearly overwhelming—clean, almost floral but not quite. I like it, but the thick, hot steam makes it hard to catch my breath.

"Lie back and breathe through your nose," Beck instructs.

There are long, built-in benches lining all the walls. I'm on the higher level while Beck stretches out below me.

I do as he says and breathe deeply until some of my anxieties loosen their grip. I don't understand what's happening. I told him everything, and he's lying here, the picture of relaxation.

"I can feel you overthinking. Relax and shut everything off for a few minutes."

Rolling onto my side, I glare down. He doesn't open his eyes, but he grins. How did he know I was watching him?

"What are we doing?"

One emerald eye squints at me. Crap. Why did I say anything?

He sits up and spins, sitting on his knees so we're face to

face. I should have kept my mouth shut, but now he stares at me as though I'm the only thing that matters in the world—like laying our truths bare has tied us together, made us one.

"What we're doing..." He reaches up and tucks a damp piece of hair behind my ear. "Is getting you to relax. You've been told so many despicable lies for so long that you believe some of them. I need your body to unwind so we can rewrite some of those pathways sending your brain misinformation."

"I'm messed up, Beck."

"You are." My gaze snaps to his. "So am I." He grins. "So is Tabby. So is Elijah. It's how we fight through the tough times that makes us a survivor to look up to. Stella?" He waits for me to give him my full attention. I blink three times to focus on him. "We can do it together."

Those words actually hurt my heart. The man has never had a relationship and he thinks he's all in now.

Silas called me stupid, and I would be if I believed this.

My face must betray my thoughts because his expression turns dark. "Just because I haven't done something before doesn't mean I can't excel at it, Stella. We need you in our lives. Me, Emmy, and Ruby."

I swallow, the saliva like shards of glass in my throat. "And what happens when you don't need me anymore? What happens when someone more suitable comes along? What happens when the girls no longer need a nanny? What happens when no one needs me anymore?"

He stands and turns a knob on the wall. The steam slows to a stop, then he holds out his hand for me to take it. When I do, he leads me out of the steam room, down a short hallway, and into another room with dim lighting. This one is hot, but it's a dry heat. He motions for me to sit, so I do, hating how the wet sheet clings to me now.

"Nothing I say is going to make a dent for you. You've been programmed to believe that all words are lies."

He paces the room, seeming unbothered by his growing erection, and I can't take my eyes off him. Every indent and curve of muscle moves in a slow dance. His cock twitches and my cheeks burn from more than the heat in this room.

"I can't help it if you stare at it like that," he says in a huff, and it almost makes me laugh. It also makes it impossible not to stare, but my gaze flicks up to his face.

Beck's breathing slows but his nostrils flare with each long intake of air. He stands there, allowing me to gape as his boxers tent, and eventually, the head of his penis pops out, coming to life right in front of me like an X-rated inflatable balloon.

"Finished?" he asks with a sly grin. I drag my gaze up his body and my breath hitches when I reach his face. "Nothing I say will resonate with you. Not until you unlearn all the trauma you've experienced."

That drains some of the heat from my cheeks. "When did you become a shrink?" I mutter. "Don't you think I've tried? I don't know what you're saying—or asking. I just—"

"I'm asking you to try, Stella. To try for real. To try for something I've never once asked for—a relationship. One where you turn to me when you're hurting. One where I ask for help. One where we share our weaknesses as much as our strengths. That's what I'm asking. It doesn't have to be a real engagement."

His brow furrows and he rolls his tongue as though something's distasteful, then he swipes a hand down his face and plasters on a neutral expression.

"It won't be easy," he says. "And we have more fucking mountains to climb than I can even count, but I know." He pounds on his chest with his fist. "I know that we can do it together. I don't know when things changed for me. I don't know when you shook my entire world on end, making all my pieces fit better than they ever have, but you did it. You've changed me, Stella, and I haven't even considered doing that for anyone else. With you, it just happened. I've trusted you from the day you picked me up in Elijah's car, and I haven't trusted anyone in a very long time."

"You're trusting Tabby and Leo with the girls," I remind him.

He lifts his arms to the air like he's frustrated. "And you think I would have been able to do that if it wasn't for you? Let me fill you in on something, sweetheart." My tummy flips at his endearment. "Not once have I had reason not to trust Tabby. Not once in all my life, but she's a Hayes so I couldn't do it. I learned to trust her again by watching you. I saw your body language around Caleb. I saw how you tense when someone makes you uncomfortable. And do you know what you do with Tabby?"

No clue. I shake my head.

"You fucking hug her, Stella. You hug her as if she's your long-lost sister. That's how I know that your body trusts her even if your mind hasn't gotten the memo yet. You're my dowsing rod—you point me to trust. Just by being you, you show me who to let in—and how. So yeah, I trust Tabby and Leo because you trust Tabby and Leo. I do it because I trust you. I need you. I want you. Do you understand now?"

Even after all the crying I've done, I'm sweating profusely, and can't remember the last time I had a drink of water. I should be dehydrated, but nervous energy keeps my body in fight or flight.

"All I'm asking is for you to try, Stella, with me by your side, and you by mine, together."

"Just to clarify," I say, and he rolls his eyes. "You want to try for a real relationship with a fake engagement—with me."

"Yes, to a real relationship, for now on the fake engagement." Blood rushes through my head like a dam breaking, making it hard to hear, but his lips keep moving and I strain to pay attention. "I want to crush anyone and everyone who even attempts to come between us, sweetheart, so yeah, I'm talking about a real relationship. With you," he tacks on at the last minute.

"How? What does that look like to you?"

I swear he growls, but he takes a step back and runs a hand roughly through his hair before spinning on me and binding me in place with his stare.

"What does it look like?" He inhales deeply but never breaks eye contact. "It looks like you in my bed and in my heart. It looks like mistakes and do-overs. It looks like apologies and most of all it looks like love the way it's supposed to be. Honest. Equal. Safe. We both know we have mountains to move before we get there. So it looks like ruining Silas. It looks like crushing Danica and watching Caleb get what he deserves. It looks like giving the girls the stability and love my sister would have given them. It looks like us, Stella. I don't know how else to tell you, so let me prove it. Let me show you with actions because words are meaningless to you, and I understand that now. I know why, so let me try."

He flops down onto the bench next to me. His shoulders rise on an inhale as though he's already fought one battle, but now he's ready to take on the war.

That war is me. The thought smacks against my skull and ribs. It thrashes and sparks. And it gives me the courage I was sure I'd lost.

"Yes," I say. Then square my shoulders and face him head-on. "I want to try—all of that."

"Thank fuck. Now will you lie down and try to relax? People pay thousands of dollars for this experience, and I've never been more stressed out in my goddamn life. Allow me to give you this—I need it, Stella. It's been a long day."

I lean forward and kiss him on the lips. It's not sexual. It's a promise. It's hope. And it might just be love.

His hands cup my face and it's unlike any other touch. He isn't trying to control me, he's not trying to bend me to his will, he simply cradles me like I'm a rare diamond, and the tension between us snaps.

"I need you as much as I want you, you know that, right?" Beck asks as he rises to his knees.

I nod, too entranced to do anything else.

He runs a single finger from the divot in my neck down to the valley between my breasts and the sheet pools at my waist.

The moment turns frantic. One second, we're face-to-face, and the next he's on top of me, letting me see everything he holds dear in his gaze.

The sheet falls away with one rough tug, then he's kissing down my body, stopping every few inches to make sure I'm still okay. But this isn't an exploration—this is a deep dive straight to the treasure. I nod once more and his tongue parts my sex, then his mouth closes over my clit. I instantly throb for him.

He's gentle but thorough, guided by desperation that hits me in my soul. No one has ever learned my body in this way, and a shudder rolls through me.

"Beck," I whimper as he slides two fingers into my pussy.

"I will never tire of hearing my name fall from your lips. You're addicting in the best way." He finger-fucks me with intent and his stiff tongue flicks my clit with the same ferocity.

I'm going to come, and time has barely moved.

I cry out, a loud, guttural sound that echoes off the walls, and Beck responds to it with a growl against my sensitive skin. My orgasm climbs higher.

When my eyes finally open, he's hovering over me, his cock notched at my entrance, waiting for permission to make us one.

"Please," I moan when he shifts his weight so his hardened length rubs over my sensitive nerves. He does it three more times before returning to where I need him most.

"Do you want me?" he asks, but I hear the subtext. Do I want him to fuck me? Do I want him to love me? Do I want him to fight for me? And there can only be one answer.

"Yes. Yes," I cry, and shock myself when I lift my hips, engulfing the tip of his dick with my body.

"When I'm inside you, I feel whole for the first time in my life," he says through gritted teeth. "I didn't want to acknowledge it, but it's true. And I'll fight every demon that comes our way to keep this feeling."

I open my mouth, but words are lost to me when he thrusts hard and deep. All I can do is moan and take everything he gives as he works my body like an extension of his own.

Hard and fast. Slow and deep. He keeps me guessing and unable to catch my breath as he fucks me straight into another orgasm that causes lights to flash, leaving me with gasping breaths and mind numbing-bliss.

I feel him moving over and in me. I hear his voice but not the words. I taste the saltiness of his skin. And I know when he comes by the punishing stab of his penis hitting the deepest part of me before everything stills.

Time holds no meaning as he drops his full weight onto

me. The heat of the room is forgotten as the fire of us together burns everything to the ground.

Eventually, he rests some of his weight onto his forearms, and I'm struck mute as he takes in every inch of my face.

"That was amazing. You're amazing. It was—"

"I blacked out." My eyes are too big for my head and my mouth is unnaturally dry, but he graces me with that crooked grin that settles everything like a magic potion.

"And you're relaxed." He flashes all his perfectly straight teeth.

I laugh, a full, body-shaking laugh that releases my fears if only temporarily.

"I am," I say through spurts of giggles I can't control.

"It makes me happy. Let's get you home. You need sleep, and we have some things to discuss."

He must feel my body tense because he kisses me, hard. "Talking doesn't mean there's anything wrong. It means we're figuring out how to merge our lives so we can both be happy."

Beck stands and offers me his hand. I take it, but he doesn't pull me to stand. He stares at my shoulder, and I leverage his hand to lift myself up. He's taking care of me even when I forget to. My gaze falls to the sheet that clings to the bench like wet plastic wrap.

"It's okay. No one else is here." He leans down to pick up the sheet. "They'll clean up in the morning, but we can toss this," he says with a waggle of his brows. "Not sure what they'd say if they knew the boss fucked his fiancée into oblivion in here."

My jaw nearly comes unhinged.

"I'm kidding." He laughs. "But they do clean everything every morning before they open."

A thought occurs to me that bubbles and swirls like battery acid in my mind. "Have you done this a lot?"

He leads me from the room toward our clothes. "Stella, I told you. I've never done relationships. This is a very relationship-type thing to do, don't ya think? I've never brought a woman here, to my office, to my home, rarely even in my car. Any interaction with them was a release and nothing more."

"That sounds...sad."

He cups my chin, and his expression turns contemplative. "Now that I've experienced this, with us, you're right. It was sad. And I don't want to scare you, but now that I've had this"—he gestures between us—"experienced the magic of us, I'll never be able to go back. So you're stuck with me."

I can't stop the small smile that tugs at my lips.

"That makes you happy," he guesses.

I fling my arms around his waist and rest my head on his damp chest. He returns the embrace with strong arms that were made for protecting and I sink into his warmth.

"It does," I admit without fear or anxiety that he'll use it against me.

He kisses my head and whispers, "Me too, sweetheart. Me too."

CHAPTER THIRTY

BECK

"All set?" I ask when Stella steps into the bedroom from the attached bathroom.

We could have showered at Crystal Waters, but exhaustion set in, and she just wanted to get home. Sailport Bay was too far away, so I brought her to my penthouse in Raleigh since it was closer.

And with her next to me, this place finally feels like a home.

She startles in the doorway. "Yeah, sorry, I didn't see you there. Why are you sitting in the dark?"

I hadn't realized I was. "I was thinking," I say.

She walks to the bed with slow, nervous strides, so I hold out a hand to her and she crawls up next to me.

We sit shoulder to shoulder facing the wall of windows. The lights from the city below twinkle against the glass.

"Why didn't you tell me about your mom?" I keep my tone light. I don't want to sound accusing, but it slips through anyway.

Her shoulder brushes mine when she shrugs.

"I wasn't sure how you'd handle it. From what I'd seen

and heard in the office, you don't do family stuff, and then when I saw you exit Cally's room in Sailport Bay, well, I was afraid you'd fire me. My mom's diagnosis is terminal. I had no way of knowing how you'd process that, and I really need this job. And the truth is, giving you a little information would have spiraled until I had no choice but to tell you about Silas, and that was a shame I couldn't bear."

My eyes prickle as though they're full of sand—it hurts. But her points are valid and what I feared.

"I'm sorry I put you in a position where you felt you couldn't trust me with something so important in your life."

"It's not just you," she whispers. "Trust and fear are hard to separate sometimes."

I bump my body into hers. "We have that in common then."

She nods, but the silence cloaks us both in regret.

"How long does she have?"

"I'm not sure. She still has some good days, but not as many. We could have months or weeks, there's just no way to know." Her voice breaks, and I pull her in close enough for her to rest her head on my chest.

This is where she belongs.

"You're close with her." I guess.

"She was my best friend—sometimes my only friend. She was a single mom, and we were a team. I've always felt like the adult because we couldn't be more different, but she was amazing, Beck. Everything good the world has to offer, and she's lost it all one memory at a time while people like Silas live and breathe cruelty into an already bitter world."

"It's not fair."

She nods against my chest, and I play with the ends of her hair. They're soft as they fall through my fingers, but I'm only stalling now. I'd already come to this decision while she was in the shower.

"Let's bring her home."

Stella's entire body goes rigid, and she holds her breath. I sit quietly until she pushes against me. Her eyes are sad. "What do you mean, 'bring her home'?"

Her amber gaze searches my face, and if I'd had any doubts left, this is the expression that would have obliviated them into the ether.

"Bring her home with us to Sailport Bay. The..." I choke when emotions stick in my throat. "The library is still a functioning hospital room. We can bring her nurse with us or hire a new one."

She's shaking her head and rubbing her temples with her fingertips. "I can't afford to do that."

Taking her hand in mine, I use my thumb to rub small circles on her soft skin, hating the marks that show on her wrists. "I'm offering you a chance to spend time with her every day. Don't you want that for however long she has left?"

"Of course I do." Her words are barely audible. "That's what I was doing, but you gave me a way to pay for Mindful Moments and I took it. You've already done so much. I'm not working three jobs. I'm sleeping. I'm—"

"Sad," I interrupt. "So let me do this for you. Then you won't have to make these long trips and it can be our first step in moving forward—together."

"Can I think about it?"

I shake my head. "Do you trust me?"

"I want to, but—"

"Then accept this gift. We have other obstacles, and my gut says we don't have a lot of time. This is an easy fix. I need you by my side—to be a united front to face down Danica."

"Did something happen?" Her voice goes from terrified to mama bear and I'd be lying if I said it didn't settle over me like a weighted blanket.

"Tabby sent a text message. She's friends with Danica's housekeeper's daughter." I give her a minute for that connection to settle in. "The word is I'll be served with papers this week. We need to prepare for a custody battle because Danica won't play fair even if Cally named me as the girl's guardian—because Danica doesn't give a shit who gets hurt."

Stella's demeanor shifts right before my eyes. The fear and trepidation of a moment ago are replaced with sheer determination and a fire I rarely get to see. And it's sexy as hell.

"She can't get those girls, Beck. She can't."

"She won't," I promise and hope I can keep it. "We'll do whatever we have to in order to make them ours, permanently."

"Ours," she repeats. Things are moving at warp speed, but that's the way things work in my world. They always have. When something's right, failure isn't an option—I don't allow it. And nothing has ever been more right than this. Than us.

"It's a lot, but we can do this," I say.

She's back to nodding.

"Are you hungry?" I ask. We grabbed burgers in the car, but I'm not sure what else she's eaten today.

When she opens her mouth to answer, she's overtaken with a yawn she can't fight.

I stand before she's even finished and pull down the covers.

"I'm not hungry," she says with watery eyes.

She's dressed for bed in one of my undershirts. Does it smell like her or me?

"I love you in my clothes, Stella Jane." Because fuck me. She's gorgeous, and seeing her in nothing but my T-shirt makes something primal roar to life. I feel it in every blood vessel.

She's mine.

"I don't think the same can be said for you," she says while slipping beneath the covers. My shirt rides up her thighs with the movement, and I climb in next to her.

"No, your clothes would not be a good look for me, but you're welcome to borrow mine anytime. Seeing you wear them—it does something to me, Stella. You do something to me. It's how I know this thing between us isn't something we can ignore."

"I'm nervous, Beck." Those three words give life to the dread that's been trying to find life in my heart.

With my nose buried in her hair, I inhale deeply, enjoying the scent of my cedar shampoo on her, and close my eyes. "I know you are, sweetheart. We're at an impasse with a fight in either direction. Things have moved too fast for us to build a stable foundation, so no matter what happens, no matter how hard things get, we have to trust each other. Always and about everything. Without trust, we'll have nothing."

"What if I mess up?"

God, this girl. I hug her more tightly in my arms and silently vow to piece her back together again—and to ruin fuckwad Silas in the process.

"We'll both mess up, but we keep a united front and do our best to fix our mistakes together."

"I don't think I've ever been part of a team before."

A smile that fills my body with warmth spreads across

my face tooth by tooth. "Someone told me recently that I haven't either. But we're not golf or tennis, Stella. We're the reward that comes from a lifetime of fighting for happiness. We're the Super Bowl of life."

Her shoulders shake against my chest. "I said I've never been on a team, but I know sports. You need to work on your sports analogies."

I smack her ass lightly, and she jerks back, pressing her ass into me, and I swallow a groan.

"Sleep, Stella. We both need it, and we should get an early start home tomorrow."

She's quiet while her breathing evens out. I'm about to doze off when she turns in my arms. "Can I ask you something?"

I open one eye. "Always."

"Are the girls okay? I overheard you talking to Tabby, but...I don't know. They've been through so much. I'm just—"

"You're worried," I finish for her. "Damn it, Stella, I should have told you, or let you talk to them yourself. My brain isn't processing all the complexities of these relationships yet. It never occurred to me that you'd be worried, but of course you are. You're you."

"I care about them, Beck, and I get attached easily, I know that, but those little girls have given me a purpose I haven't had in a long time."

"I'm sorry. We're very lucky to have you. The girls are fine. They went right to bed and Tabby has everything under control. Leo grilled hotdogs for dinner, and everyone ate without complaining."

"What's going on between Tabby and Leo?"

I shake my head. "I'm not sure. There's a lot about Sailport Bay I don't know anymore. But if that's where we'll be, I have no doubt we'll figure out Sailport Bay." I kiss her nose. "You can always call to check on the girls, Stella. You don't need my permission. Now sleep."

She kisses me gently, lovingly, casually, as if we've done it for a hundred years, and that familiarity is something I've longed for my entire life and didn't even know it.

CHAPTER THIRTY-ONE

STELLA

BECK'S PHONE RINGS, FOLLOWED IMMEDIATELY BY MINE, AND A second later his front door opens with a crash.

"Beck? Stella?" Elijah calls from somewhere in the apartment, and I feel the mattress shift as Beck stands.

It's a rude way to wake up and I'm struggling to shake the cobwebs from my mind. Too many sounds are hitting me at once. My phone goes to voicemail and rings again with a number I don't recognize. But Beck is already speaking in hushed tones on his phone, so I get to my feet and walk toward the family room.

"Elijah? What's going on?"

He takes in my appearance and a smug sort of appreciation takes over his features.

"Elijah?" I ask again.

"Right, sorry," he says, tugging on his earlobe.

"What's going on?" I peer over my shoulder at Beck's raised voice and my phone rings again in my hand. It's not even five in the morning, and alarm bells make my palms sweaty.

"Google Carolina Counting," Elijah says on his way to the kitchen. Metal and glass clatter while he pulls out coffee grounds from the pantry and starts a pot.

Thank God. I need caffeine, but I do as he asks. Carolina Counting says it's local news for the Carolinas, but truthfully, it's a gossip site similar to Page Six or TMZ for locals, with an occasional political article thrown in on slow days.

I don't even type in the entire name before images fill my screen.

Images of Silas, Beck, and me from last night. I flick through them one after another—shock rendering me immobile as I scroll.

"He set me up." I cover my mouth with my hand when vomit threatens. My heart thrashes and every internal organ shivers and shakes with the first signs of a panic attack. He must have been wearing a camera. When his bloodied face appears in an awkward selfie in the next photo, I know it's true.

"For fuck's sake, Elijah. You couldn't have warned her?" Beck spits while taking the phone from my hands and guiding me to the sofa.

"What's going on?" I choke out as Beck's phone chimes again. He glances at it briefly, his expression so cold I swear the temperature in the room drops twenty degrees. His body twitches as anger consumes him like the moment the superhero learns who killed their parents.

I'm witnessing the physical representation of a man out for revenge, and this time, I'm on his side.

Elijah stands behind us and leans over the back of the sofa, so Beck lifts his phone and we all read the text message.

Unknown Number: I warned you to tread carefully. You just never know who I have at my disposal.

Unknown Number: (Photo Sent)

I gasp at a bloodied photo of Silas. "Who—Who sent that? Did *he* send it to you? Is he threatening you?"

My world spirals. I can't allow him to come after Beck and the girls.

"Not him," Beck says in an icy tone that covers the room in frost. "Danica."

My lips press together, and I tug at my already bruised wrist. "But how—"

"What did you tell Caleb and HR about yourself when they hired you? How did you explain your previous employment?" Elijah asks gently.

It all throat punches me. Caleb knew I left the private school under duress.

"He knew where I worked, but not why I had no references," I reply flatly. I don't know what to feel anymore. "And I only told HR a little more than that."

"What is Silas getting out of this though? Didn't you say he went to extremes to cover his tracks with you?" Beck asks, but it's Elijah who answers him.

"These photos were leaked around midnight. I tried to reach you, but it kept going to voicemail, so I met Teddy at the office, and he found court documents. Silas's wife filed for divorce about a month ago, citing infidelity as the cause, and he's been wiped from the Chelsea Day School website."

Beck stares at him while he processes this information.

"It's not a stretch to assume that Caleb gave Danica the information, which she probably then told his wife," Beck mutters. "Then knowing he had nothing to lose, she went to him with this fucking slaughter campaign." He shakes his head and takes in Elijah's appearance. "You've been in the office since midnight?"

"Teddy texted as soon as he found some information. We've been digging through the mud ever since."

"I owe that fucking kid a raise already," Beck mumbles while I sit mute.

Beck's phone chimes with another picture. This one is of the Currituck County Courthouse.

"She's using this to get custody of the girls." Beck's voice is low but his jaw flexes with every controlled word.

My hand covers my mouth as I shake my head and tuck my feet underneath me. The urge to curl into a ball is over-whelming.

"That's what I thought too," Elijah says, holding out two cups of coffee. Beck and I take them gratefully, but honestly, the events of the last three minutes have given me more of a jolt than caffeine ever would.

Once he's grabbed his own mug, Elijah rounds the sofa and sits in front of us on the coffee table. "So," he says with a grin. Why the hell is he smiling? "Here's what I'm thinking. You two started dating after the office party last spring."

Beck sets down his coffee and leans forward, resting his forearms on his thighs. "And?" he encourages.

"Stella's my friend and attended the party as my guest. That would mean you were already an item before Caleb's assistant quit and I tossed her name into the hat. You were never even involved in the hiring process, Beck. All our paperwork shows she was hired by HR and approved by Caleb. And we don't have a fraternization policy, so you didn't break any rules."

"That would mean we've been together for close to a year," Beck mumbles.

My gaze ping-pongs between these two men who are rewriting our history.

Beck catches me watching and winks. "Teamwork, Stella Jane. It's not so bad after all."

And he's right. It's not. For the first time in my adult life, I'm part of something real. Something good.

"Welcome to the club, Stella. Lottie's going to flip."

Beck and I both swing our slack-jawed stares to him. "What?"

"Elijah," Beck asks, reclining on the sofa, "how do you know Lottie, and how are you connected to the hotline?"

"Easy," he leans back on his hands with sparkling eyes. "Lottie's my sister."

"Charlie?" Beck asks.

Elijah laughs. "Yeah, she stopped insisting we call her Charlie when she was about fourteen. She's Lottie now, and I'm helping her stick it to our father by using his clients for her business."

"What?" Beck and I both ask.

"Yup, you two were just a bonus, but we'll discuss that later. Right now, you both need to be on the same page. So you've been together for a year and kept it private for obvious reasons. But now you're taking it to the next level." He reaches into his pocket and hands Beck a small velvet box. "So it doesn't need to be kept a secret anymore. Of course, since I'm best friends with both of you, I've known all along. Stella's mom knows." He frowns and corrects himself. "Knew, but since neither of you have other friends, that's where it stopped. And now—"

"Now we're getting married," Beck finishes.

"Yes." Elijah claps. "Will I be the best man or the man of honor?" He hands us both a file. "This is everything you would have learned about each other in the last year. Memorize it."

I set down my coffee to open the folder and it's everything from Beck's middle name—Heath—to allergies—cats. Beck does the same thing and I peer over his shoulder.

My nose scrunches up and I glare at Elijah. "How do you know my feet are always cold?"

Beck's hand slips to my feet, testing Elijah's assertion, and he finds that Elijah's right.

"That's easy," Elijah says, clasping his hands and standing. "You put a heater under your desk. You always put on fuzzy socks when you think no one's around, and you sit with them under you when your heater and socks are not an option."

I am currently sitting on my feet. Geez! "You're better than the CIA," I mutter.

"Not quite, but we've got this. That bitch crossed the wrong team."

Beck's shoulders fall away from his ears and he holds up the folder. "She did. Thank you for this. And this," he says, turning the jewelry box in his palm.

"That's it for me, kids. Call me when you get home. I've got the office handled, and I've started the search for buildings near Sailport Bay. I'll forward them when I have all the options rounded up."

Not for the first time, I wonder about Elijah's background. He's polished, like Beck, but there's something a little reckless in him too.

Elijah leans down to hug Beck, then me, and he whispers in my ear. "You look good, sweetie. Trust the process. We've got your back."

"Thanks, Elijah. For everything." I don't know if anyone

has had more of an impact on my life than this quirky man, and for that, I'll forever be indebted.

He turns to Beck. "When do you want Laura to arrive?"

"What? How? When?" When the hell did he tell Elijah about my mom?

Beck turns to me with questions in his eyes and shrugs. "When do you want it to happen?"

"Beck. The custody case, and whatever it is Silas hopes to achieve—do you really think now is a good time?" My heart races.

"No," he answers honestly. "But we don't have the luxury of time, either. So we should bring her home to you—to us —as soon as we can, and we'll take the hits as they come. Nothing will be easy for a while, but I can make this easier for you. Having her with us will bring you the smallest sliver of peace."

My lower lip trembles. "Th—thank you. Thank you both."

"As soon as the facility can arrange it," Beck says without taking his gaze off me. "What about the nurse?"

I stare at Beck. "If Lucía will come, I'd like her. She's been with my mom the longest, and she's—she's important to me too."

He turns back to Elijah. "Make it happen."

Elijah salutes us with two fingers and turns on his heel.

The penthouse falls into an unsettling silence when he leaves. Beck and I both know the gauntlet has been thrown, and it's up to us to pick it up for the sake of the girls, and maybe for ourselves too.

He turns to me and lowers himself to the floor in front of me. "The timing isn't ideal, but maybe that's our thing, huh?" His cheeks are pink, and it's so damn attractive I bite my lip to keep from kissing him. "It's okay if this isn't what you envisioned for yourself, but I designed it with you in mind, so I kind of hope you like it. It doesn't have to be real —for now." His brow furrows, but he continues. "But while we navigate what's real, I ask that you keep an open mind because who knows what the future will bring, right? So, Stella Jane, will you wear this ring that ties you to me and me to you?"

It's not a marriage proposal. Not really, but it is an open door to the possibility of forever, and it couldn't be more perfect.

I know it's not real. I heard him say it, but I can't stop my heart from fluttering wildly in my chest or my hands from shaking. "Yes. I will," I choke out.

Beck stands and kisses my cheek, then slips the most beautiful ring I've ever seen onto my finger—it'll never be green again. It's round with two delicate rows of tiny diamonds around the center stone. It sparkles and shoots rainbows everywhere the light hits it.

My hand shakes as I hold it out, unable to stop staring. The band is two thin rings of platinum that twine around my finger in an infinity symbol and is encrusted with even more diamonds.

"What do you think?" Beck asks shyly. "Because I'll be honest, this is not something I ever envisioned doing, but when I sat down with the jeweler, I just knew this was what I wanted for you."

I can't get enough air into my lungs, so my words sound stilted, but happy. "Geez, Beck. How could I not? It's beautiful. I couldn't have picked anything more perfect myself."

"Good. Every detail from the most precious gem to the infinity band that binds your finger reminded me of you—of forever."

Happiness makes my cheeks hurt, but before he can say anything else, our phones interrupt the precious moment.

He takes my hand in his. "This is only the beginning of the madness. But we'll get through it."

"Together," I say, and this time I try to believe it with my whole heart.

CHAPTER THIRTY-TWO

BECK

It's the girls' naptime when I get off the phone with our new family law attorney. He's the best and worth every dollar it costs to fly him in from Charlotte. I walk straight to Laura's room, sure that's where I'll find Stella.

She sits beside her mother, holding her hand and speaking in hushed tones, so I lean against the doorframe and observe them.

In some messed-up way, it helps me work through the guilt and grief of knowing my sister was in this very position not that long ago—without me.

Bringing Laura here was the right move, but it's been an exhausting few days.

The baby monitor lights up when Ruby cries for five seconds, then rolls over and goes back to sleep, but the disruption causes Stella to raise her head and she meets my gaze.

Her smile is sad, and I hate everything about it because she's experiencing a hurt that has no cure. I can't fix this.

"Hey," I say, entering the room. "Hi, Laura. It's me, Beck."

I lean down and kiss the side of the old woman's head. It's awkward, but Stella talks to her, so I do too.

It's these moments when flashbacks of my mom and visions of Cally choke me the most.

"Hello," she says.

I sit in the seat next to Stella.

"What did the lawyer say?" Stella asks.

I close my eyes briefly, trying to gather my thoughts, but I'm too tense to focus. "Danica requested an emergency hearing, saying she was scared for the girls' safety."

Her beautiful face crumbles. "It's my fault."

"Don't do that. No one is to blame here except for Danica. Do not bear the weight of someone else's poor choices. We need to stay focused on what matters."

She nods and bites the inside of her cheek, then sits up taller. "You're right. When is the hearing?"

"Tomorrow." That one word sounds bitter, but it's really hiding my fear. My head is still a mess. I'm angry at my sister, and I love her. Every emotion I experience where my sister is concerned is followed by another one that contradicts it.

"What did the lawyer say?"

I'd wanted her in the meeting with me, but naptime is when Lucía takes a break, so Stella sits in here with her mom. We have another nurse who does the overnights, but she's usually gone by the time we wake up.

It's amazing really, that in just a few short days we've all fallen into a schedule that works. Well, as well as any schedule can work with kids this age, I guess.

"We'll give more statements, prove it was self-defense. Lucía signed hers before she left the clinic, and that will help. But honestly, it's going to depend on who we get for a judge. I have no doubt what Danica says is true—she does have some judges in her back pocket, but not all of them. That's what we're hoping for, that we get one she can't bribe or blackmail."

I shift in my seat so my knee rests between her thighs as we face each other.

"I'm scared," I admit. "I've wondered if the worst happens if I'll have the guts to run with the girls. How insane is that?"

"It's not, Beck. You love them, and you know how she'll treat them, so your mind is running through every worst-case scenario to keep them safe."

The doorbell rings and we both look to the side like we can see the door from here. Our cheeks nearly touch, and I inhale deeply. Her apple scent calms my racing heart.

The sound of Daisie racing through the house makes me cringe. She's going to break at least one thing before she reaches the door, and sure enough, there's a small crash before she barks at the front of the house.

Is it weird that I'm learning her barks? That's a happy one. Whoever's at the door, Daisie wants to lick.

"Are you expecting company?" I ask.

"No," she says with a heavy exhale. "Would the media show up on the doorstep?"

It's a reasonable question considering what Carolina Counting has been publishing. I don't know how celebrities deal with this shit. There are other wealthy families that garner much more attention than this, but it's never been mine.

I've always been too boring. I've never been photographed with a date, never had a wild child stage. I've been focused, so perhaps that's the appeal now.

"I don't think anyone would be stupid enough to show

up, and Daisie sounds happy with whoever it is, but stay here just in case. I'll get it."

She nods, and I kiss her forehead, then stand and warily walk to the front of the house.

"You've got to be shitting me," I mumble, stopping a foot from the front door.

"What is it?" Stella asks, sticking her head out of the doorway.

"Not today," I groan. I'm standing in the entryway while Oliver Shines waves with his entire body and a grin too big for his face through the glass. He hasn't changed at all since I was a kid.

Stella's footsteps pitter-patter against the hardwood floors. "Oh...huh? What's going on?"

I pinch the bridge of my nose, then kick the basket of shoes that Daisie knocked over out of the way. "It's the welcoming committee."

"I thought they did that with the parade," she says.

"They did. This will be the sand dance."

She bites the inside of her cheek. She's been doing it more lately, especially when she's nervous.

"Steel yourself, Stella. You're about to get a proper Sailport Bay welcome."

It's the worst possible timing for this, but if I say no, they'll just set up on the beach anyway since it's technically not private.

Rolling my shoulders, and with Stella's palm between my shoulder blades urging me on, I open the door, holding Daisie by her collar.

Music hits us first. No one knows that Oliver's radio program has been a secret addiction I allowed when I was truly at my lowest. It was the safest piece of home I could keep and still move on. But seeing him now, in my home, is a minor celebrity moment for me, and it's all I can do to rein myself in.

It's the least Becker Hayes thing I've ever indulged in.

"Becker Hayes, look at yourself," Oliver says with a slow Southern drawl. He enters the house and I'm immediately engulfed in a hug while Daisie jumps and wiggles, attempting to get free. "It's been too long, son. We're happy to have you home. And this must be the beautiful Stella Anderson I've heard so much about."

Stella cringes. "I hope you don't believe everything you read," she says demurely. I straddle Daisie and hold her with my legs and the collar.

"Oh, for heaven's sake. No! We don't believe any of that trash that girl is dreaming up."

This catches my attention. There's no mention of Danica in any of those articles and my forehead pinches in confusion.

Finally, he turns and gives Daisie the attention she wants. After a thirty-second head rub, the damn dog settles down.

"Daisie, go watch the girls," I command. She tilts her head, looks at Oliver, then takes her sweet-ass time waltzing up the stairs. She'll nose her way into Emmy's room and stay there until she wakes up.

"Don't be fooled, Stella," Oliver says while waving people down to the beach. "We've known that girl since she was a child, and it's no secret she's taking you to court for custody of Cally's babies." He cups his hand around his mouth like he's telling a secret. "Benny Johnson works in the town clerk's office, and he told Wanda who told me about the paperwork she filed. She's truly a piece of work, that one."

He walks farther into the house. "Anyway, that's why

we're here. To show our support with an old-fashioned sand dance."

"What's a sand dance?" Stella asks, moving quickly to shut the door to her mother's room.

"Oh, Stella. We heard all about your mama too. If there's anything we can do to support either of you, just say the word. We have a town-wide help network. All it takes is one phone call to get the ball rolling and before you know it meals, groceries, even books can be delivered in a flash."

"How did you—"

"I had the pleasure of running into Lucía at the market yesterday. It's still too early for tourists, so I latched onto her quickly and learned we had two new residents. She. Is. Lovely."

"She is," Stella agrees but watches me wearily.

Neither of us have the energy for this today, but I know they have our best interests at heart.

"So," Oliver says in his smooth radio host voice. "A sand dance is similar to a barn dance, but at the beach." He walks her to the kitchen and the wall of windows facing the ocean. "There's nothing like Carolina barbecue. Don't go tellin' me you're one of those veggie eaters because Ray-Ray brought over a pig he's been roasting for close to twelve hours."

Stepping behind Stella, I relax when eighty-year-old Ray-Ray starts barking orders at the younger generations to get his pig in place.

A strange mix of sadness, relief, and love fills me as this all unfolds. These used to be better than Christmas for me. Before my mom passed, she was one of the food pushers, so we were always the first to arrive, and she made it feel like a privilege to be the first to learn about the new families, new babies, or say our condolences before anyone else. It's one of the only clear memories I have with her outside of the house.

"I thought you'd enjoy this," Oliver says from my left. My throat is dry, but the grin I'm wearing is so damn right. "Sometimes we have to run away from home to find out that everything we ever needed was here waiting for us." He pats me on the shoulder and opens the back door. "Join us when you're ready. Don't forget the sunscreen on those babies. It may not be summer, but that sun will still go strong for a couple more hours."

Stella and I stand in place as he walks through the yard to the party unfolding before our eyes on the beach.

"What is this place?" Stella whispers with a hint of awe in her tone.

That's a great question.

"This place is where hearts are mended," I say, remembering one of my mother's favorite sayings.

Stella doesn't speak, but she places her head on my chest and holds me tight. The fear she's holding in seeps through tiny tremors released with every breath.

"Thank you, Stella. Thank you for entering the madness with me. Thank you for being on my side."

"I feel like I should be thanking you," she whispers. But she couldn't be more wrong. Because of her, I'll never want to be alone again.

"Let's go get the girls ready. It'll be a long afternoon," I say with my chin resting on her head. It's already late afternoon, but these people will keep the party going well into the evening.

She nods and detaches herself from our embrace. "Anyone I should be aware of out there?"

"They're good people, if not a little wacky. I think that happens when your town goes from a hundred thousand people in the summer down to less than fifteen hundred in the off-season."

More people walk along the side of the house and wave when they see us in the window.

"How do they know to come?" she asks.

"The grapevine is more powerful than Wi-Fi."

Her brows wing up.

"I'm serious. This town is better than the musketeers—they never leave a man behind."

"That's...going to take some getting used to."

Ruby chooses that moment to announce that she's awake, so I take Stella by the hand and, with a final glance over my shoulder, we go get our girls.

"Emmy's in heaven," I say, taking a seat in the sand next to Stella. Emmy's dancing in the center of a circle filled with townspeople I haven't seen in years. The sun is setting on the horizon, but the party is in full swing.

"She's very comfortable," Stella agrees. Ruby sits between her legs, sometimes throwing sand and sometimes eating it. It's fucking disgusting.

"They did this every week in Cally's last few months," Leo says, flopping down beside us.

"They did?" The words hurt like fresh sandpaper on sensitive skin.

"Yup. Tonight is as much for her as it is for you. This town still loves you, Beck. They always have. You're home-grown, as they say."

I chuckle, but it's halfhearted.

"Just remember to lean on us when things get tough. You've always tried to do everything yourself, but the girls need this. They need the community. And they need you, so every person here supports you."

"So much for town loyalty," Danica calls from somewhere behind me.

My spine stiffens like a zipper.

"I guess that Hayes name will always equate to royalty for the dimwitted." She gets closer with every word, and the crowd grows silent. She's a hurricane rolling in and people don't know where to hide—they're in the path of destruction wherever they go.

Leo and I are on our feet before she gets too close, but I keep a hand on Stella's shoulder to keep her where she is and take the strength she offers at my side.

"Beck," Stella hisses. "Let me go so I can get Emmy."

Shit. Emmy. God, I love this woman. Her priority is always the girls. I scan the crowd to find Daisie blocking Emmy's path.

I release Stella's shoulder and she stands with Ruby in her arms.

"Yes, please allow a woman of questionable moral integrity to get my niece."

Stella doesn't take the bait. Instead, she makes a beeline for Emmy and shows her strength when she hauls the little girl up one-handed while pressing Ruby into her other side. She stands with a girl on each hip, silently daring anyone to take them from her, but I saw the flash of pain when she lifted Emmy—her shoulder isn't completely healed.

Danica slides around me and heads straight for them.

"Come on, Emmy. Come to your auntie. Your *real* family." She places her hands on the little girl's torso and Stella tries to swing her away, but Danica latches onto the child's arm and attempts to rip her from Stella's hold. Daisie goes insane, but Danica doesn't let go—she's sending a message, and I'm sure it's the only reason she's here.

A local teenage boy grabs Daisie's collar and holds her back. He's probably worried she'll bite Danica, but would that be so bad?

Emmy's cry is pure terror. "No. No," she screams. "Not her. Not her. Daddy."

The air whooshes and distorts everything around me as I process her words.

"Daddy," she cries out and my feet are moving before I register the action. Her little eyes find me in the bonfire light. She's terrified, and she needs me. She reaches for me out of desperation and fear. The expression on her face has me ignoring the dangers as I hurdle flames and driftwood to get to her sooner just as Daisie breaks free.

I step between Stella and Danica. Stella's arms shake from the effort of holding both girls, so I take Emmy. She clings to my chest as though she's trying to crawl inside me, and Daisie advances on Danica in a slow prowl.

"Shh, it's okay, lovebug. I've got you." With Emmy tucked into my side, I turn on Danica.

"What are you doing here? Are you trying to traumatize them more than you already have?"

She takes a step closer and lowers her voice but freezes when Daisie growls. "I gave you the option of doing this the easy way, Becker. It's not my fault if they get hurt because of your poor decisions."

Emmy whimpers and her little nails dig into my shoulders. Why is she so scared of her?

Danica raises her voice. She's putting on a show. "It's so sad that you're turning my family against me, Becker. They're all I have left."

Thank God she's a terrible actress.

"Danica, why are you here?" Leo asks, stepping in front of me and pushing me back with his ass, and then Tabby steps to his side, creating a human wall. They're joined by Oliver and even Wanda is heading this way, so I grab Daisie by the collar and haul her back into our family circle.

The laugh that comes from Danica makes Emmy tremble in my arms. "It's a sand party," she hisses. "All are welcome."

"You've made your point, and now you should leave." Leo, for all his surfer-dude, yogi-loving personality, is another defender right now. There's a warning in his tone that not even I would fuck with.

Wanda takes up her position next to Oliver with a tsking sound that drowns out the whispers and waves. She keeps her back to Danica and addresses Stella and me. "It's been a good night, kids. You know, a storm's rolling in. Maybe it's time to take those angels inside while we handle the..." Her lips purse into a thin line. "Flotsam," she finishes. "We'll see you tomorrow. And don't worry, we've got your back."

I take Stella's hand in mine and actively focus to keep my grip light. "Daisie, come."

"What did she do to turn an entire town against her?" Stella whispers when we reach the patio.

"I'm not sure," I reply honestly. "But my gut says it has everything to do with my sister."

And if it does, I'll do more than ruin her career. I'll bury her.

When we get upstairs, I sit Emmy on the edge of her bed. Daisie jumps up and lies down beside her. "Lovebug, can you tell me why you're so scared of Aunt Danica? Did she hurt you?" The lump in my throat makes it hard to speak. I won't be able to handle it if she's hurt this little girl in any way.

Emmy's eyes well with unshed tears and her little chin quivers. The sensation that washes over me at the sight makes my fists clench. I've never once felt such all-consuming love as I do now. I would lay down my life to take away her pain.

Somewhere, somehow, that protective instinct has ingrained itself in my DNA for my girls—all my girls.

If this is what happens when you become a father, how could Davis have ever continued risking his life with shitty adrenaline-rush activities?

"She was mean to Mommy," Emmy whispers, and her tears break free. "She hurt Mommy. Mommy cwied when she was here." Daisie's whine is as heartbreaking as Emmy's tears.

"Emmy, honey. Do you know why your mommy cried?" Stella stands in the doorway, listening on with sadness surrounding her like a raincloud. She must have skipped Ruby's bath tonight.

"No," Emmy says, and any hope I had fizzles out.

What did she do, Cally? Her note about shining bright has been niggling a memory I can't quite recall, but I'm beginning to believe that whatever the clue is, it has everything to do with Danica.

"It's okay, Emmy. Stella and I will never let anything hurt you, I promise." Even before the words leave my mouth, I cross all my fingers behind my back and pray that Danica won't make a liar out of me.

CHAPTER THIRTY-THREE

STELLA

BECK AND I ENTER THE COURTROOM HAND IN HAND, BUT HE stays one step ahead of me—it's become his thing ever since he found Silas cornering me. He stands one step ahead, not because he thinks he's better than me, but because he's ready at a moment's notice to throw himself into the fire for me and the girls.

He's on high alert and his instinct is to protect us. That's not something I've ever had before and that one small gesture, more than anything else, tells me that he believes I'm lovable.

It's a rude awakening to be almost thirty and realize you've never truly felt one hundred percent safe a day in your life.

I hope Emmy and Ruby feel safe with Leo and Tabby today.

I'm lost in thought so when Beck stops short, I faceplant into his back, then take in our surroundings for the first time.

Danica sits at a table with an older man. I almost run when Silas turns a sneer my way behind her. With his face still covered in bruises, it makes it easier to maintain my strength and independence though—he's not unbeatable.

"What are you all doing here?" Beck whispers, and I peer around his large frame to the other set of benches.

"I told you, son," Oliver says with a wink. Half of Sailport Bay is sitting on our side of the courtroom. "We have your back."

Holy crap. They showed up for him. I can't even begin to imagine what that kind of support feels like.

"And you too, Stella. We've seen you with those girls. If they can't have their mother, I'm sure glad they have you," Oliver says with a watery smile.

His words make me lightheaded. I never set out to be an adoptive mom, and I thought the last few years stole my dreams of motherhood from my heart—I didn't think it was in the cards for me anymore. Not when my own mother's mind is slowly dying before my very eyes, and I've never been able to provide a stable home, even for myself.

Now I'm in a courtroom and I have no idea who they'll declare the bad guy—us or Danica. I blink back fears, but I'm too tired to do much else. There's too much going on all the time.

Beck tucks me into his side, lending me his strength and pulling me back from the brink of my breaking point.

"Where's Caleb?" I ask.

"That's a different court case, sweetheart," Beck whispers, searching my face. I don't know why I didn't think to ask these questions beforehand. "And Caleb only thinks Teddy found one fraudulent case, so Danica believes that too. They don't know what's coming for them yet, and they won't until we have a solid case. Today is just about the girls. Okay?"

I nod, but it's difficult to breathe in here.

"Of all the judges we could have gotten, this is the best option." Beck's attorney is speaking in hushed tones as we approach our side of the room. "He's known to be fair. His son is a single parent, and he has a penchant for calling out people like a human lie detector."

"All rise," someone calls from the front of the room, and it becomes an out-of-body experience. I see it all happening, but I don't feel it. I hear what everyone says, but I'm not really a part of it.

Beck has been casting worried glances my way since we sat down, probably because I can't hide the sadness in my eyes, even as I sit stone-faced. I am sad. And angry, and so fucking confused my heart aches with each beat hitting harder until the sound of it is a dull roar in my ears.

I sit through Danica's lies, and Silas's fabricated version of events where they paint me as an unstable monster, and Beck as a violent abuser. But when it's Beck's turn, he's as honest as he can be when he tells the room why he left and why he was not in contact with Cally when she died. It's heartbreaking.

"I also love Emmy's bedhead in the morning," he says, his voice resonating with conviction and command. "And the way Ruby smells after a nap. I love how they run to Stella's arms for comfort, and that she gives it freely any time they need it, sometimes before they even realize they need it."

The judge is nodding, but his expression hasn't changed once.

"My family dynamic has been messed up for the last few years, your honor. But I loved my sister and I love those girls in a way I'd forgotten was possible. They've changed me. I want to be their protector and the one who checks their closets for monsters." His glassy eyes peer down at me, and his crooked smile rights my world. "I want to watch them grow up and pick fights with me when they're teenagers, and I don't care about their inheritance. I don't care if they get it or not, I will always provide for them. Just, please don't take them from their home—or from us."

Beck falls into his chair, and Danica's scoff echoes off the walls.

"Does anyone have anything else to add?" The judge stares straight ahead, and the silence calls to me. I'm compelled to say something, anything, because regardless of how fast things move, these little girls deserve a family who loves them exactly as they are, so I raise my hand.

The movement is tentative and awkward, demonstrating to everyone that I don't really know if I want to be called on. But the judge's eyes crinkle at the corners and he gives a solid nod, then a roll of his hand for me to speak.

I stand on shaky legs and will my stomach to hold still while I find my words.

"Have you ever been in love with someone so completely that you were blind to their flaws? Or been so completely consumed by love that you forgot who you are, and that love isn't supposed to come with conditions until it's too late?"

"Your honor," Danica's attorney interrupts, making me jump.

Beck reaches out and squeezes my lower thigh, and I stop fidgeting with my hands.

"Let her speak," the judge says. "There have been a lot of accusations today, I'd like to see where she's going with this.

Me too, judge. Me too. I don't look at Beck. If I do, I'll lose my nerve. Instead, I stare straight at the judge and tell my story.

"I know this is a custody hearing, but my character has been called into question, and my character matters since I care for and love those little girls. I've never been able to defend myself, but I'll do anything for them."

He nods, and I continue. "I was lied to for so long I believed the lies." I chuckle and clasp my hands tightly in front of me. "I believed someone else's version of myself, a broken version that couldn't function without the occasional kindness from an otherwise cruel man. When my story was twisted around, turning me into the villain, I broke in ways I didn't know a person could break. I've never felt so alone or scared in my entire life. Everything and everyone I loved was leaving me."

The air is thick with tension, but the judge's face relaxes, and his eyes stay glued to mine, like he's offering encouragement.

"I didn't know where I belonged. Then I met Beck, and you should know, he was a terrible team player right from the start." The crowd chuckles behind me and my shoulders relax. "He strived to do everything on his own while I was doing everything I could to feel needed. It gave me validation and him a false sense of safety. Neither of us asked for help because we viewed it as a weakness. Even when our connection was so strong that neither of us could walk away, we still couldn't fully find a way to rely on each other."

The judge nods, and I hear sniffling in the peanut gallery while Beck shifts uncomfortably in his chair.

"Then Beck became the girls' guardian, and something snapped into place for us both. I found where I was wanted more than I was needed, and he found that being part of a team is what makes you stronger. The four of us were broken, Your Honor. We've had unthinkable heartaches and tragedies."

An image of my mom flashes in my mind and I swallow hard.

"But through all the pain, we found love. Love for each other and love for our girls. I've made mistakes. Silas was my worst, and I truly feel for his family, but I was not a willing accomplice in his games. I've lost myself more than any one person should be allowed, but I found myself with this family. I'm not a bad person, I'm simply a person who made mistakes that I've paid for. There are always two sides to every story, and this is mine."

Finally, I glance down and draw strength from Beck's steady gaze. "Your Honor, I love Emmy and Ruby. I couldn't love them more if they were my own flesh and blood. And I love their uncle, even when it's hard. Especially when it's hard because as much as he needs me, he wants me more, and the same goes for those girls. Life is so stinking hard, but when the four of us are together, it's a little more tolerable, and it's filled with more love than I could have ever asked for."

Something drips onto my hand, and I touch my fingers to my face. I'm crying and never realized it.

I snap my mouth shut and drop into my chair. That was draining. Every inch of my body is exhausted from years of running from myself.

Beck leans into my space, cups my face and kisses my forehead. "Thank you, Stella. You didn't have to tell everyone your secrets, but I can't tell you how much I love that you did."

The jury is still out on what I think about it though. I feel myself slipping. Is this just my life? Will I always feel like I'm falling?

I glance at Beck, but his attention is focused on the judge. He must sense that I'm off though because his hand slips under the table and holds mine in my lap.

Maybe he is my safety net. Across the room, Silas is

glaring at me with unadulterated hatred in his eyes. I thought he was my safety net once too.

How do I trust myself now? How do I trust my judgment?

Beck leans in and whispers, "I'm not him, Stella. I see your fears dancing back and forth between us, so if that's what's making you squeeze the blood from my fingers, you can stop now. I'm not him."

I release my hold on him, horrified to find his fingers white and the skin creased from my grip. He's quick to reposition our hands though, and this time he holds on for dear life. My mind is messed up and confused, but Mom always told me happiness and love are a choice. You can't control who you fall in love with, but the decision to stay through the good times and bad is a choice, just as happiness is a choice we make for ourselves.

It's time I started making some choices for myself.

The sound of a gavel against wood grabs my attention as Danica spews venom at her lawyer.

"File something, you fucking moron. Whatever it takes, and get me one of my judges. This is unacceptable. He cannot have those girls, they're *my* family."

We won? The judge chose us? Beck's gaze is already on me when I glance up. Does he sense how confused I am?

"We won?"

His face breaks into a smile. "We did. I'm their legal guardian, at least until the actual custody hearing next month." His brow furrows. "Stella, are you okay?"

I nod a little too aggressively, and he bends closer to study my face. "Are you okay?" he asks again.

"Yes, it's just—"

"It's a lot. You've been through a lot, but don't check out on me, okay? Promise me that you'll talk to me. You've got me on your team now, Stella. I don't know what I'll do if I get cut."

Oof. I know he doesn't mean that as a guilt trip, but dang, it hits like one anyway.

"I will." My breath comes out in a whoosh when he tugs me in for a crushing hug.

"Well done, kids. Very well done." Oliver pats Beck on the shoulder as he exits his row.

"Stella?" A woman I've never seen before approaches us nervously. She's soft-spoken and the only word that comes to mind when I look at her is gentle, from her slightly lowered head to her shoulders that seem to get smaller with each step.

"Yes?" I reply when she stops in front of me. Beck looms behind me and her gaze jumps from him to me multiple times. "Is there something I can do for you?"

"No, no, nothing like that. It's just..." She stares at Beck again. Who is this woman? "I was friends with Cally. My name is Bella Moonbeam, and I wanted you to know that I think she would have loved you."

Beck's heavy hands rest on my shoulders.

"Y—You do?" I ask, stumbling over my words.

"I do," she says with more confidence. "And she asked me to tell you something," she says to Beck.

His fingers tighten, digging into my skin. "What?" His voice is gruff and low as if he's in pain and grunting through it, like when you get a charley horse in the middle of a meeting.

"She wanted you to know she loved you."

Beck says nothing.

"And that she hopes you'll, sorry, hold on. She was very specific about this part." Bella reaches into a bag that probably weighs more than she does and comes up with a small notebook. It's a few more seconds of her flipping through the pages.

"Here." She takes a deep breath. "She hopes you'll give her girls a childhood that storybooks are made of. Help them shine bright, write their own stories, and never allow them to believe, even for a second, that they aren't loved. Help them shoot for the stars and always be their safe place to fall like—like she was once for you."

"Shine bright? Again?" Beck mutters, but his expression looks far away.

"Thank you, Bella," I say. "You were close with Cally?"

She nods sadly. "She helped me fit in when I first moved here. She did everything for everyone, and she's really missed. *I* really miss her."

Maybe Cally and I had more in common than I'd realized. A tear falls from Bella's left eye, and Beck clears his throat.

"Thank you, Bella." He isn't terse, but the air around him has changed. "Thank you for being a good friend to my sister. Did she have any—eh—other messages?"

"No." She glances at her feet. "But could you tell the girls I miss them? I used to come over on Mondays and Wednesdays to play with them. The lawyer picked them up before I had a chance to say goodbye, and dropping by unannounced made my knees shake so hard I couldn't do it. I'm, ah, not great with crowds." She glances around nervously. "Or new people."

I glance up at Beck to get his take, but his lips are moving with no sound. Whatever's bothering him has taken over his mind for the moment. "I bet the girls would love it if you came over and told them yourself. How about on Wednesday?"

The woman absolutely beams. "Cally would have really loved you," she whispers before stepping away.

"I'm sorry I never met her. Thank you...for letting us know...everything."

She nods and is gone a second later.

"Are you ready?" I ask Beck.

He smiles down at me, but it's troubled. "Yeah, sweetheart. Let's go home." He leads me out of the courthouse in silence and doesn't speak until we're in the car.

"Cally was trying to tell me something. First in the letter, and then here. Something about stars shining bright, but I can't make sense of it."

I take his hand in mine and lift it to my lips. "We'll figure it out."

His gaze softens when it lands on me. "We will," he agrees. "I just hope we're not too late. There's no doubt in my mind Danica will take the house the first chance she gets, and I have no way to stop it."

"I know it holds memories, Beck. But a house is just that, a house. It's the people you love who make it a home."

As soon as the words leave my mouth something unlocks in my chest and it's as though I'm taking a full breath after spending too long underwater.

I've spent a lifetime trying to feel safe in a home built of glass. But it was never the home that made me feel unsafe. It was the instability. Whatever happens, Ruby and Emmy will never have to move every other month or worry about where their next meal will come from. It's not the same.

Beck leans forward and his lips meet mine in a kiss meant for comfort. Our breaths mingle, and whatever we have here in this bubble settles the runaway fuse that sparked through my body searching for an explosion earlier.

His forehead rests against mine, and he cups my neck tenderly with one hand. He's holding me to him, but he's also holding on to me like a lifeline for us both, and I recognize that in him now. "We will make wherever we are home, Stella. We have to."

"Let's go do something fun with the girls this afternoon," I suggest. "Tabby's probably ready to bake something by now."

His chuckle fills the car as he starts it. Before he pulls out of the parking lot, he turns to me. "One battle down, a few more to go."

Together, Stella, together. I chant that mantra the entire way home. We will do this together. He flashes me that crooked grin that melts my heart. If this is me falling into another bad situation, I'm too far gone to stop it even if I wanted to.

"We've got this," I finally say.

He holds my hand the entire way home. Not for show, not because he had to, simply because he wanted to. These are the moments to remember—these are the moments that tell me this is real.

I just hope Silas hasn't messed me up so much that I won't be able to keep it.

CHAPTER THIRTY-FOUR

BECK

"It's time to bring in a forensic accountant," I tell Elijah over video chat. "Teddy is a wonder kid, and I appreciate the hell out of him, but we're hitting too many dead ends and we're running out of time. How does someone his age get as far as he did anyway?"

Elijah laughs. "He also has a master's degree in accounting. And he told me the same thing this morning."

"Damn. Is he willing to move too?"

Elijah has located multiple building options within a thirty-mile radius of my childhood house. The commute will suck, but moving my headquarters is the only option now. My priorities have shifted. Keeping the girls in Sailport Bay is a necessity. It's home to them, and that means making some pretty substantial changes, at least for now. I'm still fully committed to my company, but my family comes first.

My family. The words cause a brain freeze. Never in a million years did I expect those words to rattle around my mind and not cause a tidal wave of hurt.

"He might be. He's going through a bad breakup," he says.

"Hmm. That sucks."

"I'll have a list of people willing to relocate by next week and then we can start the hiring process after we secure a building."

"That's great. Thanks, Elijah. Make sure you mention the moving stipend."

"I did." The damn guy leans toward the camera, resting his chin in his palm with a huge-ass grin on his face while I shift uncomfortably. He always knows when I'm having an internal struggle and it's freaking irritating as hell.

The silence stretches, so I pretend to be going through paperwork then shake my head and ask, "Do you think I trust you?"

His burst of laughter makes me cringe. "Of course you trust me. We wouldn't work if you didn't. Trust may come with boundaries for you, but you do trust me. You have since we were ten."

Stella was right.

"Is that all?" he asks.

"That's it. I'm making some jellyfish lantern or something with the girls now."

"The girls? My, how your life has changed, Becker Hayes."

I open my mouth to defend myself, but defend myself from what? He's right.

"Relax, it's a good thing. It's a really good thing. I was worried about you for a while."

It *is* a good thing. I'm happy for the first time in years, the kind of happy that comes from making other people a priority and not just dollar signs or objects to own.

"Okay," he says, "go to arts and crafts. I'll call you after I check out those accounts you sent me."

"Thanks again, Elijah." *For everything—especially Stella.*

As if reading my mind he asks, "How's Stella?"

"She's good. She's great with the girls, but her mom isn't doing well."

"Dementia is a hard disease."

He doesn't know the half of it. I've read three damn books and none of them have been all that helpful.

My knee bounces beneath the desk. "Yeah. It is."

"You have a good thing going there, Beck. Don't screw it up with your penchant for self-sabotage."

My nose wrinkles in indignation before I can stop it. "Why do you say that?"

"Because it's how you've lived for the last few years. You don't allow people to get close, but Stella isn't just anyone—she's who you need. Take care of each other."

"I love her," I blurt. The words that used to sting like a curse are slowly beginning to heal like a promise.

"Have you told her that?"

"Yes." I sound petulant. Why does it feel like I'm talking to my father?

"Wow, I'm impressed. But remember, she's searching for stability, even if she doesn't know it. So don't do anything to fuck that up. I love you, Beck, but I love her too."

My chest heats with the possessive streak that's becoming a second skin.

"I've got to go. Let me know what you find," I say, pulling away from my desk.

"You got it. Give everyone a hug for me."

"I will. Thank you, Elijah."

He's silent for a moment, and I chastise myself for being an ass. He's been the one constant in my life for years and I fear I've taken him for granted more than once.

"You're welcome." He hangs up without saying anything else.

While we're relocating, it might be time to restructure Crystal Waters as well—fucking teamwork.

Pocketing my phone, I exit my makeshift office and find myself wandering toward Laura's room. That's usually where Stella is when the girls are napping. And if Laura is having a good day, it's where they play.

I knock softly and when I don't get an answer, I push the door open to find Laura sitting up in bed with her hands clasped in her lap.

"Hello," she says pleasantly, but gives no indication of where her mind's at. Stella told me she's been calmer since we moved her here. She hasn't lashed out, but her nurse said it's most likely a coincidence.

"Hi, Laura. Did they leave you all alone in here?"

She peers around the room as if it's all new to her. "It's beautiful here, isn't it?" she asks instead.

"It is. My mother loved it here. This was her favorite room."

"How lovely. Does she mind that I'm here?"

This disease is fucking awful. A beautiful woman is sitting here with no idea whose house she's in or why she's here. I couldn't imagine waking up each day like this. It's heartbreaking.

"No." I clear my throat and the sad direction of my thoughts. "Not at all. Are you comfortable?"

"I am. My daughter's coming to visit soon." Hope swells in my chest. Is today one of the good days that Stella's always talking about?

"Is that right?"

Her smile is hesitant, but I can imagine what it was like before her memories were stolen. The lines around her eyes and mouth show years of laughter. I hope that's what Stella remembers.

"Yes. She's away at college. She was nervous to leave me. Always worrying I would miss her too much. Of course I do, you know, but I'd never tell her that. She's a worrier, that one. A helper too."

My grin matches hers as I take a seat beside her bed.

"She sounds like a great girl."

Laura sizes me up with a quirk of her brow. "She is. She's the best. Loving and beautiful, but don't go getting any ideas, young man. You're much too old for her."

"Me?" I scoff. "How old do you think I am?"

"You're at least twenty-five, and my Stella is eighteen and going places. So you stay away from her. I know hooligans like you."

I raise my hands in defeat and grin. I've never been called a hooligan before. "Fair enough. Can you tell me about her?"

There's that smile again. It's so similar to Stella's it makes my heart skip a beat.

"It's hard being a parent, you know."

I nod in earnest because I'm learning that lesson now.

"I did my best, but sometimes she worries so much..." She stares at me for a moment and I silently pray this conversation isn't over.

"It's hard not to worry. I'm Beck, by the way."

"Beck. Right. My Stella would like you. But..." She sighs, and my soul weeps. "We moved around a lot when she was young, and it changed her. She never wanted adventure— she wanted structure." Her brow furrows as she speaks, but when she meets my gaze, her face transforms into a smile. "We chased the fun in life, you know? It's just how I'm wired, but we lived bill-to-bill, and maybe young girls do need security."

"I'm sure you did everything you could. No one has a perfect childhood, Laura."

"Did you?"

Her question startles me. But then I glance around the room, and I can't hide my truth. "I thought I did, but now I'm not so sure." *And all signs are pointing to the answer being no.*

Her eyes crinkle. "Do you have children?"

I hesitate and finally answer honestly. "I do. I'm raising my sister's little girls."

"Oh, that's a big job, young man. A big job indeed."

"Do you have any advice for me?"

Her gaze holds me hostage. "Little girls want the same things big girls want. They want to be loved and protected without someone clipping their wings. They want to assert their knowledge without repercussions and have the security that comes with knowing no matter how hard they fall, someone will always be ready to help them up."

I scratch behind my ear, and that turns into pulling on the muscles bunched at the base of my neck while she studies me.

"Oh." Stella stops short in the doorway. "Sorry. I thought you were still on the phone."

Her smile is infectious. She glances from me to her mother, who regards us curiously. But the hairs on my arms stand on end when I witness the shift happen in Laura. The confusion that blankets her is like a curtain at the end of a Broadway play—it falls heavy and final over her eyes.

"Is everything okay?" Stella asks.

"Who are you?" Laura studies my face without any signs of recognition. It stings, but when she turns the same worried expression on Stella, salty emotion clogs the back of my throat.

Suddenly the weight of the pain Stella carries sits around my neck, and it's not fair that there's nothing I can do to help her. None of this is fair. This room—all the life that gets snuffed out here. Will it always be a reminder of death?

Stella speaks in hushed tones, but I stand and back away until I reach the door, then turn and leave the room searching for fresh air. New life. And I find it when Ruby's babble radiates innocence in the monitors we have throughout the house.

I take the back stairs two at a time, desperate to reach her. Or desperate to be away from that room. I'm not sure which.

Ruby's sounds of joy and happiness wash over me as I approach her door, and when I open it, her round little face, rosy with sleep, pops up over the crib railing. The second recognition shines in her eyes, it glows around me with the power of a thousand hugs.

"Hey, Ruby-roo. Did you have a good sleep?"

She removes her fist from her mouth and drool covers every inch of it, but that smile. That crooked smile that matches my own pulls at something deep within me.

"You're going to be trouble. I can feel it."

Her eyes twinkle, but they're not like mine or Emmy's. Hers are the same vivid blue as her father's.

Davis.

Cally.

Their girls.

I have no doubt Cally is still trying to tell me something, and if I don't figure it out soon, it's possible we'll lose the only place that has ever been home to these girls.

Laura's words echo in my mind. The ones about security

and regrets. I don't want to have regrets when it comes to them, and I want to give Stella the security she deserves.

Would Stella describe her childhood the same way her mother did?

"Daddy Beck?" Emmy's words whoosh around me in slow motion.

"Hey, lovebug. You're up too?"

She nods and rubs her eyes with the palms of her hands while I pick up Ruby. When I look at Emmy a little closer, I notice that her color is off. She's holding her ear with one hand and Daisie's neck with the other.

"What's wrong, Ems?"

Her chin trembles, but she juts it out, attempting to stay strong.

"It's okay, lovebug. You can tell me. What's up?"

Emmy's strength vanishes and her face falls. "My ear hurts," she wails as Daisie nudges her chest with her nose.

I freeze. Her ear hurts. Okay. What does that mean? Temperature? Do I need to call someone?

"Stella?" She'll hear me through the monitor. I want to remain calm but I'm twenty decibels past it already.

Thank God she walks through the door before I've finished saying her name.

She drops to her knees in front of Emmy, and I stand to the side as she presses the back of her hand to the little girl's forehead.

"Oh boy. You're feeling pretty warm, sweet pea. We need to take your temperature."

Stella looks over her shoulder to confirm that I've got Ruby before she whisks Emmy from the room. I hurry to change Ruby's diaper, then follow them into the girls' Jack-and-Jill bathroom.

CHAPTER THIRTY-FIVE

STELLA

"SHE HAS A FEVER," I TELL BECK WHEN HE ENTERS THE MINT-green bathroom with baby-pink ballerinas dancing across the walls. Ruby is in his arms and...oh no. "Beck—"

Too late.

Ruby opens her mouth and projectile vomits, first on Beck's cheek, then he spins and covers me in it too.

And all hell breaks loose.

Emmy bursts into tears. Beck gags. Ruby cries for a heartbeat, then laughs before crying again.

I place Emmy on the floor, take Ruby from Beck, usher him out of the room, and turn on the faucet in the bathtub. "Go get showered," I order when he continues to retch.

He doesn't need to be told twice.

Sitting Ruby on the floor beside her sister, I remove my T-shirt, thankful my bra is only slightly damp with vomit. It doesn't help the shudder that rolls through me though. No one, and I mean *no one,* enjoys this smell.

"Why are there so many bodily fluid malfunctions with mini humans?" Beck grumbles from the other room before his voice fades away.

With my hands on my hips, I take a deep breath through my mouth and assess the situation. Emmy sits slumped forward, looking miserable, and Ruby can't decide if she's sick or if she's going to make a run for it.

Taking Ruby's temperature is first on my list, so I grab the forehead thermometer I just used with Emmy and run it across the little girl's skin. It flashes red instantly.

"Poor babies," I coo. "I'm sorry you're both sick. Let's stick you in the bath to help lower your temperatures and I'll give you some medicine."

I have no idea if taking room-temperature baths is still a thing, but my mom used to do it with me when I had a fever, and I'm running on instinct and memories at the moment.

Carefully, I strip both girls out of their clothes and place them in the tub. Neither is happy about it, but after a few minutes, Ruby splashes while Emmy sits looking utterly miserable.

I start with her, gently pouring water down her back, over and over again.

"I don't feel good, Stella." Her voice is so pitiful it breaks my heart.

"Oh, sweet pea, I know. I'm so, so sorry."

Ruby's next, and I give her the same treatment, but I use extra soap with her to rid her body of the scent of bile.

When the water cools, I lift Emmy out first, draping her with a towel, then reach back for Ruby as Beck enters the room.

His gaze hits my skin like a wildfire spreading through the forest, fast and unrelenting. Hot.

Securing a second towel around Ruby, I hand her to her uncle, and the second he holds her to his chest, she stops moving.

"How can she go from daredevil to this in the blink of an

eye?" he asks. The desire on his face from a second ago is replaced with fear.

"Don't worry, kids are tougher than us when they're sick," I say with a smirk. "Get her dressed. I'll take care of Emmy then meet you in there."

He hands me one of his T-shirts he must have grabbed when he showered and I quickly slip it over my head, soaking in the scent of him as it floats to my thighs, and then he's gone.

Emmy's lethargic and allows me to dress her quickly in the comfiest set of pj's I can find.

"All set," I say. Emmy holds her arms up to me, so I pick her up, hug her close, and cross to Ruby's room.

Beck sits in the rocking chair with Ruby held high on his chest. Her eyes are open, but her pouty little mouth is silent, a sure sign she's ill. The only other time she's quiet is when she's asleep, and sometimes not even then.

"I'm going to put you down for a minute while I get some medicine and crackers, okay?" Emmy casts her watery gaze in my direction but doesn't fight me when I set her in the middle of the bed.

Turning to Beck, I say, "I'll be right back. You okay?"

His eyes tell stories of reverence and love, and it stops me dead in my tracks because I'm experiencing the same thing.

"Yeah, I'm okay. Now," he adds.

I throw him a small smile, then hurry from the room. There was a shelf in the pantry with baby meds, so I go there first and grab a bottle of Tylenol, the tiny measuring cup that goes with it, and a syringe for Ruby. Then I grab the only crackers I can find and hope they aren't too stale.

The girls haven't eaten since snack time, and they need something in their little bellies. Opening the fridge, I search for something high in electrolytes, but only find water, milk, and orange juice. I go for the bottles of water.

What else do I need?

"Everything okay, hon?" Lucía asks when she spots me standing frozen in the middle of the room.

"Ah, I don't know. The girls have a stomach bug or something." I take a giant step back. "You better not come too close. And maybe you should wipe down the chair on the right side of Mom's bed. Beck and I were just in there."

She nods. "Okay. Do you have everything you need there?"

I glance down to my arm full of supplies. "I—I think so."

"Good. Parenting is hard, and kids get sick, Stella. They're still building their immune system, but you're doing everything you're supposed to. Trust yourself, okay? You'll make a great mom."

"I'm not sure I know how to be a mom," I whisper. "I love my mom dearly, but I didn't have the healthiest childhood. What if I repeat the patterns I grew up with? What if I'm not wired to be a mom?"

"Oh, Stella. Don't you see? You already are." She crosses the room and holds my cheeks in her palms. "Did you know that I raised five kids?"

"Five?" I gulp, and my eyes widen.

She nods. "Twins and a singleton. Then, after a failed vasectomy, another set of twins."

"Holy crap."

She grins, pats my cheek, and lowers her arms.

"My point is parenthood is just a series of surprises from the very beginning. No one starts off with a plan they actually stick to. Parenting is often simply herding children to safety until they're ready to break free and make mistakes on their own time."

I hug the medicine and crackers to my chest.

"After all my years as a mom and a nurse, I think good parenting boils down to three criteria. Do you love them?"

"Of course I do."

"Do you anticipate and meet or exceed their needs?"

It's becoming harder to swallow. "I try to."

"And do you put their needs ahead of your wants?" she asks with a knowing glint in her eyes.

This was the one place my mother failed—her wants always took precedence over my needs.

"You may not see it, but you always put them first," she says. "Those babies are lucky to have you."

"Then why do I feel like the lucky one?"

She smiles as though I've missed the point. And maybe I have. "Sometimes in life, people are thrown into your path to test you. Sometimes it's to make you reevaluate. And sometimes it's to give you a different kind of chaos so you learn to hang on to what matters in life."

"What matters?" I'm suddenly a timid little girl again.

"Relationships, Stella. Ones that make you a better person. Ones that test you and push you but never tear you down. Ones that make you view things differently and accept what you can't change. It's the ones that make your heart beat and your mind calm. It's love, Stella. Plain and simple."

Her words echo in my mind long after she's gone, but I only spring into action when I hear Emmy moan through the baby monitor.

Grabbing two large bowls, I dump all my supplies in them and head up the stairs.

Emmy is exactly where I left her, staring at the door as if she was waiting for me. I shouldn't have taken so long.

Beck is still rocking a sleepy Ruby, so I place a bowl on

the table to his right, not that a one-year-old will ever make it in a bowl. He seems to be thinking the same thing because when I back away, he smirks.

"It's worth a shot," I whisper with a shrug, and his smirk widens into a dimpled grin full of promises. His green eyes crinkle at the corners and the man looks...content.

It's a sexy look.

I grab the medicine and pour some into a little cup for Emmy, then turn the bottle upside down and measure Ruby's dose in a syringe. Emmy downs it like a champ, and I hand her a cracker.

"Can you try to eat one of these?"

She mumbles something unintelligible, but takes the cracker and crawls up the bed to the pillows. Shoot. She probably should have eaten the cracker first.

Ruby rests with rosy cheeks on Beck's chest right under his chin, so when I lean in to insert the syringe into her mouth, we're nose to nose.

"You're too good for us," he whispers.

When Ruby's lips begin sucking, I squirt the rest of the Tylenol into her mouth, then run a finger over her heated face.

"I don't think that's true," I say without lifting my gaze from Ruby's chubby cheeks.

He catches my wrist with his free hand before I can pull away, then he draws me closer and places a gentle kiss on my lips. "I don't deserve you, but that doesn't mean I won't fight to keep you."

Blood rushes in my ears and my face must be flaming because his words have the effect of a torch gun.

Then Emmy whimpers and I jump back. I'm rushing to her side, but it's too late. The sheets are ruined. It's in her hair, down her pj's, and all over the carpet.

I'm in it now, and there's no going back. Lifting her from the bed, I carry her toward the tub.

"It's going to be a long night," I call over my shoulder.

"With you, I'm ready for anything." Beck doesn't raise his voice, but his words fill the space, taking up all the oxygen.

"Teamwork," I mutter, and hear his soft chuckle.

"Come on, little lady. Maybe a shower this time." Emmy rests her head on my shoulder as though it's the only place she wants to be.

I thought I couldn't be a good mother because of how I grew up, but I can do this, and I can do it well.

I may not be her mother, but I already love her like she's mine.

CHAPTER THIRTY-SIX

BECK

WE SURVIVED THE STOMACH BUG, BUT IT WAS A CLOSE CALL. Who the fuck knew so much crap could come from such a tiny human?

Ruby was the worst. At least Emmy had some control. But I'm not really one to talk. I got it on day number two and didn't fare much better than Ruby.

Stella took care of us all. She's the true rockstar of our little family.

"Beck? Are you listening to me?" Elijah asks, drawing my attention away from my Ruby Rocket. "Does she just fly back and forth like that all day?" He arrived this morning and has been talking ever since.

"No," I scoff. "But she would if we let her. I'm afraid she has too much of her father in her already."

Elijah's expression softens. It's the first time I've allowed myself to speak about Davis, and he knows it.

The front door opens, and Emmy runs through, followed by Stella, Tabby, and Leo.

"I gots my dwess, Uncle Daddy. I gots my dwess!" Emmy holds up a bag that's overflowing with pale-pink tulle.

I push the laptop aside and open my arms, fully aware of Elijah's eagle-eyed gaze following my every move.

"Elijah," Stella cries as Emmy jumps into my lap.

"There she is." Elijah embraces her like a long-lost lover, and it's all I can do to keep my growl in check.

"Jealous much?" he tosses over his shoulder, and I fight another rumble in my chest.

"Whatever," I mutter. Emmy sticks her bag right under my nose.

"Isn't it the pwettiest?"

"The prettiest," I agree. Turning to Tabby while Leo drops even more bags in the foyer, I ask, "Is everything all set?"

Jesus. How much shit did they buy?

"I hate shopping," Stella mutters.

My jaw drops. "Who doesn't enjoy shopping?"

"It feels like a waste of money, Beck. If this isn't, you know..." She holds up her hand wearing my ring and my stomach sours.

I stand with Emmy in my arms and cross the room. "Everything about that ring is real, Stella. It's a celebration of us."

"Holy swoon," Tabby gushes.

"What will it take to make you realize how serious I am? I'm all in, sweetheart, and I'm willing to prove it however you need." I grip the back of her neck and pull her lips to mine.

Emmy, still propped on my hip, claps her hands wildly. We've kept the PDA to a minimum in front of the girls, but my self-control is running thin. Especially when there are times like this that I fear Stella has one foot out the door.

That's the worst kind of panic I've ever felt in my life. I

don't know how to live if she's not by my side because I'm no longer me without her.

"Emmy," Stella hisses and tries to pull away, but Leo takes the little girl from my arms without me asking and I deepen the kiss. The moment her lips melt against mine I know we're on the same page.

I hear Elijah and Tabby ushering the girls to the kitchen so it's just me and Stella.

"This is us, Stella Jane. Does this feel real enough for you?"

Her objections melt away as she sinks into my touch. This, right here, is when my life finally spins in the right direction.

When I pull back enough to see her, I find my entire world in two swirling pools of amber.

"It's only money, Stella."

She blinks, and Laura's words haunt me. Stella grew up living paycheck to paycheck. It's something I never thought about until I was an adult, and I need to keep that in mind.

"Let me rephrase that. It's money that I have more than enough of and that I want to spend on us. It's an investment in us, okay?"

"I don't want your money, Beck. I don't just take money. Not anymore."

Anger rolls hot in my gut. I lift her chin until her downcast gaze meets mine.

"I am not Silas, Stella. This will never be a one-sided relationship—not ever. We're equal partners, and that means what's mine is yours. That's how this works."

"It's not equal, Beck. Don't you see that? I can't contribute a quarter of what you can."

"For fucks sake, Stella. This isn't tit for tat. What I have in money you have in heart. Some things don't have a monetary value because they're priceless. What you bring to this family is worth more than any dollar amount I might have in the bank. You have to understand that. You have to believe that because it's the truth. You're our glue. You're the reason we work. You're the reason we'll get through all this shit. You're the backbone of this goddamn family. Why can't you see that?"

She juts out her chin to keep it from quivering. How do I make this stubborn woman understand? She's my pot of gold at the end of a very long rainbow.

"What happens when..."

"Don't say it, Stella. We've been over this already. Our family will grow and change just like every other family out there. We will grow and adjust with it. You will never be obsolete—but you will always be ours."

"God. I'm such a mess."

I hold her tightly in my arms. "You were broken down by the worst kind of person. I'm the lucky bastard who gets to help build you back up. I understand some of these concepts will take time to override what you've been conditioned to believe, but I have all the time in the world. Trust me, sweetheart. Trust us, please."

Her shoulders droop with a heavy exhale. "It's uncomfortable for me to spend your money, Beck. I'm not sure that that will ever change."

"Money will not be the thing that comes between us, so add it to the list of shit for me to figure out." I bend at the knees and swipe my nose along hers. "Did you have any fun at all?"

Stella's lips kick up at the corners in a way that makes my heart skip a beat.

"I don't know anyone who wouldn't have a good time trying on wedding dresses," she admits.

"Did you pick one?" After my conversation with the attorney this morning, speeding up our timeline is our best bet.

Her eyes glow and her cheeks heat. "I did. But we only got the engagement dress. Buying a wedding dress without a wedding was where I drew the line."

"Oh, honey. But there will be a wedding. It's why I'm here," Elijah says so loudly it breaks through our spell like a wrecking ball.

"Elijah," I snap, but Stella's already pulling away.

"What?" She wrings her wrist so roughly she's already created an angry red mark.

"Thanks a lot, asshole."

"Sorry." Elijah shrugs then flops onto the sofa as though he's about to watch a movie.

"I want to marry you," I begin, and the panic flares to life in Stella's eyes. "I know I said we could wait, that the piece of paper didn't matter—"

"But it does." Her voice squeaks like a cat toy.

I nod.

"Beck. This is crazy. It's too soon. Too fast. We—We haven't even been together that long."

Her head is on a swivel, and she pauses when she lands on Lucía standing in the doorway. The older woman is a mother figure to her, and since she's been in my house, I'm thankful for her too. She cares about Stella, and the girls. Hell, she might even care about me.

Lucía nods her head with a gentle, maternal smile, and Stella stops spiraling.

"I know that you got the scar on your shoulder blade on a metal park slide when you were six," I recite. "And that you didn't go to senior prom because you couldn't afford a dress."

She scowls and shoots Elijah a dark glare that could melt glaciers. He shrugs and blows her a kiss.

"That's all stuff you read in a folder, Beck. It's not the same. You shouldn't rush into anything you might regret—what if a year passes and you regret it all, especially me?"

"God, I love you, but you're more fucked up than I am."

"Mayday, mayday," Elijah says with his hands cupped around his mouth.

"That's—probably true." Stella laughs and drops her face into her hands.

"Just telling it like it is, baby," I say with a waggle of my brows when she peers up at me.

"But—how do you know? she asks.

"I don't." My expression is carefree, but she frowns. "There are no guarantees in this life, and love is not cut-and-dried. Hell, I'm not sure I even knew what romantic love was until I met you, but I've lived my life on instinct, and every fiber of my being is saying to keep you. I'm jumping into the fire with you because in my heart, I know it's right. Are you willing to do the same with me?"

The column of her delicate neck works to swallow, and I could swear an eternity passes before she speaks. The air is so thick my shirt sticks to my chest and goosebumps appear on my arms.

If she's silent for much longer I'm sure steam will billow from my ears, and I'm willing to bet she's running through every possible scenario and all the ways this could go wrong instead of how it's right.

"We're trusting each other, remember?" I encourage while taking her hand in mine. I love running my thumb over the diamond I placed on her ring finger.

She sighs and it blows the hair away from her face. She's scared, terrified maybe, but she's also determined, and it all adds up to a woman I will love until my last breath. After all the pain and betrayal she's faced, she's choosing me. She's going to trust me.

"It's not that I don't want to marry you, Beck—"

"I don't want to hear any 'but' in that sentence, Stella."

"I do want to marry you, *and* I have a stipulation."

I furrow my brows, feeling my forehead wrinkle. "What's that?" I ask slowly.

"You give me a prenup."

Back to fucking money.

"Why?"

"I want one."

Irritation prickles my neck. "Do you think I'm not serious about us? That this will end?"

"It's not that," she pleads, but I pull away and walk to the wall of windows.

"Then explain."

"I need it, Beck. I need it to quiet the voices in my head that are not my own. The ones whispering dark thoughts and darker words. The ones that tell me I'm a gold digger and a...whore," she finishes on a whisper. "The ones that sound like Silas and cut like an enemy."

I'm on her before she says another word. "You need a piece of paper to prove to an asshole who doesn't exist in our lives that you're not any of those things he's said for far too long?"

She shakes her head and I'm vaguely aware of the audience behind us.

"I need it to prove it to myself, Beck. You don't understand how confused I am sometimes. I know it doesn't make any sense to you, but it does to me." She drops her gaze to the floor and Daisie uses that moment to sit on her toes.

This fucking dog is a menace, but she protects Stella

when I can't, so I begrudgingly reach into my pocket and retrieve a doggy treat that I toss to her while I process Stella's words.

What must it have cost Stella to admit that to me? My throat attempts to close. I'm the one being selfish here, even if I hate everything about what she's asking.

"Baby," I say in hushed tones. The only sounds in the room are the girls playing in the corner. She drags her weary gaze to mine. "I will always give you what you need. Even if it pains me—even if I hate it."

Hope blooms in the crinkles at her eyes.

"But," I say. "I want to take care of you. If I'm giving on this, you agree to do it my way."

"What does that mean?"

"It means it won't be an all-or-nothing prenup, but I will give you one if that's what you want."

"I do." She nods eagerly. "So what does that mean?" She turns to Elijah, who might as well be tossing popcorn in his mouth. "What's the new timeline?" Her words are timid, and I know she's overwhelmed.

"Are you okay?" I whisper.

She nods. "It's just a lot. I'll be fine—I promise."

I glance around the room, at the people who make up our family. Tabby clenches her hands together under her chin. Leo leans against a doorframe wearing a smirk and resting one hand on Tabby's shoulder. Lucía has tears in her eyes, and Elijah sits like the cat who got the cream while Daisie circles our legs waiting for her chance to trip one of us up.

And then there's our girls.

Our girls.

"Well, here's what we need to do," I say. "You guys tell me what order to do them in."

Tabby darts across the room to an end table and pulls out a notepad. She pauses, her face morphing into sadness and possibly confusion before holding it in the air and showcasing handwriting I recognize—Cally.

"'Childhood dreams can be painted over, but the bones that make the memories will always hold our truth,'" Tabby reads.

She lifts her teary gaze from the page. "I wish she'd told me what was going on in her head. She was confused sometimes Beck, and desperate, but I have no idea where that desperation leads."

I can't speak. Instead, I motion for Elijah to pick up where I left off because my mind is a twirling firestorm of memories, and none of them make sense.

"Okay," Elijah says. "I'll take care of the attorney, filing of adoption papers, and Stella's prenup."

I hear the disapproval in his tone, but Stella places her arms around my waist, and my demeanor shifts. It calms, regulates, and settles enough for me to focus.

"We need to plan a rehearsal dinner and wedding," Elijah continues. "The custody hearing is in two weeks, so ideally, we'll get this done next weekend. Any objections?"

"Nothing too crazy," Stella murmurs at my side.

Elijah catches her eye and softens his tone. "Nothing too crazy. We'll go coastal chic, how's that sound?"

"Oh," Tabby cries. "That will go perfectly with her dress. We can totally do this. I'll call Bella. She's our local party planner."

The muscles in my body draw tight. Bella Moonbeam lived up to her name in person with her long flowy dress and round John Lennon glasses. My thoughts must show on my face because Tabby rolls her eyes.

"You're such a snob, Beck," she chides. "But trust me, she's got this."

I chance a peek at Stella. We're so in tune with each other that her gaze is already on me. She gives a shrug, and I love the laughter I find in her eyes, so I concede.

"Fine. Let's do this." Emmy appears at my side, so I bend down to pick her up.

"I gets to wear my pwetty dwess?"

"You know it," I say, bopping her on the nose with my pointer finger. This little girl absorbs so much information.

She chews on her lip, so much like Stella.

"What's up, buttercup?"

Emmy glances from me to Stella. "You'll be my new mommy?" She turns to me. "And daddy?"

The air evaporates in the room as though someone popped a balloon. And once again, it's Stella to the rescue.

She takes Emmy in her arms and carries her to the window seat, where they sit down face-to-face.

"Your mommy loved you very much, Emmy. So, so very much. That love doesn't just go away. You'll carry your mommy in your heart for the rest of your life, and no one can or should ever replace her. But I'd be the luckiest girl alive if I got to love you as much as your mom does. I'll take care of you here, while she watches you from heaven. And the same goes for Daddy Beck. How does that sound?"

You could hear a pin drop. I scan the room. There's not a dry eye in here.

Stella Jane is our savior, and she has no idea.

"I lub you." Emmy's chin wobbles.

"Ah, sweetheart. I love you and Ruby." Stella pauses, then locks eyes with me. "And Daddy Beck so, so much. That will never, ever change, okay?"

Emmy throws herself at Stella in her version of a bear hug that is felt throughout the room.

When Stella lifts her chin from Emmy's head with a deep inhale, Tabby brushes away the tears on her cheeks, then takes charge. "We've got a wedding to plan, people. Let's get moving."

Leo's gaze hasn't left Tabby's, so when she gives him a list of stuff to do, he's ready to go. But she still has messy emotions floating in her eyes, so he tugs her to him and hugs her until her breathing evens out.

Love.

I see it now. In every eye, every hug, every person in this room, and regret sinks in. This is the family I could have had all this time if only egos and miscommunication hadn't gotten in the way.

It's a mistake I'll never make again.

CHAPTER THIRTY-SEVEN

STELLA

"Breathe, Stella, breathe," I mutter while pacing beside my mother's bed.

She's sleeping. She's been sleeping a lot since we moved her here, so I miss her voice, but this is better than when she was lashing out. She always did love the ocean, and even if she doesn't remember me, I hold on to the hope that she's calmer because I'm here. It's purely selfish on my part. Need and love are still synonymous in my head.

"You're beautiful," Beck says from the doorway, making me jump.

I instantly flatten a hand down my stomach. I've been too scared to sit. This white linen floor-length dress seemed like the perfect one in the shop, but I had no idea linen wrinkled as easily as it does.

Beck stands in navy dress pants and an untucked white button-down, the sleeves rolled up to his elbows. He could easily pass for a J. Crew ad, and he takes my breath away.

Are we really doing this?

He crosses the room and pulls me to him. My worries float away on the sea breeze the second I fall into his arms.

"Are you okay?"

"Yeah, I'm just...nervous." My gaze is drawn to the wall of windows.

I have to hand it to Bella Moonbeam. She pulled this together as though she'd been working on it for months, not days.

Sheer panels blow in the breeze on the beach where she created a dance floor, and magical fairy lights shimmer in the fabric. Round tables dot the sand with navy tablecloths and silver bobbles shining on their tops. Accents in yellow are a shock of color that brings the entire scene to life.

It's beautiful.

"There's nothing to be nervous about."

"The entire town is out there."

He chuckles and it vibrates against my ribs. "They are. I told you weddings are a big deal around here, but they're here because they care. About you, the girls, me. They care about us, sweetheart."

"Did you miss them while you were gone?"

His gaze flicks over my head to the crowd gathering at the edge of the beach.

"I didn't allow myself to remember—there's so much I blocked out, Stella, and even more from my childhood that I should have memories of and don't. But the more time I spend here, the more they attempt to make an appearance. And yeah, I missed them so much it hurts. I thought that by running away the pain of betrayal would stop. It was foolish. All it did was bottle it up and fester, rotting me from the inside out."

"I'm worried about the girls," I admit. "I'm scared for the next hearing, and I can't stop thinking about what will happen to them if Danica succeeds."

He squeezes me tighter. "Me too. But I'm holding on to

faith. Cally left them to me for a reason. That must count for something."

"Knock, knock," Elijah says, interrupting our conversation.

We haven't had much alone time—ever. Not with Emmy's sudden nightmares and Ruby teething. Not with the chaos that surrounded the house the second we put wedding wheels in motion. But I don't feel disconnected. If anything, I feel closer to Beck than I've ever felt to anyone.

Maybe it's waking up in the cocoon of his arms every morning. I've never done that before. Silas never stayed over, and my previous boyfriend wasn't a snuggler. I've never felt so safe in all my life.

"Hi, Elijah." I retreat from Beck's embrace.

"She's peaceful," he says, nodding toward my mother.

"I hope so." It's the greatest gift anyone has ever given me, this time with her, and it's all thanks to the man holding my hand.

"Everything's ready when you two are."

The grin that slides across Beck's face is unlike anything I've ever witnessed before—and the way it warms me is an experience in itself. He beams like sunshine on a rainy day.

"You ready?" Beck asks. He's bouncing on his toes. Is he nervous? Excited?

"Are you?" I ask hesitantly, taking in his behavior.

"Sweetheart, I'm so ready my skin is trying to go ahead without me. I'm so ready the excitement is a ticking time bomb in my gut. I'm so ready—"

"We get the idea," Elijah laughs. "And I never thought I'd see the day."

Beck scoffs in response, but it doesn't dim his shine.

Music begins and wafts up from the beach.

"Oliver has been waiting for this day since I was a kid,"

Beck says with so much enthusiasm I'd worry he were drunk if I hadn't been with him all afternoon. "I thought I was going to be a radio DJ when I was a kid. I spent a lot of time in his studio."

I peer over his shoulder at the crowd gathering for our rehearsal dinner. Wanda stands at the very edge, staring at the sky with her finger pointed in the air while Tabby and Bella scurry between people, arranging last-minute decorations. There's a screen down the beach that will play a montage of photos we've gathered of our families and others that we've taken over the last couple of days in as many different outfits as we could manage—it's the photos of all of us that make my eyes well with happiness.

"There's nothing to be nervous about," Beck says again and when his gaze captures mine, I know he's right.

"It just feels weird. Like things are going too well. I can't help waiting for the floor to crumble beneath me."

"Nothing is crumbling tonight. Tonight is about you and me and the girls."

"And fun," Elijah adds with a sly grin. "Don't forget the fun."

"Where's Samira?" I ask.

"Oh, don't worry about her. She's down there talking yoga with poor Leo."

"I'm glad you're both here." My body heats as they stare at me. "And I, I kind of have a favor to ask."

"Oh, you silly girl. Of course I'm going to walk you down the aisle. No worries about that. And I'll be your man of honor too, since Beck has Leo and all. Tabby wanted to do it, but she'll need to help with the girls, so I told her I've got this."

"You're a pushy little man, you know that, Elijah?" Beck asks. His voice is full of teasing love.

"Oh, I know. Is that what you're over there worrying your lip about?"

I nod.

"Well don't. Not a single person on this property is going to let you go it alone. Not anymore. Got it?"

Warmth spreads through my chest. "Got it." My smile must match Beck's because Elijah falters, then pulls me into a hug.

"You look good, kid. Trust yourself, and us. We've always got you."

I hug him tighter, fully understanding what it means to have people in your corner. "I will," I whisper.

Beck tugs on my hand. "Come on. We've got a party waiting on us."

My gaze snags on my mom, who sits watching us with a small smile on her lips. There's no telling what she's thinking, but I hope it's that she's happy for me.

Releasing Beck's hand, I take hold of my mother's, squeeze it gently, then kiss the thin skin of her pale cheek. "I love you." It's a choked whisper of a confession I shouldn't make, but when I pull back, she's still smiling.

"It's nice to be loved," she says as she pats my cheek.

It's as good as I'm going to get from her, so I hold on to it with both hands, happy to see her like this, even knowing it won't last forever.

Beck pats my back and says goodnight to my mom, then we meet Lucía in the hallway.

"Are you sure you don't want to come?" I ask. "It's not too late to call one of the night nurses back."

"Thank you, but go have fun. I'll celebrate with Laura from her window." She holds up a book of poems my mother has had since she was a small girl. "I'll read to her tonight."

It feels right, but still causes a lump in my throat. "Thank you, Lucía. For everything."

"You're a good girl, Stella. You deserve happiness. I'm glad you've found someone who agrees." She winks at Beck, then leaves us to our party.

Our rehearsal dinner is unlike anything I could have ever imagined. Somehow, I've slipped into Emmy's book of fairytales and become a princess.

"Dance with me." Beck's gravelly tone causes goosebumps to appear along my shoulders. He presses his nose into my neck, just below my ear, inhaling deeply, and his heat instantly warms my back.

I turn in his arms then lick my lips. He follows the motion.

"You're killing me in this dress."

I drop my chin to my chest and peer down. It's a pretty simple dress.

Looping his arms around my waist, he pulls me to him, and I gasp when his steely erection presses against my belly.

"Told you," he says smugly.

Neighbors and friends sway around us, but he's transported me into a world where it fades into the background.

Emmy runs by with a local teenager chasing her, the peals of laughter stitching up cracks in my heart.

I scan the space and locate Bella, who has happily been on Ruby duty tonight, then find Tabby and Leo at the edge of our temporary dance floor. Tabby dabs at her eyes, and Leo hasn't torn his gaze away from her all night.

"I've never had this," I admit. He arches his back to

search my face. "This," I say, waving my arms around at all our guests.

His eyes glaze over as he takes in each person. "I'm happy we can give this to the girls." His tone is melancholy, but his desire is still making an appearance down below. It's a heady thing, knowing I affect him this way.

"Me too," I admit, then rest my head on his chest. His strong, steady heartbeat is my own metronome that calms my fears. "I didn't know if I'd ever be able to offer anyone this kind of security."

"I want that for you too, Stella. I want to make a home with you where the only time we leave is if we want to. A place you come back to every day for so long that you memorize the steps it takes you to get to the front porch and how many minutes it takes to get to town. Security is a good thing for all of us, sweetheart, and I've never felt more secure with anyone."

I open my mouth, ready to refute his claims with facts. Facts that whisper in my ear late at night. Facts that we haven't known each other very long and other insecurities that don't even sound like my own.

That's when I snap my mouth shut. Allowing Silas into my head still gives him power over me, and I won't consciously do that. Not ever again.

The song ends, and our friends clap and cheer— because that's what friends do. This town came together in a way I've only ever seen on TV, and not just because they love a good party, but because they love us—all of us.

The clapping dies down, except for one, exaggerated slow clap that eerily draws closer. It's the sound that plays in a movie before the main character dies. And when a face appears from the shadows, it's clear why.

"Congratulations, you two *love* birds." Danica spits the

word love as though someone poured hot sauce on her tongue.

Leo is faster than a ninja and blocks her from view a moment later, but he can't shield us from her words.

"Back off, Leo. I'm only here to congratulate the happy couple. I even brought a gift."

Is it me or did she just turn into Jafar from *Aladdin* with that last sentence? A sense of foreboding washes over me.

"Destruction," Beck hisses.

"What?" I whisper, not sure he even hears me.

"Wanda said destruction was in the air when she first arrived."

Wanda the weather witch. My stomach heaves, and I place a hand over it to keep my dinner down.

The large screen lights up down the beach, and my voice rings through the sound speaker that should be playing music. All the life drains from my body, and if Beck weren't holding me up, I'd fall to my knees. The world tunnels around me as the worst moment of my life begins anew.

CHAPTER THIRTY-EIGHT

BECK

"Shut it off," I bellow. Stella crumples in my arms.

Oliver appears at our side and takes her arm. "Go," he orders with a nod of his head toward Danica.

"Jesus, Beck. I got it, okay. This doesn't mean anything to you. You don't need me even if you want me, but I want to feel something, anything to make me forget, just for a little while. I understand what this is, what it isn't, and what it can only ever be— sex—a physical release for us both. Not a relationship. I got that message loud and clear."

Stella's voice is shrill through the speaker, followed by mine.

"No, I don't think you do. I can't need you. I can't need you because everything I need in life becomes cursed. I can't do that to you. I want you as my nanny, but I can never need you as more."

My gaze snaps to the screen and all rational thought leaves my head. I freeze in place as a grainy video of Stella straddling my legs plays larger than life.

How did Danica get this?

Chaos erupts around me, but I can't stop staring at that screen. The rage is so blinding I can't make my limbs move.

"That's all stuff you read in a folder, Beck. It's not the same. You shouldn't rush into anything you might regret—what if a year passes and you regret it all, especially me?"

Danica has fucking cameras all over my goddamn house.

"Shut it off," Leo yells before pushing me in the back so hard I trip over air. "Snap out of it, Becker."

My head spins to where I last saw Stella and the heartbreak, fear, and pure defeat I find on her face makes my blood boil with a hatred so real, so raw, I'm liable to kill someone—someone named Danica fucking Delacroix.

Daisie barrels through the crowd and sits growling at Leo's side, but no one is paying attention to Danica anymore.

The next series of pictures are of Stella with the girls, but there's something off about them, and I'm immobile. In this shot, Ruby's on her hands and knees in the ocean, but the angle of the camera makes it appear that Stella is far away and not paying attention.

"She'd never do that." I don't know if anyone can hear my words, or if I even spoke them. Six more photos flash on the screen, each more damning than the next.

"You know this is illegal, right?" Leo shouts, but Danica continues as though she didn't hear him.

"Seems you've been so into the nanny that you never stopped to pay attention to the safety of the girls you claim to love."

Danica's voice sends my rage boiling over and I charge her. Leo pulls me back and keeps dragging me until I'm far enough away that I can't squeeze my hands around her cunty little neck.

Tabby shuts her up when she smashes Danica's miserable face into our cake and holds it there. When she finally lifts her head, purple pieces slide down her face, and I pause.

"It's a beet cake. She's fine," Leo mutters. "That is what twenty years of bullying a person will do when they finally snap."

I twist to find Leo watching Tabby with a shit-eating grin on his face. And if this were any other time, if it weren't my woman in the middle of this fuckery, I'd smile too.

Gus, a retired fisherman, pulls Tabby off her with a low word of warning for Danica. But the woman has no off button.

"That's someone you all think should be raising my nieces?" Danica screeches. Daisie stalks her slowly with her tail pointed straight in the air. She's never once bitten anyone, but she's showing teeth, and nothing would surprise me now.

Stella's voice is still echoing in the sound system until Leo runs, rips it from its stand, and tosses it into the ocean, but the images continue to flash on the screen. Anger shows in every hard line of Leo's body, such a change from his normal attitude of even-keeled and cool calmness.

He stalks toward Danica, but she sidesteps him while wiping vibrant purple cake from her face and keeping one eye on Daisie.

"None of this is real," she shouts. "I know you're only marrying the homewrecker to fool the judge, but I won't allow it. Those girls are mine. Did you all know that Stella has a type? Her name is homewrecker for a reason."

She's completely delusional.

"What the hell are you doing, Becker?" Elijah tugs on my elbow, and I'm so off-balance that I stumble into him.

I blink to bring him into focus.

"What do you mean?"

"What do I mean? Jesus Christ."

I'm taken aback. "What are you talking about? I need to get her to shut the fuck up."

"But you're not moving, and what you should be doing is supporting your fiancée who has already been through humiliation like this once and almost didn't survive it."

I spin to find Stella and my vision tunnels. Everything fades away except the all-consuming anguish on her face. Fear has never felt so visceral. Stella breaks before my very eyes, and I feel the shatter of every crack.

Danica's shrieks cloud my head, but it's the painful vacancy in Stella's gaze that renders me useless.

Elijah's right.

Stella shakes her head and points at a picture on the screen. One that makes it appear Emmy's about to step into a busy street on her own, and new fear takes over my body.

I know this is nothing but lies, but the pain on Stella's face tells me she might not see this for what it is.

"That— It's not— I didn't," she chokes on a sob, then turns her back on me. It's like shutting down the sun at midday, and I move on instinct to reach her.

Danica grabs my forearm, stopping my attempt to reach Stella, and it's all I can do not to hurl her into the ocean with a cement block tied to her ankles.

"It doesn't have to be this way, but if you fight me," she hisses, "I will destroy everyone you love."

She presses a button in her hand and the photo on the screen changes, freezing me in place and making it hard to breathe.

Stella and Danica sit together in a coffee shop. Stella's hair is slightly shorter and Danica's laughing at something.

My heart stops beating as I study this—this betrayal. I drag my hardened gaze to Stella's. Thump. Thump. The beat starts slowly, then rolls into a raging thunder, then back to the photo. Would she have done this to me?

My thoughts shift to Silas and to the hurt that she's carried with her. When I glance back at Stella, I already know the truth—that's not the face of a betrayer. That's the face of someone who has been betrayed over and over again.

I stalk toward the screen, studying the photo as if it's a feral animal, searching for the proof that has to be there. This photo isn't real, I know it in my soul. In my periphery, Danica retreats like the snake she is, but Daisie doesn't let her get far.

Flashing blue lights streak the sky as the sheriff, Joe Carol, rolls in on a four-wheeler, and once again, it's Leo who stops my forward motion. Why is everyone getting in my fucking way?

"Go," Leo spits. "Take out the trash. I'll check on Stella."

"No, I'll go—"

"Son, a word?" Sheriff Joe appears at my side. This guy has to be pushing eighty and his speech pattern shows his years.

This is going to take forever.

"Fine, just give me a minute," I concede to Joe. To Leo, I say, "Just—just make sure she's okay. I'll be up as soon as I can."

Leo shoves me off him with two hands. I've never seen Leo this pissed. "File something with Joe. Stella's already on the move. She should have been your first priority, but instead you panicked. You let your own insecurities override what you know in your heart. You told her to trust you, yet you bought into this bullshit and froze the very first time you were tested. You didn't go to her. You didn't support her, and you let her suffer the humiliation alone. You broke the trust, Becker. Not Stella."

"I'll explain. I'll—"

He storms off, and panic seizes my lungs.

"She assaulted me with cake," Danica squeals like the pig she is.

Tabby holds a handful of purple mess above her head. She's probably considering a repeat performance.

I do a quick scan of the party to find Ruby and Emmy far away from the chaos with Bella. She gives me the okay sign, and I walk toward Tabby.

What a fucking mess.

"Tabby," I say gently. She spins, and the fire in her eyes tells me she's reacting to more than just me and Stella. This was Tabby's retaliation for a lifetime of wrongdoings. Little Tabby Hayes is a pissed-off hornet ready to sting, and I don't blame her a bit.

"Who does she think she is, coming in here and invading Stella's privacy like that? She's a wretched, wretched bitch," Tabby announces.

"Put the cake down," Joe says. I swear it takes him a minute per word.

I look toward the house, but it's too dark to make out anything in the shadows.

"She doesn't care who she hurts." Tabby's lip trembles. How much damage has Danica done to my family over the years?

Placing a hand over hers, I lower her arm, and she drops the cake.

Danica wipes her face with a napkin that doesn't belong to her, and suddenly I'm proud of Tabby's *special* baking abilities. Danica's face is tinted a deep purple, and it's not coming off.

People point and laugh, which makes this vile human even more angry.

Another officer arrives and pulls her to the side while Joe speaks with me. Just fucking perfect.

"Joe, it's great to see you, but this woman just demolished what should have been one of the best nights of my life. She hurt and embarrassed my fiancée. She's trespassed, recorded us illegally, and has been a menacing pain in my ass for the last time."

He nods while taking notes. "Illegally recorded you, you say?"

"It's my house," Danica shrieks. "I can put cameras anywhere I want as long as they're not pointed at bedrooms or bathrooms—I checked. Everyone needs to know that you're not so innocent either."

"Is that true?" I ask.

"It's not a law I'm familiar with. We've never had this issue in Sailport Bay before." Old Joe scratches his chin and looks at his notepad like the answer will jump out at him. "Nope, not one I'm familiar with at all. It'll be for the courts to decide, son. Trespassing I can do something about."

"Do it. Throw anything you can at her. I don't care if she's a blood relation to my girls, she's never going to hurt them again."

It's another twenty minutes before I can leave the beach, but the second I'm set free, I sprint toward the house with Emmy in one arm and Ruby in the other.

Elijah is sitting on the porch with Samira. Breathing is painful, and I know before he opens his mouth that Stella's gone.

CHAPTER THIRTY-NINE

STELLA

Shaking out my arms does no good. There's a tremor of doubt and insecurity rolling through my body that I can't control. My blurry eyes distort my vision as I stumble toward the house, causing me to trip more than once.

"Stella, Stella, Stella."

I stop short when I reach the side of the house. That voice. It doesn't belong here, and it sends my already shaky insides straight to my throat.

"How do you keep getting yourself into these pickles?" Silas asks.

Fear infiltrates every pore at the sound of his voice. Images flash like lightning strikes in my mind. The summer he suggested liposuction. The dinner where he ordered me a salad with no dressing in front of everyone to prove a point. The double date where he told his friends I needed training. The holiday party where he ambushed me. Me, nearly naked on top of Beck.

My neck itches, but my nails can't scratch it no matter how hard I dig. Fear and embarrassment scrape against my throat, and my breaths come in harsh pants.

"Stella," he says again, and I flinch. More memories cloud my vision. I don't even know what's real anymore. Sounds distort, cresting and falling like a wave.

Am I losing my mind?

"All you have to do is get him to merge with Delacroix Holdings and this will be over for all of us. She has me by the balls too, but you can end this. Just fucking end it." He shakes me by my arms.

When did he grab me?

"If you don't want her getting custody of those girls, walk away from them now and tell him to agree to the merger." His words sound tinny and far away, but I blink, and his ruddy face is inches from mine.

"Are you listening to me you stupid little—"

Someone yanks me away from Silas, but my ankle gives out in the grass, and I stumble into the side of the house.

"Are you okay?" Leo asks, but never takes his eyes off Silas. When I don't answer, he asks again more firmly. "Stella, are you okay?"

"Yes," I say meekly. Why can Silas still turn me into the version of myself I hate the most?

"Get out of here." Leo's voice is scarily calm. He towers over Silas.

"She did this to herself," Silas spits out. "She's always causing drama. If she'd only kept her legs closed, Danica wouldn't have gone after her—" The rest of his word vomit is cut off when Leo moves like a shadow, spins Silas around with his arm pinned behind his back and slams him into the house next to me. Silas's ego is stronger than his sense of self-preservation.

"Do you know what I hate more than anything in this world?" Leo's words send a chill down my spine. This is not the surf-loving yogi I've grown to love. This is a soldier taking down an enemy.

"Take it easy," Silas blusters.

"Men. Like. You," Leo growls. "Men who think they have a right to put their hands on a woman just because they can. Men who have no social or moral compass and take what doesn't belong to them. I hate men like you, so you have two choices. Leave now before the sheriff finds you, or stay and keep running your fucking mouth and let the sheriff find what's left of you."

Leo shoves his weight into him hard and Silas falls to the ground with a psychotic laugh. "She has no idea what's coming for her. She'll get what she deserves. You hear that, Stella?" He wipes at his nose. He must have been on the verge of tears when Leo had him pinned. "And I don't even have to get my hands dirty for it to happen. But my bed is open if you want to make other arrangements."

The echoes of our rehearsal dinner whirl in my belly, but I steel my resolve and keep them down.

A rage I've never known gives my voice a razor's edge. I am so done with being treated like shit. "You can threaten me all you want, you pathetic piece of shit, but your words no longer infect me—your poison can't reach me anymore. And you'll never put your hands on me again. Never." My words are pitched high but strong. "And you will *never* speak about those girls again, do you understand me? Just because you believe you have all the videos of you at my apartment doesn't mean it's true."

Never has a lie fallen from my lips so easily before.

"You fucking whore." He lunges for me, but Leo intercepts him with a two-handed shove that knocks him to his ass.

Silas splutters and curses. He just doesn't quit.

Leo takes a menacing step forward, and Silas retreats on his hands and knees before scrambling to his feet.

"Get out of here, Silas. I hope you get hit by a fucking bus and then vultures eat your nasty-ass carcass."

Leo raises his brow, and his lips twitch at the corners, then he kicks gravel in Silas's direction, and we watch him scramble down the driveway like a rat.

"You know," Leo says. "I don't think I've ever heard you curse before."

A humorless chuckle gurgles in my throat. "It seemed like the right time."

"Yeah, it did." His tone is gentle and filled with sympathy.

As soon as Silas is out of sight, my body spasms. I heave and drop forward with my hands on my knees. My false bravado is immediately replaced with shock as the adrenaline leaves my body in a whoosh. I have to get out of here.

Danica's voice carries over the ocean breeze. Hearing her say Emmy's name makes me heave anew.

"I have to leave. I—I can't be here." Each word cuts through my throat and burns my skin.

"Come on," Leo says, offering me a hand. "I'll take you to Tabby's."

I look up into his eyes, so kind and patient, then I scan the mess at the beach. "Beck..."

"I'll get you set up at Tabby's, then come back and give him an update. You don't need to be here for this. Let's get you somewhere you can think for a minute, okay?"

I nod, but sadness weighs me down. I don't want to leave Beck or the girls. "My mom," I say as new tears clash with old ones. I can't catch my breath. My blood is boiling in my ears and my vision tunnels.

"Lucía will take care of her," Leo says, gently holding me

up by my biceps. "You can come back tonight if you want, but I have experience with PTSD, Stella. What happened out there just now? It fucked you up. I'm only trying to help."

He's right, I know he is. And that's why I follow him to his car. "You'll tell them I love them? I don't even have my phone."

"Yes, I'll take care of everything. Get in the car, and I'll run down to let Tabby or Elijah know, okay?"

I'm nodding like a broken doll—a sad, broken doll. "Emmy will worry about me. I don't want her to be sad."

His eyes soften, and he expels a long exhale. "You're good people, Stella. You know that?"

I open the car door without answering him because the truth is, I don't feel like a very good person right now.

***

Leo pulls up in front of Tabby's Tasty Treats on Main Street and hands me my phone. He must have grabbed it earlier. It's the first time I've been to this part of town. Next to it is Cool Vibrations—Yoga and Meditations.

I turn back to Leo. "Is your shop next door to Tabby's?"

"Yup," he says, turning off the engine, then points to the second floor. "She lives above the yoga studio, and I live above the bakery."

"Huh." It's all the words I can form right now.

We exit the car and walk in silence to the side entrance of the building, then I follow him up the stairs.

When he reaches for a door, he lifts one shoulder in a shrug. "I have to grab Tabby's keys. Do you want to come in?"

He opens the door and after hesitating for half a breath,

I follow him in. It's so…homey in here. Photos of him and Tabby line the mantel. There are even some of them together as children.

"Are you and Tabby together?"

Leo's grin doesn't quite reach his eyes. "It's complicated." He holds up a key he takes from a hook on the wall, and we exit his apartment, then enter Tabby's.

Her place is decidedly un-homey. It has a sterile feel with clean lines and a minimalist atmosphere that has me spinning in confusion.

This is the least Tabby-like place I could imagine.

"She spends a lot of time at my place," Leo explains. "She only sleeps here."

"That is complicated," I agree.

"Take a seat. Would you like a glass of wine?"

"No, thank you. But I'd love some water, please."

"You got it." I sit on the black plastic sofa. Why the hell is it so hard? The only photo in here is one of them together as teenagers. It's not anything I would have imagined for her.

Leo returns and hands me a bottle of water. "How are you doing?"

My shoulders slump forward. "I'm not sure." My gaze drifts back to the lone photo and I mindlessly drag my fingers along the hard lines of the sofa. "This is not how I envisioned Tabby's place," I admit.

"No?" he asks. "What did you expect? Something more like my place?" His eyes sparkle, and his grin takes over his face.

"Well, yeah," I admit.

He takes a seat in the chair opposite me. "For good reason. I built that apartment with her in mind, and I built this one to be as uncomfortable as possible."

"You succeeded there," I mutter, glancing around at the cold interior. "Why would you do that?"

"I was trying to win her back," he says with a chuckle. "I stupidly thought that if she was so uncomfortable here, she'd spend more time over there," he says, hitching his thumb over his shoulder. "With me. But I seriously underestimated how stubborn she can be."

"What did you do?" My heart pitter-patters in my chest, but I don't know if it's from his heartbreak or mine.

"I drunkenly married her younger sister in Vegas, which is not as simple as it sounds, so that tells you just how drunk I was, and then was too chicken to come home and face her for too many years."

"Leo," I gasp. "What the hell? Were you with her when you married her sister?"

His nose wrinkles. "We were on a break."

"Oh my God. Seriously?"

"Yeah," His gaze drops to the floor. "I was on my way to California. My band at the time was trying to get our big break, but we only got as far as Vegas. Bea came out for her birthday, we got drunk, and don't remember much after the last round of Fireball. We didn't even know what we'd done until months later when the marriage certificate showed up at their parents' house."

"Oh no." My hands fly to my mouth. Poor Tabby.

"It gets worse."

"How? How could that get worse? She must have been heartbroken and felt so betrayed."

"She did, but the thing about Tabby is she always puts everyone else's needs above her own. Her parents are extremely religious and demanded we give it a try. I couldn't do it. I'd made a mistake, but knowing I'd hurt Tabby was too much, so I ran."

"Leo!"

"I know. Young and stupid, remember?"

"What happened?"

"Bea came back to Vegas. Pretended to 'work on things' for a while, but in reality, I never saw her again. I can't even confirm she was in Vegas. Then, we filed for an annulment through lawyers, and two more years passed before I got my head out of my ass."

"Her own sister?"

"We never meant to hurt her. I've loved Tabby for as long as I can remember, and it's a betrayal I'm still trying to correct."

"And her sister? How are they?"

He shrugs. "Bea moved to Tennessee a few years ago. Their relationship is okay, but it never really recovered, and that's a guilt I carry around too. Tabby lost the two most important people in her life because of one stupid mistake."

Unease swirls in my gut. "Why are you telling me this?"

"I'm not sure, honestly. Maybe because Beck made a mistake tonight and I don't want to see him lose any more years. I think he had a moment where he was scared and confused and he forgot to trust you, but I also know that he loves the hell out of you."

Once again, sounds gurgle in my ears and images of my mistakes assault me. They flash and change faster than strobe lights in a confined space.

"Stella, focus." It sounds like Leo, but his voice is distorted, so I close my eyes. Focus, Stella. Focus.

I blink through the nightmare I can't wake from. The nightmare that will always follow me because that's what narcissists want, right?

Leo's voice cuts in and out of the rising tide of panic. Is

this what my life boils down to? Haunted by Silas's words and actions—a coward in men's clothing?

Cold water hits my face and I choke on it. Gasping for breath, I use both hands to wipe the droplets from my lashes and dripping from my chin. When I'm finally dragged into reality, I find Leo standing before me with my crushed bottle of water in his hands.

"Ah, sorry." His expression is sheepish. The deep set of his brows and turned-down lips tells me he's concerned. "I know that vacant stare, and you were rocking yourself with your arms locked around you."

I drop my chin to my chest. He's right.

"Don't let that fucker win, Stella. Whatever he's done, whatever he said, it's not the truth. Believe in yourself, your heart, because the rest of us do. Regardless of the brain fart Beck had tonight, he knows you, and what's more, he trusts you."

I shake my head to argue, but Leo keeps going. "He does, and we both know it. If you, for one second, allow anything Danicruel or Fuckface said to penetrate your walls, just remember that Beck let you in because he saw the truth of your heart. Think about what trust, and the lack of it, has cost him. He's going to stumble occasionally, but he'll never fall, and he'll never allow you to either."

I'm still drying my face with the sleeve of my sweater when I lift my gaze to his. It could be stress, or the anxiety of the last hour, but when we make eye contact, all I can do is laugh—loudly.

"You threw water in my face."

He smirks. "I did. And I'd do it again. Are you here now? In the present?"

I scan the terrible decor of Tabby's apartment and my shoulders sag with relief, disappointment, and love. But most of all, with compassion and understanding—none of us are perfect. Parts of me may be broken, but isn't that what life is? A bunch of broken people searching for the broken parts of others who make us feel whole.

"What if I'm not right for them?" The whispered admission squeezes my heart and twists it until I'm not even sure if it's beating.

"They know you are."

"I'm not the person I used to be. I don't know if I'll ever get rid of Silas's voice in my head."

"None of us are who we used to be. That's the beauty of life and experiences—the good and the bad. It makes us who we're meant to be. Use your past to draw your future."

I lower my lashes as new threads of dread worm themselves into the cracks of my heart. "What if my mistakes are actually traits I'll inadvertently teach the girls?"

"There's nothing wrong with wanting to be loved," he says softly. "And if you took a moment to look inside yourself, you'd see yourself as we do. You can't keep kids from making mistakes, but you can guide, and teach, and lead by example."

"That's what I'm worried about."

"Then you're not listening to your own voice, and you're letting Silas win. You're exactly who those girls need. You're exactly who Beck needs, but if you can't see that, then maybe you're not who I thought you were."

His words puncture my walls. My chin wobbles, and I bite my lip.

"Tabby's room is through there," he says, pointing at a door to my right. "Help yourself to whatever you need and get some sleep. Text Tabby if you're missing anything, but I don't think you should go back to them until you're all in— heart, mind, and soul. Beck and those girls need you, but not part of you. They need all of you. If you can't give that to them, then walk away now."

"But—"

He shakes his head. "I'm heading back to help clean up. Get some sleep, Stella. And think about what I said."

He walks silently to the door, but I can't watch him go. The click of the lock tells me I'm alone in this cold apartment with thoughts so loud and violent in my head I can't differentiate them from my own.

If you can't give that to them, then walk away now.

If you don't want her getting custody of the girls, walk away from them now.

Everyone's telling me to walk away, and it hurts so damn much.

You're listening to the wrong voices, Stella. Find your voice, sweetheart, and trust it over anyone else.

"How do I listen to my voice when I don't even recognize it anymore?" The words echo in this space. I glance at Tabby's closed door, but I don't move. Instead, I curl into a ball, ignoring the hard surface below me, and allow all the voices in my head to wash over me. The good ones. The cruel ones. The ones I no longer recognize. Somewhere in the tangled mess is my voice, so what is it I want to say?

CHAPTER FORTY

BECK

THE SUN IS RISING LIKE AN ANGRY BALL OF FIRE OVER THE ocean, but it does nothing to warm the chill that's taken over my body. It crashed into me the second Elijah confirmed that Stella was gone.

One fucking moment of hesitation—one moment where I allowed my fears to win. That's all it took, and the pain I inflicted was etched in her face. I'll never forget her expression.

"Fuck," I mutter. My breath puffs out in a cloud against the cold morning air. Daisie sits dutifully at my side, for once not being a pain in my ass, but she whimpers at my harsh tone, so I bend down into a squat and pet her head.

"I messed up, Daisie." Her ears rise, and it's all the warning I get before she jumps up and places her heavy paws on each shoulder. We tumble to the ground, and she licks my face.

"Dang it, Daisie. Cut the shit." She doesn't stop, so I roll to my side, but she follows. It takes three tries before the mutt allows me to stand.

It's freezing out here, but I refuse to go inside. My

fingers went numb hours ago, but it doesn't keep me from obsessively checking my phone for a response. The first three text messages show as read. The next eight haven't been opened, and my gut twists with what that could mean.

My willpower and pride sank into the ocean hours ago.

Beck: Baby, please talk to me. I know I fucked up. I didn't do the one thing I've asked of you.

I stare at the phone in my hand, praying for the message to show as read or for the three dots to appear, but I get nothing.

"She's sleeping," Elijah says over my shoulder. I hadn't heard the sliding glass door open, but perhaps that's what he wanted because it creaks loudly as it closes now.

I nod but don't turn to him.

"Just give her some time, Beck. I'm sure the events of last night were just as overwhelming for her as they were for you."

"She's still at Tabby's?"

My cousin texted last night to tell me she found Stella curled up on her sofa, her face red and swollen from crying, and it cut my chest wide open knowing I did that, at least part of it.

"I'm sure she is," he says, falling into a chair, so I slide in next to him.

"I need to talk to her."

"She needs time. She'll come home when she's ready."

"But I have to tell her I trust her, that I love her." The desperation in my tone causes his icy demeanor to thaw. Not fully—he's still giving me the cold shoulder—but his defenses are slowly lowering.

It doesn't even bother me that he's on Stella's side—if anything, it makes me love the guy more.

"She knows," he says, staring out over the ocean. He's tucked into a flannel blanket, while I'm still in my clothes from last night.

I won't be warm without her anyway.

I shake my head. He doesn't understand.

One goddamn moment in time.

"Would you have noticed her if you hadn't needed her?"

My body heats as anger rises in my chest. "I've always noticed her," I say through clenched teeth.

His look burns the side of my head, but I stare straight ahead. I'm not in the mood to prove anything to him, but the words fall from my lips like a confession.

"I noticed her on the street first, outside that princess bar. I didn't want to. I'd wanted to go home, but that purple dress of hers caught my eye, and I haven't been able to look away since. She smells like apples, and she replaces my chocolates everyone pretends they don't steal. I always knew when it was her who dropped off my coffee because she would place it so the handle of the mug was at a forty-five-degree angle. I know her handwriting—memorized the swirls and loops connecting cursive letters with print. It's pretty, and conflicted—like her."

Finally, I turn in my chair to face him. "And that's just a few of the things I *noticed* before I needed her."

"What made you fall in love with her?"

"What kind of question is that?" I bark before standing and resting my elbows on the railing of the deck.

He silently joins me a second later.

"It's the way my body trusted her before my mind did," I say. "It's how she did things to make everyone around her better, but never asked for credit. And how she never knows how perfect she is. It's all of her, Elijah. It's hard to pick one thing because with Stella, it's a million pieces that she believes are broken, but truthfully, they fit my broken bits like a beautiful life-sized puzzle. She makes me whole."

He nods and uses the blanket to dab at the corner of his eye.

We stand in silence together as my mind replays the events of last night. I'm only half paying attention when he lifts his phone to his ear.

"I need a favor," he says.

I tilt my head to the left and glare at him.

"Yes, I'm very well aware of what time it is, Lottie, but I'm with Beck, and you're the only one who can help."

I lift a brow in his direction, and he smiles, places his hand over the phone, and whispers, "Remember what I said about love languages, Beck. Our girl needs you, and she needs to feel needed right now, and she's too afraid of breaking the rules not to answer a hotline call, so let's reroute your number again and let her know how much she's needed *and* wanted."

Lottie's voice is high-pitched as he puts the phone back to his ear. "I'm well aware that you're not running a match-making company, but really, it's starting to work out that way. Now here's what we need from you."

"Where's Stella?"

Turning away from the wall of windows, I find Emmy rubbing the sleep away from her eyes.

"Hey, lovebug. Are you okay? You didn't nap for very long." I crouch down and open my arms, a sense of calm washing over me as she runs on little legs into my embrace.

Her hair is mussed with sleep, and she smells like innocence.

"Stella was sad." Her words make my stomach hollow out with guilt. "Mommy was sad like that too."

The breath stalls in my lungs. "Why do you say that, lovebug? What made Mommy sad?"

"Dani."

The one word makes me flinch, and I stand quickly with her in my arms. The little blue book she carries with her everywhere falls to the floor with a thud, and I freeze with her dangling from my arms as I take in the illustration on the open page.

It shows a child's room that opens to the stars. My body reacts to it as if it's a rattlesnake about to strike. Sweat dots my hairline and I can't get enough air.

I know this drawing. I know this book. I think I made this book.

"Mommy," Emmy whines, reaching for it, and I glance from her back to the open page. There are two kids in the illustration who look too much like Cally and me to be coincidence. We lay in a fort made of pillows, and a memory blinks into consciousness.

Cally and I on the third floor, counting stars.

Grabbing the book, I stand upright. Emmy grabs for it, but I hold it open to this page and scrutinize every detail. It's the words that cause me to shake and almost crumble to the ground.

The stars shine brightly with the hopes and dreams of children.

"E—Elijah," I call. My voice is hoarse, and Emmy rests her head on my shoulder with open palms, so I hand her back her book.

"T—This is a very special book, lovebug. I see why you

love it so much."

She tilts her head to look up at me, and her smile lances my chest as another memory forms. Cally crying when my father covered the stars, and it was my fault.

"What's up?" Elijah asks. The second he sees my expression—he removes Emmy from my arms.

"I know. I know what Cally was trying to tell me."

I feel it in my soul, and there's only one way to find out if I'm right.

In the background, I hear Elijah telling Leo and Samira to help him get the girls ready for a walk.

The rain hits the windows like tiny pebbles, and I'm tucked under Cally's bed with my hands over my eyes.

"Bear? It's okay, lovebug. Come on out. We're going to get some ice cream."

I lift my head and my hands shake.

Glass shatters in the hallway, and our parents' violent yelling causes my entire body to tremble.

"Mom's not feeling well today, Bear. That's all. I know it's scary, but it will be okay."

Mom has a lot of bad days.

"You need to get help, Emily. We can't go on this way." My dad's words slice through the air.

"Don't you dare," Mom shouts back. "I'll take that little boy and you'll never find us again. You or Cally. Do you hear me?"

Cally drags me out from under the bed and pulls a blanket over me, then runs through the house and out into the rain.

My phone slides around my now-clammy hands and I turn it over and over again.

With my heart trying to escape my throat, I press the green call button and pray.

It rings three times before her timid voice comes over

the phone. "Single Dad Hotline, I'm your helper. How can I help you?"

"Hello, Jane." Stella gasps, but I push on before she hangs up. "My name is Becker Hayes, and I need you."

"Beck." My name from her lips settles the unease Emmy's book has stirred.

"I think I figured out what Cally was trying to tell me. Or at least where she was trying to guide me. But the thing is, I can't do any of this without you. If you want to call off the wedding tomorrow, I understand. I won't like it, but I'm the one who fucked up and need to regain your trust. But I need you, sweetheart. I need you now."

Her breathing is heavy and erratic as though she's just run a marathon. My shoulders tense, reaching for my ears with every second that passes.

"I need you, Stella Jane. We need you."

The sound of her swallowing makes my lips twitch because I can picture her neck working and her wide, guileless eyes searching for every grain of truth.

"Please." I'm not above begging. I'll never be above begging when it comes to her.

"I'll be home soon."

Anxiety rushes from my body in an audible whoosh. She didn't say she'll be here soon. She didn't say she'll meet us at the house. She said she'll be home soon—to our home —to me.

"I'll be waiting. I have apologies to make, and things to prove. Please don't think I've forgotten that, but—"

"The girls will always come first, Beck. Always."

"I love you, Stella."

Silence.

I pull the phone away to confirm we're still connected, and a pit forms in my stomach.

"I know. I'll be there soon."

She hangs up, and so many emotions swirl in my mind. But it's the possibility of losing Stella and the girls that keeps me focused on one step at a time. And right now, I need a sledgehammer.

CHAPTER FORTY-ONE

STELLA

"Are you sure you're ready?" Tabby asks with puppy dog eyes. "I love Beck, but it's okay if you need some time. I get the feeling you've been through hell and back in the last twenty-four hours."

She's not wrong, and I appreciate her kindness, but I'm ready to go home.

My chest aches and my mouth goes dry. For the first time in my life, I have a home to go to. One that's filled with love and memories—both good and bad. It's full of mistakes but also second chances, and it's waiting for me with open arms.

Tabby gave me space all day, while also finding excuses to check on me from Leo's apartment. But in the last twenty-four hours, I've cried. I've raged. I've felt sorry for myself. And I've decided to take control of my life, once and for all.

I'm not a victim, I'm a survivor. I'm not broken, I'm stained glass. I'm me, exactly as I am, and Becker Hayes loves me anyway.

Is getting married to a man I haven't known very long a smart thing to do? Maybe not. But I love him.

Every thought that suffocated me last night had nothing to do with Beck. It's because I didn't trust myself. I thought I was in love with Silas. I thought I knew what love was, and I was so very wrong.

In order for me to trust Beck, I have to trust myself first, and we're both worth the risk.

What Beck and I have is more than love—it's life, and I wasn't living before I met him.

"Stella?"

I blink myself out of my reverie and press my palms to my heated cheeks. "Sorry. Yes, I'm sure. I belong with him, Tabs. Last night gutted me. It hurt more than I can say, but I didn't give him a chance to explain either. Those photos looked real, even to me. If I hadn't known that my hair hasn't been that short since the fifth grade, I would have questioned them too."

She nods with watery eyes.

"We both made a mistake, but I don't think it changes us." My insides roll over because what I really mean is I *hope* it doesn't change us. "It doesn't wipe away what we're building."

Fingers crossed.

Tabby nods excitedly with her hands clasped tightly in front of her chest—barely containing her golden retriever energy.

"And I miss the girls." The reality of that statement tightens my throat. "I haven't been gone long, but I don't want them wondering where I am when they've already lost so much. It's also not fair to leave Beck with my mom—she's my responsibility."

"She's both of your responsibility, Stella. Beck sat with her for hours last night. He loves you and everything you love."

I hadn't been expecting that, and a new ray of hope surrounds my heart.

"Let's get you home." She barrels into me with a hug so tight I can't breathe. When she releases me, I see a lifetime of stories swirling in her gaze.

"Thank you, Tabby. Do you think someday you'll tell me about…" I pause, taking in her space one more time. "About all of this?"

She laughs, then tucks her hair behind her ears with both hands. I know that trick well—she's shielding herself. "I'm sure Leo told you the gist of us. He can't help himself. I swear he blabs to punish himself, but that's not who I am. I forgave him a long time ago. But forgiving and forgetting are two very different things, and sometimes forgetting is harder than forgiving."

"Yeah," I whisper. Her pain could so easily be my own.

"And sometimes forgiveness is more for yourself than it is for anyone else. Holding on to hate or the things that harm us only hurts ourselves, and we owe it to ourselves to do better than that. So I'm trying. I'll never apologize for how long it takes me, or the bumps I hit along the way. It's my journey and no one can dictate how, when, or where I find healing."

I follow her out the door while I chew on her words. Forgiving is not the same as forgetting. She's right—about all of it.

I'm not even surprised when we climb into Leo's car. These two say they don't have a label, but they count on each other for a heck of a lot. Tabby may never be able to forget what hurt her, but I do hope that she eventually finds a way to grab happiness with both hands instead of straddling it the way she is now.

She pulls out onto the road, and I grab the oh-shit

handle while peering at her with wide eyes. Is she even sitting in her seat? Her head barely breaks the top of the steering wheel. She holds it in a death grip at ten and two which means we swerve wildly every time she looks at me.

I have the insane urge to tell her to keep her eyes on the road. Note to self, Tabby is a terrible driver.

"For what it's worth," she says, taking a corner so fast I'm sure we're only on two wheels, "Beck was a fucking pain in the ass when he realized you were gone last night." *Please keep your eyes on the road!* She turns right onto the street that runs along the ocean, and my breath comes out in a whoosh. "He practically lost his damn mind. If it weren't for the girls, I'm sure he would have broken every law to bring you home last night."

The driveway comes into view around the final corner, and my anxiety releases muscle by muscle. Beck has given me the one thing I've been searching for my entire life—a place to belong.

The tires squeal as Tabby turns off the asphalt and onto the gravel driveway and we kick up dust the entire way to the house. She puts the car in park before we've stopped moving and we jerk forward, and I shove my door open and jump from the passenger seat. Who the heck gave her a license?

Shaking my head, I inhale deeply to calm my nerves. Beck has a lifetime of secrets to unfold, and from his tone of voice when he called me via SDH, he might be on the verge of uncovering it all.

"Stella," Emmy cries the instant I open the door. Relief slaps me in the face like icicles in a winter storm. Her little body slams into me a second later and I tug her close, breathe her in, and feel how wildly her heart beats against mine.

"Hi, sweetheart." My heart slowly syncs to match her breaths. "I'm sorry I didn't say goodnight last night."

A loud crash sounds above us, and my hand instantly covers Emmy's head while I duck low. But the ceiling isn't falling in. What the heck is going on?

Leo rounds the corner as Tabby enters behind me and instantly drops to the floor like a comedian in a sitcom when there's another crash overhead.

"What's going on?" I ask, covering Emmy's ears.

"Demolition," Leo says, shaking his head. He pulls a hard hat off the entry table and tries to trade it to me for Emmy, but she clings to my neck.

"Hey, kiddo," he says, rubbing her back. "Can Stella run upstairs and check on Daddy Beck? Maybe she can help him make less noise."

"My book," Emmy whispers, then hands it to me. It's tiny —just a blue square that's no bigger than four or five inches. But it's always close by.

"Do you want me to read it to you?" I ask as Beck's hammer hits wood—and maybe metal—upstairs.

She shakes her head but opens the pages.

My gasp is audible as I see crude, childlike illustrations of a little boy holding his big sister's hand.

"It triggered some kind of memory or something," Elijah explains, joining our small circle. "Come on, kiddo. I bet Tabby will help you bake something full of sugar."

Emmy bounces in my arms, but I can tell she's torn by the way her gaze darts between Tabby and me.

"That sounds like so much fun," I say with fake enthusiasm I hope sounds genuine. "Why don't you bake with Tabby, and when I'm done with Daddy Beck, I'll come taste test with you."

She hesitates for half a second before reaching for

Tabby. She keeps her gaze on mine as they walk toward the kitchen. When they're out of earshot, I glance at the ceiling. "Where is he?"

"Third floor," Leo answers. When I turn my head to the left, he's staring at the ceiling too. So is Elijah on my right.

"What's going on?" I ask.

"He either knows what Cally wanted to tell him, or he's losing his shit thinking he lost you. It's a toss-up right now," Elijah says with a wide grin. "I'm hoping it's the first."

Leo plunks the hard hat on my head, then knocks against it gently.

"Is this really necessary?" I grip the edges to keep it out of my eyes.

"If he's doing what I think he's doing, then yes." He glances down at my feet in pink tennis shoes. "Be careful where you walk, okay?"

"What am I supposed to do up there?"

Both men drop their stare to me. "Just be there for him," Elijah says.

"And listen when he says he's sorry. I've never seen that man as heartbroken as he was last night. He loves you, Stella." Leo's attention drifts to the hallway Tabby walked through, and my heart hurts even more.

"I—I love him too."

They smile at me with blinding wattage.

"Then go see what the hell he's up to before he brings the entire house down around us."

My eyes fly open so wide they actually hurt. "Is that possible?"

"No." Leo laughs. "It's a figure of speech. But he's only been up there for twenty minutes, so who knows? Go check on him."

Elijah gives me a big hug, then turns me toward the stairs. Beck's words fortify each step I take. *I need you.*

There are fourteen stairs to the second floor, each step bringing me closer to Beck. Up here I can hear the music blasting through a speaker more clearly, but I don't recognize the song. The next staircase is shorter, but by the time I reach the sixth step, my head is already clearing flooring on the third level and it's hard not to remember the last time I was up here.

Beck is across the room on a ladder. My feet hit the floor just as he takes a wild swing at the ceiling, and a cloud of dust and debris falls over him. He hits the spot again and again, only pausing to swipe at the goggles he's wearing.

He's covered head to toe in a thick layer of white dust. Based on the holes in the walls, I'm guessing it's some sort of sheetrock. His hands grasp the ladder while he chokes on an inhale, and I rush to his side.

"Beck."

He doesn't hear me—the music is too loud.

Standing in the center of the room that looks nothing like the first time I was here, I close my eyes to decipher where the music is coming from.

I follow the sound to the window in the far corner of the room, then shut it off.

Beck's head whips toward me. It takes him half a second to clear his goggles, but when he spots me, he jumps from his spot on the ladder to the floor as though he's part spider.

His strides are long and determined, and he reaches me in record time. "You came."

"I came." My cheeks heat, and I could die of embarrassment because my mind instantly conjures our night up here.

"I remember," he says with a smirk. Damn it. Desire flutters deep in my core, then he coughs, sobering us to the moment.

"What are you doing up here?" I scan the space again. Dust mites float all around, sparkling in the last remaining rays of sun like thick specks of glitter.

"Stella," he says, then coughs again.

"You need to be wearing a mask up here. You're inhaling God knows what."

He coughs so hard his eyes water, but there's nothing to drink up here.

"Let me grab you some water." I turn to go, but he catches my elbow. It's another few seconds before he's able to speak.

"I'm so sorry, baby." He moves in as though he wants to cup my face, but catches the filth covering his skin and pulls back. "I know none of that was real. I just—fuck, Stella. I froze for one damn second. It looked so real. After everything, I—I panicked. But please believe me, I love you so damn much. You're my lifeline—my northern star. I..."

He starts hacking again and I pull from his grip, run to the second-floor bathroom, grab one of the girls' cups, fill it with tap water, and rush back to his side.

He takes it and drinks deeply.

His face is covered in muck, so when he smiles, his teeth stand out in blinding white. "I'm sorry. I'm so damn sorry."

I shake my head—too many thoughts vying for the top spot. "No, I get it. I know why you hesitated, why you were confused. I was too, and I shouldn't have run. But then Silas was there, and Leo pulled him off me—"

"He had his hands on you? He..." Beck takes a step back, and his entire body shakes.

I step toward him and place a hand on his chest. It brings his gaze back to mine.

"I'm going to kill him. I'll ruin the motherfucker."

A slow grin slides over my lips because I know he would. If I asked him to, he would burn the world to the ground for me.

"What I'm trying to say is I panicked too. Old insecurities crept in, and new ones sprouted. I come with a lot of baggage, and I was so worried I'd hurt you or the girls that it took me all night to set myself straight."

His expression softens and this time, when tears slip down my cheeks, he wipes them away with gritty thumbs.

"You set yourself straight, did you? And what does that look like exactly?" His body heat engulfs me, making it hard to think, but I focus on my words.

"It looks like me coming to you with baggage that's too heavy to carry on my own, knowing you won't let it crush me. It looks like me accepting that trust is sometimes hard for you and remembering to be patient. It looks like believing you when you say you love me and allowing those words to be my mantra when everything feels uncertain."

"Stella." My name is a groan and a prayer. "I'm supposed to be the one apologizing."

"No. We wasted enough time because awful people want to hurt us and take what doesn't belong to them. I don't want to waste any more time. I want to fight for the girls. I want to fight for us—for our..." I blink as insecurity pokes at my chest, but it's time to be brave, so I steel my spine.

"I want to fight for our family. I've had enough apologies and empty words to last a lifetime. They're just words. We're more than that, Beck. We're more than empty promises and broken dreams. We're the future I've always wanted but didn't feel worthy of having. You've given me hope that that future exists and that a place to belong is within reach. It's everything I've ever wanted, and I'll be damned if I let anyone take that from me now."

His gaze drops to my fisted hands, then he crushes his body to mine, but I'm not done yet.

"So tell me what you're doing up here. Tell me how I can help. And then—" My voice breaks. I don't need an apology from him, but I do need something. I need to hear that he still wants me—self-help is a long game, and I've only just entered the arena. "T—tell me you still want to marry me tomorrow."

His groan hits my ears first, then his lips cover mine. He's not gentle, and if I inhale too sharply, my nose tickles with the dust that's still covering every inch of him. But he's mine. And I'm his. I feel that in this kiss.

"Oh, I still plan to marry you, sweetheart," he says with his lips hovering above mine. He rubs our noses together. The dust and grime grind harshly between our skin, and it's perfect. His words, our kiss, the dirt and dust between us, settling over us and filling in the cracks of our foundation caused by Danica, fortifying our bond, creating a seal, and making us stronger.

"You're mine, and I'm yours," he vows. "I'm marrying you because I want to. Not because it'll look good on paper. Not so we can get custody—we're doing that anyway. I'm marrying you because I'm not me without you. I need you and want you and will fight to keep you forever."

A piece of sheetrock falls from the ceiling, hitting his ladder. It crashes into the wall, knocking down a child's painting.

"What are you searching for up here?" I ask again. This time, the lump in my throat is happy emotions that invade every inch of my body until I'm cloaked in his words.

He stares at where the ladder leans haphazardly against

a discolored portion of the wall, but his expression is blank. He crosses the room slowly, muttering something so quietly I can't make out the words, so I follow behind him, careful as I step over debris of all sizes.

Beck holds his hand out with his palm toward me. "Stay there."

He pulls the ladder from the wall, then picks up his sledgehammer, and attacks the place where the painting had been. It only takes a few swings before it's big enough for him to put his head through.

"Un-fucking-believable," he says. But he doesn't sound pissed. He's almost...happy, maybe?

"Beck?"

He turns to me with a wide grin, reaches into the hole with his right hand, and pulls out a large plastic accordion folder. The front simply says, *For Beck*.

CHAPTER FORTY-TWO

BECK

THE INSTANT I SEE CALLY'S HANDWRITING, THE ENTIRE WORLD fades away until I'm lost in the past. One where I'm a little boy and she's my big sister, protecting me and always trying to make me laugh.

My gaze cuts to the ceiling. The glass is still there. I knew it was the second I saw Emmy's book. My book, actually. I'd made it for Cally when I was in kindergarten, and like most childhood memories, it faded with time.

"Beck?" Stella's voice pierces the silence in my head.

"I—I have to shower," I say.

She stares into my eyes and nods as though she understands, before peering into the hole I created. It never crossed my mind to look for anything else.

"Is it empty?"

Her head swishes from left to right, causing sheetrock dust to fall into her silky brown hair.

We'll both need a shower.

"Well," she calls over her shoulder. "There are light switches and a big lever or handle-like thing next to it." She pulls her head from the hole, with an extra-large ziplock bag in her hand. "Do you know why there's another wall back there?"

I nod, hold my hand out to her, and wait for her to join me, but I can't tear my gaze away from the bag in her hand. When she slips her palm into mine, she passes me the bag containing a giant ratty teddy bear.

"It's Bear," I say.

Her brows furrow.

Opening the bag, I take out the stuffed animal and the note he has pinned to his belly. It reads, "Bear protected me through college and life. Now it's time he found his way home."

"I gave Cally my prized possession when she went to college," I tell Stella. "Even though she technically still lived at home, she kept him."

"Bear? Dog? You really have a way with names." Stella laughs. It pulls a chuckle from my chest.

Then I look up, waiting for her to do the same. Her gasp is a lightning strike to my heart, jump-starting me into motion.

"Did you put a hole in the roof?"

A chuckle shakes my shoulders. "No, sweetheart. This was Cally's observatory."

Stella's forehead creases when she tilts her chin to me but keeps her head back so she can still stare at the darkening sky.

"This was her sanctuary when we were kids. She spent more time in this room than anywhere else—at least for a while. She stopped coming up here." *Because of me.*

Stella steps in front of me, no longer staring at the stars that will soon shine bright. "What happened to it?"

The truth slices my tongue like shards of glass, but I speak through it. "I happened, Stella. She lost her safe space because of me."

Her face crumbles but compassion shines in her eyes.

"Shower with me? I'll tell you the story, but I need to get cleaned up to see what she left me." I hold the file folder to my chest with a viselike grip.

Whatever's in here will change everything—it's a truth that settles into my lungs more painfully than frigid air. But I also think it's a truth that will bring us peace, so keeping Stella's hand in mine, I lead her to the stairs, ensuring she takes care stepping over nails, two-by-fours, and broken Sheetrock.

The first swing of the sledgehammer was cathartic, the last therapeutic, and together, they might just lead me home.

In the hallway, I bypass her old room and the master that's become ours in recent weeks, opting instead for Cally's room at the front of the house.

It's no longer adorned with posters of pop bands and movie stars. Now it houses his-and-her desks that face each other. Bookcases run the length of the room. One half is filled with romance novels and business how-to guides, the other half with books on nature and hiking. The bottom row is for the girls. Board books, picture books, and what looks like short chapter books run along the floor that's covered in bean bags and throw pillows.

I've been in here a few times, and the picture the room conjures doesn't change. I can so easily picture Davis at his desk and Cally at hers while the girls play and read at their feet.

It's so domestic and full of life. It's been too painful to

spend any time in here, but now I need the pain. I need to immerse myself in their life, the way it should have been, so I can understand what it was that had them scared enough to allow me to push them away.

We walk through the room, and I pause to drop the folder and teddy bear onto Cally's desk but can't remove my hand. Peering at the open door, I lift the folder to my side and carry it into the bathroom with us.

I trust every person in this house, but I can't be sure we've found every camera yet.

Leo surprised the shit out of me when he arrived back here, without Stella but with arms full of gear, and went to work scanning every inch of the downstairs with military precision.

He's led an entire life I haven't been part of, and the sadness of that fact is crushing, especially since I did it to myself. Now that I've opened these doors, the truth of what I've lost presses down on me.

Then there's Stella, who stands at the shower stall with worry written in every line of her face. She opens her arms to me as she's opened her heart to make us a family, and anger overpowers my fear at the thought that Danica could have taken this from me.

It fortifies my resolve. It makes me stronger and more determined than I've ever been in my life.

Stella reaches for the folder, and after a brief tug-of-war, I relinquish it and watch as she stashes it in the cabinet under the sink. She protects it because it's important to me.

"Tell me," she says while reaching for the bottom of my T-shirt and pulling it over my head.

I allow it. I allow her to take care of me while I work through memories that bring both pain and joy.

"The third floor was Cally's room when I was really little,

but she always let me in. She wasn't one of those big sisters who got annoyed by her younger sibling. She took care of me as though I were hers. I think I started sleeping on her floor as soon as I was old enough to crawl out of my crib. That's why there's bean bags up there."

Emotion collects on Stella's lashes, but she blinks it away and unbuttons my jeans, then removes them and my boxers in one fell swoop. I stand, immobile, allowing her to care for me while I unearth memories I've repressed.

She turns on the shower, then removes her clothes. I scan her naked form, and my body responds. I can't help it, but this isn't about sex. This is about knowing our connection, our relationship that started out with so many rocky shores, will weather whatever storm comes our way.

She tests the water, then ushers me inside. She follows and closes the glass door behind her. It's a tight fit because this shower is only meant for one person, but she maneuvers around me with ease and applies soap to my body while silently prodding me to continue.

"When I was in first or second grade, she'd gone to a friend's house for a sleepover. My dad was upset about something. It was the first time I'd heard him yell like that when she wasn't here, and I got scared, so I ran to Cally's room."

Stella places a gentle kiss on my chest, then turns me toward the spray of hot water and washes my back.

"I wasn't allowed to touch the skylights. That was a rule. One of the only rules I ever remember having, but it was cloudy, and I couldn't find the stars Cally had taught me to count when I was scared. There are a lot of windows, they take up most of the ceiling, but I couldn't find even one star. I thought if I opened the skylights, I'd be able to see them. I got up on my tiptoes and pushed with my fingertips until the heavy lever lifted."

She turns me again and drops to her knees to wash my legs.

"I think I got scared a lot back then, but that night I woke up in the middle of a raging storm and couldn't reach the handle, so I ran to my room to hide. I thought if I couldn't see it, it wouldn't be as bad."

Her eyes are damp, and I know it's not from the shower as she stares up at me through long lashes.

"Cally was gone all weekend. And it rained harder than I've ever seen. My dad was in a terrible mood. He yelled, my mother cried, and I was too scared to tell anyone. By the time Cally got home, there was so much damage to not only the room, but the roof, the floor, even the ceiling on the second floor."

I reach down to pull Stella from her knees. I can't look down at her while I recall the next part.

"I remember my father yelling, and Cally saying she didn't do it while she attempted to salvage all her books and I hid under my bed. Eventually, she realized it was me and took the blame."

I can't swallow past the lump in my throat, so I lift my chin to the ceiling. "She had to work for free for four summers at Hayes & Delacroix to pay for the damage, and my father had the observatory sealed off during construction as punishment. A piece of Cally died that day. Looking back now, I know she shielded me from a lot."

I shake my head. "She tried to shield me from it all. I grew up thinking I had the perfect childhood because she took my father's angry words, my mother's depression and detached parenting, and absorbed them before they ever reached me."

So many memories shift in my mind as I recall them as they were and not as she framed them. The fights my parents had over money and the business. The empty bottles of liquor that I helped Cally carry out of the house. Even when I was old enough to know better, I believed her excuse about cooking wine.

"I believed it all because I wanted to. I grew up in a land of make-believe while she grew up in a house of horrors."

"No." Stella's stern voice has me snapping my attention toward her. "You grew up believing in the good of your family because that's a choice Cally made. Obviously, she wanted happiness for you, and she sacrificed so you could have it. Don't diminish the fact that it was a choice, and one that probably brought her a great deal of peace she didn't otherwise have."

Rose-colored glasses. How can this woman still see the light when she's been shrouded in darkness her entire life?

She inches me out of the way to rinse her body, then turns off the shower and exits the stall. Her moves are efficient but graceful as she dries herself, then pulls down a giant robe from the hook on the door and puts it on. She hands me a towel and leaves the room. By the time I'm dry, she's returned with fresh clothing for us both.

"The girls are having a good time with all the attention they're receiving down there, so let's get dressed and see what Cally left you, okay? Then we'll make a plan."

She doesn't give me a chance to agree, she just drops her robe and steps into a pair of panties, then tugs on navy blue leggings, a bra, and one of my sweatshirts. She's dressed before I've even removed the towel and stands there with a toe tapping against the floorboards, her arms crossed over her chest.

It makes me smile. Correction, she makes me smile.

Even as my life as I knew it is crumbling around me, I know we'll rise from the ashes to build something bigger and better than I could have ever dreamed.

So I do as she requested. I dress, grab the folder that burns my skin, and follow her into my sister's old room.

CHAPTER FORTY-THREE

BECK SITS ON THE FLOOR WITH HIS BACK TO THE BOOKCASE AS I lay out all of Cally's documentation in chronological order.

It starts off strong. Pieces coming from both her and Davis, then, presumably after his death, only from her. The worst of it is you can see her physical decline by her handwriting. The last few documents have shaky chicken scratch in the margins with ink that gets fainter by the sentence.

"They've been working on this for...for years," I say, placing the final note from Cally on the floor. "It's an actual timeline going back to before you were born."

Beck nods, but he hasn't spoken in almost thirty minutes. Not since he handed me the papers and the letter from Cally. We set the letter aside to organize these documents first.

"Why? Why would she go to all this trouble and not just give it to Sterling with her other letter?" His voice is hoarse and scratchy.

"Tabby said she was really confused and paranoid in her last few months. I'm sure that played a part."

He lifts the new letter and holds it out to me.

"Do you want me to read it to you?"

He nods again, so I swallow down my emotions, take a seat next to him, and read Cally's shaky handwriting out loud.

Baby Brother,

I'm sorry for all the lies. All I ever wanted to do was protect you. In his own way, Dad was doing the same thing. He shielded you and Mom the only way he knew how—by cutting you off early.

My only hope is that you'll understand why we did it when you go through our evidence and remember who you were as a twenty-year-old—bright, determined, the best kid I'd ever met, but stubborn as hell and full of righteous indignation.

Davis found proof first. He brought it to me because, at the time, his father and sister were positioning everything to incriminate you. When Davis took over, he did everything he could to turn things around.

My tears stain the page, and my stomach hollows out, but I press on.

Vincent ran their family as though they were royalty, meaning with each child we had, the further down the ladder Danica fell. It was the perfect way to get rid of her, or at least keep her from hurting us. But when Davis died, she took over because our girls were too young.

You've done so well building what should have always been yours, Beck. I'm so proud of you. But she's been preparing for a war her entire life.

Davis and I pulled everything we could, but we know it's not enough to stop her. We're missing something, and I ran out of time. I wanted to protect you, but now I need you to protect my girls, and please make sure they know how much I loved them. This isn't how things were supposed to end. I was supposed to figure out the clues. I was going to finally get my brother back, but then cancer reached up from hell and I didn't have the energy to finish. I'm sorry for that. I'm sorry for missing out on so much of your life. I'm sorry for shielding you from the truth. In my efforts to protect you, I may have hurt you more. But mostly, I'm sorry I couldn't protect you this time.

And I'm sorry for making this harder for you. I don't know who to trust most days. The poison in my body is making things more confusing, so I have to give you what I know in a way no one but you could get it. I just pray that you're the one to find it.

In this folder, you'll find everything Davis and I were able to piece together. There's also a flash drive tucked away in Bear's secret zipper. He's always held my secrets—thank you for that. It'll be hard for you to watch, but it'll be enough to ensure Danica doesn't gain custody. The problem is, once she sees all of this evidence, she'll know we have her missing files, and she'll do whatever necessary to save herself.

I've loved you since the day you were born. I will love you from heaven, and I hope one day you'll forgive me.

I wanted to be your hero, but the truth is, you have always been mine.

Davis and I had to play the villain in your story in order to protect you in ours, and for that, I hope you'll find a way to forgive us. Emmy and Ruby need you now, more than you ever needed me, and I hope you'll shower them with all the love in the world, because that's what you've always been to me—a physical representation of pure love.

From my heart to yours,
Cally

Tears stream down his face as he takes the flash drive

and stands. He hovers over each piece of paper. The dates in the corner of each look like either Cally's handwriting or what I'm guessing is Davis's.

"Do you know what it all means?" I ask, carefully placing my hand on his shoulder blade.

"Not all of it…" He leans down and draws one of the first pieces of paper to him, then bends again to stare at the next one in the row. "It looks as though Delacroix has been stealing from investors for years." Another piece of paper, this one with his father's name on it. "It appears Dad knew and was trying to turn on his partner. When he couldn't get away cleanly, he gave Delacroix control of it all."

I gasp. I can't help it. "Did he know you'd see it as a betrayal?"

He holds up Cally's letter. "I'm guessing he was counting on it." He places the papers on the desk, then sits in one of the chairs and holds up a laptop, searching for the USB port.

I drag a chair next to him as he turns it on, navigates to the USB folder, and opens it.

The video is grainy, but I recognize Cally from the photos in the girls' rooms. She's so frail and crying on the stairs.

Beck searches for the volume and turns it up as loud as it will go.

"Where were you?" a voice screeches. Danica.

"I told you," Cally wheezes. "I was putting notes in the girls' rooms for when I'm gone."

"What's that shit all over your hands? Why did the cameras turn off this afternoon?" Danica comes into view now, her face the picture of evil.

"I fell and knocked over some of the girl's art supplies." Her voice is so weak we can barely make it out.

"She's on the stairs to the third floor," Beck whispers. "This must be the day she was hiding evidence."

"Why do you bother?" Danica snarls. "You're down to your last days, you pathetic piece of shit. Give me six months and those girls will never even remember you existed. By the time they graduate boarding school, they won't even remember they had a family. I might even destroy all your little love notes after you're gone."

Cally reaches out, but she's clearly exhausted and has no energy left to hold her arm up. "Please," she begs. "I did what you asked. I signed everything over to you, so please, leave the notes alone. Please."

Danica leans in close to Cally's face, and to Cally's credit, she doesn't back away. "I'll leave your notes—for now. Tell me, Cally. Does that break your pathetic heart knowing your daughters will never even remember they had a sister after I separate them? Or a mother?"

Cally spits in Danica's face, and the crazy woman laughs. It's an eerie sound that makes me want to vomit.

Danica gives a rough tug on Cally's foot, and she's too sick to stop the fall. We watch in horror as Cally slides down the stairs and lands in a heap at the bottom.

Emmy runs from her room, appearing to hiss at Danica on her way by. She throws herself over her mother, and my stomach does heave this time.

Beck stands from the desk with such force that his chair rolls across the room. "I'll be back. Watch the girls."

I claw after him. "Beck, don't. Don't go after her. We need you here." I don't know what Beck is capable of after seeing that, but if he feels half of what I'm experiencing, it wouldn't be a stretch to say Danica's life is in danger.

He stops in the doorway and softens his features. "I won't put myself at risk. I know what's at stake, but our attorney needs to see this, and we need to get Teddy and a team here as soon as possible."

"Beck?" Elijah calls from the stairs. "Stella? We—ah—we have company."

My heart rate accelerates, and I cling to Beck as he gathers up all the papers and sticks them back into the folder. That doesn't sound good. We walk hand in hand down the hallway toward the stairs. At the bottom, we see a woman in an ill-fitting suit, and for the second time in less than an hour, my stomach tries to revolt.

"Mr. Hayes? My name is Angela Marsh. I'm with Child Protective Services. I'm here to investigate claims made on behalf of Emmy and Ruby Hayes. This is..." The woman squints at the man. "Dr. James Montgomery. He's here to observe."

"Fucking Danica," Beck mutters through clenched teeth. Turning to Elijah, he hands him the file. "Don't let this out of your hands. If you have to piss, hold it. If you take a phone call, hold it. It doesn't leave your hands, understand?"

Elijah nods. "I've got you, Beck." His lighthearted tone is gone. He reads Beck's face better than I do.

I squeeze Beck's arm tight. "We have nothing to hide," I remind him. He takes my hand in his and we descend the stairs as one.

"Is it normal for them to be alone with the girls for so long?" I ask. I've probably already worn a hole in the carpet, but I can't stop myself. At least they have Daisie, but it's getting dark and they aren't dressed warmly enough.

Mr. Sterling arrived from his Sailport Bay office shortly after we called him. While the girls have been playing outside with Mrs. Marsh and the child psychologist, Beck has been filling him in on what we know so far.

"They will be thorough, Miss Anderson," he says dismissively.

"She's worried about them, Harold. Show some fucking respect." Beck's words are a warning, and he heeds it well.

"I'm sorry, Miss—"

"Stella. Just call me Stella."

"Right. I'm sorry, Stella. It's a lot of information I'm taking in. I should have been more sympathetic to your plight."

I hate the guy, and as more time goes on, I can tell Beck does too.

"So you're aware, Harold, this meeting is being recorded. The only people who know this information are in this room right now. Should it slip to anyone, I'll be speaking with the Bar Association."

The older man sighs. "It's not that, Becker. Not at all in fact. However, I do feel guilty for not piecing any of this together myself. I fear I'm likely implicated in some of this as I've been both families' attorney for over thirty years."

The tiniest sliver of sympathy blooms for him, but part of me wants to shout that he should have known better than to work with Danica. Instead, I shift my focus back to the window, back to the girls. Ruby's too young—stranger danger doesn't appeal to her—but Emmy's wary in her interactions.

My heart twists watching Emmy, knowing the reason—having seen with my own eyes why she's terrified of Danica.

Mrs. Marsh and the psychologist, whose name I've already forgotten, turn to each other, then look toward the house. Emmy holds Ruby's hand while Daisie keeps her nose pressed into her side. Even when the man lifts Ruby from the ground, Emmy doesn't let go of her sister. Mrs. Marsh tries to steer her toward the stairs, but she swats the woman's hand away and keeps hold of her sister.

It's enough for me to open the door with a crash and barrel down the steps with open arms.

Emmy's little shoulders sag in relief when she spots me, and the second I lift her in a hug, Ruby claws for me and the man hands her over. With them both in my arms, Emmy cries. She sobs as though the events of the last hour have broken her spirit that was just beginning to heal.

Daisie paces in a circle around us, nudging us with her nose when she can't see Emmy's face.

The adults stop to watch our interaction. When I catch them staring, I lift my chin. "I know that Danica has a reach far more powerful than my own, but I have something she'll never have—I have love for these little girls that will never be bought or broken. I hope that's enough, because it's the only thing they need, and it's the one thing she'll never be able to give them."

I feel Beck behind me before he clears his throat. "We've done as you asked. You're welcome to search the house, just know we haven't been here long enough to make it ours, but make no mistake, we will be making it ours—permanently."

"This is simply a well-check as required by law when... claims are made. Our findings are satisfactory," Mrs. Marsh says with absolutely no emotion.

"Satisfactory?" Beck snorts. It's a derisive sound, and I elbow him in the gut.

"An emergency custody hearing has been brought before the courts, however—"

"Again?" Beck growls. "How many false claims can someone make before they're held responsible?"

"I can't answer that, but we'll have our findings prepared

for the courts before the hearing. I suggest you make preparations to win." Her tone sounds like it's a warning, or a strongly worded suggestion—perhaps she knows Danica too.

If everyone knows who the devil is, why does it feel as though we're all on opposing sides? She can't possibly be blackmailing everyone, can she?

"I won't accept anything else." Beck's words are a promise as he takes Emmy from me. She molds herself around him so tightly I'm not even sure air could get between them. "It's okay, lovebug. I've got you."

Daisie whines at my feet, and I lower my hand to her head. She's as protective of our family as I am.

Good dog.

My gaze drifts from Beck to the people sent here to put cracks in our foundation. But never again will an outside presence tear us down. From this day forward we're a united front, a steel barricade that will protect these girls from everything and everyone wishing them harm. And from that bond, my love twists and turns into an all-consuming living, breathing entity—not only for the girls, but for my entire family, and that starts and ends with Beck.

"Do you need anything else from us?" I ask. Ruby squeezes her thighs and bounces up and down on my hip with a fist full of my hair she's now trying to eat. I deftly pull it free, and she flashes a gummy smile.

I hug her close but speak to the strangers still tracking my movements. "They may not be my blood, but I love them like they are. All of them. Their uncle, the girls, and everyone attached to them. I'll lay down my life before anything hurts them again. Can Danica say the same?"

"The girls feel your love, Stella." The psychologist speaks for the first time, conviction clear in his tone. "That was evident within five minutes. They're lucky to have you. There will be hiccups—they've been through a lot, so always know you can reach out to their pediatrician or therapists if the need ever arises. But the best thing you can give them right now is your unconditional love, and you've done a fine job so far. These visits are generally conducted by the social worker, but I was asked to come along as a favor to an old friend."

He winks, and there's something familiar about him that I can't put my finger on.

He must sense my reluctance because he quickly adds, "That's a good thing, Stella. You'll see. We'll show ourselves out."

I don't move until they're out of view and I'm sure they're gone. Then I take a babbling, drooling Ruby to find the rest of our family.

I've been through so much in my twenty-nine years, but today I'm finally strong enough to fight, and more than that, I'm strong enough to win.

CHAPTER FORTY-FOUR

BECK

STELLA'S WEDDING DRESS HANGS ON THE BACK OF THE DOOR in our bedroom. She should be getting her hair and makeup done today. Instead, she's on the floor with the girls while an army of attorneys takes over our home.

Never in a million years would I have thought I'd be mourning a wedding that started out fake, but now want more than my next breath. That's what she's done to me since the first moment I laid eyes on her in that purple dress —she makes me want those moments that make life worth living.

With a heavy sigh, I join them, standing just behind Stella. Emmy loves to paint, and she has her mother's talent. Ruby sits next to her sister with some kind of nontoxic book that creates colors with water. She studies Emmy intently and mimics her motions.

Emmy's so much like her mother. She holds out her paintbrush and adjusts the one in Ruby's hand. It lasts all of ten seconds before Ruby sucks on the end of it.

Was I like that with Cally? Copying her every move?

"Do you know I had no real memory of this room before we moved in here?"

Stella leans back on her hands to peer up at me, then pats the floor beside her. I'll always heed her invitations, but instead of sitting beside her, I sit behind her, wedging my right leg between her and an unhappy Daisie, wrap my arms around her middle, then rest my head on her shoulder.

When she melts into me, the anxiety tying my stomach in knots eases. "What did you remember of this room? I'm assuming it was your parents."

"Yeah."

Ruby hears my voice and looks at me with a string of drool falling from her double chin. There was a time when that might have repulsed me. Now I hope it's a memory that will never fade.

Leaning into Stella, I swipe the drool from Ruby's chin, but she laughs and tries to bite me. "You're a little vampire, you know that?" I wipe the slimy goo on my pant leg. "The room always smelled like lilacs, but I have no recollection of ever being in here. Not even as a teenager. My mom was always in the library. Cally's the one who made sure I'd done my homework and came home at curfew."

I chuckle, but it's full of sadness. "Cally showed up to a house party when I was a junior in high school. She was older than me, so she had already graduated college, but she still lived at home."

Was that because of me?

Stella rests her head on my chest and hugs my arms.

"Anyway, I thought I'd ignore curfew. She had other plans." The memory comes alive in my mind. It's so real I can hear her voice, and a laugh full of love and sadness fills the room. "She showed up with a baseball bat at three in the morning and broke up the party, then hauled my ass home. I don't know if I've ever been so hungover in my life, but she didn't let me get away with it. The next morning, she woke me up at six and handed me a pair of work gloves and a push mower. She signed me up to mow everyone's lawn within a mile radius of our house—and it was one hundred degrees outside that day. I threw up in the bushes twice."

Stella's body shakes with a belly laugh. "Did you ever miss curfew again?"

"Hell no. Never."

"She loved you, Beck."

I move my chin to the top of her head and allow myself to soak in the love and emotions the memory evokes. "I know. How did I miss so much?"

"You didn't," she whispers. "You lived the life they all wanted for you—you can't feel guilty for that."

It's easy to say, not so easy to do.

A knock at the door has Stella reaching for both girls and Daisie jumping to her feet. It gnaws at me in unimaginable ways because I know Stella's scared, terrified really, and there's not a damn thing I can do about it.

I place a hand on her shoulder. "I'm sure it's one of the attorneys." We'd holed up in here with the kids because Stella was worried all the commotion would scare them, and she's right. It's a lot, even for me.

Kissing the side of her head, I rise and walk to the door. When I open it, I find Teddy and Elijah standing shoulder to shoulder. Teddy bounces on his toes like a kid who's had too much sugar, while Elijah wears an unreadable mask. Daisie barrels into them both, jumping and prancing and licking their hands while they shoo her away.

"Come in." I usher them forward. The girls love them.

It's the rest of the crew they could do without. "What's up?" I ask, resuming my spot behind Stella. "Daisie, sit."

The damn dog gives me the side-eye then meanders back to her spot next to the girls like she's a ninety-year-old grandma—she takes her sweet-ass time.

"Hey, Teddy." Stella flashes him a small smile, but the tightness around her eyes relays her fears.

"Hi, Stella." He paces beside us, and the girls stop painting to watch him. He waves at them, then lifts a laptop in his other hand. "I found the proof. Davis had it here the whole time but didn't know what he was searching for. And the best part is, it matches what was happening at Crystal Waters. I couldn't follow it to the end because I didn't have the beginning. The beginning is right here," he exclaims, each proclamation becoming more animated than the last.

My brows furrow into my line of sight. "What do you mean?"

"Oh, shit, Mr. Hayes. You won't believe it."

Being called Mr. Hayes in my father's old bedroom gives me the heebie-fucking-jeebies.

"Jesus, Teddy. You're standing in my bedroom. Call me fucking Beck."

His face explodes in various shades of red, and Elijah hands Emmy a ten-dollar bill.

"Now tell me what you found."

"This has been going on longer than I've been alive, maybe even before you were born too."

"I'm thirty-five, not eighty."

"Oh, then definitely since before you were born. Your father started keeping a second set of records almost forty years ago, then Davis found a connection on his side, and then your sister—dang, man. She should have been in the

CIA. She pieced it all together even with the missing pieces. My IQ is 120, but she spanked me."

"Spankin' is not allowed," Emmy says, staring at Teddy as if he's her very own Prince Charming.

That's a hell no, Emmy! There will be no dating in this house.

His face deepens to near-purple now and he tugs on his collar. "Ah, no. No, it's not."

It's so absurd that I laugh. It sets off a chain reaction that feels a hell of a lot like relief.

"What he's trying to say is, Cally had it mostly laid out," Elijah says. "She'd been working on it for years, but she got too sick to finish what she started, and even as confused and paranoid as she was at the end, she started making these plans on the days when confusion didn't cloud her thinking. Tabby said the only time she was alone was when she took the girls out for playdates, so Cally did all of this, pushing her body to the limit because even in her most paranoid times, she knew you would take care of them. She's handing it all to you on a silver platter, and you're lucky enough to have boy genius here to follow her trail."

"But what is the trail?" Stella asks. "What did they do?"

"They've been embezzling money for half a century," Teddy explains. "We're talking millions of dollars they've stored in various accounts, rolling it from one to another so it never really appears to be gone because the bottom line always adds up, but they had a plan to take it all and run."

He takes a deep breath, then continues. "It looks like they were waiting until they got a big enough deal, but I can't even begin to imagine what that would be because Miss Delacroix has doubled down in the last four years. She alone has skimmed nearly two hundred million, and that's just with a cursory glance—it's probably much more."

Stella flashes a small smile in my direction. Teddy is talking faster than any man has a right to speak.

"But," he says with a grin, "about six months ago is when she managed to get to Caleb. I don't know what that connection is, but the files in Caleb's office align with the money trail in Cally's files. I think Caleb was trying to alter your files to make it look like a merger would be financially irresponsible to ignore. But what Miss Delacroix was really doing was setting it all up so when she took the money, you would take the fall for it all."

"A cursory glance?" Stella laughs. "Teddy, come on. Your IQ must be higher than 120."

He shakes his head violently. "No, and honestly, I wouldn't even be on this track if you hadn't gotten the ball rolling. This is all because of you."

Her laughter disappears instantly, and she stands even quicker. "No, I didn't do anything."

"You did a good deed because it was the right thing to do," I remind her. "And now you might have saved our family."

"No, Teddy did. Cally and Davis did. I'm just—I'm just the—the…"

My head nearly explodes. "I know it's been a hell of a few days, but going forward, if you ever refer to yourself as 'just the' anything other than my wife, my partner, their auntie, mother, or simply Stella again, I will lose my ever-loving mind. Got it?"

"Mommy said I'd get a new mommy who loved me like an angel," Emmy throws out as if she's reciting the weather. "You'll be Mommy Stella, he'll be Daddy Beck, and I'll be Emmy Hayes. That's how it works."

I'm not sure what's happening with my face, but the color drains from hers and it's a perfect picture of how I feel.

It's not the first time Emmy's said something similar, but it's the way she says it that hits hard—as though it's a truth she's known her entire life.

"Who told you that, Emmy?" I ask, falling to my knees beside her.

"Mommy did. Mommy and Daddy lubed us and now you lub us too." She looks at Stella and grins. "Stella too. Mommy didn't know Stella's name, but she pwomised she'd come."

"I need a freaking truckload of tissues in this house," Elijah grumbles.

"You're not s'posed to curse 'cause we is just kids," Emmy says with a roll of her shoulders, then her attention is lost to her painting. Daisie is snoring in her lap.

"We don't have much time to prepare, but we have enough evidence to drag out anything Miss Delacroix might be planning." Teddy speaks as though he's in a race with himself.

"Okay, what do you need?" I ask, rising to stand next to Teddy.

Stella squeezes my arm, then returns to the girls on the floor, but it's a silent promise that passes between us. One that says she'll protect the girls while I protect our future, and it's a plan I'm wholeheartedly committed to.

"I called my dad," Teddy says with a shrug. Is it normal for grown men to call their dad for help? Who the hell knows anymore. Maybe in his world, it is. "He's a corporate trial attorney. The best, if you ask me. He's on his way. I'm sorry to make a snap judgment, but to be honest, I was concerned I was in over my head and Elijah said it was okay. This is—this is too important to let any detail slide, so I'd feel better if we had a checks-and-balances system until things settle down."

I nod with a smile. "I'd like to meet the man who raised you, Teddy."

This seems to fluster him more. "Oh, okay. Well, he'll be here in about an hour. Then Mr. Sterling brought in a defense attorney for any claims Miss Delacroix might make. There's a litigation attorney here from Crystal Waters but not hired by Mr. Fairfax, two law assistants, Elijah, and me. As I said, not a lot of time to pull it all together, but I believe it's enough to thwart her evil plans."

He nods twice in quick succession, then tries to hide a grin.

"When is the last time you slept, kid?"

"Ah, well…"

"Go take a nap. Elijah will show you to a room, or a sofa—something. We'll wake you when your dad arrives."

He starts to shake his head, but I glare at Elijah. "Did you give him my coffee?"

Elijah smirks. "He likes it."

"Go," I say, opening the door to find a startled Tabby with her fist in the air.

"Ah, hey. Um, Stella's mom's awake…and she's asking for her."

Stella barrels into my back a second later while disengaging Daisie from her legs. "Dang it, Daisie. Sorry," she mumbles. "My foot fell asleep, and Daisie's all up in my business."

Glancing down, I find our dog is in fact, sniffing her ass. Freaking dog!

"I'll stay with the girls. Go." Tabby points with her head. "And I'll keep Dang-it Daisie with me too."

I chuckle while Stella backtracks to kiss the girls. "I'm going downstairs to see Laura for a few minutes, okay? Tabby will play with you."

Emmy holds up her arms, and so does Ruby. Their wide eyes and trembling hands tell us everything we need to know about their emotional state—they'll be attached to us for the foreseeable future, and I can't think of a better place for them to be.

I pick up Emmy, and Stella reaches for Ruby. "Elijah, come get me if you need me for anything."

He salutes me, but it's not mocking. His features are soft, and his gaze is watery. He approves of who I'm becoming and, if I'm being honest, so do I.

CHAPTER FORTY-FIVE

STELLA

Beck sits to my left, closest to the girls, while I hold my mother's hand. Tears flow freely and I'm unable to stop them. This is the most lucid she's been in months. It's a small miracle when I needed one most.

"Why are you crying?" she asks again.

"It—It's just a good day, that's all, Mom."

I think she tries to wink, but she doesn't have control of those muscles anymore. "I'm guessing it has something to do with the hunka bubble-yum holding your hand with a ring that could put an eye out if you're not careful."

She always could make me laugh. It's her superpower.

Beck's deep laugh rumbles from his body to mine and fills the air with a rich warmth we'd been missing.

"This is Becker Hayes, Mom. Do you remember?" It's an unfair question, but I'm surprised by how much I want her to know him.

She squints and smiles. "He feels familiar. I'm sure he came by to ask my permission at some point or other."

"Oh, I did, Mrs. Anderson. I sat right there where Stella

is for hours, and I told you all the ways I love your daughter."

I tilt my chin in his direction. Did he really do that?

"What?" he asks. He must read the skepticism on my face. "I did."

"I believe you." If Beck has proved anything, it's that he's a man of his word.

When I turn back to my mother, she's crying. It's usually a sign that we're about to lose her, and I nearly scream at how unfair it all is.

"Mom, don't cry. What's wrong?"

It takes her a long time to answer, but after Beck hands her a tissue and helps her dry her eyes, she finally says, "You're going to be such a beautiful bride. I hope I get to see it."

A sob breaks from my chest, and Beck coughs to hide his emotions. "No, Mama," I say through the salty taste of tears. "You'll see me. You will."

She nods, then pats my hand, because we both know it's a lie.

"Hi, Auwowa," Emmy pokes her head up on the other side of my mother's bed. No matter how many times we tell her that my mother's name is Laura, she won't have it. To her, she's Auwowa because Aurora is Sleeping Beauty.

And tonight, it fits. Laura Anderson has always been beautiful, but tonight, she glows, and somehow, deep down in my soul, I know our days are numbered.

"Now there's a princess no one could forget."

Emmy beams at her, then rounds the bed and climbs into Beck's lap. Ruby doesn't want to be held, so I keep a close eye on her as she plays at our feet.

Emmy and I tell her about my dress, and for a brief moment, I consider running upstairs to try it on for her, but fear keeps me in my seat. If I go and she doesn't remember me when I get back, it'll crush me.

So instead, the four of us sit and talk. We laugh and I brush away silent tears. She tires too soon and when she blinks slowly, then pauses between each one, I know it's only a matter of seconds before I'm erased from her life again.

It will never get easier. Even knowing it will happen, it's still a loss, a mourning, every time it happens.

"I love you, Mom."

Her gaze struggles to focus, but one side of her face smiles. "I love you, my sweet girl."

She's told me she loves me all my life. But this one, tonight, is the one that binds all my heartache and revives my soul. I needed to hear this from her, and I'll cherish this moment long after she's gone.

Her eyes close, and this time she falls asleep. I scan the entire room, committing every detail to memory. This is the moment I'll recall when I remember her. This one blip in time when she saw me happy and healthy and surrounded by love.

"It's getting late," Beck whispers, tucking me into his side. "Why don't you take the girls to bed? I'm going to check in with the Teddy brigade, then I'll join you."

I don't fight him because I have nothing left to fight with tonight. The wave of emotions never seems to end. It's exhausting, and I'll need all my strength for court tomorrow. So I kiss my mother goodnight, then lift a yawning Ruby into my arms. Emmy slips her hand into my free one, and we head upstairs to sleep.

THE BED DIPS ON BECK'S SIDE AND MY ARM SNAPS OUT TO catch a child. It takes me a few seconds to get my bearings and understand that Ruby is still asleep on my chest and Emmy is tucked under my other arm in between us. The movement has Daisie stirring at the foot of the bed.

The stinking dog isn't supposed to be down there, but she managed it tonight.

"Shh," Beck whispers, carefully dragging Ruby from my grasp and placing her between us. "I can't believe she slept through your snoring."

My nose scrunches up and my jaw hangs open. Even in the dark, I can see he's trying to suppress a laugh.

"I was not snoring."

"You were, but it was cute. It also shows how tired you are. Go back to sleep."

"What time is it?"

"Four."

"In the morning?" I nearly roll out of bed.

"Shh. Yes. Four in the morning," he whispers.

"What's wrong? What can I do?"

He shakes his head, then reaches over the girls to seek out my hand in the dark. When he finds it, he entwines our fingers, and rests our clasped hands over my heart.

"Nothing's wrong." He glances down at Ruby, then over to me and Emmy. "In fact, nothing has ever been more right. I stayed up with Teddy because Elijah got him high on my coffee."

"Oh no." My body shakes with laughter, and it's nearly impossible to remain silent.

"It all worked out. He and his dad walked me through every single document they'll present to the judge tomorrow."

Emmy flops over and laughs in her sleep. My heart flutters in my chest.

"If she can laugh in her sleep then I think we're doing something right," he whispers.

I roll over so we're face to face. He looks as tired as I feel. My sleep has been fitful at best, and I'm not sure when he actually slept last.

"I'm sorry about our wedding day." The emotion in his words tells me the guilt over it has been weighing heavily on his shoulders.

"Beck. I don't care about a ceremony. To be honest, I've never really been able to picture my wedding anyway. This, right here, is where we were supposed to be today—fighting for these little girls—fighting for us. I'll never regret that, so you have no reason to apologize. Well, you may want to apologize to Bella." I cringe. "No one called her, and she waited at the church for over an hour for us."

"No," he groans.

"She finally called Tabby, who let her know what was going on, but she worked really hard to pull everything together. I feel terrible."

"We'll make it up to her, after we get through this."

We're silent for a long moment, listening to Emmy's deep breaths and Ruby's gurgled noises.

"What are you thinking about?" he asks.

I learned a long time ago not to speak my fears because they generally come true, but when he squeezes my hand, then leans over the girls to kiss my lips with a heartbreakingly gentle touch, I open my heart. "We will get through this, right? The four of us, together?"

He nods, but never breaks eye contact. "It could be a difficult few months, but I'll spend every dollar to my name to make sure they get what they deserve—and it starts with

Danica. She's the mastermind behind all our heartache, and karma is finally on our side."

Ruby kicks in her sleep and gets him right in the chest. She's strong for such a little thing and he grunts, then lays his head back on his pillow.

"Yes, Stella. We'll get through this. I'll make sure of it."

Call me crazy, but I believe every word he says.

<hr>

Morning came too quickly, and the girls could sense something was off from the moment they woke up next to us.

And it all went downhill from there. When Emmy realized we were leaving for the day, she complained of a stomachache, then an earache, and that her heart had broken so she needed me to stay home with her.

Ruby just wailed and screamed, feeding off her sister's energy.

Leaving them, even in the loving care of Tabby and Leo, is one of the hardest things I've ever had to do, and that includes living through Silas's gaslighting and abuse.

But that's how I ended up in the courtroom with my skirt on backward, a blob of applesauce on my right boob, and two different shoes.

Beck didn't fare much better. Although he does have matching shoes, his shirt is wrinkled, and he may have used Emmy's glitter gel instead of his hair gel this morning.

"We'll break for lunch in about twenty minutes," Mr. Park, Teddy's dad, whispers to my left. Beck sits on my right, and Teddy next to him. Behind us is an entire row of attorneys, and behind them, our Sailport Bay family.

Danica and her team have held court all morning. Teddy

and his dad thought it best to allow them to dig their own grave, so we've sat through every demeaning, fraudulent claim she could dream up. All the while I stewed and imagined horns sprouting from her skull that I could use to swing her around and toss her ass-first into a firepit straight to hell where she belongs.

"How can she be allowed to submit photos that are artificially generated? That's not even me up there," Beck hisses.

Another lawyer leans forward to answer. "We're documenting it all. When it's our turn, we'll prove their lack of authenticity."

"I'm checking everything myself," Teddy assures us for the fourth time. "And my dad is checking what I've checked. I promise." He smiles over us, and when I look at his dad, his expression is one of pride for his son. That's how it's supposed to be.

And that's the kind of parent I want to be. That's the kind of parent I will be for our girls.

Please, God, if you're up there, just give me the chance to be that kind of parent to Emmy and Ruby. Please.

"Are you okay?" Beck whispers into my ear. I nod emphatically even though I'm anything but okay.

He holds up our joined hands tightly and I gasp, drawing curious stares, when I glance down and find my nails have broken skin on his knuckles. He quickly tugs our hands under the table.

"I'm so sorry. I'm nervous. Really nervous."

He rests his forehead against mine. "Breathe, Stella Jane. Breathe."

Our breaths mingle as we share the air between us. After a few haggard attempts, my body finally relaxes, and I loosen my grip on his hand.

When we lift our heads, I find the judge watching us, but

his foreboding glare does nothing to ease my fears. It's not the same judge we had last time, and that's setting off alarm bells in every corner of my mind.

He doesn't flinch when Danica screeches something and points at me. Or when he slams his gavel and calls a recess.

But there's a slight tilt of his lips as he descends the stairs and exits the courtroom for his chambers.

Please let that be a good sign. Please.

"Stella?"

I bolt upright in my chair and only stay seated because Beck has a hand on my shoulder holding me steady.

A delicate hand reaches out and hands me some wipes. Bella. "They'll get that stain right out. I tried to get it to you earlier, but you've got a big, ah, group here today."

I offer her a kind smile while Beck gives our apologies and I stand up to attack the dried applesauce. She's a miracle worker because it comes right out with hardly a wet spot to be seen.

"Thank you, Bella. Honestly. Today has been...trying."

"You're doing great, Stella. Really. Here." She hands me a brown paper bag, then reaches into her oversized purse and pulls out six more to give to each of our attorneys. Too curious not to peek, I open it and find it full of snacks. She shrugs. "It could be a very long day."

She approaches Teddy next, but she drops the bag, he fumbles to catch it, and they collide headfirst in the mayhem.

"Crap. Sorry," she mutters, holding her head.

"No, it's my..." His mouth falls open and he doesn't finish his sentence. Beck notices the awkward exchange and nudges him in the back, but he jumps into the air like a horse who's seen a snake and plows forward into Bella, knocking her over. Luckily, she lands with a thud in my vacated chair.

"Bella?"

"Teddy?"

"Wait," Beck says, pinching his nose. "You two know each other?"

"Um, we sort of dated in high school."

It's official. Teddy's face is not capable of turning any redder.

"I can't believe I didn't recognize you," Bella says with a strange grin and aggressive shake of her head.

"Well, you only saw me from behind…"

Something happens between them, making Teddy spin in place and Bella practically jumps over the table.

"Great to see you, Teddy. See ya." She sprints from the room, leaving a trail of snacks in her wake.

"What the hell was that about?" Beck asks.

Teddy closes his eyes, and his father laughs. "Teddy and Bella had a rather embarrassing skinny dipping encounter their senior year. I had to pick them up at the station." His laughter is rich and welcoming, and even Teddy's mortification brings a sense of normalcy to this stupidly messed-up day.

"Go take a breather," Mr. Park says. "That was just the warm-up. It'll be a long day still."

Beck doesn't need to be told twice. He takes me by the hand and practically drags me from the courtroom.

CHAPTER FORTY-SIX

STELLA

WE EXIT THE COURTROOM AND BECK LEADS ME DOWN THE hall to an open bench. He holds my hand while I sit, then joins me so every inch of my left side is touching his right side. There's not a breath of space between us, and we just sit and watch people walk by.

Slowly, the muscles in my body uncoil, and Beck seems less tense next to me too.

"It's pretty intense, huh?" he finally asks.

"It is," I agree. "I've never had anything so valuable to fight for before. It's like the possibility of her getting our girls is shredding my heart, and it hurts, Beck. What if—"

"There are no 'what ifs,' Stella. It's you and me and Emmy and Ruby." He sighs. "Fine, and Dang-it Daisie too."

I laugh and it feels so good—like a release.

"We're going to be okay."

I lean my head on his shoulder. I'm suddenly so tired— the kind of tired that's bone-deep. "I know. But it'll be better when it's all over."

"Becker?"

I straighten my spine and stare up at the men standing before us. My hand clamps tighter to Beck's, but when I look over, Beck is smiling.

"Judge," Beck says in greeting, before turning to the other man. "Is this what you meant by being a good thing?" Beck asks James—the child psychologist—and all the pieces fall together.

"This is your son, the single dad?" I ask the judge.

"The very one. I hope you can forgive my father's meddling," James says. "I don't generally accompany Mrs. Marsh. However, her husband has been known to do Danica's bidding occasionally."

"Sending James ensured the report was accurate." The judge winks. "Danica may believe she has a hand in every pot, but I've been in this town longer than she's been alive. She's not the only one who has strings to pull. I can't say for sure, but I do believe you'll have a fair outcome. The judge presiding over your case is known to be fair. Now, I have court myself, so I'll leave you two to your break, but know we're rooting for you."

The judge turns to go, but James stays put.

"Your sister was very special, Beck. I—she left quite an impression on me. We helped each other out a lot. I'm a little lost without her, to be honest. Single parenting isn't easy, so I'm real glad you two have each other."

"Are you... Do you need help?" Beck asks.

James waves him off. "No, I'm in the process of finding a nanny, but it's—"

"A real pain in the ass," Beck interrupts. He points to the notebook James is holding. "May I?"

James shrugs and hands him the blank notepad and a pen.

I lean forward to see he's writing Lottie's email address and the Single Dad Hotline on it, and I smile.

"Email this woman. She runs the Single Dad Hotline." Beck casts a loving gaze my way. "She's really good at her job, and she'll find you the right person."

"Huh," James says. "Never heard of it. Thanks though. A personal recommendation always eases a little of my worries." He takes his notebook back and nods. "I'll see you around, and thanks for this." He holds up the notebook, then turns and disappears into the people milling about the hallway.

We sit in companionable silence as minutes tick by— our minds decompressing by people watching.

"We should probably get back in there," Beck finally says. "Are you ready to tell our side?"

I suck in a deep breath but stand and hold my head high. "I am. I just need a minute alone."

"Stella," he says, worry etched into his face.

"I'm okay. Really. I'm just going to walk the halls for a minute and release some of this anxiety." I shake out my arms for effect.

"You sure?" He's definitely not convinced.

"Yes. A few laps of the hallways and I'll be good to go."

He laughs, then leans in to kiss my cheek.

"Go," I tell him. "I'll meet you in there."

He glances around. "You're positive?"

I nod. Even if I were to run into Danica now, it's not like she could do anything. "I'm sure. I'll head into the court-room in a minute."

I wait until he enters the conference room we were assigned, then head in the other direction. I have no idea where I'm going, but I do need to move. My skin is itchy, and anxiety is making my muscles hurt from being so tense all day.

I'm on my second lap when I look up and stop cold. Caleb is headed straight for me. I spin in a circle, hoping he hasn't lifted his eyes from his phone yet, and dart into the nearest unlocked room.

When the door shuts, I inhale deeply, then release it slowly. It's some kind of conference room that's currently pulling double duty as a storage room.

"In here," Caleb says on the other side of the door, and my heart races so fast I become dizzy. The only place to hide in here is behind a small folding partition along the back wall, so I run to it and duck down just as I hear the door open.

Hushed words filter in a moment later, and alarm bells ring like a warning, but my ears still strain to listen.

"Did you even check to make sure this room was empty before barging in?" Danica hisses.

I press my back into the cool cement wall and try not to make a sound as I reach for my phone in my bag. Can't a girl catch a freaking break around here?

"There's no one in here, see?" Caleb sighs heavily.

Wait. Did he not see me enter?

My heart thuds in my ears, but I wake up my phone and hit record. Surely it can't be this easy—nothing is ever this easy.

"What do you want?" Danica demands.

"You haven't been home in a week. What did you expect me to do?"

It takes so much effort to hold in a gasp, but it helps that I might not even be breathing.

"Don't be ridiculous," Danica scoffs.

"I love you."

"And you're a fucking fool." The vitriol in Danica's voice has my heart clenching painfully. I know that kind of abuse.

"Am I? Was it all a lie?"

Danica's laugh is cruel. "It's a good thing you're so pretty because you're an idiot. You were a means to an end and not even a very good fuck."

"That's not what this was, and you know it."

Their steps are muted from the worn carpet, but their feet make swishing sounds that alert me when they're close. Someone is pacing.

"Wasn't it? Tell me, does this sound familiar? 'But Caleb.'" Danica's voice changes, it's quieter, more fragile sounding. "'He's going to ruin everything I've worked for. He's going to destroy me. I won't be able to carry on if that happens. I can't. You have to help me.'"

Silence.

"You see." Danica's voice is back to her normal tone of hatred. "You really were a means to an end, and you're no better than fucking Stella—so desperate to be loved you fell for every line I fed you. You did my dirty work. You got me into his company, you made my plan possible, and if I crash and burn, guess where the fingers will point?"

Oh my God.

"While Becker was busy building a *luxury* brand, I diversified into other opportunities. I expanded on what my father had built. I made it better. He stole from our investors for years, but I took it to the next level. Hundreds of millions of dollars sit with my name on it and now, with your help, I'm not only going to tear Becker's company down while leading the blame straight to his doorstep before I disappear, but I'll get those girls too and ruin every last remaining heir to the Hayes line—young, impressionable minds are so easy to poison. Don't you agree?"

She's fucking insane.

"Was the bullshit about your father all a lie too? How he groomed you to be this vile version of yourself that no one could love?" Caleb sneers.

The sound of a slap reverberates against the walls, and my head snaps to the side as though I were the one struck.

"Don't speak about my father. Ever. You're lucky I gave you as much time as I did. You really are a useless piece of shit, but fuck it. You scratched an itch."

She's disgusting.

"You have no regrets? You're ruining lives, and none of that matters to you?" Caleb asks.

"The only regret I have is not making you beg more—"

"That's enough." Caleb's voice doesn't waver, but it carries a tone I've never heard from him before.

"Are you going to cry?" Danica hisses. Her tone makes my stomach turn. "You know how much I love it when you cry. Do you want to talk about your wife some more? Will that make this easier for you to swallow?"

"You're sick," Caleb snaps. His tone is lethal. "But you're also wrong about where the fingers will point. I may have screwed up accounts in Becker's office, but I never did more. I'll take a hit to my reputation, they'll say I've lost my touch, or possibly had intent to do more, but I didn't. You, on the other hand? Your downfall will be brutal. Maybe, if I'm lucky, someone will make you their bitch in prison. I hear they also like to see people cry."

The door opens to loud voices, and it drowns out anything else Danica and Caleb might say.

I stand frozen for a long time until the room falls silent again.

"You can come out now."

I suck in an audible breath, and after my shock wears

off, I count to ten, then slowly slide along the wall. When I exit my hiding spot, I jump in surprise.

Caleb leans against the opposing wall, waiting for me. All the fears Silas instilled in me come rushing back, and my gaze darts between him and the door. He seems to sense my fear and slowly walks to the side, so there's a clear path to the exit. I can do this. He will not intimidate me like Silas did.

"You knew I was in here?" I glance down at the phone in my hand. Should I keep recording?

You will no longer do what makes things easy for others at the expense of yourself. The voice I hear in my head is my own. It's not entwined with Silas or my childhood bullies. It doesn't sound like my mother or a father I never knew—it's just me, strong and taking up all the space in my mind. It's a reminder to take up space wherever I am.

My shoulders roll back, my head lifts, and I face Caleb head-on with my phone still recording.

"I saw you enter. Hopefully you have half a brain cell and recorded all of that."

My jaw hangs open. Why would he let me witness this kind of encounter?

He shakes his head. "Don't tell me you panicked and didn't record that."

His words feel cruel, but his tone betrays his pain. "Is Danica why you lash out at people?"

Caleb's lip curls into a snarl, but it's lacking its usual bite. "No, sweetheart. That's just my DNA."

"Why? Why did you do this?"

"For fuck's sake. Be more specific," he barks.

"All of it."

He glances at the phone in my hand, then back up at me. "I needed an outlet for my grief, and she was there. I thought I loved her. And I thought I could make a merger happen without crossing the line into the illegal—I didn't," he snaps. "I may have fucked with records, but I didn't ever cross that line."

"You gave a competitor information, Caleb."

He grins, and I take a step back. "Did I?"

"Didn't you?" I'm seriously the worst detective in America.

He shakes his head slowly. "Danica is right that I have a pretty face, but I'm also much smarter than she gave me credit for. The only thing I'm guilty of is trying to bring her into all those deals with Becker under her different entities' names, but it was all aboveboard."

"No, we found—"

"You found mistakes, just as I've said, and I'll take those repercussions. But the rest of it? That's all her."

He glances away, but not before a hint of pain shows itself in his gaze.

"You really did love her."

His eyes narrow, but he nods, once. "I wanted to, but it wasn't anything like my marriage. I foolishly hoped that a merger would be enough for Dani—that's all she wanted in the beginning, or so she said. As time went on, I hoped it would, at the very least, put her in a position where Beck could facilitate her getting some help. She played me emotionally, but no one ever fucks with my career. So," he says with an arch of his brow. "It's kill or be killed."

"You gave this to me to save your own ass."

"Think what you want." He adjusts his tie, but his hand trembles. It's the only outward sign that he's not holding it together as well as he'd like me to believe, and I feel a flash of empathy he probably doesn't deserve.

"You're a smart man, Caleb," I say quietly. "You know that's not love. The way she speaks to you is not love."

He lifts a shoulder and walks toward the door. "Hurt people hurt people, Stella. I hope you're the one to break the cycle."

His words knock me back a step. "If that's true, why did you tell her about Silas?"

A flicker of real emotion casts his face in shame before he drops his gaze to the floor. "I told her about you when I first hired you. In a 'guess what happened at work' kind of way. I never could have anticipated things playing out the way they did."

"Would you have told her if you knew how she'd use Silas to hurt me?"

He stares at me blankly. "I can stand here and lie to you, but the truth is, I don't know—I can't say what I would have done. And it's a waste of fucking time to think about it."

With that, he walks out the door, and a second later, Beck barrels through it.

"Are you okay?" he asks, breathing hard and gripping my biceps to inspect every inch of me. "I couldn't find you, then I found Danica glaring at the door, and then Caleb walked through it. I just had a bad feeling about it all. Are you okay?"

I blink.

"Stella?" Beck asks again. "I swear on my life, if they did anything to you…"

"No, I'm—okay. But—well, listen to this." I press stop on the recording, then play. It's not the best quality, but there's no mistaking their voices.

"No way," Beck says, then leans against a vacant table.

An older woman enters and does a double take when she finds us here, but she shakes her head, muttering under her breath, and grabs a stack of chairs piled up next to the door.

I drag him out of the room by his sleeve.

"He knew you were in there?"

I nod.

"He came clean." His brows pinch as he scans the hallway.

"Maybe he thinks the court will go easy on him because he did?"

"What was he thinking?" His hands clench at his sides, and I can tell this information upsets him. He can deny it all he wants, but he feels the sting of his betrayal because he trusted Caleb.

"We should get this to Mr. Park, right?" This snaps him out of his fog, and he nods. "Yeah, Cally's video should be enough, but this will give us a win in the corporate suit too."

We enter the courtroom and hand my phone over to Teddy's dad. Beck does most of the talking, and my gaze wanders around the room, landing on Danica more than once.

Hurt people hurt people.

It's a truth I understand, but refuse to participate in. At some point, you have to take responsibility for your own actions. My issues are my own, just as Danica's are hers, and Caleb's only belong to Caleb.

Perhaps that's what sets me apart from them. I'm aware enough to know this, and I'm strong enough to act on it.

So in my head, I reframe a new mantra. One that will carry me and the girls for a long time to come.

Hurt people can only hurt you if you allow it—and I won't allow it.

I'll fight every day to know my worth, to make sure our

girls know theirs, and if someone doesn't see our value, we'll know it's okay to walk away from what hurts us.

Never again will I allow someone else's opinion of me to shape who I am or who I can become.

Beck squeezes my hand, and I follow him to our seats. But this time, when the gavel cracks down, I'm here, in the present, ready to take on our future.

A future filled with love notes and lifelines.

EPILOGUE

Beck
One year later

"Are you ready?"

There's something about Stella's voice that settles me, especially now. I turn from the windows to find her propped against the doorframe of the library.

It no longer holds a hospital bed, or the scent of death. Now it's a place for new beginnings and life. We spend more time in this room than anywhere else.

After Stella's mom passed away, I wanted to burn this room to the ground, but Stella had other plans. She's always been able to change my perspective—it's a gift I'm grateful for. When I wanted to set fire to the entire house, she convinced me to give it a facelift and add new memories to the ones that already live in its walls. That included opening the third floor to the stars again. Now it's Emmy's favorite place to paint.

Memories and experiences brought us here. I don't want to

erase what we've been through. I want to celebrate that we've made it.

So we did. We cleared the room, painted the walls, bought new furniture, and decorated it with memories of our lives. Photos of my parents, Cally and Davis, Laura, Tabby and Leo, Elijah and Samira all fill the space. And at the center of it all is a photo of the four of us—me, Stella, Emmy, and Ruby. Though Ruby does appear to be giving us the finger in it, it's my favorite—even with Dang-it Daisie jumping in midair beside us.

It was taken right after I was awarded full and permanent custody of the girls.

Today, we'll make them both of ours—officially.

"You look beautiful," I say.

She's wearing the same dress she wore to our rehearsal dinner because she insists on creating new memories in it. And today she will. Today she'll become my wife and the girls' mother in a single ceremony, and I've never been happier or more fulfilled than I am in this moment.

She crosses the room with the fabric of her dress flowing around her legs. "Are you okay?"

"Of course I am. I'm excited and happy. Are you?"

It's been one year since the night I almost lost everything. One year since our rehearsal dinner went sideways and everything changed, but I've spent every single day of that year falling more madly in love with her.

There's a certain amount of fear that comes with loving someone this much, but the love overrides the fear every time I'm on the receiving end of her affection, and she gives it freely.

She stares out at the ocean and the mob of people putting together our reception for later today.

"This is the best day of my life," she says with watery eyes.

When she falls into my arms, all is right with the world.

"Are the girls ready?"

She nods against my chest. "Emmy made a valiant effort to get Ruby into that pile of tulle, but she wasn't having it. We compromised with a little yellow sundress."

That draws a chuckle from me. "We should get going then before Ruby spills something on it."

Stella squeezes me harder, and I do the same. I know she's counting to ten before she releases me. Just like the love notes we leave throughout the house, physical touch is our talisman—it centers and calms and feels like home.

"I found it," Emmy yells, bursting into the room. Stella mentioned once that she wanted to teach her to live loudly. I didn't know what she meant at the time, but I do now. Emmy's face is pure sunshine. The shadows that chased her have eased over the past year, and she's no longer the little girl cowering in the corner.

She's independent, and stubborn as hell—just like her mother. Both of them.

I smile and my heart rate picks up speed. It took six months for the case with Danica to come to a close, and six more months for us to settle into our new normal, but we've done it. We're living proof that love is the secret to happiness.

Therapy has also helped. We all go individually to work on our specific trauma, then we go once a month for maintenance family therapy, and I'm grateful for it—we're grateful for it.

"What did you find, lovebug?" I ask, crouching down in front of her.

She holds up a lavender sticky note that has *Hayes Family Love Notes* printed across the top. Stella drew flowers and hearts around the name Hayes and under that it says, *love from heaven, love from me, all around our family tree.*

My throat closes up. Stella leaves love notes for the girls every day, and she usually finds a way to include Cally.

"I found mine too," Stella says with a smirk, and I feel my cheeks heat.

My love notes to Stella are not safe for little eyes, and she calls me out on it in front of Emmy, knowing it'll make me flush. But it's not a lie. I can't wait to fuck my wife tonight.

Stella sidesteps me and pulls Emmy into a hug. "This is my favorite one," she says, caressing the little note in Emmy's hand.

Emmy nods with a grin that takes over her entire face. "Tabby read it to me. Can we start now? I'm ready and I want to go make you a Hayes. Daddy, please can we start?"

We've lost the Beck in my name this year, and Stella is Mama thanks to Ruby. I glance over at the portrait we had painted of the girls with Cally and Davis. It's moments like this that guilt hits me. Guilt that I get to be here—I get to be their daddy—and he doesn't. But it's a guilt that serves no purpose, so as I always do, I offer a silent prayer of thanks and a promise to keep them safe.

That's when I notice Stella's note to Cally. She leaves them near her picture sometimes, like a reminder of sorts. This one says, *I promise to love and protect them with my whole heart—Stella*, and I know she's overcome with the same sense of guilt sometimes.

"Daddy!" Emmy scowls with her hands on her hips. "Pa-lease can we start?"

Ruby toddles in with Tabby following closely behind.

I scoop her up, and then kiss Emmy on the head. "Yeah, lovebug. We can go make Stella a Hayes now."

She claps and runs from the room, and Tabby laughs, but it's full of wild emotions.

Tabby fans her face. "I'm literally a month pregnant. I shouldn't be this emotional."

"You should be whatever you're feeling," Leo says, entering the room and hugging her from behind. His hands rest possessively over her belly. He lifts his gaze to Stella and me. "Elijah, Teddy, and Bella are here. You guys ready?"

"Oh, I'm ready." I take Stella's hand and tuck Ruby onto my hip. "Did she agree to move in yet?" I ask, winking at Tabby.

Leo frowns. "Not exactly."

"What does that mean?" Stella searches Tabby's face.

"Ugh, fine. I said we could tear down a wall that separates our apartments. Baby steps, you know?" she says with an annoyed shake of her head as we walk down the hall.

"No," Leo corrects. "What you said was I could put in a door that separates our apartments."

"Same thing," she says with a shrug, then stops when we enter the kitchen.

Judge Montgomery stands in front of the open windows facing the ocean, and our Sailport Bay family is behind him waiting for us to make our way down to the beach.

To his left, Lucía stands hand in hand with Oliver Shines. A happy side product of their union is that Lucía has stayed part of our Sailport Bay family.

On the other side of the room, Teddy and Bella speak in hushed tones while she spins the new ring on her finger like she's afraid she'll lose it. Elijah and Samira stand next to them with the smiles of proud parents even though we're the same age. Stella says it's because they're old souls.

Even Daisie sits like a lady with bows on her ears, but I still keep an eye on her—who knows when she'll freak out.

This is the family we've built. This is the family that will fill this home with love for years to come and the emotion of it nearly knocks me over.

"Are we ready?" Judge Montgomery asks.

"Yes. Yes, we're ready," Emmy squeals, bouncing around the room.

Everyone laughs. There was a time when all this little girl knew was sadness, and this is something Stella and I have done too—we've given her a childhood she won't have to forget to survive. If I accomplish nothing else in my life, this one thing will have made my life worth living.

Stella and I walk closer to the windows, and I hand Ruby over to Tabby. There's not a dry eye in the room, and I bet if I looked outside where everyone is eavesdropping, there wouldn't be one out there either.

I nod for the judge to begin.

"I've participated in a lot of gotcha days," he begins. "But I don't think any have ever been as special as this. Beck and Stella have gathered here today to unite four souls—Beck and Stella in marriage, and their adoption of Emmy and Ruby. That's one heck of a gotcha day, if you ask me. And it's one that will be celebrated by all for years to come."

My gaze drifts to Stella, then to our girls, and I commit this moment to memory. I brand it on my heart.

This is the day I let go of old pain and open myself up to a future filled with love, loyalty, and a happily ever after.

Carolina Counting, BREAKING NEWS:

- Caleb Fairfax avoids jail time by delivering details of the Delacroix's dirty deeds: Will it be enough to avoid disbarment? Time will tell.
- Danica Delacroix is sentenced to twenty years in a federal penitentiary. She's currently in lockdown for assaulting an officer. Her attorney has no comment.
- Chelsea Day School cleans house, hiring all new teachers and renaming the Dean's building after Stella Hayes. The Anderson building boasts mental health care facilities specializing in abuse.
- Silas Weaver is released for good behavior but will never work in education again. Our sources say he's working the drive-through at a fast-food chain in the middle of Maine.
- Carolina Counting's favorite sweethearts, Becker Hayes and Stella Anderson, tie the knot in a secret ceremony. Keep reading for a glimpse into their special night.

* * *

Eight months later

"Welcome to *The Love Line*. I'm your host, Oliver Shines, and today we have a very special invitation for you all. The Sailport Bay Big Baby Bonanza is taking place in the town hall this Saturday at 2 p.m. Come celebrate Leo and Tabby, Becker and Stella, and our newest residents, Teddy and Bella, as they embark on this next phase of their lives. There's no registry, but the couples request donations be made in Cally's name to Cally's Constellations, opening near the boardwalk next month. This is what it's all about, love liners—life, and love, and hope. Thank you for listening."

BONUS SCENE

Stella

"I think I'm going to be sick," Tabby groans. We waddle side by side into the restroom. "Who thought a baby shower was a good idea when we're all so pregnant?"

My expression clearly says, *are you serious?*

"Elijah," we hiss in unison.

Bella enters behind us with green and yellow ribbons stuck to the bottom of her shoes and tears in her eyes. "I'm too big. I can't get it off," she wails, pointing to the ribbon.

"Bella, we told you to let someone else do the decorating," I say gently.

Tabby is ready to pop any day. Bella is a couple of months behind her, and I'm due two weeks later, so that means I'm the one who will have to remove the offending decorations.

"Come here," I say. The thought of crossing the tile floor exhausts me. Bella is the only one of us who manages not to waddle. "Okay, hold still." I hang on to her arm for support because my balance has gone to hell, then step on the ribbons because there is no way I'm bending all the way down to grab them.

"Take a step forward."

She does, but the ribbon slips from beneath my shoe.

"Good grief," Tabby grumbles. Pregnancy has not been kind to her, and her days of spewing rainbows are on hiatus. "Maybe we should call one of the guys to help."

"NO!" Bella and I nearly scream.

I take a breath. "No, I need a minute. If Beck hovers over me for one more second, I might lose my mind. He wouldn't even let me walk down the stairs by myself."

"Same," Bella says dreamily. "Teddy is afraid I'll burn my belly, so I'm not allowed to use the stove or the oven. It's sweet but—"

"It's too fucking much," Tabby fills in.

"Way too much," I agree. "All of them. I swear they have secret meetings on ways to keep us safe. Don't they realize women have been having babies forever?"

"Oh, they realize," Elijah says, sticking his head into the restroom. "They're just freaked the fuck out."

"Elijah," I say, and my shoulders relax. Since he partnered with Crystal Waters and took over the Raleigh office, we don't see him as much. "I've missed you."

He engulfs me in a hug, but it's awkward with my big belly in the way.

"I've missed you too. You're looking good, though." He lifts his gaze to Tabby and Bella. "You all look good. How the hell did you all end up pregnant at the same time?" he asks through his laughter.

Tabby rolls her eyes. "I'd given up trying and bam. One night. That's all it took."

"Well, I hope it's been more than one night, Tabby. That

man stares at you like he's trying to eliminate all your clothing with eyeball lasers."

Her face flushes. I know for a fact they're getting down and dirty. Pregnancy hormones are no joke, and Tabby finally confided in me because she was afraid something was wrong with her. But nope, all three of us have been chatting like we're members of an old-school locker room. It's been...interesting.

"Our condom broke," Bella says shyly. "But we're happy."

"Of course you are, sweetie," I say, and Elijah wiggles his brows my way. "No story here, we were ready and just stopped trying not to get pregnant."

"Well, you ladies better pee. You have approximately three minutes before those men come looking for you."

Our collective groans bounce off the tile bathroom.

***

Beck

"How's Lottie?" I ask, but keep my eyes glued to the exit. I'll give Stella five more minutes before I check on her.

"Stella's fine, Beck. She has to pee. Cut her some slack," Elijah says with a knowing smirk. I know damn well he just spent fifteen minutes with her in the restroom. He glances over his shoulder at his sister.

So much has changed in a year—for all of us.

"And Lottie's finally figured out that she has a knack for placing happily ever afters." He chuckles.

"Why is she talking to Sebastian Walker?"

I don't necessarily care that he's here, but I was under the impression he was only in town to sign some papers. Elijah cringes, and I give him my full attention.

"Sorry about that," he says with a scrunched-up nose. "I had him stop by to talk to Lottie." I raise a brow and wait for him to continue. "Well, I knew she was here interviewing you and Stella to make improvements on her survey for the Single Dad Hotline, and that guy needs all the help he can get."

I cross my arms over my chest and watch him. "Why?"

"He's going through a tough divorce."

"Are any of them easy?" I ask.

Elijah chuckles darkly. "Probably not, but he didn't see this one coming until his wife fell through a middle school curtain with his business partner's dick inside of her—during their daughter's talent show—while their daughter was performing on stage. Luckily, they were tangled in the curtain so you couldn't see anything, but there was no mistaking what they were up to."

My mouth drops open. "Christ. That's…"

"Savage," Elijah says wearing a frown. "His daughter's a mess, his company is unstable, and his life basically just imploded, so I strong-armed Lottie into helping him because we need his properties to be fully functioning next year."

"That's really awful," I say. "Lottie's okay with helping him?"

"I pulled big brother rank."

I raise my brows in suspicion—Lottie never caves.

"Okay, I begged…just like I begged with you and Stella, and look how that turned out? Next year is too important for our deal to go sideways because his business partner is a turd gobbler. He's a great dad, but he can't be in two places at once so I thought maybe Lottie's new partnership with the local summer camp would be a great way for him to actually get his shit together."

"Her what?"

"She just signed the deal yesterday. It'll be like a mixer to kick off the nanny phase of SDH. Families will be able to interact with, and hopefully choose, a nanny at the end of the week."

"And you think this will work for him? He's very… particular."

"It has to," Elijah replies. His eyes never leave his sister and our newest partner.

We do need Sebastian at the top of his game this year. The thought of what's to come sends excitement rushing through me. It's going to be a good year for Crystal Waters. "Then let's hope Lottie has some more magic in her nanny arsenal. How's everything going in Raleigh?"

"Raleigh's good, but you know that because we spoke over Zoom yesterday."

A flash of color crosses the hallway leading to the restroom, followed by two more. The women are hiding again. It's amusing, but if they think Leo, Teddy, or I can control these protective feelings that have taken over our personalities, they haven't been paying attention.

"You're a good man, Becker Hayes. It's nice to see you trusting people again."

The drink in my hand pauses halfway to my mouth. Teddy is now my right-hand man in the local office. That was a no-brainer after I got Elijah to come on as a partner, and Teddy has exceeded all my expectations.

"Good people get good opportunities," I say.

"What the hell is taking them so long?" Leo asks, not caring that he's interrupting our conversation. "Tabby could go into labor any day now. Any. Day."

"They're fine. They're hiding in the hallway." I gesture

and he follows my line of sight. The three pregnant women scatter.

"Why are they hiding?" Teddy asks, joining us. He's the calmest of the dads-to-be, but that's not really saying much.

"Because the three of you are driving them insane," Lucía says, leaning in for a hug. "Give them some space. It's hard carrying babies."

A balloon pops, and it sets off a chain reaction that has all three women in question entering the room.

I turn toward the sound to find none other than Ruby standing on a chair with a fork as confetti in shades of pink and blue falls all around her.

"Oh, shit." I take off toward her, but Emmy beats me to it. "I've got this, Daddy." She holds up her palm to me, turns to Ruby, and scowls, then wags her finger. "Ruby Anne Hayes, give me that poker."

Ruby's grin widens and she stabs at the three remaining balloons with manic motions.

"Ruby, you ruined the surprise," Emmy scolds. Ruby ignores her and tosses the fallen confetti into the air.

"Oh no. How will we know who's having what now?" Stella asks. But there's a smile on her face as she watches our girls. "Ruby, that wasn't very nice."

Ruby showcases an almost convincing sad face. "Wub you, Mama." Unfortunately for Ruby, Stella isn't as much of a sucker as I am.

"It's okay," Bella says behind us. "I have a backup plan." She hands me, Teddy, and Leo envelopes while we all stare at each other.

"Well, open it," Stella demands. "I can't believe I let Tabby talk me into waiting this long."

Slowly, they open their envelopes, and hearts fill Teddy's and Leo's eyes.

"Seriously, Leo," Tabby grouches, "if you don't want to sleep on the floor tonight, you had better tell me what we're having. Right now."

His smile splits his face in two. He's been this way since they started building a house a mile down the road from ours. "We're having a boy, Tabs. It's a baby boy."

Hoots and hollers fill the town hall, and he lifts her off the ground in a hug.

"What about us?" Bella asks quietly.

Teddy stands with tears streaming down his face. He's not shy about showing his emotions, and when his dad squeezes his shoulder with tears of his own, I know why. He was raised to be a good man. A man unafraid to show just how much he loves the people around him.

"We're having a boy too," he chokes out. Happiness fills Bella's face, and he kisses her hard.

It's then that Stella's nails bite into my forearm. "Seriously, Beck. Open the dang letter."

I do as she asks and pull out the pink slip of paper. "We're having another girl," I say, though the words feel thick and get stuck in my throat. "Another girl."

Emmy grabs Ruby's hands, and they dance together in a circle. "A sister. A sister. We're having a sister," she sings.

"A girl?" Stella asks, and I nod. "A girl," she repeats as a smile grows on her face. "We're having a girl?"

"Yeah, baby. Are you okay?" I glance around at our friends and family celebrating, but Stella stands frozen.

I tug her to me and hold her tight. "Stella?"

She lifts her gaze to mine. "We're having a girl, Beck. Another girl."

"Yeah, does that upset you?"

Stella frowns. "No. Not at all. It's just, now it feels real. I know that's silly. We've seen her. We've heard her heartbeat. But..."

I open my mouth to say something, but her body trembles in my arms, then she breaks into a laugh.

"We're having a girl, Beck. A house full of girls. Did you know I always wanted sisters? It was a dream I would think about every night before falling asleep."

"Are you happy?" I'm so confused. I can't keep up with the mood swings of pregnancy, but I'm trying.

"I'm so, so happy, Beck. Thank you for giving me... everything."

"Oh, sweetheart. I only gave you myself. You did all of this—you created this family of ours, and you hold us together every day."

She shakes her head. "Don't you see? You gave me you— all of you. You let me in. You trusted me. You loved me. And now, we have our happily ever after."

"It's more than I could have ever asked for," I admit just as a loud crash brings the party to a complete standstill.

On the other side of the room, Ruby and Daisie stand covered in blue punch.

"Dang it, Daisie. Who brought you here?"

Stella pulls away and won't make eye contact.

Busted. "Baby, you know what a menace that dog is. How did you get her here?"

"Elijah, but don't be mad at him. I thought she'd keep Ruby occupied."

"Oh, yeah. They're a great pair, the two of them." I laugh as Daisie licks punch off Ruby's face. "Come on, looks like I've got a mess to clean up."

"I'm sorry," she says, and I squeeze her hand.

"I'm not. This is life, Stella. Happy, messy, crazy life. I'm just lucky you let me tag along for the ride. I love you, sweetheart. So very much."

Her glassy gaze finds mine. "I love you more than I ever thought possible."

"Oh, shit," Leo mutters a little too loudly, and we all turn his way.

Tabby stands with wide legs and a puddle below her.

"Ah, my water just broke," she announces, and all hell breaks loose.

Our Sailport Bay family rushes to clean up the punch, while the rest of us hurry to waiting cars.

It's a clusterfuck of chaos—but it's mine and I wouldn't have it any other way.

ACKNOWLEDGMENTS

To my friends and family: Thank you for believing in me and supporting me, even when I'm cranky, in need of a shower, and weepy. And a special thank you to Mr. Maxwell who has to put up with me through it all.

To my TWSS family: Thank you for helping me spread my wings with each new release and always encouraging me to enjoy the ride.

To my agents, Flavia and Meire: Thank you for taking me in new and exciting directions.

To my team: Thank you to everyone who helps with every step of my process, even when my process changes like the wind. Rhon, Joyce, Tammy, Lona, Liz, Marie, Sara, my street team, my ARC team, sensitivity, and beta readers —it's because of you I can create stories with heart.

To HEA Author Services: Thank you for pushing me, teaching me, and helping me be my best. I measure my success by how much I'm able to improve, and because of you, I have. Kimberly, thank you for adjusting your edit to work with my bullet-point-loving brain. Jess, thank you for always making time to work with me, to answer my millions of questions, and for walking me through all the things I don't know. Emily, thank you for fixing all my commas and for your research skills.

To the readers: Thank you for taking a chance on me and my books. I'm only here because of you.

Hello, Luvs!

Want to hang out with me? I'm in The Luv Club every day sharing my chaos, my mess, my life. Pop in to say hi, meet the other luvables, and stay a while. It's the happiest, kindest, messiest, most inclusive group on the internet and I'd LUV to see you there!

https://geni.us/AverysLUVclub

Standalone Romance:

Without A Hitch

Your Last First Kiss

Falling Into Forever

The Westbrooks Series:

Book 1 - Cross My Heart

Book 2 - The Beat of My Heart

Book 3 - Saving His Heart

Book 4 - Romancing His Heart

Book 5 - One Little Heartbreak - A Westbrook Novella

Book 6 - One Little Mistake

Book 7 - One Little Lie

Book 8 - One Little Kiss

Book 9 - One Little Secret

Single Dad Hotline Series:

Book 1 - Love Notes & Lifelines